OPERATION: BLOODBATH

"We can't hold our position! We're taking incredible incoming!" came the tacomm voice of Capt. Lew Pagam.

Colonel Curt Carlson saw it. The new enemy force was on his tac display, coming in fast four hundred meters to the east.

"Battle tanks!" Carlson said.

They were big, heavily armored, and gunned. And, they were attacking. That's what mattered most.

"Okay. Engine leader. Let's pop a little smoke at them!" Curt ordered.

"Roger, Colonel!" Suddenly an old robot Jeep dashed out in front of the attacking force, spewing dense clouds of smoke. The tanks began to stop, unable to use their sensors to proceed.

"Guard your eyes and i-r sensors. Fire at will!" the colonel commanded.

The explosions were deafening, lighting up the mid-morning skies with destruction.

"Move in! We've got 'em!"

WARBOTS

#11: WARRIOR SHIELD

G. HARRY STINE

PINNACLE BOOKS
WINDSOR PUBLISHING CORP.

To:
Eugene Wesley Roddenberry, former captain, USAAF

PINNACLE BOOKS

are published by

Windsor Publishing Corp.
475 Park Avenue South
New York, NY 10016

First printing: February, 1992

Printed in the United States of America

"In the last analysis, success in battle is a matter of morale. In all matters which pertain to an army, organization, discipline, and tactics, the human heart in the supreme moment of battle is the basic factor."

— Ardant du Picq
Battle Studies (1868)

One

The red telephone rang.

It really wasn't a red telephone. It was a beige multi-line set on the stand next to the President's bed. But it was the "red" line that lit up and the attention-getting "red" tone that sounded.

The President stopped what he was doing, rolled over, and noted that it was 1:44 a.m.

"The red line," he muttered.

"That means real trouble.

"Probably. If not for me, then for whoever is making the call." The President was vexed. It wasn't often that he could enjoy himself after a state dinner. And it wasn't often that the first lady was out of town visiting her parents.

Historically, the affairs in the family quarters of the White House didn't always involve family. Some administrations had gone to great lengths to keep the White House image pristine even though its occupants weren't. Many chief executives had had voracious appetites.

The present President was one of them, although no one might have suspected it from his true-blue Ivy League background.

"This is the President speaking," he intoned into the instrument.

"Mr. President, this is Dan Gram."

The President hunched himself up straighter in the bed. When his national security advisor called him on the red line, something was indeed coming unbonded somewhere in a world that never seemed to stop fighting. This bothered the President a lot. He'd tried very hard by diplomatic and economic means to eliminate armed conflict from the world. He hadn't succeeded. It seemed that some people liked to fight. He didn't understand that at all. And the more he cut back the United States military forces as well as overseas commitments, the worse things got. He was proud of the fact that nowhere on Planet Earth could the United States of America be perceived by anyone as a military threat to world peace.

But some people didn't seem to want world peace.

"What's gone wrong, Danny? And it had better be important. It's almost two a.m.!" The President tried to sound stern.

"Thirty minutes ago, Malitanian armor and warbot forces crossed the Senegambian border in force at Nayé. Generalissimo Modibo has invaded Senegambia," the former army general reported.

It took the President a moment before he could locate Nayé and Senegambia in his mind. But he knew the tall, acerbic Tuareg "President for Life" of Malitania.

And this bothered the President even more. "Damn it! Modibo promised me he wouldn't do that if the Senegambians would ship food to him instead of exporting it elsewhere!"

"Well, Mr. President, it seems that Generalissimo Modido Ould Daddah Sidi Ahmed has forgotten his promise," the national security advisor said. "He's coming on television in twenty-two minutes to explain what provoked him to take this action."

"What *provoked* him? He has no provocation! He's simply invading another country!" the President shouted.

"Sir, I agree with you. And I'm merely reporting what the Malitanian telecommunications minister reported to the embassy over on R Street. And in his exact words, by the way. I apologize for waking you, but it's my duty to inform you at once of such happenings, especially when they may affect the national security of the United States," Gram replied stiffly.

The President sighed. Gram was a good national security advisor. The President believed that the retired general understood well the chief executive's academically-bred aversion to war and the military. Although Dan Gram was a re-

8

tired general, the President believed he could trust him.

Gram had therefore done an outstanding job of camouflage. He himself harbored none of his chief executive's pacifistic philosophies. The former general officer in charge of defense intelligence operations, Gram had been carefully maneuvered into the position of national security advisor by politically-minded military colleagues. The Gun Club, as it was known unofficially, thus would have a trusted comrade in the highest of high places. Gram had no problems with the fact that he was a two-way messenger. He carried the President's latest anti-war dreams out to his comrades while subtly inserting his colleagues' policies and principles into national security affairs.

"Danny, I don't see where the invasion of Senegambia in Africa has the slightest impact upon the security of this country!" the President told him. "I don't believe it warrants any action on my part at this point in time . . ."

"Sir, the Senegambian diplomatic transmission we intercepted to their embassy indicates that the Malitanian troops are slaughtering Senegambians in Nayé. It's a replay of the blood bath of the Mali-Mauritanian Anschluss."

"The generalissimo assured me that he was merely putting down an armed rebellion against the peaceful unification of the two countries!"

"Yes, sir . . ." Gram knew better than to argue with his boss. Gram had seen the tapes of the blood bath in Mauritania a year ago. So had the President, but the chief executive had either refused to believe those tapes or his mind had literally blocked the memory. In light of the invasion of Senegambia, Gram knew the next few days were going to be difficult. Very difficult indeed. This was the sort of thing that caused Gram to kick himself in the ass for listening to his friends on the JCS instead of moving out to Fort Ord where he could devote his full attention to his wife, grandchildren, and small arms collection.

"Sir, this is quite different from the Malitanian Anschluss when the generalissimo set up a puppet government in Mali which then invited him to unify the two countries. This is naked aggression," Gram reminded him. "For many decades, the

9

United States has had an extremely strong anti-aggression doctrine as a linchpin of foreign policy. The UN Secretary General will certainly call before breakfast and ask you if you intend to instruct our UN ambassador to bring the matter before the Security Council . . ."

The President lost his temper. This happened quite often when the rest of the world didn't behave the way the chief executive believed it ought to. Especially in the military sphere. "Damn it, General, let's be patient! Get with Al Murray and General Wool. Work up a complete brief for me. Make sure I get to see the videotape. I want to hear what the generalissimo says. But I'm certainly not going to make a major foreign policy decision at two in the morning with no more information than you've given me! The morning schedule's tight, but I'll get Mary to put the three of you on early before I meet with the quality of life people. Danny, you're doing an outstanding job. Thanks for the heads-up, but I'm not going to lose any sleep over it. Good night!" He hung up and turned back to his companion.

"I'll squeeze them in at eight. Consider it done," the President's companion murmured in his ear.

"Better let me call you officially at seven, my dear. I want a record of it. I can always trust my Secret Service bodyguard, but some of the staff members would sell out . . ."

"Not easily," she told him. "The President's secretary does indeed know where a lot of bodies are buried, you know. After all, we've played this game for years; I know who we can trust and how to control those we can't. Don't worry about that. Worry about me instead. That telephone call interrupted things just as they were getting hot . . . and I haven't cooled off a bit, honey! Just the opposite! Come here!"

The bedclothes concealed what the bright White House exterior security lights shining through the window would otherwise have revealed.

Two hundred kilometers away, those bright lights and the rest of the shining electric jewel that was the nation's capital provided yet another romantic backdrop for a tender liaison.

"Alzena, you're right."

"Curt, I'm always right."

10

"You're pretty sure of yourself."

"I pay attention to my market analyses."

"Always the businesswoman!"

"Not always. Why do you think I asked you here?"

Col. Curt Carson, United States Army, had to admit that the Sultana Alzena Mahathis bint Muhamad, daughter of the Sultan of Brunei, was not just intelligent and sophisticated. She was also one of the most beautiful women Curt had ever known. And he'd known many. But in the orbital weightlessness of her latest business venture, a luxury hotel called The Three Dolphin Ranch circling two hundred kilometers above the blue planet below, Alzena was more than stunning. She was breathtaking in her overt sensuality.

It had something to do with the visual effects of weightlessness. Without the persistent tug of Earth's gravity, the human body took on a slightly different appearance. It was hard for Curt to pin down these effects, but Alzena looked absolutely ravishing with her long, dark hair exploding out around her head and her small body reacting only to the tension of her smooth skin and soft muscles.

Or it might have been Alzena's ability to take advantage of the world's most advanced biotechnology in Brunei. For eight years, he'd enjoyed one of the loveliest and most romantic relationships of his life with the elfin Muslim princess. He knew he'd grown older, but the gorgeous Alzena seemed to become younger and ever more beautiful. It was as if she'd enhanced every sensual and exotic feature and ability . . . and she had always had plenty of those attributes.

"Well, the invitation requested my presence as a family member for the marriage of the Gen. Sultan Ahmad Mahathis bin Muhamad and former Maj. Alexis Morgan of the Washington Greys," Curt reminded her. "The only way I could get leave and take advantage of a spaceplane trip to your orbiting fleshpot was to claim family business . . ."

"You were once awarded the Sultan's Star of Brunei for outstanding service to my father," she reminded him. "You are indeed an intimate part of the sultan's family . . . my dearest brother. Besides, I wanted to get intimate with you in some place other than that dreary Fort

Huachuca and your regimental responsibilities."

"You've never needed an excuse before," Curt told her.

"Nor have you. Until recently." Her slightest touch brought them languidly together in intimate physical contact. Done slowly and sensually, Alzena's caresses kept them together.

"You just wanted to get me up here in zero-gravity to find out how brotherly I really am, right?"

"I've told you often, my dear, how glad I am that you're not my real brother! And how much you've taught me. . . . Umm . . . And how much pleasure we've shared . . . Oh! . . . So I had to learn with you if zero-gravity was any improvement . . ."

It was so much easier to do things without gravity, Curt decided. Staying together was no real problem. Alzena seemed to know what to do. "But you've obviously been practicing."

"Not in orbit . . . in the neutral buoyancy water tank we built at Kota Kinabalu . . . for research purposes . . . due diligence, you know . . . oh, Curt, do that again! . . ."

The artfully cushioned alcove had no lights, but they didn't need lights. Even as the orbital hotel swung through the night sky over the United States, enough illumination for their purposes came through the window. But when the habitat crossed the populous east coast of the United States, they separated briefly but only enough to take in the incredible panorama below them.

"Those must be the lights of Washington down there," Alzena remarked, turning her head slightly and brushing her long, dark hair back from her face. "Beautiful."

"Yes." But he wasn't referring to the lights of the nation's capital. And his tone was suddenly somber.

Alzena noted the subtle change in Curt as those lights passed below. "Curt, my dearest, your President and generals can't see us up here. Please forget your cares and concerns about your job."

"I can't, Alzena," Curt had to admit. "I can't see those lights without remembering I have a responsibility. It's called the Third Robot Infantry Special Combat Regiment of the Army of the United States."

Alzena peered deeply into his eyes with a questioning look

12

in hers. "I know that. Years ago I agreed to accept you as a soldier in the service of his country. You accepted the fact that I have no aspirations to raise a family because of my cultural situation, that I chose the French approach, the art form of love as both a hobby and a way to compensate for motherhood."

"And you're very good at it," Curt admitted both honestly and tenderly. How could he be anything but tender with someone like Alzena, certainly one of Allah's loveliest creations?

"You're very troubled. I saw that days ago when you arrived in Bandar Seri Begawan. Want to tell me why, Curt?"

He hesitated. "Yes and no."

"Why?"

"Because your father might be the cause."

This confused her. "Please explain, Curt. Please," she pleaded.

Curt sighed. He knew the matter was going to surface sometime. Might as well be now while they were enjoying a tender rhapsody with the completely new sensations of zero-gravity love. "Since we retreated from Yemen over two years ago, I've had to fight for every replacement officer and NCO, every warbot, every aerodyne, every round of practice ammo, and every spare part! That's because someone down there in that jewel of lights sent us to do something we couldn't hack. And then someone ordered us to retreat, someone who believes the world will disarm and behave itself if America sets a shining example. The only shining example seems to be that canopy of lights we just orbited over!"

She reached out her small, smooth hand and caressed his shoulder. "You made an honorable evacuation from Yemen."

"Evacuation, hell! Retreat! Under orders! And I've never got a straight answer about whether or not we were there protecting an iron mine your father owned!"

Curt was very bitter about the last campaign of the Washington Greys. They'd been deployed to Yemen under the provisions of a mutual military assistance treaty. Their orders were to guard the world's richest iron mine and its facilities against Yemeni terrorists and guerrillas. But the rules of en-

13

gagement allowed them only to shoot back. That was a hell of an assignment for a "special combat" regiment trained and equipped to carry out the most devastating form of mixed human-warbot assault warfare ever devised. Thanks to the professionalism of the Washington Greys and the three other regiments of the 17th Iron Fist Division in the Yemen Expeditionary Force, they'd gotten out of Yemen with only thirty-five percent casualties and the loss of a lot of equipment. During the withdrawal, they'd tangled with an unknown mercenary force equipped with Chinese warbots and other East World military hardware . . . and broke that force to bits in what turned out to be one of the classical battles of recent military history. At least, it was being studied carefully now at his old school, West Point. And since then Curt and the other regimental commanders had fought an endless bureaucratic battle to rebuild their regiments.

"Curt," Alzena said, drawing him gently closer to her in the floating environment of zero-gravity, "I didn't lie when you asked me. My father isn't involved with the Yemen operation. But it could have been any of the family. We have thousands of business ventures all over the world. Some of them are consortiums. We manage fifty trillion dollars that belongs to the people of Brunei, not the sultan and his family. If we don't manage it right, hundreds of thousands of Bruneis won't enjoy the world's highest standard of living."

"With that much money, Alzena, why the hell were the Greys called in to defend that investment? We lost people in the process! Your brother leads the Royal Brunei Legion. Your Gurkhas would have been the perfect outfit for the Yemen mission . . ."

It was obvious to Alzena now that Curt's bitterness ran deep. She realized it would take a lot of loving care to bring it all out of him. "The Sultan's Sixth Royal Gurkha Rifles and the rest of the Royal Brunei Legion have their own jobs to do keeping the jackals away from Borneo and maintaining order in southeast Asia. On a worldwide basis, that's your job, too."

Curt shook his head slowly to prevent the zero-gravity disorientation that accompanied sudden head movement. "No, my oath is to support and defend the Constitution of the

14

United States against all enemies, foreign and domestic," Curt corrected her, recalling from memory the solemn oath he'd taken upon graduating from the United States Military Academy two decades ago. "Not to fight other people's battles for them. My God, we learned our lesson about that back in the last century!"

"Look at it another way, then. Our countries are allies. 'The enemy of my friend is my enemy.' But you were also fighting for your adoptive family's possessions." The intimate contact of her body was both pleasurable and erotic, and Alzena maintained it in this strange weightless pillow talk.

And Curt knew that Alzena was doing her very best to get his mind off Yemen. He knew he was obsessed with that failed campaign. Curt Carson didn't like to lose, even when he was ordered to do so. "I would have been perfectly willing to fight to protect my family's possessions. But in Yemen, I had to order my friends into deadly combat. They aren't part of your family, Alzena."

She slowly shook her small head, and her Eurasian features were suddenly illuminated by light from the sun rising over the eastern limb of the Earth below. In a low voice, she remarked, "As I recall, a battle streamer flies from your regimental colors signifying the receipt of the Sultan's Royal Star and Crescent of Brunei. The Washington Greys are 'family,' Curt, and every member will be treated as such at any time by any of us."

Curt knew there would be no resolution to the situation here and now. So he backed off emotionally but not physically. He resumed a lighthearted approach. "Quite frankly, my dear Alzena, you're doing your lovely best to confuse the hell out of me. Under the circumstances, I'm enjoying being confused in this manner, especially by you."

"Dearest Curt, you are indeed such a manly warrior! And you Americans have a strange compulsion to believe in what you're fighting for." She turned and looked out the window over Curt's shoulder. "Don't be bitter, my dearest. With all of its death and destruction, it's still a beautiful world . . ."

The orbiting habitat had crossed the Atlantic Ocean while they'd talked. Now they looked down together at dawn breaking over the west coast of Africa. Because of a peculiar set of cloud bands hugging the land and sea below, the scene was blood red along the coast.

Neither of them realized it was an omen of things to come. Distance lends enchantment. They were looking down at the city of Dakar on the western tip of Senegambia.

Two

Generalissimo Modibo Ould Daddah Sidi Ahmed paid no attention to the bloody, bleeding, and dismembered human bodies on both sides of the railroad track. Some were wounded and screaming in pain. Others lay silent, becoming fetid corpses in the hot Senegambian sun. A large number of the dead wore uniforms; they were the remnants of the 12th Lébou Infantry Regiment, Senegambian Republican Army; they had fought a gallant but hopeless holding action at Tambacounda against Chinese Red Hammer warbots and Malitanian assault infantry. Most of the others, however, were civilians, including children and infants, now dead beside their mothers. Earlier in the day, these had been healthy, well-fed, well-dressed inhabitants of a country that was a prime example of an emerging nation in twenty-first century Africa. These Senegambian soldiers and innocent bystanders had been killed only hours ago during the Malitanian Army's rapid sweep westward.

But the scene already smelled of death and fetid decay. The corpses were beginning to bloat and decompose in the hot September sun.

The railway and the roads stretching back to the Malitanian border that hot, sunny day were strewn with the bodies of Senegambian people. Most had been shot, usually in the head. Others had been bayoneted. Some had been run over by Malitanian vehicles and Red Hammer warbots; a few of them were still alive. None appeared to have been tortured; the invaders hadn't had time. Torture would come later when

17

the soldiers had completed their conquest. Those Senegambians who had put up any sort of resistance to the Malitanian warbots and infantry were hanging from any tree or pole over which a noose made of rope or wire could be draped.

This trail of grisly death led back from the train's present position near Tambacounda to the Malitanian border 170 kilometers to the east. The rails of the Bamako-Dakar railway were bathed in blood. The roads were covered with it. The command train's locomotives had trouble maintaining traction with the blood. Even the Red Hammer warbots of the Malitanian robot infantry found it slippery going on the asphalt road that paralleled the railway.

Generalissimo Modibo viewed with approval the results of his blood bath invasion.

The dead were Senegambian people he wouldn't have to worry about now. They would offer no further resistance to the Malitanian occupation of Senegambia. But, more important, he wouldn't have to feed them. The food they would have consumed was now available for his army and his people, in that order of priority.

The evidence of brutal butchery and utter carnage didn't bother Generalissimo Modibo. Death had always been a part of his life. It had been all around him for more than thirty years in the barren and decaying Sahel region south of the Saharan Desert. That former savannah was now a barren wasteland because of generations of misuse by the farmers and herdsmen of Mali. Malitania was rich in many ways, but the people couldn't eat the gold of Mali or the iron ore, magnesium, and crude oil produced in Mauritania, the most recent addition to his domain. They needed the corn, meat, potatoes, rice, fish, sugar, peanuts, sorghum, and millet that were cultivated with professional, scientific care on the savannahs of Senegambia.

And the burgeoning industrial base of the St. Louis-Dakar-Banjul coastal strip was nothing to be passed off lightly, either. Modibo was getting weary of paying premium prices for military equipment and advisors from China, India, Burma, and Annam. He looked forward to being able to produce his own warbots, guns, and other implements of war. He had an appe-

18

tite for power that reached beyond Malitania and Senegambia. Someone, he told himself, had to unify sub-Saharan Africa. He also told himself that he was that person.

He didn't even bother to look the other way when some young Senegambians tried to board his moving presidential train to plead for help. Three of them slipped and fell under the wheels of his palace car. The train didn't even slow down. This part of Africa had too many people for its agricultural resources to support, anyway.

Generalissimo Modibo's appearance wasn't that of the typical African military leader and "President for Life." His background was mostly Tuareg. He was two meters tall, a skinny ectomorph with a long, cruel face dominated by deep, dark, heavily-browed eyes that had come from ancestors who had scanned the far horizons of the Sahara. But because no one could really claim or prove "pure" descent from the many peoples of the southern Saharan region of Africa, some Bambara blood also flowed in his veins. Some of Modibo's long-dead forefathers had been Songhai Berbers who had brought Islam across the Sahara to Timbuctu in the eleventh century. However, in spite of the cruel nature of his personality, he could speak several languages, mesmerize a crowd, and look very good on television.

The carriage door behind him opened. He was joined on the platform by Col. Godavari Singh Pratihara, one of the military advisors provided by the East World to help him properly manage and lead his armed forces, which were equipped with all the latest military exports from India, China, and Annam. The turbanned Sikh was one of many in Malitania because the Sikhs were able to mix well with the Muslims of the region, lowering the possibility of any sort of religious confrontation. East World found the Sikhs to be outstanding military advisors for that reason, plus most of them were certainly no strangers to massacres or even individual killings.

But even Colonel Pratihara was aghast and sickened by what he saw as the train rolled along.

"Generalissimo," the colonel ventured to suggest, "all these decaying corpses are going to pose a serious health problem for our troops. They really should be buried very soon."

Modibo looked down his long, aquiline nose at his military advisor, the one he'd chosen to assist the military occupation of Senegambia. "I do not wish to waste perfectly good fighting troops in the task of burying the enemy! We must first consolidate our military objectives. Other Malitanians will follow in the next few days to occupy and farm this beautiful savannah. They can do it as part of cultivating this land. They won't waste the corpses. They'll use them where needed to fertilize the fields!"

Colonel Pratihara had come from a country where cleanliness and hygiene meant better health and a longer life. The dead were either interred or cremated as quickly as practical, even on a battlefield. Sikhs were a clean people who'd learned to remain clean in order to stay alive in a hot climate. The average life span of a Sikh in the twenty-first century was over seventy years, in contrast to the forty-two years of the average Malitanian. Pratihara now knew that it was more than malnutrition that kept the Malitanian life expectancy so low.

The colonel recalled why he'd come out on the platform to report to the generalissimo. "Sir, we've just received word that the First Malitanian Robot Armored Division has broken through the Senegambian Republican Guards' defenses at Thiès and made contact with your regiment, the Third Special Infantry, who are holding the Aéroport de Dakar-Yoff."

This news elated Modibo. "Excellent! The strategy worked!"

"Yes, sir!" It was Colonel Pratihara who had suggested it and based his planning on a long-forgotten campaign. "An Arnhem operation done properly! I always felt that Viscount Montgomery was right. Operation Market Garden would have succeeded if it had had good intelligence and better weather. We had both!"

Modibo hadn't paid too much attention to military history. He was a political leader who also fancied himself a military genius. In his rise to power in Mali, he'd fought and won against units that had been poorly equipped, poorly led, or poorly motivated. His Muslim followers were led by Tuaregs with the help of some Riffs, people who knew how to fight battles of maneuver while outnumbered and with little fire-power against adversaries who were far better equipped. Modibo had rewarded his lieutenants well with important positions in the Mali government. After the Anschluss with Mauritania, many of them had been given important positions in the expanded government. And then slowly eliminated if they showed any possibility of confronting him in a struggle for political power. Few of his old lieutenants remained, which is why he had to depend so heavily upon East World military advisors now. But a military genius he wasn't; he'd just been lucky, merciless, and ruthless.

Modibo wanted to make the most of this. He'd planned a show of force upon capturing Dakar, the Paris of West Africa and the old French colonial capital. "Have the generalissimo's Guard relieved by the First Armored. I want to lead the Guard in the triumphant parade through Dakar tomorrow! I presume that our schedule still holds?"

"Yes, sir. Your train is scheduled to arrive at the Gare de Dakar at twenty-two hundred hours today," Pratihara confirmed. "However, we may have a slight delay. Nothing that would change the schedule for the parade tomorrow, of course. Irregular Senegambi units have ambushed the Tenth Airborne Regiment north of Kaolack. We've had to divert the Seventh Airborne Regiment from its mission to subjugate Banjul. The railway may be blocked temporarily if the Seventh Airborne cannot dislodge the guerrillas by sixteen hundred hours."

"Guerrillas?" This astounded Modibo.

"Partisans," Pratihara explained. "Armed civilians."

The response from Modibo was immediate. *"Crush them! I will not tolerate partisan activity! The populace must be convinced that I will not tolerate that sort of paramilitary activity in my rear! All partisans are to be slain; we will take no prisoners!"*

Pratihara didn't comment. The general orders issued to all units of the Malitanian Army were simple: *Kill everyone! Leave no extra mouths to feed!* Except in the cities, of course, where specialized expertise was needed to keep civil domestic services running. The urban experts were to be convinced to continue

21

to do their jobs. The Malitanians planned to see to it that these Senegambian professionals did so by the simple expedient of herding their families into detention camps as hostages against proper and vigorous performance.

So Colonel Pratihara did what all soldiers everywhere do when given an irrational order by their superiors. He saluted and said, "Yes, sir!"

The situation was actually somewhat worse than Colonel Pratihara had reported to the generalissimo.

The town of Kaolack lay along the Saloum River on the humid semi-tropical coastal plain only sixty kilometers from the Atlantic Ocean. The terrain was quite different from the savannah over which the Malitanian Army rolled along the railway westbound, connecting with the airborne forces that had landed at Tambacounda, Kaolack, Banjul, and Thiès shortly after sunrise.

Not all the Senegambians had been surprised by the Malitanian invasion. The Senegambian armed forces had been both outnumbered and overwhelmed by the unorthodox strategy of Malitanian airborne troops leapfrogging by air into important airports. There, these airmobile forces pinned down Senegambian forces while the main Malitanian heavy ground offensive surged westward along the railway. The Senegambian army units fought bravely and valiantly. They were still doing so. The Senegalese had a long tradition of French militarism with its emphasis on *élan* while the Gambian units had a similar heritage of dogged never-say-die, an attitude imbued by the British Army.

But both the French and British colonials of the last century had also given the Senegambians another legacy: an armed citizenry.

In a situation where it's apparent that the regular military forces are losing or in danger of losing, one or more partisan armed resistance movements usually are formed and begin waging guerrilla warfare.

This is precisely what was going on in the Dakar-Kaolack-Banjul triangle where the vegetation was thick and visibility was limited to a few meters. This was not the sort of combat environment in which Malitanian troops had trained.

22

Furthermore, the area was the "high rent district" of Senegambia, populated by wealthy people who had learned the ways of the market economy. They were the venture capitalists, the business people, the agro-managers, and the artistic intelligensia of the nation. They'd chosen to live near Dakar but not in that bustling city. They were the Senegambian suburbanites. With them were the supporting tradespeople and service technicians that move out from the cities with the suburbanites. It was no different in Senegambia than it had been in the United States during the twentieth century.

The Malitanian Anschluss of several years before hadn't gone unnoticed by these people. They were smart enough to figure out that Senegambia was next on Generalissimo Modibo's list. They had prepared for it. Three centuries ago, slavers had raided the land and taken the people who weren't able to defend themselves. The French colonial administration had brought an end to that. But the end of colonialism had meant the resumption of tribal warfare and the need for self-defense. These people had it, and they had the organization necessary to make it effective.

And they were prepared to fight for their country.

A rump contingent of about one hundred Senegalese irregulars ambushed the Malitanians at the Saloum River crossing between Kaffrine and Guinguineo northeast of Kaolack. Both men and women were involved. They were a strange mixture of young and old, veterans who had seen combat elsewhere fighting alongside ordinary citizens who had never been shot at before. Some of them were retired Senegalese Republican Army personnel who still had their French Fusil Attaque MAS rifles; others were armed with highpowered hunting rifles and shotguns. Since the Malitanian invasion had occurred before they'd expected it, they didn't have as many grenades, anti-warbot rockets, or explosives as they'd planned for. But they had enough to give the invading Malitanians a very hard time.

Furthermore, the Senegalese resistance fighters knew the terrain and made use of every bit of the spare cover along the river. The Malitanians were caught on the railway and the road, out in the open on the grassy, flat savannah.

However, the Malitanians had Chinese Red Hammer war-bots whose firepower and accuracy was massive and deadly. When a Red Hammer got a target on its visual, infrared, or radar sensors, its 53-millimeter high-velocity high rate gun didn't miss.

It was a slaughter on both sides. Strangely, because of the ability of the resistance fighters to use cover and stealth, the Malitanians took far more personal casualties.

The Malitanians left their wounded to die. These were forward assault forces operating without bio-tech support. And the generalissimo hadn't wasted resources on bio-tech units and supplies anyway. He had too many Malitanians to feed as it was. And he knew his army outnumbered the Senegambians by three to one.

The resistance fighters did have bio-tech support in the form of local doctors and nurses who'd donned the white tabard with the red crescent front and back. These valiant people worked right up at the forward edge of battle.

The Malitanians paid no attention to the rules of war regarding bio-techs wearing tabards. They not only shot them along with the resistance fighters but slaughtered them instead of taking them prisoners.

The fight at the River Saloum didn't stop the Malitanians. It did slow them down by about an hour. The resistance fighters didn't press their luck; when they saw they were losing, they withdrew to fight again. The Malitanians pursued and caught some of them; they emasculated the men before killing them; they raped the women before impaling them on bamboo skewers by the river.

It was a minor skirmish in terms of twenty-first century combat. Certainly, other engagements fought around the volatile world had been far larger with many more people killed and wounded. But the Battle of the River Saloum became one of the icons of brutal, barbaric warfare, an image of madness and blood and ruthlessness that quickly became symbolic around the world.

Generalissimo Modibo had video crews travelling with units of his army as they swept into Senegambia. But the images that would be made available to the world from that coverage would be very carefully selected and edited.

Modibo hadn't counted on any Senegambian coverage because his troops had struck first at communications facilities.

But one had been missed.

Jasper Duckworth Greenway was a free lance British videonaturalist who'd carefully hidden himself in a blind along the River Saloum. He had one of the best Batavian videocameras with a 5000-millimeter lens and an image steadier. The videocamera also had a very sensitive long-range shotgun microphone. "Ducks" Greenway was an electronic birdwatcher. He hated his given name, Jasper, and reluctantly accepted the nickname "Ducks" that had been given to him by his schoolmates at Eton. Ducks Greenway had always been a loner, and he liked to travel to far off places to photograph birds. He'd sold a lot of footage, which had supplemented his independent upper-class English income. So he'd planted himself along the River Saloum to get pictures and sounds of the fire finch and Senegalese snake bird, species which others hadn't yet documented.

Instead, he found himself a hidden witness to the bloody Battle of the River Saloum.

Ducks Greenway was a non-violent, anti-war person. He'd never even seen a pub fight, and he'd run from fights at Eton. Now he saw one of the goriest, brutal, inhuman activities imaginable. Certainly, no one in the rest of the civilized world would have believed him if he'd reported it verbally.

Three motives drove him to aim his 5,000-millimeter lens at the slaughter, the cruelty, and the ruthless, wanton carnage. It reviled him so deeply that he could think of nothing but taping it to prove to himself later that he had indeed seen it. Secondly, his non-violent personal philosophy told him he could use this tape some day to promote anti-war causes. And lastly, he knew he probably had broadcast quality videotape and audio for which the news media would pay handsomely . . . if he could get it transmitted via satellite to London.

Duckworth Greenway's videotape was to change the world and cause far more death than he ever imagined.

Three

"What do you mean, 'We haven't got the funds'?"

"Major Clinton, that's only the first reason." Lt. Col. Wade Hampton, commander of the Service Battalion, was unhappy, too.

"Only the *first* reason? We need those warbots repaired and operational!" Kitsy fumed.

Maj. Kathleen B. Clinton was having an unusual amount of trouble in her assignment as temporary regimental commander. She was the "low icon on the totem pole" insofar as her assignment in the regimental TO&E. She was only a company commander.

When Col. Curt Carson went on leave, it had become his practice to assign different senior officers as temporary commanders. So it wasn't Kitsy's first shift "in the barrel." She was slowly growing used to the trials and tribulations of regimental command. She was good at company command and believed herself ready for battalion command. However, regimental command was something that still tended to overwhelm her, even with her aggressive, positive attitude of "everything worth doing is worth over-doing."

It was generally understood among the Washington Greys, the 3rd Robot Infantry (Special Combat) Regiment, that the colonel was training potential replacements. He'd chosen to create competition between his potential successors. Everyone originally believed that Maj. Jerry Allen was the anointed one; then Curt had given the job to Kitsy and Maj. Russ Frazier in turn. In many outfits, this could have led to interpersonal tensions. However, even though the morale of the Third Herd was outstanding with few personal enemies among the Greys, Curt had made it clear to his senior officers that any reported attempts to sabotage a temporary regimental commander would be reflected in the next evaluation reports. In short, cooperation with a potential rival was considered to be as important as performance in the temporary leadership role.

"Yes, ma'am," Hampton replied. "Quartermaster reports the parts are out of stock, no longer being stocked, or unavailable on the commercial market even if funds were available."

Kitsy shook her head in frustration. She didn't like to be frustrated. "How in hell can those terminal twerps in Quartermaster do this to us?"

"Easy," was the comment from Maj. Harriet Dearborn, commander of the logistics company and regimental S-4. "If I know Quartermaster — and I do because I have to deal with them constantly — they're probably sitting on tons of stuff. Why? Because their orders are to maintain inventory! If they can't replace inventory, they won't draw down what they've got!"

"That's ridiculous! It's their job to support combat units like the Greys!" Kitsy knew the supply officer was right.

"Sure, but the non-fighting army doesn't think that way," Harriet reminded her. "Their mission is clear, but their responsibility is to keep the paperwork clean . . ."

"If I had my way," Kitsy muttered, "I'd have you send them back some of the ten thousand cases of toilet paper they just unloaded on us. Accompanied, of course, by an official letter telling them to keep that paperwork clean instead!"

"No, that would just complicate the situation," Hampton guessed. "Unless we could get Major Gydesen and some of the other bio-tech types to send them some dysentery bacteria, too."

"Sorry," Kitsy apologized. "I get uptight when some of the non-combatants figure the Army exists for and because of them. West Point attitude, I guess. But, dammit, our present situation puts us in Readiness Status Three. We're supposed to maintain Status One because we're ALO One. We have to

27

be ready to deploy within twenty-four hours."

"Not with the present commander in chief recalling units to the ZI as fast as any excuse permits," Hampton reminded her. "The current United States' foreign policy is one of diplomatic negotiation in lieu of military power. So I think we can look forward to sitting here in Fort Huachuca in a training mode for the next year or so. That assumes a new administration gets elected next year. But that gets us into a political discussion . . ."

"And we'll save that for the Club," Kitsy added. "But don't count on us sitting on our asses here for that long. If you saw the news this morning, you know it's getting messy in Africa again. The Malitanian-Senegambian sheep screw may require us to go out and get shot at. Sort of like another Bastaard Rebellion, another Namibian embassy rescue operation. I wasn't aboard for Namibia, but I've studied the operation."

She turned to Harriet Dearborn. "Look, you know the paper chase, Harriet. Can you invoke any sort of emergency status for those parts orders?"

Dearborn shook her head. "We have no emergency authorization."

Kitsy thought about all this for a moment. It seemed that the Third Herd was hemmed in by bureaucracy and the Army way of doing things. *Dammit, Kitsy, they tried to teach you to think at West Point. They tried to teach you to be flexible and show initiative. They tried to teach you to try a different approach if the initial assault went to worms,* she thought to herself, glad that she didn't have to rigorize her thinking as required when running neuro-electronic warbots and tacomm. *What would Curt Carson do? How would he handle this?*

Then she suddenly realized what Curt would do because the regimental commander had been taught far more after he'd left West Point. His teachers in the real world of the Army had been the NCOs who really ran the show.

And she then knew that Curt Carson wouldn't handle it. He would delegate it. And she knew to whom he would delegate it.

Reaching over the top of the terminals embedded in the

28

desk top, she passed her hand over the interoffice intercom switch. "Sergeant Major Kester, please report to the regimental commander's office ASAP!"

The old soldier was standing in the doorway less than thirty seconds later. He saluted. He didn't have to, but he did. It wasn't a matter of following military protocol. He saluted out of respect for the perky officer with whom he'd served for nine years as she'd come up the ladder of promotion. Furthermore, she'd been severely wounded in Iraq and managed to recover totally in spite of the pessimistic prognosis of the experts at Walter Reed Army Hospital. Henry Kester liked Kitsy Clinton. So did all the other Greys. "Reporting as requested, Major."

"At ease, Henry," Kitsy told him. "We've got some parts availability problems . . ."

"Yes, ma'am. With Jeeps and the Mary Anns." Kester was obviously on top of the problem already.

"You're the regimental master scrounge. Where can we get what's needed?"

"New or used, ma'am?"

"New if possible. Used if necessary."

"Well, Major, if it's okay with Colonel Hampton here, I can probably have used parts available by the end of the day. They should tide Major Otis and his people over until a swap for new parts can be arranged with another regiment somewheres." Kester said it flatly and without emphasis as if it was just another deal that could easily be arranged between friends.

He looked at the regimental S-4. "Major Dearborn, if you'll let me know what's needed, I'll get on the hooter to the detail I sent up to the Davis-Monthan boneyard this morning to pick up those aerodyne parts for Major Worsham's Chippies. They can swing by the Army Annex later this afternoon. I gave Flight Sergeant Tomasio enough of our surplus Mark Seven-Eleven gigabyte memory cubes, I think. The boneyard people always need more file storage capability. If he needs more cumshaw trading stuff, I think we can probably unload a couple of truckloads of old nine-mike-mike Hornet rounds. The Air Farce security police are always running short of that ammo for requalification target practice. We've still got a warehouse full of the old stuff now that we have our 7.56 millimeter Novias. That is, if Major Dearborn can arrange to 'expend' that ammo on the books . . ."

Dearborn waved her hand. "Consider it done! Expendables like ammo I can always expend. It's the non-expendable stuff that I've signed for that gives me ulcers . . ."

"Major, Sergeant Manny Sanchez knows a lot about how to expend the non-expendables," Kester advised her.

"Because you taught him, Henry?" Dearborn knew what the score was. But she asked anyway because she was always interested in the sort of answers Kester gave.

He didn't disappoint her. "Yes, ma'am. Somebody has to maintain the traditions, Major!" Kester's faced remained impassive as usual, but there was a twinkle in his eye. After more than thirty years of service, he knew how to work the system every which way, including loose.

"Well, Major Clinton, there you have it," Hampton told her. There was no rancor in his voice. He was an old hand on the service side of the regiment, and he knew that Kitsy had to learn the ropes of regimental administration by herself. She had to learn to call upon the NCOs of the regimental staff—Regimental Sgt. Maj. Henry Kester and the top tech sergeant, Sgt. Maj. Edwina Sampson. He and Harriet Dearborn couldn't mother-hen her. . . . Officially, that is. The two of them had responded to Kitsy's reaction to their morning reports indicating the usual problems of parts. She'd called them to her office to talk about it. Down at the company level, Kitsy probably realized that Master Sgt. Carol Head, the huge Moravian who was her first sergeant, really ran ASSAULTCO Alpha, "Clinton's Cougars," but she obviously hadn't fully realized that the same procedure worked all the way up the line to regimental headquarters, division headquarters, and thence even to the hallowed halls of the Pentagon. "Harriet and I will go back to managing and administering our units, seeing to it that the work gets done. As for solutions to the real problems and doing the real work, we'll carry on as always and count on our NCOs for the answers."

Kitsy realized what had taken place: Another training session of Regimental Command 101. No wonder Curt Carson was assigning various officers as temporary regimental commanders when he was on leave. She knew that being in the barrel was the only way to learn. And she was learning more every time it happened.

"Wade, Harriet, thanks for coming in and shedding some enlightenment on the situation," Kitsy told them. "You're dismissed, but don't fail to let me know if something comes unbonded in your units for any reason. I'll go up the line if we can't do anything about it. And I don't want to hand Colonel Carson any more of a can of slime than he left for me to deal with! Henry, stick around for a moment, please."

Kester did, and after Hampton and Dearborn had left, Kitsy moved around the desk to sit with Henry without anything between them. She'd seen Curt do this when he wanted a down-and-dirty person-to-person without protocol getting in the way. "Henry, I'm worried," she confided in him.

"Lot of things out there to worry about, Major," Kester told her gently. "What's the big one?"

"I've been in the Greys long enough to know that when something goes to slime in the world, we're sent out to piss on the brush fire, ready or not."

"Yes, ma'am. That's why our Stand-to theme song is, 'Send In The Washington Greys!'"

"Or 'The Sierra Charlie's Lament,' " she reminded him. "My big worry is that right now the Third Herd is in miserable shape . . ."

"Morale seems to be fine, Major," Kester pointed out.

"That's because we're the Washington Greys, and we've had two years to recover from the debacle in Yemen. We're not tired. But we're short-manned and short-botted."

"We can do our job if called on, Major," Kester assured her in a fatherly manner.

"But not well. Dammit, Henry, we've got no regimental artillery company left to speak of! We've got the Saucy Cans, when we can keep them running, but we're short four sergeants there!"

"Captain Hall and Lieutenant Taire are experienced. Sergeants Barnes, Carrington, and Jouillan are competent and combat hardened. They can bring the new officer, Lieutenant Kyger, up to speed real fast. And they can run multiple Saucy Cans easier than we can run multiple Jeeps and Mary Anns," Kester tried to assuage her concerns. "Colonel Carson spent a lot of time with everyone shifting the T-O-and-E around so that empty officer slots were filled with good NCOs who'd accept commissioning. And so that all new officers and mustangs were supported by experienced NCOs. Does the T-O-and-E bother you, ma'am?"

Kitsy shook her head. "Not if it doesn't bother you, Henry. Does it?"

"No, ma'am. It's the best that we can do with what we've got," he confided in her. "And we ain't gonna get any more than what we've got. So we do what the Army's always done: Do the job with what we've got and fergit that we're short of everything except the enemy."

"Do you expect it to change any time soon?"

"Do you mean, will we ever get back to a situation where the armed services have the high-level support we need in order to do what we're paid to do when the high level calls for us to go out and get shot at? Sure. Probably. But I don't know when, ma'am. That's not my responsibility. Or ours. I been through at least five periods when military people were treated like third-class citizens who were a drain on the tax base," he went on carefully.

Henry Kester had his definite opinions about the role of the military in American life and in the twenty-first century world. But he kept them to himself. An NCO could bitch and moan a lot more than an officer, but it didn't help an NCO's career to have the reputation of being a political animal. An NCO might get away with openly criticizing the President or Congress where an officer wouldn't, but the exercise of such freedom would certainly find the NCO not being offered the chance to re-up when the time came.

Both Kitsy and Henry knew what they were really talking about. The present administration was solidly anti-military. The President had pulled the Third Herd out of Yemen just when General Hettrick and Col. Curt Carson had figured out low to keep from losing because they weren't permitted to win. In the pull out, they'd taken losses in people and equipment they hadn't made up for yet. And it didn't look like things were going to get better. The Washington Greys were being held together by scrounging and swapping techniques. They were keeping their old warbots running by fixing parts they would normally throw away, by scrounging used parts off old warbots, by substituting parts from industrial robots, and by swapping what they had lots of for things they had little of. Other warbot outfits—the Wolfhounds and the Cottonbalers at Fort Huachuca with the Greys—were going through the same drill.

"Henry, are we ready to deploy if we have to?" Kitsy asked. She thought she knew the answer, but she wanted his expert opinion.

"Depends where, Major. And to do what."

"You heard the news this morning?"

"What nasty sheep screw do you mean? Several going on out there in the Big World."

"Senegambia."

"Not much news about that, is there?"

"Enough for me to know that we've got another madman loose. Overt aggression. Invasion. Probably end up taking diplomatic hostages when they occupy Dakar."

"You're thinking maybe another Namibia?"

She nodded.

Kester shook his head. "Different circumstances, Major. That was an internal rebellion. This is just another invasion."

"I've been reading a lot of history," Kitsy admitted. That had never been her strong subject at West Point. But in Yemen, Curt had advised her to bone up on it because the path of promotion was restricted if one didn't know the mistakes of the past and use those mistakes to keep from making the same ones over again. She knew what he meant. Curt Carson was a master military historian and tactician. He had learned that from his mentor, Gen. Belinda Hettrick, when she was commanding the Third Herd. "It could be another Korea. And we'd probably be the first to go, even at Readiness Level Two or Three. So I think we'd better start thinking in

33

that direction, whether or not we have orders in hand. When it happens, it could happen fast."

"I sure can't argue with that approach, Major," Kester admitted, thinking that Kitsy was beginning to show glimmerings of the sort of leadership he'd known under Belinda Hettrick. He leaned back and looked up at the ceiling, then mused, "I sorta think I oughta increase our efforts at scrounging up to the best readiness level we can possibly sustain, given that the warbots are wearing out and the aerodynes are showing their age. Come to think of it, with the proper backing, I think that Sergeant Sampson and I can probably even make a few improvements here and there that weren't exactly reg when times were a lot more plush than they are now . . ."

"As only the temporary regimental commander, I'm not sure I can give you the authorization to go ahead on that, Henry."

"Ma'am? Authorization? You mean somebody's really looking at what's going on? From higher than General Hettrick's staff, that is?" Henry Kester tried to look innocent as he usually did when he was up to something on the sly.

"Yes, Sergeant Major. I'm looking."

"You really shouldn't, you know. You'll be responsible if something hits the impeller, Major."

"So? I've already had my neck broken once. It won't hurt so bad the second time . . . I hope." Kitsy reflected on what was happening here. Then she went on, "I've seen Colonel Carson do similar things that Hettrick didn't know about. It saved our butts multiple times. So let me tell you something, Henry: If you and the other NCOs are going to do interesting little things to the warbots, I damned well want to know about it. I'll be out there in the field beside them taking incoming. Anyone higher than the company level shouldn't give a damn what non-reg mods are in the warbots. All the warbots have to do is work reliably and hit what they shoot at."

"Major, you're in the line of fire if the IG decides he's got a hot one," Kester warned.

"Not exactly, Henry. I don't want to know exactly how you and Edie Sampson do what you do, and I won't ask you again about it," Kitsy explained. "I'll depend on Carol Head. He's a

34

good man. It will be impossible for the IG to trace all the non-reg scrounging and mods and changes to Uncle Sam's equipment through the NCO network. At least, if you do it right. And I know you will."

"Yes, ma'am. If you'll excuse me, I think I'd better get busy."

"Remember, Henry. We're going to try to have an outfit here that's good to go and hot to trot, regardless of what the bean counters and striped pants brigade in Washington try to do to us," Kitsy said as Kester rose to his feet. "And we'll build the damnedest Third Herd ever. How much do you think we can get done by the time the Colonel is due back in two weeks?"

Henry Kester wasn't a big man, but even he could look down on Kitsy Clinton, who was really petite. "How much do you want to get done, Major? The minutemen gathered over-night for Lexington."

Kitsy smiled in her pixie manner. "I suppose you ought to know, Henry. I presume you were there?"

"I remember it well," Kester returned her kidding. "An outstanding example of early partisan warfare . . ."

They were about to become embroiled in another such war.

Four

"This is Doctor Henri Mermoz. May I speak with Lat Dyor, please?" The male voice was cautious and spoke in French.

"Lat Dyor is speaking." The person who replied was a tall, very shapely, and extremely beautiful Senegalese. But Lat Dyor wasn't her real name. Nyamia Lébou was her professional name as one of the top fashion models in Dakar; she was married to Wade Abdoulaye, a photographer. She was emotionally distraught that evening. Her husband was in Dakar. She knew from Sundiata Linguére, her intelligence chief, that the Malitanian Army had occupied Dakar in a bold airborne move. All communications out of Dakar had been cut. She didn't know whether her husband was alive or dead. But she did know that she had a job to do now. The only way to get him out or to avenge him, depending on what had happened that afternoon when the Malitanians had swept through Dakar, was to do that job she had voluntarily taken upon herself.

She was also the de facto leader of the Garamandes. This group had formed itself as a civil defense league several months ago when it became obvious that Generalissimo Modibo intended to invade Senegambia. Overnight, it had become one of the Senegambian partisan resistance groups.

That is why she replied cautiously on the telephone. The Malitanians hadn't moved out of Dakar into the suburbs such as Mbour where she happened to be that day, resting in their beach home.

But she knew she was talking to another Garamandes

36

member. He had used her partisan code name.

"I have a patient with something that you should see," Dr. Mermoz told her with equal caution. "Can you drop by in the next few minutes?"

"Can it wait, Doctor?"

"No, I'm afraid it cannot. It has to do with the lethal plague that infected the area along the Saloum River. I need to send it out for analysis as quickly as possible."

She remembered that the doctor had a satellite dish. He often sent data to Paris or Phoenix for expert analysis, and he also used the satcom system to maintain independent communications ties with colleagues overseas. Mbour's local beautification ordinances didn't permit a resident to tarnish the lush landscape with such "ugly" artifacts as satellite dishes, so Mermoz had carefully hidden his. This capability made him the logical choice for operating the Garamandes' overseas comm links. Now these would be needed.

"Expect me," Nyamia told him and hung up. She grabbed her pocket phone, checked its operation, discovered with relief that the Malitanians hadn't yet seized the local node, punched in her call-forwarding code, and left the beachfront house.

Dr. Mermoz's combined home and office was only a few hundred meters inland. There she found the biotechnician sitting in his living room with a pale and trembling man. Speaking in English out of courtesy to the man, Mermoz introduced her to Duckworth Greenway.

"Haven't I seen your wildlife films on the BBC?" Nyamia asked him, recognizing his name and replying in Gambian-accented English.

Greenway nodded. He was obviously very shaken and out of sorts. "I was under cover along the Saloum River this afternoon when the Malitanian Army was attacked by a guerrilla outfit," he replied uneasily, speaking with hesitation as if he really didn't want to recall what he'd seen.

"The Kaolack contingent," Nyamia remarked. "It was not a good afternoon. I got the reports about an hour ago."

"I had my five thousand millimeter lens on my videocamera. The usual sort of equipment a videonaturalist uses, of course." Greenway was talking a bit more freely now. As with anyone who has witnessed something that shocks them right to their inner being, Greenway found that it was surprisingly easy to talk about it once he got started. And he felt better as he talked more, even though he was deathly afraid of the beautiful Senegambian woman. He'd always been afraid of women. The beautiful ones terrified him. But the terror he'd seen that afternoon overwhelmed the fright he felt now.

"You got tape of the battle?" Nyamia suddenly asked.

"Yes. It was . . . ghastly. I'm not sure I can bear to review the tape," Greenway admitted, his face sweating far more than necessary in the humid evening air. After a moment's hesitation, he went on, "But the world needs to see the tape. They need to know what's going on here in Senegambia. They need to stop these madmen from Malitania. So . . . so I remembered meeting Doctor Mermoz."

"We became acquainted at one of Fulani's dinner parties," Mermoz added. "I offered to let Ducks use my satellite link if he ever had to get something transmitted to London in a hurry and didn't have time to get into Dakar to do it."

Nyamia thought that "Ducks" was a highly appropriate nickname for an electronic birdwatcher. "Have you transmitted it, Henri?"

"No."

"Why not?"

"I reviewed it. As a medical man, I'm rarely affected by the sight of blood. But this tape is so powerful that I almost reacted as I did the first time I saw abdominal surgery. I was afraid that if we just transmitted it blindly to London or Paris, it might not get the sort of attention it deserves. It can certainly do a great deal to inform Senegambia's friends and possibly bring help. So I wanted to get your recommendations. You must certainly know the proper people to send this to," Mermoz explained carefully.

"If it's as powerful as you say it is, Henri, you're probably right. I certainly do know who needs to see it. But I need to see it myself to know for certain."

"I hope, my dear, that you haven't yet had dinner," Dr. Mermoz remarked.

"I haven't. There's been no time to eat."

"Good."

When the tape ended with a video screen of noisy snow, Nyamia had grown pale. It was only by means of incredible will power that she kept herself from becoming ill as a result of the very graphic and explicit scenes of the Malitanian soldiers' brutal and utterly ruthless murder and rape of the Senegambian resistance unit's survivors who didn't get away.

She regained control only because she forced herself to think about what to do with this incriminating piece of evidence.

"First," she finally managed to say, "we transmit it. Many times if we can. Then we duplicate it . . . many times. I want copies of that tape for Garamandes' use. And I want other copies of it carefully archived and hidden. It must not be lost to history. Henri, can you select the satellite and transponder you wish to use?"

"Naturellement!"

"Very well! But first I need to affix an introduction to it," Nyamia told him. "Mr. Greenway, can you make a videotape of me right now?"

"Ah, yes, of course," the naturalist replied with a slight stammer. He was still awed by her beauty, which reinforced his psychological fear of women. He found himself behaving in a way and agreeing to things that otherwise would have caused him to make a reticent withdrawal into his introverted shell. "I think I have a lens of normal focal length with me . . ."

Nyamia Lébou knew that she could get one satellite transmission out of Senegambia. Perhaps two or more could be sent, depending on the effectiveness of the Malitanian electronic warfare capabilities. And how fast the invaders could either locate the Mermoz sat dish or jam it. So the first transmission with its personal introduction by Nyamia had to go to the one person in the world she knew would be able to do something about it.

After she'd finished making the introductory and summation tape, Nyamia went into the bathroom and became sick to her stomach.

Then she returned to the task she knew she had to do. And she returned with even greater resolve than before.

Dr. Henri Mermoz not only transmitted the tape up to the satellite transponder Nyamia had identified, but made transmissions to London and Paris as well.

However, as Nyamia had pointed out, the important transmission was the first one. The others would serve as backups.

Gen. Albert W. Murray, USAF (Ret) and Director of the National Intelligence Agency in Langley, Virginia, had fretted all day. He had many subjects to occupy his time. Intelligence data flowed in from all over the world. Most of it was filtered according to a priority system. He saw only that information which got through the filters he'd established in weekly meetings, plus special tidbits of information that his top staff people and analysts believed would be of interest to him.

He'd set up an open filter on anything emanating from Malitania, Senegambia, or adjoining countries. Murray knew that all hell was breaking loose there, just as he'd predicted. His analysis of the Malitanian invasion had been off by only twenty-four hours. It came one day later than he'd thought. All the escalatory elements had been there. He'd watched the situation grow and fester for months. He had his agents lined up. Now the expected invasion had happened, and he was fretting because he wasn't getting enough data.

Murray knew the United States would somehow become involved in the Malitanian-Senegambian War. It was an outright invasion, an act of overt aggression. American policy stood firmly buttressed by numerous UN resolutions and more than half a century of foreign policy that even the current President hadn't had time to dismantle completely.

And he knew it would be a bloodbath because of the underlying and unvoiced Malitanian justification: hunger.

The stats were burned into his mind. The Malitanian population growth rate was near four percent per year. Nearly twenty million people lived in a country whose agricultural output could support one third of that number without malnutrition running rampant. The Malitanians were reaping the whirlwind of land mismanagement. The sands of the Sahara Desert had been slowly creeping southward across the country while the Malitanians continued to rape the savannah by over-grazing and over-planting. Year by year, the Malitanian food imports increased. Year by year, the value of their iron, copper, and coal exports had decreased. This imbalance further compounded the national debt incurred by importing more and more food. The situation couldn't continue.

Generalissimo Modibo had taken over the government of Mali in an attempt to straighten things out. In order to do that, he'd engineered the merger of Mauritania with Mali. He bought a few years there. Finally, because the Malitanian government was unable to control the country's population growth, the only answer was to race against time, using the exportation of natural resources to buy military capability.

Murray had watched as Modibo built up a starving war machine. The intelligence chief had tried to anticipate the direction in which the dictator would strike. Would he go after more resources to the east and south? Or for more food in the well-managed savannahs of Senegambia?

Two months ago, Murray stumbled on Modibo's obvious strategy: Move into Senegambia, slaughter the Senegambians, resettle his excess agricultural population, and thus ensure the Senegambian food supply for his population.

Murray would not have paid a great deal of attention to this if it had not been for a factor that affected the national security of the United States as a seafaring power:

Modibo couldn't have done it alone. He was being supported by the East World power block in its efforts to gain control of resources and trade routes.

But the intelligence chief was unable to convince his chief executive, the President, that Modibo's seizure of Senegambia had an additional consequence. It would mean that Malitania—and East World—would also control the Paris of Africa, Dakar. That city sat on the tip of Cape Verde, the easternmost point of Africa. With a naval base as well as an air base for long-range maritime aircraft at Dakar, the nations of East World could interdict most of the shipping routes of the Atlantic Ocean, including those used by oil tankers from the Middle East bound for North and South America as well as

41

Europe.

At 1600 hours, Washington time, Murray got his information. But it wasn't what he expected.

It came via messenger from the communications section. A videotape cassette had a scrawled note with it:

"Chief: Couldn't help but monitor this as it came in via satellite. Hope to hell you've got a strong stomach. And you may not sleep very well tonight. Signed, Chas."

His subordinate was correct. When the beautiful Nyamia Lébou's image faded from the screen as the end of the tape, Murray found himself shaking. Of all people high in the federal government, he knew how violent, vicious, and ruthless parts of the world still were. But he had to go into his private bathroom and do something he rarely did: take a tranquilizer pill.

This didn't really affect his extremely high anger level, however.

That sonofabitch Modibo has got to be stopped! Right now! he told himself. But who was going to stop him? Who could stop him? What country or group of countries had the diplomatic clout and the military might to halt the bloodbath? The United States of America qualified in the former area, but its military might had been deliberately allowed to deteriorate in the past two years. Furthermore, missing was the will to use military action in the classical tradition of Clausewitz.

He sat back down at his desk and started to think. Murray decided he had to initiate a clandestine operation. And he had to do it quickly. He had to overturn the foreign policy of the United States of America. If this act ever came to the attention of anyone in the White House, he might or might not survive as chief of NIA. He did indeed have a lot of inside information about personal activities of high-level people. They didn't know exactly what he had. This allowed him to keep his job. And he was highly dedicated to doing the very best job he could. Intelligence work was something that was distasteful to most Americans, although even Gen. George Washington had employed spies. So it took a very powerful man to hold the position of "chief spy" through several administrations. Murray often didn't like what he had to do to keep the job. But, thus far, he hadn't had to destroy a person's reputation. His own reputation was so apparently impregnable that no one had dared attack him. And he operated in such a way that his overt actions were beyond reproach. In short, Albert Murray was very, very careful.

So he didn't take notes; written notes could later be damaging. Nor did he think aloud; he was 99% certain that his office wasn't bugged, but one could never be sure of the uncertain 1%. So he thought about what he had to do.

The intelligence chief was well aware of the current left wing, anti-war, anti-military climate of "negotiate" that prevailed at high levels in the government at the time. He had to work around that. He decided he would have to orchestrate a scenario that would force the administration to take what was the honorable, correct, and traditional American response. He had to build a case for active response in a short period of time, and he had to do it in the National Security Council and with the full support of congressional leaders.

His first telephone call was to a philosophical comrade, one who thought as he did. Adm. Lewis S. Joseph, Chief of Naval Operations, came on the line at once when Murray punched in the secure personal number. "Lew, I need the Navy's side of Tiffany this evening. You're invited."

Having thus arranged an extremely secure meeting place that could be entered surreptitiously by high-level government officials, Murray called the Secretary of Defense, former Adm. Nelson J. Fetterman, and National Security Advisor Dan Gram. They were on the same side when it came to this sort of thing, even though they had to openly behave in accordance with the prevailing political climate in order to maintain a role in the game.

Then he played his hole cards.

He was holding a political IOU, and he called it in. Sen. Dan G. Bancroft of Ohio was Chairman of the Senate Armed Services Committee. Bancroft didn't like Fetterman very much, but Murray had some privileged personal information about Bancroft that caused the senior senator from Ohio to be extremely cooperative.

His other hole card was a new man on the Hill, one who

had been elected to represent the 3rd Congressional District of Arizona after he'd retired, having held the lofty position as Chairman of the Joint Chiefs of Staff. Situations like Senegambia were familiar to the man, the Honorable Jacob O. Carlisle (R-Az) and General, AUS (Ret.).

Five

"My God, I wish I could believe that was only very realistic special effects!" The Secretary of Defense was white-faced with horror and revulsion.

"And I wish to hell they *were* only special effects," NIA chief Al Murray muttered. He was nearly as upset over seeing the Duckworth Greenway tape for a second time that day as when he'd viewed it earlier in the evening in his office.

The super-secure Naval Operations Strategy Room in the ultra-secret Tiffany defense complex was silent except for the sound of the air coming from the environmental control ducts.

Tiffany was a relic of the ballistic missile age. It was so deep and so hard that it could withstand a 50-megaton deep penetration thermonuke detonation directly on top of it. It still housed the basic defense computer complex and strategic warfighting command of the United States.

Most people knew about Cheyenne Mountain. Fewer yet knew about Tincup. Some amateur spooks had guessed that Old Hickory was located in the roots of the Appalachians near Front Royal. But Tiffany was located where no one would ever suspect it, where comings and goings of both uniformed military personnel and high-level government officials were commonplace: deep, deep under a Washington Metro station called "Metro Center." It had been excavated when the Metro was built because who would notice additional digging? Those who had built it were now not only retired but long dead. And it was the place where the *real* warfighting work would be done.

"Not even Hollywood would dare be as graphically explicit as that tape," was Dan Gram's acidic comment. "How the hell did you get that tape out of Senegambia, Al?"

"Danny, you know as well as I do the only explanation I can give. We did it with 'national technical means,' " Murray told him. Even in this super-secure, debugged warfighting center, Murray didn't want to talk about his sources, although he trusted all of these men except, possibly, one.

"Which means you don't want to compromise your agents," Sen. Dan C. Bancroft snapped. He was the one Murray wasn't sure he could trust. But Murray knew that his presence in the elite group that evening deep in the bowels of Tiffany was absolutely essential to what had to be done.

Bancroft had come a long way since his days as a staffer on the Hill. He'd clawed his way up the greasy pole of politics until he became White House Chief of Staff under a previous administration. What he'd learned in his upward voyage through the corridors of Washington had gotten him the financial wherewithal and backing to run for the Senate. His power then had catapulted him rapidly to the lofty position of Chairman of the Senate Armed Services Committee. No one crossed Bancroft. He wasn't just a wily political infighter; he played dirty and went for your balls.

"That's correct, Senator!" Murray replied with a smile. The NIA chief was invulnerable, but he tried not to act that way. However, occasionally a man like Bancroft had to be reminded that even a senator's power could be topped, capped, and blocked.

"Outstanding agitprop. Most propaganda stuff is well-faked these days. As Nelson said, that tape could be damned good special effects. I know several SFX people in Hollywood who could do as well. So I don't for a minute believe that tape's the real stuff!" Bancroft suddenly said.

"I wish I couldn't believe it," was Fetterman's rejoinder. "But I know if Al called us together like this, he got it from an authentic source somewhere in Senegambia. I have to believe it's real although I don't like it. I spent my whole naval career trying to stop military rapacity like that and keep us out of war . . . and I'm still doing it."

"So what's the pitch, Al?" Congressman Carlisle put in. "You didn't call us in here just to make us heave our suppers."

"Very simple," Al Murray told the freshman congressman who also had an outstanding military record as CG of the 17th Iron Fist Division and Chairman of the Joint Chiefs. Carlisle had been too good at diplomacy and at political maneuvering to be left wasting and puttering in his garden in Sun City. He was a war hero in an era of war-hating. "How do we get the President to act?"

"About this supposed Senegambian bloodbath? Why the hell should we get involved?" Bancroft wanted to know.

Murray had anticipated that reaction from the senator. The former White House Chief of Staff had damned near ruined the Borneo operation, turned victory into defeat in the war with the Kurds, and hobbled the Sakhalin Police Detachment operation. He was a dove — except when it came to the cut-throat political warfare of Washington.

"Because our nation has a history of standing up to naked aggression, Senator," Murray replied in straightforward and unambiguous terms.

"Our interests aren't at stake in Senegambia!" the Senator objected.

"Senator, with all due respects, sir," Admiral Joseph put in deferentially, "more is at stake than just an overt aggression accompanied by brutality . . . although God knows that in itself is bad enough. Generalissimo Modibo is backed by the East World nations. Our intelligence on this is very good. When Modibo took Dakar today, East World suddenly got itself a strategic base of incredible influence on world trade."

"World trade? Hell, nothing comes out of Senegambia but a lot of peanuts!" Bancroft snapped back, revealing his general ignorance of West African affairs and economics.

"Senator, Dakar sits at the tip of Cape Verde with a wonderful harbor and an outstanding airfield. It's only twenty-eight hundred kilometers from South America," the naval flag officer reminded the solon. He rose to his feet and stepped over to the world map on the wall. As he went on, the Chief of Naval

47

Operations indicated the places he spoke of. "Based at Dakar, any submersible worthy of the name can easily control the narrowest part of the entire Atlantic Ocean. From the Dakar airport, any maritime aircraft with a modicum of range can reach out as far as Gibraltar, the Azores, Brazil, and all the way down to Saint Helena Island and the mouth of the Congo River. That sort of range allows the air and sea interdiction of five important sea lanes—Gib to North America, North America to Rio and Cape Horn, North America to Capetown and points east, Europe to South America, and western Europe to Capetown. Talk about the capability for sea control! The importance of sea control lies in the fact that the real bulk cargo of the world economy moves by ship. Those five sea lanes are half of the top ten oceanic trade routes of the world! And they could be cut by East World operating out of Dakar with extremely modest boats and aircraft!"

When Joseph resumed his seat, silence engulfed the room. "Lew, you've certainly studied your Mahan," was the comment from Gram.

The SECDEF, a former naval flag officer himself, observed, "All graduates of the Naval Academy have carefully studied the work of our earlier shipmate."

Bancroft's thoughts suddenly turned to those individuals and corporations who kept his political action committee well-funded. Then he said, "Okay, you've got a valid point there. So what the hell can we do? Stage a counter-invasion to take and hold Dakar? You're talking about starting escalatory warfare."

Using the stilted terminology he'd learned over in the south wing of the Capitol Building, Carlisle put in, "I believe my esteemed colleague from the Senate may assume that we have only one option. We have many. Human decency aside, first we must send a strong signal that we won't tolerate an East World military or naval presence at Dakar."

Bancroft reacted in a similar manner, mocking Carlisle's phraseology, "And how does my esteemed colleague, the congressman from Arizona, propose that we send such a signal to the sort of people who would carry out the kind of ruthless action we've just seen on the videotape? Seems to me Modibo has a very short memory. Why, just last week he promised the President that Senegambia wouldn't be touched if more Senegambian food was sent to Malitania to head off mass starvation there . . ."

"It isn't the first time a dictator has broken his word," Gram commented. "Or the last time, either. If we don't bat these bastards down every time we catch them lying, they won't get the message that their behavior is no longer acceptable in the world. Then maybe one of these days they'll wise up . . ."

"But some way must exist to get that message to them without going to war with them!"

"Sure as hell is," Murray ventured. "It's called a 'police action.' "

"Not another Korea!" Bancroft objected. "We got our ass whipped there!"

"Senator, it stopped an invasion . . . permanently," former General Gram reminded the man.

"Korea was the first military action that was called a police action, and it was accurately described," Murray went on to explain rather pontifically. It was obvious that Bancroft really didn't know history. Or fully understand the new role the United States' military and naval forces were playing in the twenty-first century world. So he continued his lesson, "When the cops catch someone breaking the law everyone's agreed to follow, the punishment should be swift and public to set an example and deter other renegades. But sometimes the circumstances require that it be quite restrained. Perhaps it's only a warning to the miscreant that he'd better watch his step in spite of power and position. Like the warning tickets some elected officials have gotten from time to time from the District Police." The intelligence chief needed to say no more.

Dan Bancroft *knew* that Murray *knew* exactly how many warning tickets the senator had received, for what infraction of the rules, where, and when. Some of them would make juicy copy for the sensationalist media or a damning indictment if someone was really out for his political hide. The information wasn't hard to get; the national data base could be accessed by nearly any law enforcement agency in the nation as well as by the intelligence community. It was a fairly simple

49

hack. Any bright teen with the proper terminal could do it. Most people didn't bother. With a plethora of information available, individuals were very busy keeping track of what they needed to know. It was one of those things you simply didn't have time to mess with. Who bothers to look up a neighbor's credit rating just for the hell of it?

"So what are you proposing to do, Al? Or you, Jake?" the Secretary of Defense wanted to know, cutting right to the heart of the subject matter of the meeting.

"Knowing you, Al, I suspect you've worked through a scenario pretty well," Carlisle remarked to the intelligence chief. "It may match what I have in mind. Why don't you lay yours on the table so that I can pick at it from the viewpoint of a person who's had to order friends and colleagues into combat quite recently?"

Murray, a graduate of "Blue U" at Colorado Springs, had learned years ago to like and trust this West Pointer. Their friendship had become stronger while Carlisle was CJCS. But he couldn't help ribbing his friend. "Jake, you just want me to lay my neck on the line so you can run over it with a warbot, don't you? Never mind! Don't answer that!"

This sort of black military humor disturbed Bancroft. He didn't understand it. "Dammit, are you joking about the possibility of going to war? That's sure as hell not what I would expect from some of the highest military and naval leaders in the nation! As for myself, I find the prospect of going over to Senegambia and taking part in that kind of a truly bloody war pretty damned frightening and downright distasteful! Civilized people shouldn't have to fight one another!"

"Maybe we've learned to joke about it, Senator, because it's even more frightening and distasteful to us . . . and we've learned that humor is one way to keep both our sanity and our perspective, sir. In the last century, a very fine author named Arthur Koestler wrote the seminal book about just that sort of thing." Adm. Lew Joseph had not only been an outstanding and highly decorated naval aviator and commander of the U.S.S. *McCain*, the Navy's first carrier submarine, but he'd spent his off-duty hours writing best-selling action-adventure war novels under a pseudonym. Thus, he always had a way of expressing himself that belied his extensive reading of world literature.

"Agreed, Senator. Civilized people shouldn't have to fight one another. But not everyone in the world is civilized yet. It's possible to refuse to loan money to someone, but if he wants to fight, you've got to oblige him. Now, let me get back to the subject at hand," Murray remarked. Then he went on, "I'm willing to make book on the accuracy of my scenario. As you might guess, I've got a lot of inputs. Anyway, the Senegambia bloodbath is going to get worse. Much worse. Every corpse is a mouth that Modibo doesn't have to feed. Soldiers operating under a leader like that usually aren't very gentle when they take over a country. They've got orders to spare the nation's infrastructure—the roads, buildings, telecommunications, transportation, industrial base, and especially in this case the agricultural facilities. Dakar is known as the 'Paris of Africa.' But what the Malitanian Army will begin to do there—if they're not already doing it—will make the Reign of Terror in Paris during the French Revolution look like a tea party. No looting and pillaging, but lots of raping and killing. It's going to get out of hand. Modibo may be saying that all foreign nationals in Senegambia are safe and that he's going to let all of them leave unharmed if they want to go. But I don't think he's got that sort of tight control on what his soldiers will do. Some Americans are going to be slaughtered along with the British, French, German, Italian, and Japanese who are in Dakar for business and diplomatic purposes."

"Another Namibia," the SECDEF muttered.

"Not exactly, Nelson," Carlisle interjected, and he knew a lot about that. "That was an internal uprising led by the Bastaards and Ovambos. This is an invasion. Totally different situation, although I agree that on the surface it seems very much the same sort of thuggery. Both involved outright butchery, but this one isn't based on racism or ideology. Overtly, its cause is hunger brought about by land mismanagement; covertly, it's a strategic move that's masked by the overt cause."

"Okay, Jake, since you said you wanted me to go first so you could take pot shots at me," Murray got them back on the sub-

51

ject. "Because you were the one who assumed joint operational command in Namibia, what would be your next step?"

Jacob Carlisle's reply was immediate: "Send in the Sierra Charlies accompanied by air and naval support as the shock force. Then hold Dakar with warbots and warbot brainies, restore law and order, and get our people out. Depending on how that operation went, I'd then tell the Generalissimo we'd occupy Dakar as a police unit base of operations to restore civilized behavior. I'd stay in Dakar until he sat down with the Senegambian government and negotiated his way out of his hunger problem. We did that in Chad, Sfax, and Iraq. And other places, too."

"Beirut," was the one word Gram uttered.

"Sort of. But I'd use warbots to hold the place. They're excellent at that sort of thing, as we discovered in Europe."

"You assume, I take it, that we're going to be doing this alone?" Fetterman asked.

Al Murray shook his head. "Initially. It should be a UN operation. But it takes a few days to thread the needle of a UN resolution and longer than that to get a multinational force deployed. We haven't got a few days. We're going to have to go in first on our own, then seek UN support. We haven't done that before, but time is of the essence here. So this is going to be a new one to work out—we go in first then convince the UN to follow us."

"Risky as hell! Puts the United States way out on a limb from the policy standpoint. I don't think it's going to work," Bancroft complained.

"Why not, Senator?" was Murray's simple question.

"It's a de facto war. Congress will balk. Believe me. Even if I could support it, I'd balk. It involves the constitutional principle of the separation of powers. And without Congress, the President stands little chance of getting a UN resolution." He paused, then went on, "Besides, you know the President. He isn't going to do it. He will not send in troops. He'll try to negotiate. I think that's the way to go. I think he'll win if he does so and sticks to his principles."

"If that's the way to go, Senator, then those who decide to take that path will cause a hell of a lot of people to be murdered. Most of them will be butchered just the way you saw on the videotape," Murray insisted.

"You military types always want to go in and shed blood! War is what you've trained for, and war is what you know how to do! You don't know how to wage peace!" Bancroft had said this many times before.

The retired Aerospace Force general who was now the nation's intelligence chief sighed. "I've spent my life trying to prevent wars, killings, slaughter, all the rest of the uncivilized list of nasty things people do to one another. I'm going to try my best to stop it in this case. I couldn't live with myself if I just turned my back on it. I've got to try."

"We're not the world's policeman!" Bancroft insisted.

"Senator," Carlisle interrupted his political colleague in a quiet voice, "I'm afraid America *is* the world's policeman. This violent world *needs* a policeman to maintain law and order. We're the only country strong enough to do it, and we're repaid a thousand times over by the benefits of peaceful trade that result. Now, a policeman doesn't go around bullying and shooting people; he patrols his beat in peace. He doesn't pick fights with people; he encourages them by example to behave in a civilized manner. But if someone shoots someone else, he goes after them." Those words were not only prophetic, but they would be heard again in times to come.

"So we have to convince the President to do what needs to be done," Murray finally said after Carlisle's words had soaked in. "Or we have to figure out a way to do it and then get his approval on it."

"Al, if I were you, I'd be very careful," Adm. Lew Joseph warned him. "Sounds to me you're advocating sedition. If that's what it turns out to be, I'm out of here. At once."

"Sedition? From the five of you? That's ridiculous!" Murray exploded. He looked around the table at the men he'd chosen to invite to this special meeting. "We're six people who can be trusted. We're six people who know *how* to make things happen and *can* make things happen. Our lives have been involved with leadership. That's the art and skill of imposing one's will upon others in a way that commands their respect, their confidence, and their whole-hearted cooperation. We're all leaders and damned good ones. Or we wouldn't be where we are. And none of us would be sitting in this room tonight. What we have to do is not to seize leadership and command. Our task is to help our commander in chief exercise leadership in a situation where he might not be well-equipped to do so. The President needs our help. It's our duty to let him know that and to convince him we're right.

"If that's sedition, then we'd all better retire to our rose gardens and wait for Armageddon because this nation and the world will very quickly go down the chute!"

Again, the room was silent for a moment while everyone thought about what had been said. It was finally Gen. Dan Gram, the National Security Advisor, who piped up, "Al, I think that if we want to get the President on our side, we need a little more help."

"How? Who?" Murray fired back.

"The Vice President."

"What? She's supposed to be as anti-war as the Man himself!"

"Aren't we all?" Fetterman reminded them. As if anticipating the senator from Ohio, the Secretary of Defense turned to Bancroft and remarked, "Contrary to the beliefs of some people, Senator, military and naval people are probably the most anti-war of all groups. They're the ones who are going to be shot at if war starts."

"Dan, I'm surprised at your suggestion that Henrietta Hamlin might be an ally," Murray went on. "Some of her public statements have been strongly in support of the President."

"And what else can a Vice President be but supportive when not quiet?" The National Security Advisor knew the lady long before the President had tapped her for his running mate. She had confided in Gram several times. "The Vice President is anti-war, but she isn't anti-military. She doesn't talk about her family's service."

Jacob Carlisle, the former CJCS, suddenly nodded in agreement. "Of course! Now I remember! Her daughter was wounded in Trinidad. And she lost a son in Yemen with the Wolfhounds. Her surviving son serves as a major in the Fifty-second Robot Infantry Regiment, the Ready Rifles."

"Henrietta Hamlin is in politics for the same reasons I've stayed in this Washington rat race: To keep war from starting if possible and to stop it if it does without giving away the firm," Gram explained carefully. "She has a clandestine motto: Peace through superior firepower. The President doesn't know that. He really doesn't care because she chairs only the National Space Council and does a lot of administration legwork. Now the rest of you know why you've gotten at least some support from the White House. But don't talk about it; it would undercut her effectiveness."

"You're sure you can get the Vice President, Dan?" To Murray, this was a coup of the greatest magnitude.

"I will talk privately with her tomorrow morning . . . early," the National Security Advisor promised.

"In the meantime, I think I can get a few things ready to roll," the Secretary of Defense mused.

Six

"Thanks for coming up on such short notice, Bill. In answer to your question about what's up, that's why you're here. We've just received the goddamnedest 'request' order that I've ever seen come down the chain."

Gen. Jeffrey Winfield Pickens really didn't like to deal with Lt. Gen. William D. Bellamack. They weren't close friends. They were colleagues in the highest levels of U.S. Army command. As Deputy Chief of Staff, Operations and Plans, Pickens was forced to work with Bellamack in this situation.

"I figured something was stewing on the catalytic burner," Bellamack told him because he knew exactly what was going on. He had his own network. You don't get to wear general's stars without developing one. He'd clawed his own way up the greasy pole of promotion in the Army in spite of Pickens. Years ago in the Persian Gulf Command, Bellamack had blown the whistle on an arms scam in the 21st "Gimlet" Regiment in which both of them were serving at the time. Pickens hadn't been implicated in the resulting IG investigation. And Bellamack had no reason to believe that the man had been involved. However, Pickens had always acted defensively around Bellamack.

The commander of the U.S. Army Forces Command at Fort Stewart never lost any sleep over Pickens. Wild Bill Bellamack had established his own career path in spite of the Gimlet incident. The powers that be knew he couldn't stay in the Gimlet Regiment. So they'd given him command of the Washington Greys after Namibia where Belinda Hettrick had been wounded and hospitalized. It was with the Greys in Iraq six years ago that he'd made a lash-up neuroelectronic linkage with a Soviet Spetsnaz soldier. It had resulted in Neuroelectronically Induced Psychotic Syndrome that took him out of the game temporarily. But he'd beaten that, too.

"It's not every day I get a call from you at oh-dark-thirty with a request to shag my ass up here," Bellamack went on. It was also unusual, Bellamack knew, to be asked to come unaccompanied by the key members of his FORSCOM staff. Thus far, the meeting between the two generals in Pickens' Pentagon office was following the usual informal protocol of polite social small talk at the beginning. "By the way, thanks for sending your Sabredancer. Mine's AOG. Parts are hard to get these days in a budget constrained environment."

"Don't mention it. It was important to get you up here today. And as you damned well know, we're not budget constrained. Hell, the funding's there. Appropriated. Authorized. But unavailable." Pickens didn't have to expound further on the situation. Just because Congress makes money available doesn't mean that the President has to spend it. The Commander-in-Chief wasn't spending most of the defense appropriation because it was against the man's publicly announced anti-military policies. The DCSOPS then remarked, "However, that may all change here shortly."

Bellamack said only one word: "Senegambia."

Pickens nodded. Folding his hands in his lap, he looked across the coffee table at Bellamack and explained, "That's why I asked you to fly up this morning. But please understand that we don't have orders yet."

Bellamack knew what was going on, but he had to let Pickens pass the word to him. Bellamack hadn't seen the unedited Greenway videotape, only those expurgated versions that had splashed across worldwide television news programs last night. "Another Zahedan. Or another Namibia. At worst, another Trinidad."

"None of the above," Pickens said. He got to his feet and went over to the credenza where a pot of hot coffee sat slowly steaming on a cat heater.

As he picked up the coffee pot, Pickens went on, "It's not

just an invasion. It's a bloodbath. The scoop from the spooks is scary. The Malitanians are butchering the Senegambians. Fewer mouths for the conquerors to feed. The ostensible reason for Modibo's action is simple: His people are starving, and the Senegambians are exporting their surplus food at a profit instead of giving it away to the Malitanians. That's the overt situation."

"My doting grandpappy once advised me never to believe the headlines. He said I should look behind the hype and figure out who was doing what to whom and who was paying for it . . ." Bellamack put in as Pickens poured him another cup of coffee.

"Modibo's army won't confine the bloodbath to the Senegambians. We've both spent our time in the trenches in the Islamic countries. We've seen how levied armies act when they start on a killing spree. No one's going to be immune from slaughter in Dakar, for example. The bloodbath will extend to anyone and everyone who doesn't wear a Malitanian Army uniform. Including our diplomats and business people. In fact it may have already started." Pickens put the coffee carafe back on its heater, returned to the couch, and sat down across the low table from the FORSCOMM commander.

Between careful sips of the hot coffee, Pickens went on, "Let me quickly bring you up to date because a lot happened this morning while you were flying. Senegambian President Leopold Sedar addressed the UN Security Council and requested military assistance. The latest hot skinny around here says that any resolution brought forth in the Security Council will be vetoed by guess who?"

"The same gang Belinda Hcttrick's division tangled assholes with in Yemen two years ago." Bellamack didn't even have to guess on that one.

"Hell, that was a rhetorical question, but you get a four -oh anyway," Pickens admitted. Anyone who believed that Generalissimo Modibo wasn't backed by the East World gang had to be living on another planet. "East World stands to gain a lot by controlling Senegambia. The United States will act because of the bloodbath; that's the emotional issue. But we'll be doing it because of the sea control consequences of East

World sitting on Cape Verde."

"Okay, so when do I have to move on them?" Bellamack asked in anticipation. He was an old warbot brainy who'd become a Sierra Charlie the hard way by taking over and leading the Washington Greys. He was a combat officer in his guts. He was also highly suspicious of the rest of the world. That was a psychotic trait left over from his linkage with the mind of a Soviet soldier which the therapists simply couldn't dislodge. However, this mild paranoia didn't affect Wild Bill Bellamack's overall performance as a military leader. In fact, it ensured that he had better intelligence sources than many other commanders. Army spook specialists fought to serve under Bellamack.

"Whenever the order comes, which it will. But it hasn't come yet. When it does come, it will involve an extremely rapid deployment. Better get ready."

"Jeff, you sound like you believe it's inevitable, even with the current administration's policy."

"Indeed. I do believe it's inevitable," Pickens admitted. "You've got to take my word for it, Bill. A very powerful movement is gaining momentum here. Very powerful. We'll go. Soon. The reason for bringing you up here is to get you up to speed in as quiet a manner as possible at the moment. That's why I didn't simply call you on a fiber optic line."

"I figured as much when the call came at oh-dark-thirty."

"What I've told you here is classified about ten levels above Cosmic Magic Top Secret, Destroy Before Reading, Suicide Immediately. The Warfighting Directorate has already started on the basic strategic operational plan. My staff is beginning to sweat the Army side. I need your input as FORSCOMM chief."

"I wish I'd brought my staff."

"You'll be back at Bragg tonight. Then you and your staff will have the enviable task of pulling off an all-nighter. Or two or three. This has to be a joint services operation. Complex as hell."

"What's the basic objective?"

"Overtly, to get our diplomats and citizens out of Dakar."

"We've done this sort of thing before. We can do it again."

"Maybe. Each of those operations was different. And, between you and me, be advised that once we're on the ground there, someone may decide to hang on to what we've paid so highly to get. We may have to stay there to make Modibo behave himself. Depends on what the UN finally decides to do about it."

"And The Man at sixteen-hundred Pennsylvania."

"We're not paid to worry about that part of the operation."

Bellamack figured that somehow the fix was going to be put in around the White House. He didn't inquire further. He could find out later. Because it was apparent from Pickens' request for input that Bellamack was going to be intimately involved, he asked, "What do you have in mind as an overall plan?"

"We'll be out-numbered and out-gunned. The Malitanians have Chinese Red Hammer warbots. So we have to conduct a highly surgical mission with fast reaction time. We can't telegraph our punches. So it will have to be an airborne strike force to grab Dakar Airport, followed immediately by seaborne forces coming off the Navy's *Raborn* Class submarines, which are the only fast-reaction troop carriers the Navy has left. And lots of air interdiction and support from the bluesuiters, of course. As for details, well, hell, we've just started thinking about what sort of an operation might work. That's where you come in."

Bellamack thought about that for a moment, then nodded. "If we had the airlift capability, it would be easier to eliminate the carrier submarines. Seaborne support only makes the operation more complicated."

"The Aerospace Force no longer has enough strategic airlift capability," Pickens reminded him unnecessarily. "We have to use carrier submarines. They scrapped the old submersible landing craft we used in Trinidad."

Bellamack shrugged. "So, as usual, we do the best we can with what we've got. Which isn't much these days. Four robot infantry divisions, three robot armored divisions, and three light armored cavalry divisions. All of them operating at between sixty and seventy-five percent of full strength with old, creaky equipment we should have junked five years ago."

"Based on the skeleton ops plan I just laid on you, what have you got available?" Pickens asked. He knew where those ten divisions were.

Bellamack had already thought about it on the plane ride north. It's a general's job to think about that sort of thing. And it doesn't hurt to have ready answers when someone in the Pentagon asks the questions. "I'd use the Fiftieth RI as the main holding force because they're finishing revitalization at Fort Bragg and aren't committed. A robot armor division takes too long to deploy, so I'd use the First Cav out of Fort Riley to give armored support because they're airmobile armored. And the obvious choice for the initial strike force is the only special combat unit we have, Seventeenth RI. . . ."

"Still got a hard-on the Big L, don't you?" Pickens observed.

"It was the Gimlet's division, Jeff. We both served in it," Bellamack reminded him. He didn't like Pickens' conversational use of the common soldier's slang at this level of command. To him, it denigrated the serious nature of what their jobs involved: the commitment of human lives to deadly combat. Grant, Patton, and other great combat commanders might have gotten away with it, but this was the twenty-first century. "And, face it, neither of us likes to order our friends into combat. So it isn't the old crap about 'fighting tradition' and such. I wish I could use the Twenty-sixth Division out of Europe because they've trained heavily in urban warfare. However, the Big L can hack it if they have to. And as for the Sierra Charlies of the Iron Fist, have you got any suggestions for any better unit to send in as the light, mobile, maneuverable strike force? The Sierra Charlies are trained and experienced in those areas. I helped write the Sierra Charlie book when I was with the Greys. They cut the catsup in Sakhalin, Sonora, and Kerguelen where both mobility and firepower were demanded. But not on warbot patrol operations like Iraq and Yemen. The initial strike force mission of Operation Bloodbath is exactly what Sierra Charlies do best."

"Okay, so do it," Pickens told him bluntly. "You've successfully operated with foreign forces in Brunei and with the Navy in Operation High Dragon. I'm recommending that you be named joint operational commander in chief of Operation Bloodbath."

What Pickens didn't tell Bellamack was that he hoped the man would fail. Such a command disaster would bring Bellamack's career to a halt. It would remove Bellamack as the one who might — just might — be able to clobber Pickens some day. Pickens wasn't exactly sure just how much Bellamack really knew about that old arms scam deal. Pickens believed he'd covered his tracks well; not even the IG had suspected.

Pickens wasn't deliberately sabotaging Operation Bloodbath. If Bellamack failed, he knew that Maj. Gen. Belinda Hettrick of the 17th Iron Fist Division could and would save it because she'd be on the ground in Dakar first. Hettrick was one hell of a good combat commander. And she didn't have a gotcha on Pickens.

Bellamack wasn't stupid either, but he was highly suspicious. He knew if he was the overall commander of Bloodbath, he would have to damned well pick the best people he could get and refrain from operating with the questionable ones if he could. He would use people he already had contracts with or could quickly generate contracts with others as required. This was something he had learned well while commanding the Washington Greys. Picking the right people who wouldn't screw him to the flagpole when the going got slimy would require him to use his network of little black spies to its utmost. It would cost him lots of political chits. But it would be worth it. Bloodbath might be the last operation of his career, even if he got another star before he retired. He determined to make Operation Bloodbath the high point of his Army career.

"Okay, Jeff, if I'm going to run this show, let's get with the briefing. Time may be short, and I don't want to have to operate with less than a full dossier of data. What time do you think I can wheels-up at Andrews for the return to Bragg? I'll need to call my chief of staff and have her alert the rest of the people to be prepared to work all night . . ."

"Forget the briefing," Pickens told him suddenly. "That was just an excuse to get you up here so we could have this face-to-face. Considering all that we've been through in our careers, I needed to be absolutely sure you were the right man to run

Bloodbath. I'm now convinced you are. And that's what I needed to know. My Sabredancer is equipped for full neuroelectronic speed briefing. I'll give you the briefing cubes. You can get up to speed in linkage on the return trip. You are up to NE linkage, aren't you?"

Bellamack had no trouble with straightforward neuroelectronic linkage of the sort used to operate warbots in the regular robot infantry regiments. What had brought him to grief in Iraq was attempting mind-to-mind linkage with a Soviet Spetsnaz soldier. Because he read and spoke Russian fluently, he'd thought at that time he could thus get inside the Soviet NCO's mind and communicate directly. He'd tangled with a phenomenon that NE experts could have warned him about. People always think in terms of the language they learn first, their "milk" language. That determines the basic programming of an individual's mind. Learning another language allows a person to add what amounts to a conversion utility on the basic mental operating code. But a second language cannot change that code. Once an English-speaker, always an English-thinker. Or German. Or Russian. Or especially Chinese.

Bellamack smiled. He thought this might be a chance to start developing a contract with Pickens. He hadn't been able to do this before because they hadn't even been in the same batt when they served in the Gimlets. So he replied lightly, "Jeff, I might have damned near gone KIA in Iraq, but I don't recall enjoying it at the time. I got all my circuits rewired and functioning properly afterward, thanks to a lot of help."

However, he still didn't totally trust Pickens. This private meeting in Pickens' office was an opportunity for Bellamack to try to conclude his own contract with the man. So he went on, "Jeff, we'll be working very closely together during Bloodbath, if we get the orders to proceed. I hope we won't, but I don't see any viable alternate outcome to the situation. In the Army, we proceed with a lot of 'givens', but I want to make sure we understand one another. There's been some strain between us for years, and we managed to handle it because we weren't involved together on an operation or mission. Now we are. I want to guarantee you right here and now that I won't

63

shoot into your goal if you don't shoot into mine. I'll keep you informed of what I'm doing, and you can trust my reports. If I think I've got a problem, I'll let you know. We've got a big game to play here that can be a win-win for both of us. I intend to play it square with you throughout."

Pickens was a bit surprised at this. But it had been brought before him by another general officer who was junior to him. Bellamack's offer of a contract didn't cause Pickens to change his mind about having set this up so that if Bellamack failed, the mission wouldn't collapse. Pickens wasn't a vindictive man, just cautious. Caution had saved his ass in the past. Having a fall-back position in case of command failure was just a precautionary act, he told himself. So he played that same cautionary card again and replied, "Bill, I didn't get four stars by climbing up other peoples' backs with my golf shoes on. I keep my spikes in my locker over at the Army-Navy Country Club. You've got the Bloodbath job, and that includes my support. Now go do it."

Pickens didn't add that he would shift his support to a winner if Bellamack wasn't one.

Seven

"I don't know how you do it, Pappy, but you manage to find me even if I'm not on this planet." Col. Curt Carson looked tired and disheveled. Six hours ago, he'd been 200 kilometers out in space, orbiting the earth in Brunei's second space station. The Royal Brunei Airlines spaceplane had made a special stopover at Ajo Aerospace Port. Liquid hydrogen was available there to refuel it for its next jump to its original destination in Brunei. Lt. Nancy Roberts had been waiting for him with a UC-21A Chippewa aerodyne. The ride from Ajo to Fort Huachuca had taken almost as long as getting back from orbit.

"That's my job, Colonel," Lt. Col. P.G. "Pappy" Gratton replied. "A good adjutant should always know where the regimental personnel are, even on leave. Welcome back!"

"Well, thanks for nothing, of course," Curt told him. "I'm just glad that I didn't have to pony up the hundred thousands of dollars it cost the Sultan of Brunei to drop me off in Ajo on the way back."

"Yeah, the regimental funds would have taken a beating on that one, all right," Gratton admitted, then added, "and we've got no authorization to expend additional funds while going to Red Alert."

"So who's doing what to who out there in the big, nasty world?" Curt wanted to know, preferring to get a personal update from his adjutant rather than attack the files of messages waiting for him on his desk terminal screens. "Why the hell did we get the order to cancel all leaves and passes?"

"I wasn't told, Colonel. You'll have to talk to General Hettrick about that. She gave Major Clinton an order, and your temporary regimental commander told me get you home ASAP." Gratton had spent a decade as S-1 in the Greys; most people spent their entire careers in the same regiment in the twenty-first century Army. He was a good adjutant. Furthermore, as an RPC 40 Personnel officer, he didn't have to double as an RPC 11E Sierra Charlie infantry soldier. But when the situation went to slime, he could shoot a Novia with the best in the regiment and take incoming, too. He was authorized to wear the Combat Warbot Badge, had qualified for the Expert Marksman Badge, and had earned the Purple Heart the hard way in Brunei. "Actually, Colonel, it was easy to find you. Major Clinton seemed to know. And she also issued the recall order with a certain amount of relish."

"She would!" Curt muttered. "I imagine she got her belly full of regimental command again and wanted me back to take the monkey off her back."

"Kitsy does a good job as temporary CO, but I don't believe that was her motivation." Then Gratton asked in a confidential tone, "Tell me, Colonel, just between us boys: Is it any better in weightlessness?"

"Yes and no. Depends a lot on the compartment padding," Curt admitted, then added, "and the companionship, of course."

"I understand that it's difficult to maintain contact. Lot of restraint aids required. And I'm not really into bondage."

"Nor am I. Let's just say that I required no support equipment." Curt might have gone on at somewhat greater length about it, aware that he probably should use this opportunity to polish up his stories before Stand-to. But he was interrupted by a knock on the door.

It was Maj. Kitsy Clinton, Maj. Jerry Allen, and the rest of the regimental staff.

Curt remained seated behind his terminal desk. After several days in the weightless condition of orbit, the presence of gravity again bothered him a little bit. And the ride down from orbit has been a little rough. In order to land at Ajo, the pilots had had to make several high-gee cross-range maneuvers. It took extra hydrogen fuel to do that. The sultana had okayed it because of the urgency of Curt's recall order.

He waved his arm. "Everyone come on in! Excuse me for staying on my ass here, but I've been back in gravity for less than three hours."

Lt. Col. Joan Ward, chief of staff, stifled a brief cough with her right hand and said, "Yes, sir. We understand, sir. I'm sure that Major Gydesen will confirm that's the cause."

"I wasn't aware that you were that badly out of shape, Colonel," was the brief comment from Capt. Dyani Motega, S-2.

"He wasn't when he left, and leave is supposed to relax and rejuvenate a person," Maj. Kitsy Clinton commented.

It was obvious that some of the ladies of the Greys were getting a little sweet revenge. Rumor Control had suitably embellished the possibilities of an official family matters leave. Because he was officially a member of the family of the Sultan of Brunei, Curt had received an invitation to Alexis Morgan's wedding with all expenses paid. Few military people could afford that sort of a trip. Furthermore, the ladies of the Greys were more than slightly green with jealousy because weddings were high on their interest priority list. And, like men and women everywhere for the last hundred years, they'd heard stories about the potential joys of love-making in the absence of gravity.

Jerry decided that this wasn't the time and place for the ladies present to have a little fun at the regimental commander's expense. That's what Stand-to was for. As far as he was concerned, it could wait until then. "We got to see a little bit of the wedding on TV, Colonel. About twenty seconds' worth on the evening news. Alexis Morgan looked terrific!"

"Yeah, that was sort of romantic, being married to the son of the richest man in the world in an orbital luxury resort," Master Sgt. Edie Sampson said wistfully.

"But we're glad you're back, sir, because you were missed," Regimental Sgt. Maj. Henry Kester chimed in.

"And because it sure as hell looks like things have gone to hell in Senegambia," Maj. Russ Frazier, S-3, added. "That's the only reason I can figure out for Fort Fumble on the Potomac putting us on Red Alert."

Kitsy stepped forward and saluted Curt. "Colonel, it is with great pleasure that I return command of the regiment to you. I'm glad you've got it again. And I'm glad you're back." She was sincere in saying those things. Kitsy was always jealous of the sultana, being unable to match her for sheer exotic beauty and wealth. On the other hand, along with the other ladies of the Washington Greys, Kitsy knew she had more opportunities. Furthermore, she believed she could certainly handle the competition which was in the form of Dyani Motega. But that was just Kitsy's outlook on life, perhaps best summed up by the fact that Kitsy believed anything worth doing was worth overdoing.

Curt returned her salute with a crisp snap of his arm. "Very well, Major. Now, I want a full and complete briefing on the regimental status as well as the Red Alert order. Can you do it here, or shall we go to the conference room?"

"Colonel, it's fifteen-hundred hours," Kitsy complained. "Do you want to delay Stand-to?"

Curt nodded. "Stand-to can wait until I get up to speed. If we're on Red Alert, I need to know status and anything else you can report. Like right now. A deploy order could come at any time."

"Then I guess we can do it here to save time," Jerry remarked.

"I'll get Colonel Worsham and Colonel Hampton," Gratton remarked.

"We'll start without them. Everyone find a place to park it. Major Clinton, you were temporary regimental commander," Curt said needlessly, "so you can lead off."

Curt's office was a mini-conference room. At right angles to his terminal desk was a terminal table capable of seating seven. Other chairs were arrayed around the walls. The wall opposite Curt's terminal desk contained both a screen and a holo-tank. So the people in the office took their usual places with the seven staff members at the table and Jerry and Kitsy at side chairs.

Kitsy didn't sit down. She went to the lectern at the far end of the table and turned equipment on. The regimental TO&E appeared on the wall screen. Picking up a laser pointer, she reported briefly, "The regiment encountered no unusual or unanticipated problems during your absence on leave, Colonel. We participated in two divisional staff conferences that led to a series of scrounging operations to Davis-Monthan. Within the division, we swapped some supplies and parts with the Cottonbalers and the Wolfhounds. We are at sixty-six percent of authorized manpower. Most of our personnel shortage is in NCOs. The regiment is at fifty-two percent of authorized strength in warbots, sixty-nine percent in vehicles, eighty percent in aerodynes, and seventy-three percent in expendable supplies. We are listed as ALO One but we're actually at ALO Three."

"Why?" Curt snapped.

"General Hettrick has been told by Sixth Army that the criteria for ALO One have been revised so that we technically qualify."

"Do you know who bucked down that order? Who changed the standards?"

"Unknown, sir."

"Fort Fumble, I'll bet!" Curt groused. It was September. That meant it was budget authorization time on the Hill. The Department of Defense was trying to make things look good. Either that or SECDEF was covering the demolition of the military services with a scam of reducing standards. Curt didn't know or care which, but he didn't like the games the government was playing. He was trying to earn his pay properly by keeping the Washington Greys in a condition to fight as they were supposed to. If something went wrong in the world and the Third Herd was sent somewhere to piss on a brush fire—as had happened again and again in the recent past—Curt didn't want to be forced to order his close friends into deadly combat when they were outnumbered, out-gunned, or out-botted. So he asked the next obvious question, "Out of those percentages you just flashed on the screen and related to me, what's our actual operational strength? What's working that we could put into the field right now if the whistle blew?"

"I was hoping you wouldn't ask me that," Kitsy admitted. "The staffers have the exact numbers. I'll defer to them for the precise details in their individual briefings. But it's an average of two-thirds of the equipment percentages. We could fight with the regiment if we didn't go up against anything more than a Chinese reserve regiment. Actually, we could take on anyone's full non-warbot regiment if we could stand a shortfall in regimental artillery support. Division says our request for NCOs with RPC-thirteen just hasn't gotten any action at DCSPERS."

Curt said nothing but ran his right hand over his chin in contemplation. He decided he needed a shave before Stand-to. It had been nearly 24 hours since he'd shaved. Or had it been longer? His circadian rhythm was certainly all screwed up. Jerking his thoughts back to the present situation, he came to a conclusion he didn't like. The Red Alert sure as hell meant that the Third Herd was about to be sent somewhere in the world in a hurry to do something nasty to someone who wasn't behaving. From the sound of Kitsy's report—which told him that nothing much had changed for the better since he'd departed on leave—the Washington Greys were going to have to do the job with whatever they had or could scrounge up in whatever time was left.

Without revealing his gloomy thoughts, he told Kitsy in a firm, commanding tone, "Thank you, Major. I appreciate the fact that you not only held the unit together well during my absence but that you apparently spearheaded progress toward putting the unit back into fighting shape."

That caught Kitsy off guard. "Uh . . . I did? I mean . . . Oh! Yes, sir! I did my best, sir, but I had good people supporting me all the way!"

Curt knew all that he had to know. However, common courtesy from a commander required that he let each staffer report in turn, then listen to reports from the three batt commanders. These reports didn't add to what Kitsy had explained except to fill in a few details that were of minor consequence to the major problem: The Washington Greys weren't up to full strength. Even after more than two years, they hadn't recovered from the debacle in Yemen. The funding hadn't been there, and support from the administration was totally lacking. Thank God that Gen. Belinda Hettrick had handled most of the congressional visits and fact-finding tours as well as the inquiries from members of the influential Arizona congressional delegation. The only time that Curt became involved was when Congressman Jacob Carlisle, former 17th Iron Fist Division commander, showed up for a visit. Carlisle had once served in and commanded the Third Herd. Once a Grey, always a Grey.

Curt expected Pappy Gratton's report. "We're fully staffed with officer personnel," the older man explained. "That's mainly because your recommendation for field promotion came through for Harley Saunders. The three new lieutenants are working out well because of your plan to promote experienced NCOs to serve directly under them as platoon sergeants. Pearson is being backstopped by Trumble. Mikawa has Jim Elliott . . . although she doesn't need help. I suspect Major Clinton will fill you in on Mikawa later. Kyger is being handled by Vic Jouillan, but you should get a private briefing from Captain Hall about how he's restructured a badly undermanned GUNCO to operate short four NCOs or forty percent of his T-O-and-E. We're undermanned, Colonel, but we're short mainly in the lower ranks and files. We could fight if called upon to do so."

Lt. Col. Wade Hampton's report on the logistics, supply and maintenance side of the house was controversial, however. "As Major Dearborn noted in her report, we can't get parts, and we can't get replacement equipment through normal quartermaster channels. So we've organized several scrounge details. Most of these were forays to the boneyard at Davis-Monthan."

"How the hell did you get in there without authorization?" Curt asked, although he'd already guessed the answer.

It was Regimental Sgt. Maj. Henry Kester who responded. "Colonel, we managed to get the authorizations. They were signed by General George Ducrot, Deputy Chief of Staff for Logistics, by order of General Terry Balzoff, commanding."

"I see," Curt said and pressed no further. He knew exactly what Henry, Edie, and the others had done.

General Ducrot didn't exist and had never existed except in a computer database. The same was true of Gen. Terry

Balzoff. But this was known only in the combat units of the United States Army. Normally, either general would have retired more than 50 years ago. Somehow, their ages kept being revised in the databases. And they both had serial numbers, computer access codes, and computer passwords. It was a secret that was about as closely guarded in the infantry regiments as the highly classified warbot linkage technology. Therefore, no one really knew how many requisitions and authorizations bore the approval signatures of these two.

And Curt didn't want to know. Nor did he want to know who among the NCOs had initiated the computerized paperwork. In fact, he wasn't supposed to know officially about Ducrot or Balzoff. But he wouldn't have become regimental commander, much less a company commander, if he didn't.

"I'm a little concerned," Curt put in, "about the reliability of any components obtained in the boneyard."

"Colonel, we check 'em out real good when we get them back to Huachuca," was the comment from Edie Sampson, the chief tech NCO. "If they pass the smoke test, we run full diagnostics on them. About forty percent of the stuff fails before it ever goes into a warbot or vehicle. Sixty percent for the aerodyne parts because Ron Knight in AIRMAINCO has much tighter test criteria. He says he's never seen a warbot or an ATV fall out of the sky and make a smoking hole in the desert . . ."

Curt agreed that the aircraft maintenance people did indeed have a point. But he went on, "How about the Mod Seven-Eleven parts? None of those should be in the D-M boneyards. And when I left, the supply situation for those modules didn't look exactly good."

"Colonel, remember Owen Pendleton?" Jerry asked.

"The techie hostage we brought out of Zahedan with us? The one who accepted a commission and went to work at McCarthy Proving Grounds? Hell, yes! Been years, but . . ." Curt recalled. Owen Pendleton was just about the sharpest neuroelectronics expert Curt had ever met. In the years since, the man had become a real expert in neuroelectronics, bioelectronics, and artificial intelligence interfaces. He was still at McCarthy working under the now-retired but still professionally active Willa Lovell. "Got in touch with him," Jerry admitted. "The guy is now a full bird colonel, but he hasn't lost any of his urge to rise to a technical challenge. Ahem! Not that full colonels ever lose anything they formerly had, I mean!"

"I'm glad you qualified that, Major," Curt said, trying to sound stern but laughing inwardly at Jerry's unintentional gaffe.

"Anyway, sir, when I told him our problem, he flew over one day. He's strapped budget-wise, too. But he's got one hell of a big cultch pile over at McCarthy," Jerry explained, using the ancient New England term for "useable junk that's just too good to throw away because we might find a use for it a few years from now." The Greys had their own hoard of cultch quietly stashed away. It was useful when it came time for swaps with other outfits. If the Army ever had tried to run its logistics by the book, it would have collapsed a couple of centuries ago into a pile of rusting muskets and mess kits. "So he got excited about being able to bootleg some research on how to upgrade the Mod Seven-Eleven AI units. Said he could 'turbo' the existing Seven-Eleven modules with some of the new nano modules that just came on the commercial market."

"Sounds like a lash-up, a make-do," Curt observed. "Could be dangerous if we have to depend on it."

"I feel confident in anything Pendleton does," Jerry replied.

"Henry? Edie?" Curt asked the two most obvious techie experts in the group. "What do you think?"

"Colonel, it's non-reg as all hell, but I'd rather have it non-reg and workable when the metal jackets start to fly," Kester said slowly.

"It's working, and some of it is slicker than all hell," Edie added quickly.

"Wade, will Benteen and Otis and their people be able to handle the Level Two repairs on the stuff if we happen to go into a fight and it goes tits-up?" Curt wanted to know.

Wade Hampton grinned. "Colonel, Fred and Woodie are just about as deep into it as their people. They're real happy because now we've got a non-reg supply channel through McCarthy Proving Ground that bypasses all the crap that Harriet usually has to dig through."

Curt looked at his S-4. "Harriet, do you have any heartburn about this?"

Maj. Harriet Dearborn replied brightly, "Why should I, Colonel? It's my job to make sure the regiment has what it needs. I'm just delighted with all the help I'm getting from my colleagues. And most of the stuff that comes in from D-M and McCarthy on swaps and cumshaw doesn't get listed in my databases. That means I don't have to account for it!"

The Washington Greys were one hell of a unified team, Curt decided. But they'd always been that way. As regimental commander, one of his biggest jobs was to keep the team functioning as before. He also had to improve it where he could, impossible as that might seem to be at any given time.

After all the briefings were done, Curt decided that the Greys were ready. Ready for what, he didn't know. He had to find out. "Okay, sounds like we could handle the usual sort of sheep screw we normally get sent to. And Red Alert means better than a fifty-fifty chance that we'll be going out to save the free world once again. Joan, give Wilkinson a call up at Division. My compliments, and find out when I can see Battleaxe so I can be brought up to the same level of ignorance and confusion as everyone else around here! The rest of you, thanks for your update. Now get back to your jobs and assume we'll be moving somewhere in the world on a few hours' notice! It won't be war, of course, but it could be just as deadly!"

Eight

"They're not murdering *everyone!*"

Nyamia Lébou hadn't had very much sleep for several days, ever since the Malitanian invasion. So she reacted to this report from the Garamandes' intelligence chief, Sundiata Linguére, with some sharpness in her voice. "But *nearly* everyone! Hundreds of thousands now! Who are they sparing? Collaborators? If so, we must know who they are so we can . . ."

Linguére slumped into a chair. The beachfront home of Mariama Fulani was now serving as the temporary operational headquarters for the Garamandes. The partisan movement had gained considerable momentum and members since the Battle of the Saloum River. The Greenway videotape had been pivotal in marshalling the citizenry of Senegambia as well as world opinion. But no outside help had come to Senegambia yet. The Senegambian Army had disintegrated under the onslaught of the Malitanian ground and air forces. So the irregulars, the Garamandes, knew that they were the only factor left in the equation. They were the only ones who might possibly halt the bloodshed. At least, that's what the Garamandes thought. Reality was something else.

"Managers and workers in critical public service positions are being spared," he told her. "The Malitanians need to keep the water works, sewage systems, medical facilities, electric power, and communications networks running."

"Until they can bring in their own managers and technicians," Mariama Fulani snarled. She was a doctor, but she

75

hadn't reported to the Pasteur Institute in Dakar since the invasion; it was overrun with Malitanian troops. The reports said that the hospitals were being looted and the patients being shot in their beds. Therefore, Dr. Fulani could do nothing in Dakar except perhaps get shot. And someone had had to step in to command the growing legion of the Garamandes Irregulars because the former commander had been slaughtered at the Saloum River. Fulani took the job, although she was a doctor and knew little about military matters. She was, however, a leader and a manager. And that's what was needed at the moment.

"How can the Malitanians possibly get any cooperation?" Nyamia wondered. "If any of our people voluntarily cooperate, we should establish a database for future use. Collaborators must not be allowed to live . . ."

"Nyamia, my dear," Linguére interrupted her, "Georges Damas reports to me that the Malitanians have set up concentration camps. One of the first ones was Parc de Hahn zoo. The zoo specimens have been slaughtered. Those animals that couldn't be eaten had their carcasses dumped in the harbor. The families of the managers and technicians have been rounded up and placed in the zoo cages. That's supposed to be a temporary detention measure. The Malitanians are constructing other detention camps in the Zone de Reboisement northeast of Cemberene. The managers and technicians are being told that if they continue to do their jobs well, their families will not be harmed."

"Do they believe this?" Nyamia wondered. "People are going to die in those filthy zoo cages without adequate sanitation. And in the concentration camps as well! The Malitanians have no intention of allowing Senegambians to live! They intend to slaughter us all so they don't have to feed us!"

The Garamandes' intelligence chief nodded with a grave look on his face. "I know that. You know that. And I've passed along this information to outside intelligence agencies with whom I've maintained contact. That's about the only way we can get information out now. Modibo's forces are preventing any foreign media crews from leaving their aircraft at the Dakar-Yoff International Airport. The forces are sending the crews back to Europe and America. The reporters and camera crews that were already in Dakar . . . well, we don't know exactly what happened to them, but my guess is that we'll never even find their remains. Modibo's minions are controlling every scrap of news that gets out . . . except through our Garamandes' satellite comm links with the outside world, of course."

"We'll kill the bastards! We'll kill them all!" These words seemed totally inappropriate, coming from the beautiful Nyamia Lébou.

"No, Nyamia, that's not the answer." These quiet words came from an older man who had been sitting quietly in one corner of the living room. He'd been looking out over the waters of the Atlantic Ocean and listening to what had transpired in this temporary Garamandes' headquarters. In his younger days, Léon Keita had fought with honor and distinction in Sierra Leone and Liberia when the Senegambian Republican Guard had responded to calls for help from the governments of those countries. Thus, he had been sought out by Nyamia Lébou to advise the Garamandes because of his honorable service in the military forces of Senegambia. As part of the Garamandes' leadership, he was looked upon as the Grand Old Man, the wise one who should be listened to when he spoke. So the people in the room, their tempers hot and flaming as a result of the reports of the Malitanian atrocities, stopped and listened.

"We tried that in Liberia, and the Liberians hounded us out of the country. We couldn't kill all the evil people in Sierra Leone; tribal loyalties were more powerful than the sense of nationhood," Keita explained, getting to his feet and walking into their midst. His two-meter height was commanding, and he knew how to command. When the French still ruled a colonial empire in Africa, his forefathers had fought with valor for France as an officer of the Senegalese troops in both world wars of the last century. "Therefore, our strategy must be two-pronged. First, we must continually harass and kill their leadership. The Malitanians are a mixed bag, mostly very individualistic Moorish-like Berber nomads as well as

77

Songhai and other black tribesmen. Their loyalties are to their leaders, not to Malitania as a nation. So we must continually go after their leaders. Assassination must become our trademark. Georges Damas is an expert in such terrorism; he learned about it the hard way while fighting with us in Sierra Leone."

"Two things bother me about your suggestion, General Keita," Mariama Fulani interrupted. "It will take too long; we'll be decimated before we can kill all the Malitanian leaders. Secondly, we're badly outnumbered. And probably under suspicion as well. I wouldn't be surprised if we had to shoot it out with Malitanian troops here within a matter of days."

"You didn't wait to hear the second part of my suggestion, Mariama," Keita said in mild rebuke. "We can't do it alone. I know that. We need help from the outside. So that's the second part of my suggestion: Call for help."

Linguére snorted. "We got President Leopold Kairaba Sedar out of the country with his cabinet so he could appear for help at the UN. He's in New York now. Under constant guard, by the way. The Malitanians have already tried to assassinate him right outside the General Assembly building. That fact had absolutely no impact upon the response to his pleas for help yesterday in the Security Council. The PRC vetoed a very mild Security Council resolution condemning and deploring the Malitanian invasion. Forget about the General Assembly doing anything. And all the General Assembly is willing to do is talk, talk, talk! And condemn the blatant disregard of human rights by the Malitanians!"

"Sundiata, my friend, you don't fully understand the politics of the situation," Keita said quietly. "The UN will blather about human rights' violations for years and do nothing. However, human rights aside, the important fact is that Senegambian resources will no longer be available to those who provided the venture capital to exploit them. They must either write off their investments or protect them."

"They took no action in Sierra Leone!" Linguére reminded him.

"And for very good reasons. The diamonds, the gold, the bauxite from Sierra Leone kept flowing through the government's corrupt bureaucracy to the market economies. The financial and business interests of the West World had no reason to expend resources to secure continued access to Sierra Leone's resources. They continued to get them at prices they were willing to pay. This is different. Senegambia's resources will be diverted to the East World. So when we ask for help, we must ask the right people."

"And who might those people be?" Linguére wanted to know.

"I believe you've already asked them," Keita told him. "It won't take them very long to react. So be ready to help them when they come. And let's continue our assassination pressures on the Malitanian leaders. Don't go for the hands and feet; go for the brain! That's a simple rule of warfare. And this is warfare, not 'armed conflict.' I wish that UN phrase wasn't being applied to activities that really amount to war!"

The telephone rang and Nyamia picked it up. "Fulani House," she said into it.

She didn't hold it more than ten seconds before she replied, *"Bon!"* and hung up. With smooth and rapid motions, she began gathering hard copy print-outs and maps that covered the dining table. "We must move! Quickly! We'll head inland to Soussoum, then to your base at Fissel, Keita!"

"Visitors?" Keita guessed.

"One of our sentinels reports a company of Malitanians is heading south on Road N-One! They'll be here in thirty minutes or less! And we have no forces ready to ambush them! So . . . Sundiata, diskcopy the data and zap the memory cubes! Mariama, gather what you can of your things; I doubt that the Malitanians will leave much behind for you after they loot this place!"

The true nature of this war suddenly broke on Mariama Fulani. She'd studied hard in Paris, sweated through an M.D. degree, worked hard at the Pasteur Institute in Dakar, and had finally achieved status and prosperity in the form of her beautiful beachfront home. "Thirty minutes? I can't gather up all my things in thirty minutes!"

"Then, my dear Mariama, I suggest you get the critical items you'll need in this war—your FAM rifle, lots of ammu-

79

nition, and all the food you can carry," Keita advised her, turning to pick up his own automatic weapon and military pouch. "I'd also suggest you take a medical kit. We're going into an area that's somewhat primitive. And we'll all need not only your good shooting but your medical expertise as well!"

They weren't quite fast enough. Or the Malitanian company travelled faster than the sentinel had estimated. As they were preparing to leave, the front door to the house was suddenly slammed inward by two burly Malitanian corporals armed with A-99 assault rifles.

Both Nyamia and Keita responded instantly, wheeling to bring their FAM rifles to bear on the door. Neither wanted to waste ammo, so they each fired a three-round burst in the general direction of the door. The six bullets did their assigned jobs.

In the ensuing confusion of the remaining troops outside, the four Garamandes departed through the large doors overlooking the beach and ocean.

However, the Malitanian company commander wasn't totally stupid. He'd sent a detachment of four troopers around the north side of the house just to make sure no one would or could escape. What these four tall Malitanians weren't expecting was an armed citizenry getting out of the house. Thus far, the Senegambians they'd encountered along this stretch of the *Petite Côte* had been older professional and business people who were unarmed. They didn't expect the four Garamandes. Nyamia, Keita, and Linguére fired first; Fulani, not being totally comfortable yet with a personal firearm, was the last to shoot. As a result, her rounds went into the trees high above the heads of the Malitanians.

"Not down the beach!" Keita snapped a warning as Fulani headed in that direction. "Into the vegetation! To the left! Come along now!"

"My Toyota Big Horn is garaged a hundred meters this way!" Nyamia revealed, her breath coming in gasps. She was hyperventilating. The excitement of the fire fight had started adrenalin pumping through her brain.

That caused her to hesitate for a split second as another group of four Malitanian soldiers came around the other side

80

of the house and blocked their path to the garage.

One of the Malitanians fired in haste. His fully automatic burst went high and to her right. Even trained soldiers have a tendency to shoot high when firing in haste on full auto. Thus, she wasn't hit by bullets. But when the A-99 rounds hit the tree, splinters flew. Some of them hit her.

She screamed in agony as her beautiful face—a visage that had graced the covers of magazines and video screens in Senegambia and Paris—was suddenly covered by her blood. She dropped her FAM rifle as her hands went to her eyes.

Linguére shot from the hip, blowing the four Malitanians backward as rounds found their chests and exploded out their backs accompanied by eruptions of blood, flesh, and bone. The Garamandes' intelligence chief had loaded soft hollow-point hunting rounds, not military steel jackets as required by the Geneva conventions. As a result, the Malitanians almost exploded.

More soldiers were coming. Keita scooped Nyamia's rifle off the ground and grabbed her left arm while Fulani took her right.

"Go for the garage!" Linguére yelled. "I'll cover your rear!"

By the time the Malitanian captain realized what had happened, the Garamandes group reached the garage and piled into the all-terrain Big Horn truck parked therein. Nyamia was in no condition to drive, but the keys were in it, and Keita took the wheel. Fulani got the screaming Nyamia into the back seat while Linguére took the right front seat. He yelled to Fulani and Keita, "Go! I'll provide fire support! Drive this heap, General! Mariama, take care of Nyamia! Is she all right?"

"No," was the only answer Dr. Mariama Fulani could give at the moment.

Within a minute, General Keita had the truck out on the unpaved road lined with baobab trees and was roaring away from the house that had nearly become their death trap. Keita needed no instructions on how to get to Soussoum. No roads were shown on maps, but he didn't need a map. He'd grown up in this region. He knew it. He also knew the best places for ambush, and he turned off the rutted road and crossed the tree-dotted savannah to avoid them.

It wasn't a smooth ride on a four-lane super-highway. Fulani's job tending to Nyamia's wounds wasn't an easy one. However, Nyamia stopped screaming in pain as the doctor gave her a pain-killing injection to knock her out. Only then was she able to gauge the exact nature of the beautiful woman's wounds.

Nyamia was by then unconscious from the effects of the trauma and the pain-killing injection. Her head, shoulders and colorful blouse were soaked in blood.

Dr. Mariama Fulani didn't like what she saw when she'd gotten Nyamia's bleeding stopped and the wounds cleaned up as well as possible under the circumstances.

Once the chances of being overtaken by the Malitanian patrol had become slim, Linguére turned in the right front seat. "How is she?" he wanted to know.

Fulani shook her head sadly. "Splinters. Wood splinters from where the bullets hit the tree next to her. I've got most of the bleeding stopped." She sighed heavily. "Plastic surgery will eliminate most of the scars to her face, neck, and shoulders. But, oh my God, I can't save her right eye! Not when a splinter's gone right through the cornea and pierced the retina as well! If I could get to the Pasteur Institute, I might try reconstruction."

"The Pasteur Institute is in the hands of the Malitanians . . . and they've looted it," Linguére reminded her.

"She's going to need a hospital," Fulani remarked. "I don't know how in God's name I'm going to be able to maintain asepsis in the sort of rugged conditions we're going into. I'll have to enucleate her eye to prevent infection."

Even though he was concentrating on driving, General Keita had heard the conversation clearly. He shook his head sadly and remarked, "She's such a beautiful woman! What a shame! What a pity! But war is never kind to anyone. Is she going to be able to continue as the Garamandes' leader? Or should we make other arrangements?"

Fulani shook her head. "I don't know. I just don't know. She wasn't wounded elsewhere. Most of the splinters just cut her. Her eye is the serious wound. If I can get any sort of clean place to keep her for the next few days, I might be able to head off gangrene or worse. I have to enucleate that eye before that splinter infects the entire orbit and spreads infection directly to her brain. If I can prevent that, she'll only lose her eye. Not her life."

Keita tried to keep his attention on driving. "My place on the savannah is about as clean as we'll find in the bush. We'll just have to get there as quickly as possible. And you'll have to perform a medical miracle, Mariama."

"I'll try. Nyamia is too important to lose."

"And she won't be the first military leader in history to have only one eye," Linguére added.

Nine

"It isn't often that I get invited to dinner by a general," Curt quipped as he entered the suite in the Thunder Mountain Inn.

Maj. Gen. Belinda Hettrick wasn't one to mince words with friends. "Oh, really? Then you've forgotten all the occasions when a mere colonel invited you to dinner? Or when that same person bought you drinks and a meal when she was wearing railroad tracks?"

"I always figured that stars made a difference," Curt admitted. He could speak in such a light vein with Hettrick when they were in private as they were then.

"Have silver birds made a difference in your case?" Hettrick retorted. Her words might have seemed sharp, but she spoke them in a way that was almost coy.

Curt nodded, realizing that she was merely trying to get him to drop his façade of military formality. General's stars were a formidable social barrier. And a full colonel's insignia was also formidable; it was unique in the American armed forces. No other rank has a single silver eagle. Not gold. Not doubled or tripled. But a single icon. A silver bird is a silver bird, period. Oak leaves came in two colors, but eagles came only singly in silver. Stars came single or in groups up to four. Only a colonel had a unique badge of rank. "You know damned good and well they have! You've been there yourself."

"They have a tendency to turn you into an old fuddy-duddy if you let them, don't they?"

"Not exactly. But one tends to become a bit more cautious," Curt admitted. "At least, in my case."

"Pardon my non-generalistic language, but *bullshit!* You've never been known for excessive caution, Carson! Especially when it came to meeting a lady off-post at her invitation. And *why* are you cautious? Cautious over *what?*" With a smile on her face, it was obvious that she was kidding him now in retaliation for his lighthearted quip.

"Cautious as to why we're meeting off-base." Curt had found a message from Hettrick for him to call her after his staff meeting and "how-goes-it" session ended.

"You'll find out!" Hettrick was older than Curt by many years. She'd often reminded him in the past that there might be frost on the roof, but there was still steam in the boiler. Since this get-together was off-base, informal, and unofficial, she was wearing a skirt, blouse, and low-heeled pumps. Thus attired in something other than Army Green, she was an attractive middle-aged woman. The effects of her extensive medical fight against a Namibian Bushman's poisoned arrow many years ago were no longer evident. Furthermore, she kept in shape, although as a general officer she wasn't required to crawl on her belly in the mud any longer. Hettrick was no rear-echelon type, and she always considered that she might have to go out and get shot at if circumstances required it. In Yemen, the sheep screw there had indeed demanded it.

Curt knew the general wasn't putting the make on him. It had been many, many years since they'd done close-order drill together. That had been back in the days of Hettrick's Hellcats when neither of them were field grade officers. Occasionally, Hettrick liked to play games with him, and this might be one of those times. So he grinned as he replied, "Rumor Control could have a feeding frenzy over this."

"Great! Let them! It will divert their attention from other hot rumors that we can neither confirm nor deny until we get the Ungarbled Word from Higher Headquarters." She settled back comfortably on the sofa and told him, "However, we're really going to play it cool, Mister Salley and Cashier will be here momentarily. But I wanted to talk to one of my favorite subordinate officers first. And you can be about as subordi-

85

nate as they come when you want to be. Wet bar is over on the left there. Help yourself."

"It must be Super Cosmic Top Secret, Destroy Before Reading," Curt commented, pouring himself three fingers of good scotch at her invitation.

"Well, let's just say we haven't got any orders yet," Hettrick admitted. "That doesn't mean that we shouldn't anticipate by doing a little advanced planning J-I-C among us highbrass types. I didn't want the four of us to meet in any of the on-post clubs. That would only add to the speculation that's currently running rampant in Rumor Control Headquarters."

"Senegambia?"

"My lips are sealed until Maxie and Rick arrive. Then I can bring all of you up to the same level of ignorance and confusion that I enjoy," Hettrick explained, then added, "I asked you to come early so we could talk a little bit first."

She settled comfortably on the couch with her legs tucked under her. "Sorry I had to interrupt your little family gathering in orbit. I'm also sorry I couldn't be at Alexis Morgan's wedding. She certainly caught herself a rich one, didn't she? Especially after spending years denying that the affair was anything but just good clean fun."

"Former Major Alexis Morgan has always been her own woman, General."

"Yes, she has. And even more so once Dyani was commissioned."

"No, it started long before that. If I knew then what I know now, I might have changed the course of affairs, so to speak."

"Well, I often wondered why you and Alexis didn't make the arrangement permanent. But," she said with a shrug, "apparently, it just wasn't meant to be. I finally believed that fact when I saw what was going on between you and Dyani. You changed. A lot. When are you and Dyani going to make it permanent?"

"Not while we both have jobs that expose us to combat," Curt admitted. "Took a while for the two of us to work that one out. Thanks to a lot of help from Jerry and Adonica, by the way. Dyani and I had role models to work from. And I've never been hesitant about asking for help from subordinates."

"I watched you go through the wringer. With a lot of concern on my part for you, by the way. Glad you got it worked out between you because if you thought Jerry had it bad, you were worse."

"I discovered that," Curt admitted, recalling the sheer hell he'd put himself through when he'd become smitten by Dyani, couldn't figure out what had happened to him, and found himself nearly out of control when she'd gotten into a potentially deadly situation with a religious space cult in Battle Mountain, Nevada. "But I'm surprised to find you so interested in my private life."

"If I wasn't, I wouldn't be worth a damn as your commanding officer," she told him frankly. "I don't want to pry or meddle unnecessarily. You've got your job to do with the Greys and your private life to handle as you see fit. I don't need to become entangled in either one unless you have problems with the professional one or need a sympathetic ear with the private one. However, in case you never noticed, I've always been interested in what you're doing, my friend," Hettrick told him frankly.

Then she went on in mock seriousness, "And knock off the honorific crap. Ain't no one here but us chickens. And some of us aren't such young chickens any more, either! But we can cackle with the best of them. By the way, I'm going to give you only one more order tonight, then you're officially off duty. Order: Sit down because I know you've been back in gravity for less than eight hours."

Curt sat. "Thank you. Is it that obvious?"

"You forget, Mister, that I knew you when you were a newly minted brown bar fresh out of West Point and Benning. And we've been through a fracas or two since then."

A strident series of raps on the door were followed by the arrival of Col. Maxine Frances Cashier, commander of the Cottonbalers. After greeting them and pouring herself a drink at Hettrick's suggestion, Maxie sat down and remarked to Curt, "Carson, you look like hell! What's the matter? Your zero-gee gymkhana too much for you?"

Curt grinned. Maxie Cashier was hell on wheels with turbo-boost. She was a very attractive woman who forced the world to play by her rules when she could. She always wore cosmetic makeup, even in combat. But her bright blonde hair was always done in a male-style high-and-tight crew-cut. Blue Maxie, as her tacomm code call tagged her, intimidated a lot of men because she had a very strong and demanding personality. But Maxie was always a lady. Thus, she respected the fact that Curt had his own liaisons within the Washington Greys, especially with Dyani. As a result, Curt treated her with the same respect and admiration as he would any of the ladies of the Greys. The two of them could work together very well when their regiments were in combat alongside one another in the 17th Iron Fist Division. Yemen had proved that. "Hell, no, Maxie! I was in good physical shape when I went up there, and the experience helped me stay in shape. You ought to try it sometime yourself!"

"Damned well have half a mind to do it the next leave I can wrangle for myself . . . and providing I can find suitable companionship," Maxie decided. Curt often wondered what kind of a man she would consider to be "suitable companionship." One thing for certain: He would have to be all man to stay even with Blue Maxie.

Maxie went on in her no-nonsense way, "Well, glad you're back, Curt! Missed you in the recent war games. That little major of yours — Kitsy Clinton — she's a pistol! She made mistakes, but not many of them. She made up for it in other ways. Jeez, it's tougher than hell to beat such enthusiasm. And, General, I figure we'll be needing a lot of enthusiasm pretty quick. I know we haven't got orders yet. Otherwise, you wouldn't have called this private palaver off-base . . ."

"Have another drink and loosen yourself up, Maxie," Hettrick told her easily because she liked and respected Maxine Cashier. In many ways, Cashier was a far less inhibited version of a younger Belinda Hettrick. Both were ladies. Always ladies. But Hettrick had developed a far higher level of tact and diplomacy in the way she interacted with the world. The general went on, "Not that you need it. But I'm sort of curious what might happen if you shed the few inhibitions you might have left. And, as I told Curt, this is a private party. Knock off the rank crap. If it makes you uncomfortable, use my code

88

call. But don't be offended if I call you Blue Maxie in reply."

"As you wish, Battleaxe!" Maxie wasn't intimidated by general's stars. In fact, she wasn't easily intimidated by anyone or anything. On the contrary, she was usually the one who intimidated others. It made her a worthy military adversary.

When Col. Rick Salley of the Wolfhounds showed up a few minutes later attired in slacks and a turtleneck sweater, Hettrick went into action. "Get yourself some ethanol, Rick. Then relax. I've already ordered dinner for us. You're all highranking field commanders, so you automatically eat whatever's put in front of you anyway because you're too damned busy with affairs of higher command, right? No sense in burdening you with just another decision. We're dining here in the suite tonight."

"Aha!" Salley remarked. "Super Cosmic Top Secret stuff, I see. Must be about Senegambia."

Hettrick shook her head in dismay after she'd phoned the order to serve down to room service. "Goddammit, what the hell is leaking through to Rumor Control? Everything?"

"Only that a Red Alert without specific orders to back it up means someone is working hard on the Oval Office right now to send the Iron Fist Division into Dakar," Salley replied easily. "Marty Kelly had an ops plan worked out for the mission within thirty minutes. He figures that if the Malitanians are slaughtering the Senegambians, we ought to go into Dakar and slaughter a few Malitanians ourselves."

"My God, Rick, don't tell me you haven't managed to housebreak 'Kill-Em-All' Kelly *yet?*" Hettrick asked.

"No. I don't think anyone could. And I'm not sure I want to. In fact, I'm glad I've got him. He's a good S-3. Sort of counterbalances me. I'm rather a devout coward, you know," Rick Salley replied.

Salley was anything but that. The way he'd led the 27th Robot Infantry (Special Combat) Regiment into combat at Battle Mountain and in Yemen belied his personal evaluation of himself and revealed his self-deprecating sense of humor. Rick Salley acted like a laid-back gentleman from South Carolina. But his Wolfhounds were like Maxie's Cottonbalers and Curt's Greys; they would follow their colonels anywhere, knowing that they had regimental commanders who were not only one of them but also took good care of them.

The twenty-first century American Army was an all-volunteer group of highly-motivated, highly-trained, and very adult people. They knew they were warriors, people who didn't mind fighting because someone had to do the job. They all ascribed to an unwritten warrior ethic whose trappings were only partly revealed in Army traditions, protocols, and behavior. They were professionals in the classical sense of putting ethics, codes, and honor ahead of other personal interests. They weren't professionals because they got paid for doing something as opposed to amateurs who did it for its own sake. A true professional trains hard every day, maintains high standards of performance, and can be relied upon consistently to do the very best possible job. And they were professionals because they earned their pay, often by putting their lives in jeopardy.

They bitched and moaned and complained like soldiers everywhere have done at every time in history. But when they were called upon to do their professional work, they went ahead and did it. Inside, they hoped the world would no longer need warriors someday. But until Utopia became reality, they knew someone had to fight for those who didn't believe in it. Otherwise, the whole world would be in the hands of the Attilas.

Thunder Mountain Inn wasn't a posh place. It didn't have robutlers. Because it was in an Army town, a good labor pool was available, and the management wanted to help those military people and dependents who needed some part-time work. So dinner was wheeled in on a table by a teenager, not a robot. He paid no attention to them; they weren't wearing uniforms or rank insignia, so they could have been tourists. Just four men and women, none of whom looked special or were demanding special treatment. Thus, this private dinner took place with good security.

"Haven't had seafood like this since I was in the Vee-Eye with the Cottonbalers," Maxie remarked.

"I doubt that this can beat that, but they fly this in daily from San Diego," Hettrick told her. "And, by the way, this is

90

just dinnertime small talk, understand. Nothing official. How ready are your regiments?"

"For what, Battleaxe?" Maxie asked.

"Rapid deployment to Dakar."

"I thought so!" Salley remarked. "What sort of a mission?"

"First order of business: To get our diplomats and any other American citizens out," Hettrick told him.

"Uh, Belinda, it's probably going to be more than just another personnel extraction mission," Curt put in, savoring the abalone.

"Do you see something else in the cards?"

"I do. I saw an unedited version of the Greenway videotape," Curt explained. "The Brunei defense minister had it. It was also sent to Bandar Seri Begawan in Brunei. The sultan has some investments in Senegambia."

"That figures," Hettrick remarked. "So what did you see on the unedited videotape that leads you to believe we'll carry out more than a straightforward personnel extraction mission?"

"I won't try to describe that tape over dinner. But it was rough. Very rough. Only time I thought I'd lose my lunch in zero-gee," Curt said, pausing to take a sip of the very smooth white wine that accompanied the meal. "Basically, the Malitanians are butchering the Senegalese. You might call it genocide."

"Yeah, I track you, Curt," Salley put in. "That's really a food war over there."

"You've got only part of it, Rick. That's what will marshal public support in the news media. But the Malitanian invasion of Senegambia also puts the East World in control of Dakar, which is a strategic sea control point," Curt told him.

"Damn! Why didn't I see that?" the commander of the Wolfhounds exclaimed, slapping his forehead. "Yeah, we'll have to take Dakar and hold it! At least until Generalissimo What's-His-Name promises to behave himself and withdraws his troops from the country."

Maxie shook her head. "That won't happen. Modibo won't do it. He's Muslim. Shi'ite Muslims don't like to retreat. They'll go down in flames first. If they capitulate, they'll be

91

drummed out of the corps, so to speak. If they fight and die, they'll go to paradise."

"So we'll have to take Dakar and hold it to prevent Modibo's troops from killing everyone there and taking it over for themselves," Hettrick agreed. She thought about this for a moment before she went on between bites, "The intelligentsia will demand it. Dakar is a miniature Paris. Sort of like Paris must have been back in the twentieth century. Lots of artists. Booming fashion industry. Fountainhead of biotechnology research second only to Brunei. A growing industrial center. And a robust banking industry for western Africa."

"Belinda, are we going to get involved in another one of these goddamned warbot-type operations?" Curt wanted to know.

"What do you mean? Guard and patrol duties?"

"Yes. That isn't our bag. We're Sierra Charlies. We're best at shock, strike, maneuver, that sort of operation," Curt reminded her unnecessarily. Belinda Hettrick commanded the only United States Army division made up of three Sierra Charlie regiments. The other divisions and regiments were pure warbot outfit where soldiers lay on neuroelectronic linkage couches well to the rear and fought through war robots kilometers away. Pure warbot doctrine didn't work in a lot of tactical situations, and it couldn't easily be modified to handle them. Thus, the Washington Greys had been the first to put humans back on the battlefield alongside warbots. The Cottonbalers and Wolfhounds had followed. "Our performance as Sierra Charlies on warbot-type patrol and guard missions has always been miserable as a result. Didn't the massive losses and casualties we took in Yemen have any effect on the people in Fort Fumble on the Potomac?"

"They're all warbot brainies up there, Curt," Hettrick reminded him. "I spent my time in the trenches on the Pentagon's OSCAR desk, which was a sop to those of us who exposed our precious pink bodies to incoming fire. I know that trying to get those warbot generals to understand the Sierra Charlies is next to impossible. They think of us as supernumerary troops they can send in like the old Commandos, Rangers, and Green Berets. But my time behind the OSCAR desk in DCSOPS helped me find out where a lot of bodies are buried. So all is not lost when it comes to us getting the slimy end of the pole every time. And to the best of my knowledge, this fracas isn't being officially backed topwise yet. The Red Alert telephone call I got wasn't from DCSOPS. It came from Wild Bill Bellamack at FORSCOMM."

Curt grinned. "Well, maybe there's some salvation here yet. Wild Bill knows what Sierra Charlies can and can't do. He discovered the strengths and weaknesses of Sierra Charlie units for himself in Sonora and Iraq. We couldn't get anything done in Mosul until Bellamack did an end run around Pickens. Then we configured Operation Iron Fist to take advantage of our mobility and fire power! Is he in charge of this show?"

"There is no show . . . yet. Wild Bill will probably get the joint command. It will be a mixed bag if ever there was one. Sierra Charlies and warbot brainies. Navy. Aerospace Force. Hell of a combined operation," Hettrick explained between bites. "More wine, Maxie. This doesn't come our way often, and we may have a lot of fighting to do before we can convene again like this. So, Rick, assuming we were indeed to get orders to take and hold Dakar, how would you do it?"

"Well, Battleaxe, you just about laid the ops plan on us. Airborne strike. Followed by the Sierra Charlies because we're air-transportable," Salley suggested. "All our Chippewas have air-to-air refuelling capability now. They can hack the range situation."

"But the Malitanians have a powerful air force, Rick," Maxie reminded him. "We'd have to go in with better protection than our Harpies could give us. That means Aerospace Force participation."

"Or the Navy's carrier submarines," Rick shot back. "Matter of fact, the whole operation could be staged off a couple of carrier subs."

"With two and maybe three full divisions?" Maxie asked incredulously. "Get serious! We'll have to charter the QE-Five or something to carry all the troops and equipment in there!"

Curt was mulling over in his mind the complex factors that would be involved in what looked like a multi-division operation involving all three services. It wasn't going to be easy to pull off, especially on short notice. "Rick, Maxie, this isn't going to be a simple operation," he warned them. "The Aerospace Force or the Navy — probably both — will have to catch the Malitanian Air Force on the ground. We'll have to go in by Chippie simultaneously because the air strikes will alert the Malitanian defenses. That means we take the airports first. I don't recall the geography of Dakar real well at this point, but I think the city is on sort of a peninsula."

Maj. Gen. Belinda Hettrick knew exactly what she was doing in hosting this very informal and private dinner off-base. It was better than a full staff planning session. In the first place, it wasn't strapped down by military protocol or the need for people to posture or protect turf.

Her three regimental commanders were, she believed, the very best in the business. They combined audacity, leadership, tactical savvy, a knowledge of military history, a grasp of strategic doctrine, a make-it-work approach, and the sort of personal intensity and drive that was required to make a complex military operation work with the least effort and the fewest losses. Furthermore, they worked together with no jealous turf guarding.

She hadn't received any orders to implement Operation Bloodbath yet. But Bellamack had told her that it wouldn't hurt to do a little planning. That didn't cost anything and could save a lot of panic later when the balloon went up. So that's exactly what she was doing. For the price of three good meals, she was exercising the sort of leadership she knew would work.

These three colonels got deeply into the problem. Rick Salley began sketching on the tablecloth. Maxie Cashier moved wine glasses and tableware around on a mock battlefield. Curt watched, listened, committed it all to memory, and added his particular talent for tactics based on the lessons of history.

So she sat back, enjoyed the rest of the meal, and watched. And she knew that these three wouldn't sleep very well tonight if they even bothered to hit the sack at all.

Operation Bloodbath was planned in a motel room in Sierra Vista, Arizona, 9,421 kilometers from Dakar. Later, the division and regimental staffs would fill in the details.

It could have been worse, she decided. Operation Husky, the Allied invasion of Sicily, had been sketched on a damp mirror in a men's latrine in Cairo.

"You realize, of course, Rick, that this tablecloth is now highly classified," she finally pointed out to Col. Rick Salley.

Ten

The President preferred to keep his evenings free for "contemplation, planning, and study." He'd risen through the ranks of academia because he took this time when he could, but he used it for scheming more than contemplation. His evening "mentality time" had resulted in his appointment as head of the political science department, then dean of the liberal arts school, then chancellor of the university. With his influence thus extended into the state educational system, he'd moved into politics. So he didn't like to have his evening personal time usurped by conferences with members of Congress. But he had no alternative in this case.

Sen. Dan C. Bancroft was a power broker in Washington. Furthermore, Bancroft was on the chief executive's side on most foreign policy matters, especially those where the armed forces played a role. Bancroft was second on the President's list of those he worried about. Bancroft knew where bodies were buried.

For the same reason, NIA Director Al Murray was number one on the President's list of people to worry about.

But the President couldn't fathom why Senator Bancroft had requested that Congressman Jacob O. Carlisle of Arizona be included in the conference "as a personal favor." Carlisle was a retired Army general, a former Chairman of the Joint Chiefs of Staff, and a freshman congressman from a financially powerful state. For more than eighty years, people had retired to Arizona and brought their nest eggs with them for deposit in the local banks. The investment of several trillion dollars by these banks had turned the Phoenix-Tucson metroplex into the eastern financial hub of the Pacific rim.

Thus, Carlisle's constituency was inherently very conservative and very business-commercial minded. State politics was and had been low comedy; voters preferred just enough bureaucracy to run the state and stay out of the affairs of the business and financial communities. On the national scene, the state had wielded enormous political clout ever since it had been admitted to the Union.

Carlisle was *not* on the side of the President or Senator Bancroft when it came to foreign policy. The President suspected that Carlisle still maintained deep contacts within the defense establishment. Therefore, the congressman was an enigma to the President. Why would an honorably retired four-star general voluntarily give up full retirement pay and perks to serve as a congressman at a much lower salary? It didn't make sense.

However, the President tried to be pleasant. He really had nothing else planned for that evening, the First Lady having returned from her trip. And the Chief Executive had to maintain a certain level of decorum with people on the Hill.

The meeting was held in the Oval Office where it could be surreptitiously and discreetly videotaped as all such meetings were. Most of the videotapes never saw the light of day again. However, they were always available J.I.C. so the President could play C.Y.A. (Washington is a city of acronyms.)

Once his guests were seated on the other side of the fireplace, the President asked, "Dan, you were insistent upon meeting with me tonight. But you wouldn't give me an agenda. This is most unusual, but I'll consider it a favor to you."

Bancroft knew he'd used up several political IOUs to get this meeting. But, for the first time in many years, he was

97

acting on personal conviction as much as politics. "Thank you, Mister President."

"What can I do for you? What's the problem?"

"Senegambia."

"I thought so." There was a hint of distaste in the President's voice.

"Then you know that the unedited Greenway videotape is circulating widely in spite our attempts to embargo it . . ."

"We should never have allowed direct broadcast satellites!. That was a mistake!" The President had never been in favor of permitting widespread and easy-access video broadcasting into the United States without the regulatory oversight of the FCC. Anyone who could buy the inexpensive window-ledge antenna was able to receive television from satellites. The public could tap whatever anyone in the world wanted to beam into the United States from space.

The President, of course, was one of those who believed that an intelligent elitist corps should run the country and could determine what the rest of the people needed to know.

"Mister President, the horse is out of the barn and down the road. It's too late to worry about what should have been done," Congressman Carlisle put in gently but firmly. "I know the opinion polls today show ninety-two percent of the American public to be in favor of an immediate police action in Senegambia. But I can speak only for my constituents. Their mood is one of revulsion and of taking action. They're asking me why the United States isn't slapping down this madman Modibo. Our country has always stood for the principles of life, liberty, and the pursuit of happiness. We've often had to fight to maintain these principles. And we learned our lesson about trying to save other people by imposing our ways on them, in spite of their desire for what they understand is democracy. But we can and have stepped in with honor to stop naked aggression and squalid butchery."

"General, most of those historical examples you have in mind involved supporting one dictator or monarchy against another. The drivers were financial," the President reminded him.

Carlisle knew what the President was doing by using the congressman's former military title. Carlisle no longer used it because he was now an elected representative. He decided to let the remark pass although the President had strongly objected to others using the title of "Chancellor," during the election campaign—for reasons that might have been obvious only to a political scientist.

Senator Bancroft stepped into the breach between the two men by stating, "Mister President, we have the support of today's UN resolution condemning Modibo's actions. The American public strongly supports a police action on our part. And this isn't a racial or religious matter, either, although some of those special interest groups are mulling over ways they could use it to their advantage, depending upon which way the United States' government moves. The news media is beginning to get nasty because Modibo's troops killed a videonews team today in Dakar and have restricted all correspondents to the Dakar Hilton. The Nigerian embassy was occupied and looted. Malitanian troops have been deployed around the American embassies in both Dakar and Bamako. Our ambassadors and the American legations have been told to stay inside the embassy grounds. Therefore, our own diplomats and citizens are exposed to terrible danger. Some of them have already been slaughtered in the streets of Dakar by the Malitanians . . ."

"I know what our ambassadors are reporting! And Modibo has apologized to Ambassador Haley for the unfortunate accidents in Dakar . . ." the President reminded the senator.

"Apologies are cheap talk, Mister President. Actions belie Modibo's expressions of regret. His army continues to butcher people indiscriminately," Bancroft went on. "But that's only what's happening on the surface. We know that Modibo is backed by the East World bloc . . ."

"But we have no proof! We have only intelligence reports," the chief executive pointed out.

"And either we believe them, or we'd better build a new

99

intelligence activity that we can indeed believe," Bancroft remarked. "But that would take more time than you have remaining in office, sir. And we'd be without eyes and ears in the world while it's being done. As a student of history yourself, Mister President, I'm sure you're aware of what's happened in the past when intelligence data have been dismissed as unbelievable. It cost hundreds of thousands of American lives."

"And if East World is behind Modibo, then the Malitanian occupation of Dakar has severe strategic consequences that impact vital American trade interests. It gives East World potential control of the Atlantic Ocean's major sea lanes," Carlisle added.

"I can't buy that hypothesis. Even if it were true, it certainly doesn't justify a military reaction on our part. And I assume from the conversation thus far that you're leading up to a request for military action. Well, I can't and won't authorize that! It's not only against the policies of my administration, but I don't have the power to commit the nation to war."

"But Congress does, sir. We could authorize limited military action and direct you to carry it out. Similar Congressional action has been taken before," Bancroft told him bluntly.

"I am not a warmaker, gentlemen. Nor am I here to get American business interests out of trouble," the President declared firmly. He knew the power that was arraigned against him. His intelligence system on the Hill had reported it to him. But he was playing mainly to the hidden videocameras.

Carlisle crossed his legs, sat back in the chair, and folded his hands in his lap. They weren't convincing the man. So he played a trump card. "Mister President, Dakar isn't just another little capital city in the Dark Continent. It's a cosmopolitan, civilized city. It's a financial, educational, and artistic center; the people who make it so are being butchered. Artists, educators, and businessmen everywhere are revolted by that. The Senegambians have matured into civilized, peaceful, and very likeable people. But the Malitanians are basically nomads and tribesmen who were never really civilized by the colonial French. They're doing what invading barbarians have done throughout history. So it's not just a matter of an African chief wiping out another African village. Modibo's thugs are looting the Pasteur Institute. They've burned the *Ecole de Dakar* with its collection of paintings and sculpture. They've occupied the University of Dakar and turned it into an army casern. God knows what's happened to the library in the Dakar Museum. Or the other educational institutions. Even during the worst war of the last century, the Germans spared Paris and its citizens in 1940, and the rapacious Red Army spared Budapest, Vienna, and Prague."

Carlisle's words did indeed get to the academically-minded President. He was silent for a moment while he thought about all this and tried to resolve some of the conflicts within his own mind between his personal beliefs and the reality of the outside world. Finally, he said quietly, "I see your point, Congressman. But is it up to America to save civilization?"

"Mister President," Carlisle told him bluntly, "America *is* the world's policeman! This violent world *needs* a policeman. We're the only country strong enough to do it. The cost? We're repaid a thousand times over by the benefits of peaceful free trade that result. Now, a policeman doesn't go around acting like a bully and shooting people indiscriminately. He patrols his beat in peace. He doesn't pick fights with people. He encourages them by example to behave in a civilized manner. But if someone shoots, he's got to shoot back."

"You said that on the floor of the House this afternoon," the President observed dryly.

"Yes, sir, and I'll say it again whenever it's necessary," Carlisle maintained.

"I don't believe your analogy has a one-to-one relationship with world affairs," the President told him, hedging his position. Then he went on pontifically for the benefit of the

101

hidden cameras, "However, it doesn't conflict with my administration's policy because it's an unvoiced consequence of much of the best of our historic legacy."

Carlisle knew he'd won.

Bancroft was astounded. He'd expected to have to work a lot harder to get the President to commit to Operation Bloodbath. He'd even decided he would have to do some serious arm-twisting in the Oval Office, and he'd spent a lot of time that day arranging an alliance that would have tested the Constitution: A congressional semi-declaration of war by a bare majority, instructing a reluctant chief executive to engage in a military operation.

But a freshman congressman had pitched the President in a way that the President couldn't shrug off. Bancroft then realized that Congressman Carlisle was a man who was going to go places. The former general had a way of reducing to simple sound bites some of the most complex questions of the day.

The senator didn't realize that Carlisle had had a lot of practice doing just that as a leader of military units.

"Dan, you say that Congress will back my decision to send in a rescue force?"

Bancroft nodded. "Yes, sir." He didn't add that he'd already set it up. He needed only to trigger it. "It can be done tomorrow morning. I presume we'll receive your request early?"

"Better than that. I intend to address a joint session tomorrow whenever Mike can arrange it with your people."

Bancroft wished he could smile. The President had to do it that way in order to save what was left of his pacifistic, anti-military foreign policy. Furthermore, this was going to be historic, and Bancroft believed he would be cited for playing a major role in making it. His own self-interest caused him to overlook the fact that Jake Carlisle would also be noted in the process. That was going to cause a lot of trouble before Operational Bloodbath was completed. Bancroft didn't like to share the spotlight, especially with a junior congressman who was already a military hero in the minds of many Americans because of Namibia, Sonora, Iraq, Sakhalin, and Battle Mountain.

The President turned in his chair and pushed a button on the telephone sitting on the side table. "Mike, I want to convene an NSC meeting. Now. . . . Yes, now! . . . Sometimes these things can't wait. Serving on the NSC isn't an eight-hour flex-time job! . . . Yes, it's about Senegambia. Ask Fetterman and the Joint Chiefs to assemble their staffs and get cracking on a plan I can see ASAP. . . . And you'd better not figure on going home tonight yourself. People are being killed even as we talk, and the historic legacy of western Africa is being vandalized. I won't stand by idly and allow that to happen!"

Eleven

As Curt drove up to his quarters, he saw a light on inside. Although he was fatigued as a result of the long operational planning session with the other regimental commanders, he suddenly felt excited and wide awake. So he quickly shut off the car, got out, and went in.

Curt knew that Capt. Dyani Motega had to be there. Dyani had her own quarters, of course, but she also had Curt's door code. In fact, she was the only one to have it. No one else could have left the light on.

Also, it was an old signal between them.

Relationships between men and women in the twenty-first century Army were far less narrow and confining than in the preceding century and almost libertine in comparison to the Army of the nineteenth.

Love and war have always existed side by side. The people of the Washington Greys had learned how to mix the two without unduly restricting either. The infamous Army Regulation 601-10, "Rule Ten," restricted physical contact between people of opposite sex while on duty except where performance of duty required it. The Third Herd could live with that. And every Grey who had formed more than a casual relationship with someone else in the regiment or the Army was almost religious in following Rule Ten. No one wanted to screw up a good deal.

But the life of a combat soldier is uncertain. Some couples decided they wanted a family and opted out or asked for transfer to non-combat branches. Those who were warriors in their guts had worked out personal agreements, especially about what to do if either of them bought it on the battlefield.

Dyani and Curt had gone through such an assessment period. It had been tougher for Curt than Dyani. Underneath the military bearing and discipline of Col. Curt Carson lay a romantic and virile man. One can't be a warrior without being an internal romantic. Dyani was also a warrior, but her romantic personality was more carefully controlled. She'd been raised in a proud Crow Indian family that had served in the United States Army for nearly two centuries.

When he opened the door, Curt didn't really know what to expect. Dyani usually surprised him. But this time, his quarters were silent. Making as little sound as possible, Curt went into the living room.

Dyani was sound asleep on the couch.

She wasn't wearing much of anything, and what she was wearing didn't obscure much, either. On duty, she usually wore her long, heavy, sensuous black hair tightly coiffed on her head. But she'd unpinned it so it lay around her in a dark halo.

Curt could do nothing for a moment but stand there and look at her. He wondered how and why he'd been brought together with such a lovely woman whose beauty was both inside and outside.

She detected his presence, opened her eyes, and smiled. "Hi!"

Curt knelt down next to the couch. "Hi!"

"I tried to see you before you went to dinner with Battleaxe."

"I know. We ran out of time."

"We have time now."

"It's oh-dark-thirty in the morning," he reminded her.

"So?" She was a woman of few words. But she said things with her eyes that other women wasted time putting into words.

"So what are we waiting for?" He scooped her up in his

arms and carried her into the bedroom.

Some time later, when they were doing pleasant little things for one another, she asked him, "Did you have a good time with the sultana in zero-gee?"

"What do you think?"

"I think that I will always be able to compete with her, with or without gravity. I also see you more often."

"So what did you do while I was on leave?" he asked her.

Dyani smiled. "I got to know Russ Frazier better."

A twinge of jealousy raced through Curt. He didn't have Dyani's non-spiteful, rich outlook on life. "How much better?"

"A lot better. He's a warrior, too. But he's different. Now I appreciate you much more."

"I'm just a bit jealous," Curt admitted. Their relationship was built not only on physical attraction but openness. Dyani's role was that of the scout, "truthbearer of the tribe." That meant Curt could treat her without guile in the same manner.

"Relax. Jealousy doesn't fit you very well." Dyani was being true to form, as usual. "Or should we go back to page one and review that lesson?"

"It's hard to teach an old dog new tricks."

"But the old dog tries."

"I'll always try. But I know I'll never really understand you."

"That's good."

"First among equals, right?"

"More than just first, Kida."

Their sensuous pillow talk was interrupted by the insistent chiming of the telephone alongside the bed.

"Some things never change!" Curt grumbled. Over and over in his Army career, the sound of a telephone had interrupted pleasant off-duty affairs. Now it was almost a joke between Dyani and Curt. But they took their jobs seriously because they were warriors, and that meant they didn't work an eight-hour day. "Want to bet it's another damned call to go out and save the free world from destruction?"

106

"I'd lose," Dyani admitted quietly. She disengaged herself so he could roll over to pick up the handset.

He tried to sound sleepy as he said into it, "Colonel Carson here!"

"Colonel Ward here. Priority One from Battleaxe, Colonel," came the feminine voice of his regimental chief of staff. "We have a Dee-Oh-Dee Execute Order with revised plan from Operation Bloodbath chief, Wild Bill. Oscar brief in the snake pit at oh-three-hundred."

Curt glanced at the glowing red numbers of the clock. It read 0224. "Receipt confirmed. Concur. I'll be there. I'll notify S-2."

"I thought you would." Lt. Col. Joan Ward was an old friend of Curt's, but their relationship that had begun at West Point was brother-sister in nature. On occasions in years past, it had gone farther. But that was long before both had risen to field grade.

Dyani was out of bed before Curt could hang up. When the whistle blew, she toggled over instantly to her persona as an efficient, motivated, knowledgeable combat scout, commander of the RECONCO, and regimental intelligence officer.

"No time for a shower," Curt remarked.

She looked askance at him. "No one else has time for a shower, either! Here! Use this moist towelette."

"I didn't expect any execute order this fast. It must really have hit the impeller in Senegambia," Curt remarked as he cleaned up and started donning fatigues.

"Senegambia. Desert or jungle cammies?"

"Wear what you've got. We'll figure that one out later. Khakis will do. They're universal for the Senegambian savannah."

Although it was indeed oh-dark-thirty, the Washington Greys didn't look too shabby as they convened in the snake pit in the regimental headquarters building. The Third Herd's briefing theater had screen and holotanks showing the snake pits of the Cottonbalers and the Wolfhounds. The holotank connected to the 17th Iron Fist Division snake pit

107

was still a blank black. So was another one that now bore the identification label, "Operation Bloodbath command, FORSCOMM."

Precisely at 0300, Maj. Pappy Gratton stepped up on the stage surrounded by the tiered seating rows of the snake pit. "Ten-HUT!" he snapped. The cammie-clad people in the room came to their feet. Gratton's eyes swept over the assemblage. Then he turned to Curt who was waiting down on the floor and saluted. "Colonel Carson, the Third Robot Infantry, Special Combat Regiment is assembled. All present or accounted for, sir!"

The ritual was traditional. A friendly camaraderie existed among everyone there—fragging comrades literally or by innuendo was unthinkable in the Greys; anyone who didn't fit in or didn't have all their mental marbles lined up, collated, and counted was quickly but gently transferred out. Maybe they could fit better into another outfit. The Greys were professional warriors in the traditional sense: people who had a higher purpose for their activities than merely making a living. Rituals and traditions continued to remind them of this as a glue that helped hold them together in the face of death. Few non-military people understood this.

Curt returned the salute and stepped onto the stage. He picked up the meter-long pointer stick and held it in both hands in front of him. He could have used a laser pointer or other modern high-tech briefing gadget. However, the pointer was like the riding crop still carried by British Army officers who had never ridden a horse in their lives. The pointer and the crop were symbolic swords of command. "Thank you, Major Gratton," Curt acknowledged his adjutant, then looked around the room. "Ladies and gentlemen of the Washington Greys, please resume your seats."

A brief rustle of sound accompanied the personnel of the regiment resuming their seats. In a full warbot regiment, they would have been lying on couches, and all the briefing would have taken place via direct mind-to-mind neuroelectronic linkage. But the Washington Greys were Sierra Charlies who had developed the new Special Combat doctrine where humans fought in the field alongside warbots. They were fiercely proud of the different, "old fashioned," face-to-face model in which their orders' briefings were conducted.

"Thank you all for coming here at oh-dark-thirty on such short notice," Curt went on, sensing an electric tension in the attitude of his people. So he continued in a light manner, "I realize many of you had to rush in order to get out of a warm bed and go home to pick up the uniform of the day . . ."

The room erupted in a brief explosion of laughter. It was a sound of tension released. Everyone knew that an 0300 Oscar briefing meant that serious and deadly work was ahead. Everyone knew that the Senegambian bloodbath was the reason. They also suspected that the Greys would be sent in to do something about it. Rumor Control Headquarters had been active with that speculation ever since the Greenway tapes had been broadcast.

Curt glanced at his watch. He knew he had five minutes before Battleaxe and the division staff came up on the screens. Such a delay was planned to give the regimental commanders time to talk briefly with their commands before the full Oscar brief began.

"We're probably going to deploy to Dakar," Curt began. "That should be no surprise to any of you. In the last twelve hours, you've performed miracles in anticipation that we'll be called to conduct a rapid deploy. Until only a few hours ago, I was in a long planning session with Battleaxe and the two other regimental commanders. We have a basic plan. I suspect we'll have to modify it to match whatever comes down from higher levels. That should come as no surprise, either. We've been through this exercise many times before. What does come as a surprise even to me is the extremely fast pace events have taken. This Oscar briefing should bring us up to date and let us know what's expected of us. Once we know that, I have no doubts that the Washington Greys will perform as everyone expects us to . . . and beyond what we expect ourselves capable of doing."

Sgt. Maj. Edwina Sampson, the regimental technical sergeant in charge of communications, signalled Curt.

"Sergeant Major Sampson?"

"Sir, Battleaxe requests immediate contact."

Curt looked at his watch again. He'd used less than two of his allotted five minutes. But when the division commander forwards a request, it is more than just a request; it is an order.

"Roger, Sergeant Major. Put Battleaxe on screen!"

The image of Maj. Gen. Belinda Hettrick flicked onto the holoscreen behind him. Curt turned and, as the regimental commander, saluted her.

Hettrick returned the salute. "Colonel, I have a request from the commanding general of FORSCOMM Bloodbath Headquarters to speak with your regiment briefly before commencement of the Oscar briefing. Ladies and gentlemen of the Washington Greys, may I present an old friend and colleague of many of you, Lieutenant General William D. Bellamack!"

When Bellamack's image built up on the other holoscreen, the members of the regiment came immediately to their feet without an order being given.

Nine years ago, then-Colonel William O. Bellamack had assumed command of the Washington Greys and had led it in Sonora, Kerguelen Island, Brunei, and Iraq. The general had been and therefore always was a Washington Grey. The Greys rose to their feet in a signal of respect for the man who had led them so well until he'd been mentally wounded six years ago in Iraq.

Curt hadn't seen Wild Bill Bellamack for several years and was somewhat surprised by the change in the man's appearance. His horselike face had filled out as he'd grown older. It had taken on the lines and wrinkles of "character," although Curt believed it was really caused by normal aging. Bellamack's fight to regain his mental stability combined with the stresses and concerns of higher command were evident in the man's changed appearance. To Curt, Bellamack was now an older man, a father-like personage. But a sparkle still showed in the man's deep, dark eyes.

110

The voice, however, was indeed that of Wild Bill Bellamack. "Thank you. Thank you. Please resume your seats. I see many old friends among you and some whom I have yet to meet. In some ways, I envy you, Colonel Carson. You're standing on that briefing stage in command of one of the greatest outfits I've ever had the pleasure and privilege of being associated with. There have been times when I wish that I could stand there again and command the Greys.

"I asked General Hettrick to arrange this short pre-briefing interlude so I could tell you that I'm extremely proud that I'll have a small role in leading the Greys in the upcoming Operation Bloodbath. But I'll be a couple of levels up the chain of command." A smile came to his face as he went on, "Some of you joined the regiment after my unfortunate relinquishment of command. I just wanted to let you see the sonofabitch who's going to be blamed for causing you all sorts of problems in the days and weeks to come!"

In the moment created by the ripple of laughter that ran through the Grey's snake pit, Bellamack glanced at his watch. "Thank you, General Hettrick. Thank you, Colonel Carson. I look forward to seeing many of you in person in the days to come because I do not intend to lead from the rear. Commanding the Greys taught me to do otherwise. I salute you and wish you well. Now, to the business at hand . . ."

With that, Bellamack's image faded from the holoscreen. And the Oscar briefing got under way right on the tick. Hettrick brought in Colonel Salley and the Wolfhounds, then Colonel Cashier and the Cottonbalers. Their snake pits were practically right next door at Fort Huachuca. So was the smaller snake pit of the 17th Iron Fist Division a few buildings away. All the briefing rooms of these Sierra Charlie units were basically the same.

It was only when the briefing rooms of the other warbot divisions' regiments came on-screen that Curt suddenly realized how far the Sierra Charlies had progressed from their days as full NE warbot units.

The commanding general of the 50th Robot Infantry Division, the "R.U.R.," and the 1st Cavalry (Robot Armored) Division appeared as computer-generated images along with their regimental commanders. Their divisional and regimental computers lip-synched these images with the verbalized thoughts put into the system by neuroelectronics. Curt knew that everyone except those in the 17th Iron Fist Division were lying on their backs on couches with full NE head and back harnesses on. It had been ten years since he'd fought as a warbot brainy in Zahedan. It struck him now as an alien and almost unthinkable way to fight, much less to plan or be briefed.

He and the Sierra Charlies now operated in a far more intense and personal environment with much greater risks. The Sierra Charlies fought physically in an old-fashioned way with warbots as tools that accompanied and assisted them, not as extensions of their minds. Being a Sierra Charlie meant being a real warrior who could be killed deader than hell if the Sierra Charlie was stupid enough to let it happen. To Curt, it made warfare much more like other non-warbot soldiers around the world had to fight it. It gave him a better understanding of all those non-warbots troops and commanders against whom he was called upon to fight.

Being a Sierra Charlie was not only frightening as hell but equally intense after surviving combat. It was living and fighting at the limit. Curt wondered why he liked it more than being a warbot brainy. He decided that the adage was right: *"The nearer the bone, the sweeter the meat."*

But he couldn't understand why he did it so coolly and dispassionately. That was not the way of Russ Frazier or his old nemesis, now S-3 for the Wolfhounds, Colonel Marty "Kill 'Em All" Kelly. And perhaps he would never understand why some of the ladies of the Greys were so very good at it. Every time he thought he had it figured out, some new datum surfaced and blew away his hypothesis. Dyani was the only woman he felt he could really fathom because she was so forthright, and then there were other times with Dyani . . .

Curt was mulling over these thoughts in one part of his mind while another part was absorbing the information from Operation Bloodbath Command in an almost automatic mode.

Briefly, the ops plan started very much like the one he and the other Iron Fisters had put together six hours ago.

The 17th Iron Fist Division would stage out of the Cape Verde Islands, using the airport at Praia on São Tiago. The Washington Greys would be airlifted into Dakar-Yoff Aerodrome. The mission of the Greys: Take and hold the Dakar airport. Landing zone air coverage would involve Harpies from the Greys, the Wolfhounds, and the Cottonbalers. They would be assisted by deep interdiction Aerospace Force aircraft that would strike further inland to prevent Malitanian reinforcements from coming along the Dakar-Bamako highway and railway.

Because of the shortage of operational Chippies and the 700-kilometer distance between Praia and Dakar, some Chippies had to be used as midair refuelling tankers.

(The Aerospace Force no longer had midair refuelling tankers; hypersonic strategic strike aircraft no longer required them. Any place in the world could be covered from ZI bases by Mach-10 hypersonics with a striking range of 10,000-kilometers or by orbital skip bombers with unlimited range. But those weapons systems were unusable in the Senegambia campaign which was supposed to be a surgical strike and extraction mission.)

"The Wolfhounds and the Cottonbalers will constitute the second and third waves of airborne strike forces landed at the Dakar airport," the G-3 from Bellamack's staff went on. "They will arrive at Dakar Airport at plus eight and sixteen hours. The Cape Verde Peninsula will be sealed off by the Seventeenth Iron Fist Division and the harbor made safe for the *Raborn* Class carrier submarines. Then the First Cavalry light robot armored division will be landed on the beaches of Dakar harbor to clear the city and force the Malitanians into caserns there. The carrier submarines will commence evacuating American and other endangered foreign nationals. This will be followed by the landing of the Fiftieth R-U-R Division which will be sealifted to Dakar by chartered ocean liners and freighters. When the First Cavalry and the Fiftieth Robot Infantry divisions are in place as a guardian force to protect Dakar, its citizens, and its cultural treasures, the Seventeenth Iron Fist Division will depart via the chartered sealift vessels . . ."

When Curt heard this, he came to full alert.

This was *not* the ops plan put together by the Iron Fisters six hours ago.

Curt, Hettrick, Cashier, and Salley had worked through such a scenario. It could turn Operation Bloodbath into a bloodbath indeed for the Washington Greys.

Twelve

Maj. Gen. Belinda Hettrick got to her feet at once. Curt, Maxie, and Rick rose almost in unison.

The G-3 colonel from FORSCOMM was a warbot brainy operating in linkage at the moment. His computer-generated image on the screen reacted the way the FORSCOMM computer decided matched his mental activity of surprise. His screen image, therefore, looked like a cartoon character who'd just had something unsuspected done to him. It would have been hilarious except that this was a very serious situation. And the G-3 knew it. Through video sensors, he'd seen a general and three colonels come to their feet. That signified either a serious question on their part or, worse yet, a strong objection. This was unprecedented in the Robot Infantry.

But the warbot brainies of the Robot Infantry didn't have their pink bodies exposed to fire out on the battlefield like the Sierra Charlies.

"Uh, General, do you have a question?" the colonel asked.

"No, I have an objection!" Hettrick fired back. She looked at her screens and saw that her regimental commanders had also risen to their feet. "And I believe my unit commanders also have a problem with this ops plan."

General Bellamack's computer-generated image replaced that of his ops staffer. He was now in neuroelectronic linkage so he could communicate with the warbot brainy commanders of the 50th R.U.R. and First Cavalry Division. He was also plugged in to the naval and Aerospace Force commanders of Operation Bloodbath. In addition, General Pickens was monitoring from the Pentagon.

"Thank you, Colonel Rathbone," Bellamack said to his ops staffer. "Please stand down for a moment. I want to find out about this problem. General Hettrick, what's bothering you?"

"The ops plan calls for putting too few Sierra Charlies and worn-out Mary Ann warbots up against too many Malitanians and Red Hammer warbots," Hettrick snapped. "General Bellamack, for the record, would you please repeat your G-2's best guess concerning the strength of Malitanian forces on the Cape Verde Peninsula?"

Being in NE linkage gave a person the ability to access data quickly. The information Hettrick asked for was in the Operation Bloodbath databank. Bellamack could call it up with a thought command. He did so and reported, "The Malitanian armed forces presently have an infantry division of an estimated eighteen thousand troops and about five hundred Red Hammer warbots in Dakar. Satellite photos of Dakar Airport show an estimated air strength consisting of a fighter interceptor squadron, a maritime reconnaissance squadron, and two tactical transport squadrons . . ."

"Thank you, sir, that's exactly what I heard," Hettrick replied cautiously. "General, I'm not many years up the ladder from regimental command. So I see real problems here. The proposed ops plan pits the one-hundred-twenty-five Sierra Charlies and fifty warbots of the Washington Greys against a division of Malitanian troops and Red Hammers. I don't complain about being outnumbered; our warbots are a damned good force multiplier. And the Sierra Charlies have never really fought one-to-one engagements anywhere. But the way this ops plan reads, the Washington Greys will be hanging on with their fingernails at Dakar Airport for seven hours before being reinforced. The second wave won't have the advantage of surprise, nor will the third wave that's due sixteen hours later. From my own experience, this plan amounts to sheer suicide. In addition, I'm reluctant to order the Iron Fist Division into action on an ops plan which splits our already meager forces.

"We're outnumbered roughly ten to one, even accounting for the warbot force multiplier. Based on what we know about

116

rapid strike tactics, we must conduct a multi-pronged assault. Our Iron Fist ops plan recommended that the Wolfhounds and Cottonbalers come ashore from *Raborn* Class carrier submarines at the same time the Greys land at the Dakar airport. The Wolfhounds would land at Hann Plage on Dakar Bay. The Cottonbalers would come ashore at Camberene Beach on the north side of the peninsula. Our Harpies would provide direct tactical air support for the Sierra Charlies. The Aerospace Force would provide interdiction to prevent reinforcement of Dakar by the Malitanian Army. Once Dakar Airport was secured, the Aerospace Force could operate from there. Navy air from the submarine carriers would provide combat air cover over Dakar.

"Our plan would cut off Dakar in one blow. Furthermore, we'd confuse the hell out of Modibo's boys by coming at them from several directions at once. Once we free up our Chippies from the initial landing of the Greys, we can send the transport aerodynes back to Praia. They can then help the First Cav airlift into the Dakar airport in a constant stream. After all, the First Cav has Chippies, too. So why bring the First Cav in by slow boat?"

Bellamack's image held up its hand. "General Hettrick, I fully understand the reason for your objections. However, we can't conduct the seaborne portion of your excellent tactical plan."

"May I ask why, General?"

"Of course. And I'll allow the Operation Bloodbath deputy commander for naval operations to expound on what's happened," Bellamack's image replied. "This is Rear Admiral Thomas Weaver. He'll tell you why the Iron Fist plan was rejected."

The man whose real image appeared before them—the Navy didn't use a lot of NE technology to run a ship—was vaguely familiar to Curt. He'd met the admiral eight years before off Kerguelen as a commander who was the executive officer of the U.S.S. *McCain*. The uniform of the United States Navy hadn't changed in a long time. It was still a plain navy-blue suit with a minimum of insignia and badges. The only decoration on the uniform was the gold braid of rank on both sleeves. The man also wore both naval aviator wings and a submariner's dolphins.

"General Hettrick, C-N-O has no problem taking the *McCain* and the *Cromwell* inshore at Dakar to discharge Army troops," Weaver explained. "We'd precede such an action with heavy naval air strikes on Malitanian shore and harbor defense installations such as guns and missile launchers. However, when the plan was presented to the National Security Council at oh-one-thirty hours this morning, N-S-C determined that using the *Raborn* class boats in the initial assault was not a cost effective way, risk-wise, to assault Dakar. Therefore, Bloodbath Joint Command and the Navy were given a direct presidential order not to place the expensive submarine carriers at risk by bringing them near Dakar until the harbor had been sanitized. That's why we had to fall back on Plan B. I hope that's an adequate explanation, ma'am."

Bellamack's computer-generated image reappeared. "That's the story, General. We can't use the carrier submarines during the initial strike. Now I know you have strong objections to the ops plan, but . . ."

"The word 'strong' doesn't exactly describe my feelings," Hettrick retorted. It was obvious to all who watched that the lady was enraged at the NSC-approved ops plan. And she was resisting an order that she strongly felt would send her regiments into a situation of certain defeat. General officers often argue violently among themselves over the details of operational plans and tactics. However, this is usually done in private. Hettrick was taking her stand in full view of her troops. And she knew it. Insofar as she was concerned, she wanted this controversy to be discussed in the open. The lives of the Washington Greys were at stake. The Wolfhounds and Cottonbalers would he next into the abattoir of death. "With the present plan, Dakar will be Yorktown, Balaclava, Gallipoli, Dieppe, Anzio, and Dien Bien Phu all over again. Only worse. Maybe my military history professors were right. Maybe history repeats itself because we didn't learn the first time! If we salute, follow orders, and go into Dakar according to the approved ops plan, it will indeed be Operational Bloodbath. Our bloodbath!"

Bellamack knew that, too. But his staff had told him that he had no option. Time was short. Action was required. He'd commanded the Washington Greys as Hettrick had. The only reason he was running FORSCOMM instead of a Sierra Charlie division was because only one SC Division, the 17th Iron Fist, existed. And Hettrick had gotten there first to command it when Jacob Carlisle had been kicked upstairs. FORSCOMM was the best spot for Bellamack, according to the Old Comrades Club at the Pentagon. Bellamack had combat experience in both RI and SC outfits, and he'd served in Europe, the Gulf, and other overseas assignments. Furthermore, when he'd been behind the OSCAR—Office of Special Combat Assault Robotics—in the Pentagon, he'd used his power and position well. But he was still a Sierra Charlie fully qualified to wear the blue tam.

Bellamack's staff was made up of warbot brainies. Few Sierra Charlies had made it up the ladder to Army command staff level yet. The Sierra Charlies were too new. Therefore, it was too soon and too early in their careers to expect them to be up at Bellamack's level. Hettrick had managed to build her divisional staff with Sierra Charlies, often by sweet-talking a lot of former combat officers such as Col. Joanne Wilkinson who'd finally burned out.

So Bellamack felt his staffers didn't fully appreciate the Sierra Charlie outlook on this plan. Warbot brainies weren't at risk when they thought-controlled their warbots in battle while lying on comfortable linkage couches inside vans well to the rear of the action. The Sierra Charlies clearly and literally had their butts in the line of fire.

Bellamack understood the reaction of Hettrick. And he knew why Curt Carson had come to his feet in protest, too. What surprised him was the fact that Col. Maxie Cashier and Col. Rick Salley had done the same. The Sierra Charlies were sticking together.

So he couldn't ignore their reaction. Nor could he pass off the extremely strong rejection of the plan. These four people had literally risked their careers doing what they'd just done. But Sierra Charlies were used to taking risks that others never had to consider.

119

"Very well, General Hettrick, what are your recommendations?" Bellamack asked her.

"I'd revise the operational plan," Hettrick fired back without hesitation. "Tell me what you want me to do in the broadest terms. Then tell me what I can't do, what the rules of engagement are. Then let the Iron Fist figure out how to do it. How much time have I got?"

"You heard the J-C-S Execute Order, General."

"Would you please post its text?" Hettrick asked, knowing full well that she could quickly retrieve it from the Operation Bloodbath data base. But she wanted the record to show that the order wasn't just read as part of the routine protocol of an Oscar briefing.

Curt knew what she was doing. It was precisely what he would do. And what his Greys would do, because he'd taught them as Hettrick had taught him. All of them wanted to know precisely what the order said and in what terms. They were looking for slack, for looseness, for specifics concerning what they were directly ordered to do and what portions of the operations plan had been left to their judgment and planning.

Sometimes orders from the White House or JCS were more advisory than precise. The Sakhalin Police Detachment orders had been loosy-goosy because that operation had been mounted in one hell of a roaring hurry; the Greys had been in the air over the Pacific when the Congress of Pacific Rim Economies had authorized the operation. However, occasionally an Execute Order amounted to micromanagement as it had in Yemen.

Everyone wanted to analyze the Execute Order for Operation Bloodbath. They needed to find the loopholes that would allow them to do what they were told to do without being slaughtered.

"Here is the text of the Execute Order," Bellamack said. His image faded and was replaced on the screen with text:

"This is an Execute Order. By authority and direction of the Secretary of Defense. This is Execute Order JCS-OP-39-3. This message is classified SECRET."

This wording told Curt that the action order had proceeded directly from the President who was the only person responsible for the commitment of American armed services to armed conflict. The decision had been made by the chief executive on the basis of advice from the National Security Council. The order had then gone down the chain of command to SEC-DEF then to JCS. It had been bucked down to FORSCOMM and Bellamack, who was transmitting it to the Army divisions, naval units, and Aerospace Force commands responsible for taking action.

"Objective in support of U.N. Resolution 1302 is to take and hold Dakar and Cape Verde Peninsula, to restore civil law and order, to protect Senegambian cultural heritage and educational facilities, to permit evacuation of all American and foreign personnel requesting same, and to restore Senegambian sovereignty. This operation is code named Operation Bloodbath. This Operation is classified SECRET.

"Course of Action: Option Two is approved for execution as quickly as possible. U.S. Army FORSCOMM is designated as Joint Command of Operation Bloodbath. U.S. Army 17th Division conducts initial landing at Dakar, Senegambia. Second wave is U.S. Army 1st Cavalry Division. U.S. Aerospace Force 8th Air Force supports Operation Bloodbath conducting deep air interdiction of railways and highways east of Dakar. Transport of forces to Dakar is developed by U.S. Army FORSCOMM Operation Bloodbath. U.S. Army and U.S. Aerospace Force provide initial transportation of units to Dakar. U.S. Navy to provide transportation for Army units to Dakar in carrier submarines once Dakar harbor is secure. U.S. Navy provides air superiority cover over Dakar from carrier submarines for remainder of operation. 50th Robot Infantry Division is transported to Dakar by U.S. Navy carrier submarines as third wave. 17th Iron Fist Division is withdrawn upon arrival of 50th Robot Infantry Division.

"Rules of engagement: Cooperation with remaining Senegambian government is mandatory. Cooperation with Senegambian Garamandes resistance movement is mandatory. Operation Bloodbath units return fire only when and if fired upon and then only to the level and intensity of incoming fire. Prisoners to be taken and exchanged as quickly as possible. Civil facilities not being used for Malitanian military purposes to be considered as non-targets.

"International assistance and cooperation: The government of the Republic of Cape Verde Islands has agreed to permit United States' military, naval, and air forces to utilize the facilities on the island of Sao

Tiago for staging Operation Bloodbath. United States' military, naval, and air forces authorized to defend the Republic of Cape Verde Islands against any aggression that may be attempted by foreign interests.

"This is Execute Order JCS-OP-39-3. End of message. End of message. End of message. This message is classified SECRET."

Curt grinned when he read it. The order had slack. Lots of slack. It sounded like the sort that would come down from Jacob Carlisle when he wanted the 17th Iron Fist Division to figure out an ops plan and buck it back up the line to him. He wondered if Carlisle had had a hand in this one. It sounded very much like the retired general.

It was obvious that Hettrick had seen this, too.

And Bellamack now seemed to view it in a different light.

"General Bellamack, may I suggest that this Oscar brief be temporarily recessed?" Hettrick asked. "We were given no time deadline in the Execute Order, just a directive to accomplish it 'as soon as possible.' "

Suddenly, General Pickens' image appeared on the screen. "General Bellamack, pardon me for intruding, but J-C-S expects immediate action."

"General Pickens, Operation Bloodbath Joint Command *is* taking immediate action," Bellamack fired back. Then turning his attention again to his command, he went on, "I am assuming command of the Army elements as acting deputy chief of staff to myself for Army ops. I'm the only available general officer who's also a qualified Sierra Charlie, and this is primarily an Army show. General Hettrick, prepare to airlift the Iron Fist Division to the Cape Verde Islands at once. Let me know your ETA for Praia. I'll get you some combat engineering assistance from Fort Belvoir. General Palmer, prepare to deploy the First Cavalry to the Cape Verde Islands; coordinate your airlift capability with General Hettrick and with my operations staff. General Chappick, deploy the Fiftieth Robot Infantry to Charleston. Admiral Weaver, move at once to get the *McCain* and the *Cromwell* to Charleston to receive the Fiftieth Division. General Willcox, continue your planning for the Eighth Air Force to conduct interdiction per the Execute Order; move any necessary aircraft to Praia within twenty-four hours. And see if we can get some CRAF airlift support for the Iron Fist and the First Cav.

"I'm canceling the ops plan that was previously presented. The orders I've just given do not constitute a new ops plan. What I've done is to order the various units into the positions they'll occupy prior to the action regardless of the details of the final ops plan. During the next twelve hours, I'll entertain inputs through the chain of command for a revised ops plan from any commander involved. I'm not going to tell the individual commanders how to do what we've been told to do in the Execute Order. You tell me what you can do and how you'll do it. I'll convene a Papa briefing of all deputy commanders and division commanders by telecommunications at nineteen-hundred hours Zulu time today. This Oscar briefing is hereby adjourned. Commanders, take charge of your units."

His image faded from the screen, but Hettrick's remained. "Iron Fist Division, heads up! I'm calling a Papa brief immediately at division headquarters for the regimental commanders and their staffs from the Washington Greys, the Wolfhounds, and the Cottonbalers in two hours. Regimental commanders, use those two hours to get your regiments ready to move out in your Chippies. I want to be ready to wheels-up on one hour's notice. We may have more time than that, but don't count on it! People are being slaughtered in Dakar even as we speak. When we work out an ops plan we can live with, it may not take very long for General Bellamack to approve it. Regimental commanders, dismiss your units."

She paused, looked at her watch, then went on, "Add an hour to that. Get a hot breakfast. Never go into action on an empty stomach."

Thirteen

"Haven't you caught that bitch Lébou yet?"

Although the Presidential Palace was a sumptuous and luxurious place to live, Generalissimo Modibo Ould Daddah Sidi Ahmed was unhappy. Outside the window, the ocean-going traffic in Dakar harbor was at a standstill. No ships moved to or from the docks and quays of Dakar Marine. Those ships that had been docked when the Malitanian dictator's troops had overrun the city were being held for payment of much higher port fees. And no ships were inbound.

"No, Your Excellency, we have not." Col. Abdul Karim Kassem, the military commander of the Malitanian province of Dakar reported. "The Garamandes' resistance movement has gone deep underground. No one will tell us anything about it."

"What about the Garamandes' terrorists you've captured?" The generalissimo stroked his long chin with an equally long, thin hand. His nomadic Tuareg blood lines were very much evident even though he, among all the people of Malitania, had plenty to eat.

"They either knew nothing, or they died under torture," Colonel Kassem reported dispassionately.

"What of the report that she has lost an eye as a result of the attempt to pick her up?" Modibo wanted to know. "Do any of the hospitals in the area have a record of her?"

"The report is just hearsay. We haven't been able to confirm it. We did check all the hospitals," Kassem said. "And we attempted to round up all the known medical doctors."

"Did any of the doctors break under torture?"

"Your Excellency, we have a shortage of medical personnel in Malitania. You specifically ordered our troops not to kill or physically torture such highly trained technical specialists."

Modibo told himself that it was easier in the earlier days before he swept out of the Sahara and took Timbuctu. His band of picked warriors and their camp followers were hardened desert people then. After they'd captured Bamako and then thrust through Mauritania to the sea, they'd become soft. At least, that's what he believed. He knew nothing of modern hygiene or public health. He didn't understand that contact of his nomadic tribesmen with civilization brought with it exposure to diseases and personal health hazards unsuspected by nomads from the desert. Yellow fever, AIDS, hepatitis, malaria, typhoid, and cholera had decimated his original followers while they pillaged and raped.

He was a man from five hundred years out of the past. Now he sat in control of one of the biggest African empires of the twenty-first century. He simply didn't understand some of the facts about modern public health and hygiene his East World advisors were telling him. Modibo paid attention mostly to what he was told by his military advisors such as Col. Godavari Singh Pratihara.

"It used to be simpler," Modibo complained. "But at least we now enjoy the very best, eh, Kassem? By the way, you are free to close the Christian churches and Jewish synagogues, but don't lay a hand on the mosques. Especially the Grand Mosque. I have never had such a magnificent building in which to pray."

Colonel Pratihara stepped through the huge door and saluted. "Your Excellency, the American ambassador wishes to speak with you."

Modibo's visage darkened. "The one from Bamako?"

"No, sir, the one from the American embassy here."

Modibo sat up and turned the huge chair so his back was toward the huge French doors opened to overlook the harbor beyond. It was time to confront this man and put him in his proper place. Insofar as Modibo was concerned, Senegambia no longer existed as a sovereign nation qualified to have embassies from other nations. It was time to humble the American ambassador and send him packing for home. Then Modibo could order the other ambassadors out and close their embassies, too.

"Send him in!" Modibo snapped.

Dr. Luther M. Jones came in. He was a tall, proud man who had been delighted to accept a diplomatic post in the land of his remote ancestors. Without hesitation, he walked confidently up to the huge desk, gave a little bow, and said, "Good morning, Your Excellency. I am Doctor Luther M. Jones, ambassador to Senegambia from the United States of America." He proffered a small blue folder containing copies of his bona fides.

"Why are you here?" Modibo asked brusquely, not even reaching for the blue folder.

"Because I am the ambassador from the United States to Senegambia, and I have a letter to you from the President of the United States." Jones opened his attache case and extracted a long envelope which he offered to Modibo.

The President for Life, the Savior of the Sahel, and the Chief of the Military Forces of the United State of Malitania made no move. Instead, he growled, "This document should have come through the American embassy in Bamako. The nation of Senegambia no longer exists. Senegambia is a province of Malitania. Therefore, Senegambia cannot legitimately have an American embassy or ambassador. Therefore, I refuse to accept this communication from you because it did not come through proper channels."

This set Jones back. "Your Excellency, I shall have to report this to my government."

"Do so! And advise your President that if he wishes to communicate with me, he must do so through his embassy in Bamako."

Jones was visibly angry at this point. But, as a political scientist who had learned diplomacy the hard way under the present President's administration, he held his temper. "Then it will indeed be forwarded to you through our embassy in Bamako. However, I should inform you that the letter states the intention of my government to support United Nations' Resolution Thirteen- Oh-Two."

"I do not recognize that resolution. It was reportedly debated and discussed in the Security Council. I did not have the opportunity to be in New York City at the time to engage in the debate. Therefore, the resolution has no validity to me. And I am the final authority of the Malitanian government." Modibo made a steeple of his long fingers before him as he rocked back and forth in the enormous leather-covered chair.

Then before Jones could reply, Modibo stopped rocking, leaned forward, and slammed his hands down on the polished wood desk top. "I order you to depart Malitania immediately! Your building is no longer subject to diplomatic courtesies. It will be occupied by the Malitanian Army at four o'clock this afternoon. Any resistance or disobedience will be dealt with severely. I am giving you some leeway here in deference to your former status as an ambassador. However, you are now merely a foreign national on Malitanian soil and subject to all my rules and regulations. Act accordingly and you will not be harmed. Nor will members of your staff."

"Your Excellency, my chargé d'affaires has been told that no airline flights will be departing Dakar Airport until further notice. He has also been told that we will be required to obtain exit permits and pay a fee for them! Not only is this contrary to international law, but it raises the question that I cannot answer: How can I comply with your declaration of me and my staff as *persona non grata* and leave Senegambia?"

"That is your concern! I have more important matters to worry about. I must feed my people. Colonel Pratihara, you showed this man in, so you can show him out!"

Jones stood up, anger welling up within him. His emotions overcame his diplomatic good sense. "Generalissimo Modibo, your ancestors sold my ancestors as slaves. But my country freed its slaves a long time ago. From the actions of your soldiers during this invasion and your attitude here today, I can certainly see that your approach to the world isn't any different from your slave trading forebears! Good day!"

As the Sikh officer accompanied Jones through the door, Modibo merely turned to his military governor and snarled, "I will not tolerate insults! Wait until he is well away from

127

here. Then kill him!"

The invasion was over, but the bloodbath wasn't.

Modibo had forgotten that United States' embassies are closely guarded by members of the United States Marine Corps. And he didn't know that Jones was accompanied by Marine bodyguards wearing unobtrusive civilian clothes. Furthermore, Jones himself was wearing American military body armor. He carried a well-hidden Gnat submachine gun, and he knew how to use it. He wasn't afraid to use the cold steel of the knife strapped to his calf. Jones might have been an ivory tower academic, but he was no wimp. He'd grown up on the streets of the District of Columbia. In his undergraduate days at Howard University, he'd been a member of the varsity rifle and fencing teams. But he didn't discuss these personal matters with his diplomatic colleagues.

Orders moved slowly through the chain of Malitanian command. So Jones was safely in the American embassy before the word travelled from Colonel Kassem down the line.

But orders moved far more quickly in the defense establishment of the United States of America. C^3I — command, control, communications, and intelligence — was a primary factor in American military, naval, and air operations. Thanks to space satellites, earth induction, and VLF communications (as well as other "national technical means" not discussed outside very high and privileged circles on the Potomac), people almost anywhere could talk to people anywhere else. Planet Earth wasn't totally wired, but the space above it had built-in "wiring" for this sort of work.

Thus, Curt and his staff could continue their last minute fine-tuning of the operational plan even while they were airborne in a UCA-21C Chippewa of "Timm's Tigers," the airlift company of the Washington Greys. Furthermore, Curt was able to make sure everything and everyone was where they should be for the critical overseas airlift part of Operation Bloodbath.

The inside of a Chippie wasn't comfortable. And it wasn't quiet. Col. Cal Worsham and Capt. Ron Knight had worked hard to make sure the flight sergeants and tech sergeants had removed all equipment that wasn't absolutely necessary for the task of hauling Sierra Charlies, warbots, vehicles, and supplies. Gone was nearly all the sound-muffling and temperature insulation. Next to airworthiness, range and payload were the top priorities. Anything that didn't contribute to these had been stripped off and left in Fort Huachuca. The in-flight refuelling equipment installed five years before for the transpacific deployment of the Chippies and Harpies had been retained and retested.

Curt checked his watch. *Ten minutes out of Charlotte Amalie,* he remarked via the NE tacomm staff channel, sub-vocalizing his thoughts into a form that the NE skin pickups in his helmet could respond to. It was far too noisy in the Chippie to carry on a normal conversation. *Then we can stretch our legs . . ."*

And take a pee, Col. Joan Ward added. *I'm sorry we had to ditch the on-board toilets . . .*

Gave us another hundred kilos of payload, Maj. Russ Frazier reminded her.

Russ, the ladies of the Greys can't go as long as macho types. We tend to fill our piddle packs sooner. We have slightly different plumbing, Joan fired back.

Believe me. I am profoundly aware of the fact and grateful for it. 'Vive l'difference!' Russ came back lightly.

Better remind all the ladies to do a special job of draining before the next leg, Curt put in.

Yeah! Eleven and a half hours from Charlotte Amalie to Praia. Some of the girls will have to change piddle packs en route. And take other measures to prevent chafing and irritation. I'm glad Dr. Ruth came with those special tropical and desert feminine hygiene kits, the Grey's chief of staff remarked.

Don't bitch to me! The inflight refuelling was Kitsy's bright idea, Russ reminded her.

And a damned bright idea, too! Worsham's still kicking his own ass because he didn't think of it first. There was a hint of laughter in Joan's thought message. Sometimes such human emotional nuances did indeed get picked up by the NE tacomm system.

Well, Kitsy thought it through like she's been taught to do it, Curt pointed out.

I was surprised that Jerry didn't think of it. You've taught him, too. Joan didn't miss very much. She knew that Curt was in a long-term selection process for his replacement as regimental commander. Modern management techniques clearly stated that a person couldn't move up the ladder without having someone ready to fill the slot. Curt had expanded that slightly by going a step farther. He'd decided to conduct a subtle competition by quietly pitting Maj. Jerry P. Allen against Maj. Kathleen B. Clinton. Those two officers were the only ones really qualified by education, training, and temperament to take over the Washington Greys at some point in the future when Curt either retired or was kicked upstairs.

Joan Ward knew it wasn't in the cards for her; she was a brave and competent leader who'd served her time in command of a platoon, a company, and a batt. But Joan really didn't want to wear the eagles and run the regiment. Her career path was clearly one of a staffer, and she accepted that.

Maj. Russell B. Frazier hadn't at first. He had the education, the training, and the motivation. However, he had too much motivation. His mentor had been the legendary Marty "Kill 'Em All" Kelly, now G-3 for the Wolfhounds. He was too aggressive, too eager to fight. However, often command requires moderation and the willingness to try to win without fighting. Curt had had to learn that from Belinda Hettrick. And Curt was very good at it now. Russ had shown that he was a basic warrior; he liked to fight. He would rather fight than negotiate. The Army needed people like him, however, and he had been super-valuable in the past because of this. But the only way up the ladder for him was as a G-3 staffer whose aggressive tendencies could be damped by the chief of staff or the commander. He might indeed make it to general officer some day, but even with stars on his shoulders he would never be allowed to operate without careful oversight by a more moderate superior. The license to use physical violence to its utmost, the legendary license to kill, had to be carefully supervised in a world of awesome and deadly weapons such as warbots.

Jerry's smart, too, Curt admitted, but he didn't add what he considered a comment on the man's biggest weakness. Curt knew that sometimes Jerry's encyclopedic memory got in the way of his willingness to think. Jerry was an outstanding officer and leader who remembered everything, but sometimes his eidetic memory made him a little lazy.

On the other hand, Kitsy was eager and played everything for all it was worth. She had enthusiasm. Her incredible self-determination had permitted her to overcome the consequences of a broken neck suffered in Iraq. Kitsy had recovered so thoroughly that Maj. Ruth Gydesen could find no evidence of the trauma now. Kitsy had also started to listen to what Curt told her—she hadn't always done so—and she tried to follow through. Curt had pegged her as a potential regimental commander if she could learn to temper her gung-ho approach and read enough to keep her from reinventing the square wheel.

Curt thought it might be working for Kitsy. She was certainly a person who was willing to try. When she'd come up with the breakthrough idea that made the transatlantic airlift possible with Chippies, Cal Worsham had asked her derisively if she could fly an aerodyne. Kitsy replied that she didn't know because she'd never tried. And then she asked Worsham if he'd teach her.

Curt liked Kitsy . . . a lot. If Dyani hadn't come into his life, Kitsy would have been number one with him. Kitsy knew that, too, and continued to maintain that she would be the best damned number two that she could. But that was just the way Kitsy Clinton assaulted life.

If she was number two with him, she'd certainly become number one with the suave ladies' man of the Washington Greys, Capt.Hassan Ben Mahmud.

Well, Kitsy cut out all the crap and got through to the basic elements of the situation, Curt pointed out. *She may not be an aerodyne driver, but she knew that an aerodyne can keep flying with more weight than it can handle if it tries to lift off with it. She also figured out that an empty Chippie configured with internal tanks could land on a replenishment ship, pick up a load of aircraft fuel, lift off, and refuel several Chippies in the air as they go past. So the Navy has managed to position two A-Os in the Atlantic between the Vee-Eye and Praia. Two midair refuellings where we tank to the slots, and we're there without having to land en route.*

Damn, but I hope the rest of the ops plan works out as well! Joan replied cautiously.

It will! was Russ's quick response. *We're going to hit Dakar at the airport along with the First Cav. When we get through moving out of there with the One-Three-Two Engineer Batt, we can seal off the peninsula and sanitize the harbor.*

And the quicker we can do that, and then have the Navy bring in the Fiftieth, and have us extracted from Dakar, the happier I'll be, Joan said.

What's the matter, Joan? Forget your woolen socks?

That remark from Russ was uncalled for, and Joan retorted quickly, *You're a staff officer now, Russ. Your job is to figure out how everyone else is going to kill 'em all. When you have to send your friends out to do it instead taking it on yourself, I think you might get a different outlook on fighting.*

Stand by to land! came the tacomm call from the Chippie's crew chief, Flight Sgt. Barry Morris. *Welcome to the beautiful Virgin Islands! Except it isn't going to do most of us any good . . .*

Fourteen

Two hours before dawn was a sleepy time of day. The eastern sky hadn't even started to brighten with morning twilight yet.

The Malitanian Army lieutenant in charge of the security at Dakar-Yoff Airport yawned and tried to keep from going to sleep. He was tired of standing the 0000 to 0800 watch. Nothing happened then.

The gates to the airport were securely shut and locked. A squad of armed soldiers stood guard at the highway gate. Two other squads were stationed along the fenced perimeter, walking guard posts all night unless they were caught sleeping. Occasionally, the report of an assault rifle broke the silence, and a sergeant reported in by tacomm that he'd shot a sleeping guard. But the shots were the only sounds that occurred during the night.

Senegalese air traffic controllers continued to staff both the control tower and the terminal radar approach control room. An armed Malitanian sentry was on hand in each place to make sure that no one went to sleep. The guards themselves were sleepy. As for the controllers, they sat around playing cards, craps, or dominoes because there was absolutely no air traffic. The airport had been closed to commercial air traffic for days. Except for Malitanian Air Force aircraft, no airplanes had come in or left.

Up in the control tower cab, the controllers could barely see the somber shapes of the four grounded commercial aircraft sitting in a powered-down condition on the passenger ramp.

Three more aircraft sat forlornly on the cargo ramp farther down the tarmac. The airport lights were either turned off or dimmed on these ramps. The Malitanians saw no need to waste electricity on non-functional activities.

But across the airport runway rows of Chinese-made Shenyang J-22 interceptors of the Malitanian Air Force sat bathed in bright lights. A squadron of Hindustani H-224 maritime patrol aircraft had gaps in its line; two were out on patrol north and south along the West African coastline.

The only activity at the airport was among the bulky Marut MC-11 transport aircraft where Generalissimo Modibo's personal plane was parked. From the tower cab, the controllers could see that it was being prepared for departure. Probably another flight back to Bamako, they figured, so Modibo could get a day's work done in that scrawny excuse for a capital city. Then Modibo would fly back to Dakar late in the day. Dakar was a cosmopolitan city, not like the wretched town of Bamako that had been neglected for decades. It was apparent to those who knew that Modibo would probably move his government to Dakar.

As they watched, they saw a convoy of cars pull onto the military ramp. Apparently, the Generalissimo was getting an early start on the day.

Down in the Dakar TRACON radar room, a controller who'd been idly glancing at the radar screen between hands of cards saw something. Without saying anything or making any moves that might alert the sleepy Malitanian sentry, he kept shifting his eyes to it. Gently, he nudged his companion, but he didn't say a word.

Almost due west of Dakar a series of brief, transient smudges appeared on the screen at a range of about ten kilometers. Then they disappeared. They were very indistinct and intermittent.

One of the controllers was a former military air controller for the French Armée de l'Air. He knew the radar signatures of partially stealthed military aircraft. It wasn't possible to totally stealth a big transport aerodyne because it had too much surface area. But it could indeed be stealthed to the point where it didn't show up until it was very close to the radar antenna and almost in the main bang. These targets were in close and coming fast.

His companion shot the former French controller a querulous look, whereupon the man simply shrugged and replied, *"Mouette."*

Sea gulls.

The Senegambian controller also guessed what the indistinct targets were. He didn't like the Malitanians invading his country. Furthermore, he didn't like being forced to work at the point of a gun. It was obvious from other activities in Dakar that no Senegambian was going to be allowed to live very long, anyway. Once the Malitanians got East World technicians and professionals into Senegambia, no Senegambian would be spared the mass graves.

So the Senegambian kept his mouth shut and tried to decide what he would do when the bullets started to fly in a few minutes.

But bullets weren't the first lethal objects that came out of the sky.

Streaks of yellow and green suddenly appeared over the western horizon. To an untrained eye, these might have been caused by meteors. But they weren't meteors.

The controllers in the TRACON saw the bright radar return from these trails. They knew then what they were. It's impossible to stealth the ionized trail of a hypersonic Mach-10 penetration strike aircraft.

The French controller said a silent prayer to Mother Mary that the air control building wasn't the target because it was too late to do anything but watch. It was even too late for a telephone call to anyone. The incoming hypersonics were covering more than 3 kilometers every second. Within ten seconds of the appearance of their ionized trails of hot gases on the radar screens, the hypersonics released their war loads. Then they were overhead and gone.

The building holding the radar room and topped by the control tower suddenly shook with the double concussion of a sonic boom.

Every pane of glass in the control tower cab disintegrated into a shower of shards and tempered pebbles.

Something hit the military ramp across the runway. It wasn't a chemical or nuclear explosion, yet it acted that way. Two projectiles hit, and the result was a sudden release of energy. It created a brief burst of light and a sharp concussion wave. This was followed by a lethal rain of molten metallic pebbles, dirt, rocks, and pieces of concrete ramp that fell all over the airport.

Two more double booms rolled over the airport, followed by the concussion of four more objects hitting the military ramp, throwing metal and other debris in their aftermath.

The Mach-10 Black Bart hypersonic bombers of the United States Aerospace Force were gone over the eastern horizon almost as fast as this happened. Their hot, glowing, ionized trails only showed where they'd been before the trails began to disperse.

Ordinary bombs had not hit the military ramp. When they'd been released from the Black Barts at Mach-10, they'd been 10-meter lengths of steel with guidance fins on the rear and a cheap mass-produced smart robot guidance system in their noses. The Black Barts had simply released these projectiles from their weapon bays. When these steel poles hit the military ramps, they were travelling at more than three kilometers per second. The enormous kinetic energy had instantly converted to heat. The effect within a hundred meters of impact was of the same magnitude as a one megaton nuclear weapon. But there was no lethal radiation from these hypersonic telephone poles. Just the conversion of their energy of motion to heat energy was enough to do tremendous damage.

The coordination of the air attack was incredibly good. Within thirty seconds after the Mach-10 kinetic kill weapons had hit with unerring precision, the incoming USAF SAB-40 Blue Arrow bombers were over the western marge of the airport. They were decelerating to subsonic speeds so their navigational/bombing systems could more accurately place ordnance on the military ramp. At the last instant, the human pilots fingered the targets and facilities that hadn't been demolished by the hypersonic kinetic kill weapons.

Generalissimo Modibo hit the ground the instant he heard the first double boom of the shock wave. He'd fought battles all his life. He knew what an explosion was, and he reacted almost

136

automatically in the identical way of every soldier in the world: He hit the deck without hesitation. A few seconds or minutes later, he could learn what happened and move to do something about it, but his first priority was to save his ass. His sixth wife, a Songhai from Timbuctu, was a Muslim woman who expected orders and would obediently follow them. She wasn't a hardened, self-sufficient Tuareg who'd known war and fighting all her life. As a result, she was caught standing alongside the Generalissimo's limousine by the intense heat pulse from the first kinetic kill weapon. Modibo didn't even see her body caught in the shock wave, riddled by fragments of flying concrete and steel, then tossed like a limp doll across the tarmac, her ear drums broken and her face a pall of blood from the rupture of the capillaries in her nose and ears. She was dead before she struck the ground where her body rolled over and over on the ramp.

The shock wave from the second kinetic kill weapon caught Modibo's limo head on. The huge Chinese copy of the Mercedes 770SLE was picked up and tossed fifty meters against a brick wall before the wall collapsed from the overpressure of the concussion shock wave.

Nothing touched Modibo. After the third rail weapon hit, he heard the sound of the incoming subsonic SAB-40s. He'd gotten out of his limo close enough to the military hangar so that he had time to get to his feet and dash to a nearby stairwell leading down to an underground bunker. That act saved his life when the smart bombs from the first SAB-40s hit the remaining aircraft on the ramp and the accelerated penetrator weapons from the second SAB-40 took out the temporary TAB-V hangars containing four J-22 interceptors.

The SAB-40s missed seeing or detecting the old French ammo bunker between the hangars. Once used to store the anti-submarine depth charges of the French Navy maritime patrol planes of World War II, it had been converted into a ready shack for Senegambian interceptor and maritime patrol pilots. The Malitanian Air Force had taken it over as a ready room for the J-22 aircrews.

Col. Godavari Singh Pratihara knew it was there. He'd accompanied Modibo in the limo from Dakar, so now he grabbed the tall, slender man's arm and shouted, "Into the bunker! We're under attack!"

"I know that, you idiot!" Modibo shouted back. "Do we have communications in there?"

"We should!"

"It's your head if we don't!"

The smart bombs and penetrators weren't targeted on people. So they didn't go after Modibo and Pratihara. Instead, the weapons went for aircraft on the ramp and for hangars that might hold aircraft.

The initial air assault was unbelievably intense and concentrated. It was all over within five minutes.

But it had been deadly. Those who hadn't been killed were badly shaken and terribly confused. Modibo and Pratihara found themselves in the underground bunker with the flight leader and three Malitanian pilot officers who'd been on Zulu Alert. The interceptor pilots were still in bed because they hadn't received any scramble call. The emergency bunker lights were now on. The bunker had been shaken by the incoming weaponry, but it was intact. So were its telephones.

Close on the heels of the SAB-40 attack came eight AC-40C Harpies of the Washington Greys' TACAIRCO. Their pilots were looking for ground fire because their job was to finish the task of sanitizing the airport.

Capt. Paul Hands was flying the lead ship. He didn't want to have to go back to Praia with ordnance aboard. In fact, he didn't want to go back to Praia at all. He wanted to land the Harpies at Dakar and base there once it had been sanitized. As a tacair aerodyne driver, he wanted to be close to the action so his Harpy group could scramble quickly and get on the targets fast.

The eastern sky was growing lighter now as dawn approached. But it was still too dark to see clearly. That made no difference to the Harpy drivers. They were plugged into the sensor suites and scanning for targets. Anything that moved was fair game. Any military hardware was also fair game. The Mod 7/11 artificial intelligence units in the Harpies could pick it out. They'd been recently uploaded with all the characteristics of Malitanian military vehicles, missile launchers, and long guns.

Pick your targets and take them out! Hands signalled his other seven Harpy pilots by air-to-air neuroelectronic tacomm, thinking his orders into the circuitry by sub-vocalizing them. *But keep a cool stool and a hot pot. Retain situational awareness. I don't want any of you hot jocks running into one another.*

Some Malitanian gravel grabber at the airport heard the Harpies. He decided that here was a target that was moving slow enough to hit. So he shouldered a tube rocket known to the U.S. Army as a Calcutta Cutter, and fired it. Its heat-seeking guidance system locked onto the infrared image of one of the Harpies and went for it.

A Harpy isn't as large as a Chippie. It's a ground pounder, a mud-mover, a gravel maker. It's small and maneuverable. In long and exhausting war games down in southern Arizona, Cal Worsham and his aerodyne drivers had learned an interesting fact of life: a Harpy can outmaneuver nearly every shoulder-fired tube rocket in the inventory of the world's military forces. An inexpensive contract funded from regimental monies with a consumer rocket company in Nevada had produced the Vegas Viper, a harmless cardboard tube rocket simulator that could be fired in war games. A Vegas Viper flew like a Smart Fart, Soviet Ossah, or Calcutta Cutter. Worsham, Hands, and the rest of the aerodyne drivers had a lot of practice dodging the Vegas Vipers. Now they had no trouble with the Calcutta Cutters.

Wiz! Cutter coming at you! was the instant message from Harpy pilot Bruce Mark.

Got it! No problem! Jinking now! It's gonna miss! Rick Cooke replied with unbelievable calm for someone who was being shot at.

And I've got the launcher pegged! came the thought call from Stacy Honey. *I'm going for him!*

This time, I'll let ya! Mark snapped. *I got one or two of my own.*

Yeah, don't get piggy, guys! Check out the airport approaches if you can't find targets at the airport! Hands told them.

I can't find any targets! Jay Kennedy complained. *I thought Cal said this would be target-rich environment.*

The Aerospace Farce guys got first pick of the juicy stuff. Looks like they did their job, Hands remarked. *Hey, the airport perimeter fence isn't a target! If we leave it be, it just makes life tougher for the Malitanians. They can't easily get to our Greys on the ground! Warhawk Leader, Harrier Leader here! The landing zone is clear. Or are we doing this for our own glory? Where the hell are the Chippies?*

They're right on schedule, Harrier Leader! Goddammit! I'm taking ground fire! Cal Worsham wasn't specifically part of the tactical air sanitation strike. He was aloft with a Harpy trying to keep track of the airborne part of the operation.

Quad fifty! On the approach end of Runway one-niner! Right where he can pop easy at anything on approach. Must be one at the other end of the runway, too. I've got him! Cooke snapped.

The hell you say! He's mine! He had the balls to shoot at me! Worsham growled. *Wiz, take the one on the other end! Here, follow me to mid-field. Split mid-field. I'll take the south. You take the north. Come at them from behind. They'll need time to slew the guns.*

Roger! I see you on i-r, Warhawk Leader. Gotta roll in now!

Rolling with you, belly to belly. Rolling out. Got my target. How about you?

Got it! Using a Smart Fart on him. Want to save twenty-five ammo for possible air defense.

Shit! I just lost two turbines! I can't maintain altitude unless I dump ordnance and fuel! came the distress call from Lt. Stacey Honey.

Put it down on the commercial ramp, Stace! Point toward the military ramp so you can still get some utility out of your twenty-five on the ground! were Hands' instructions.

I can hover in ground effect! I can train in azimuth that way!

Do it!

Warhawk Leader, this is Grey Ops! came the NE tacomm voice of Maj. Russ Frazier, G-3 ops calling from one of the inbound Chippewas. *Speaking of air defense. I'm relaying a heads-up from Iron Fist Ops who just got data from Bloodbath Air Ops. Eight Malitanian Juliet-two-twos just scrambled off Saint Louis up north. Course is southbound to Dakar.*

We're configured for tac ground, not air cover! Worsham replied. *We'll look for them, but we need some help from Cotton Air. Aren't they configured for air cover until the brown shoes show up?* Worsham was referring in jargon to the naval air cover that was supposed to come from the carrier submarines. Unless a listener is really familiar with the English language and the slang terms used by a particular military service, jargon is as secure as code words and a lot more meaningful. (See Appendix IV, Glossary of Robot Infantry Terms and Slang.)

Roger, and they're vectoring to intercept. Juliet targets coming on your data bus now.

Okay, I see the Juliets on tac display! Tell Cotton Air to vector direct Dakar and intercept here. They can't make a rear quarter intercept on the Juliets. The Juliets are inbound Mach Two. Cotton One can't catch them.

Roger, but Cotton Air may need your help. They've got only the same twenty-fives and Smart Farts you've got!

We'll be bingo fuel by the time the Juliet-two-twos get here. If we stay to fight, we'll have to squat at Dakar. We won't be able to hack it back to the tankers. Unless you move the tankers in closer.

Grey Head says to stay and fight. The tankers are busy bartending the Cav Chippies. Once the Greys are on dirt, they've got Smart Farts and the twenty-fives on the Mary Anns to back you up, Frazier told him.

As long as they don't shoot at us!

That's why it doesn't pay to make enemies of your friends. Just hope none of the Greys on the ground owes you money!

By the way, when you gonna pay me what I won in that last poker game in Huachuca three nights ago?

See me when this is over.

I'm losing Seven-eleven! was the call from Lt. Jay Kennedy. *Infrared gone! Losing situational contact with my Harpy!*

Get it on the ground, Jay! Fast! I don't want you to go KIA! Worsham ordered him.

I'm taking small arms ground fire from several locations! Gabe Neatherly reported. *Need help! Lot more than I can handle!*

Okay, I see it! Grey Head, this is Warhawk Leader! Hold in hover! We haven't got the field sanitized yet!

Warhawk Leader, this is Grey Head! came Curt's response. *We're already over the northwest corner! Spot those dirty sites and we'll try to take them out when we land!*

Christamighty, Grey Head! We're taking a lot more now! All around the perimeter fence! Must be sentries! We'll go for them, but be advised you're gonna be touching down with small arms fire all over you!

141

Fifteen

The electromagnetic spectrum used for communication and air traffic control around Dakar International Airport was immediately blanketed by intense electronic counter-measures. Tiny "eyelets" were left at carefully selected frequencies to allow tacomm frequency-skip communications between elements of the incoming Operation Bloodbath units.

The first Chippewa on the ground at Dakar Airport opened its cargo doors almost the instant the landing pads touched the concrete tarmac.

Out rolled eight M60A Airborne Mobile Assault warbots, Mary Anns. Their M300 25-millimeter cannons were loaded and their sensors seeking targets.

They were followed by the three Sierra Charlies of Hassan's Assassins led by Capt. Hassan Ben Mahmud. With the Sierra Charlies was Sad Saddam, Hassan's M33AZ General Purpose warbot or "Jeep."

Immediately following them were eight more Mary Anns, a Jeep, and the three Sierra Charlies of Lt. Matsu Mikawa's Marauders. Mickie Mikawa was a new officer making her first assault. She was getting more attention than normal because of this. Alongside her was Capt. Lewis C. Pagan, ASSAULTCO Bravo commander accompanied by Master Sgt. Robert Lee Garrison. Pagan wasn't worried about his other platoon officer, Hassan, a blooded officer; Hassan could handle his new NCO, Sgt. Maria Lunalilo. But Mikawa also had a new NCO, Sgt. A.W. Guilford. So

Mikawa's Marauders were, in effect, a green outfit.

If Jerry Allen and Lew Pagan were worried about Mickie Mikawa, Col. Curt Carson wasn't. Born in Honolulu of parents with Japanese ancestry, Mikawa was a doll-sized samurai with a sweet social demeanor and a deadly fighting attitude. During martial arts training, she'd clobbered such big men as Capt. Larry Hall and Master Sgt. Carol Head.

The assault was made in total tacomm silence. Everyone knew the plan. No one needed to be reminded of orders or objectives.

Besides, they were all too intent upon the attack. They were worrying that maybe one of the Mary Anns would go tits-up or wondering where the first rounds of incoming would go.

It was a situation with a very high pucker factor. All airborne Chippie assaults were. They probably always would be. Airborne assaults can make opposing forces keep their heads down and become confused . . . sometimes. But once the initial shock of the assault wore off, that confusion never lasted very long.

But this was a strange assault. None of the Sierra Charlies of the Washington Greys met incoming fire during the first long minute.

The second Chippie grounded thirty seconds after the first. It disgorged another sixteen Mary Anns along with Sweet's Stilettos and Lt. Dan Power's Panthers. Major Kitsy Clinton accompanied Power, her new platoon leader, covering him J.I.C. (Just In Case).

The Pumas went for the military ramp which was covered with flaming, smoking debris.

The Cougars directed their attention to the commercial side of the field and the terminal building.

Alleycat Leader, this is Puma Leader! No incoming fire! Pagan broke the tacomm silence by reporting to Maj. Jerry Allen, the TACBATT commander who was in the third Chippie just touching down on the airport.

Mustang Leader will find some for us, Puma Leader. Jerry promised in reply, trying to project cool and couth in his directed thoughts to the neuroelectronic tacomm system. *She's going out the door now with Saunders and SCOUT. Black Hawk birdbots will be up as soon as we can get their ACV out of Chippie Number Five when it lands.*

Alleycat Leader, do you want us to draw fire for you? We'll do it! Dyani's tacomm voice came back with equal composure. Dyani rarely got rattled. She kept herself under control in combat. But she let it out afterwards in private with Curt. She led her Jeep, recently promoted Lt. Harlan Saunders, Sgts. Tracy Dillon, Sid Johnson, and new man Zeb Long across the runway in a skirmisher formation. The platoon headed for the military side of the airport.

Chippie Number Four grounded next. Out came Capt. Larry Hall's Hellcats and the five Saucy Cans' warbots that made up the regimental artillery. The 75-millimeter Saucy Cans' guns on their Light Artillery Mobile Vehicles not only had a range of fifteen klicks with rocket-assisted projectiles if needed. They could also be elevated to high quadrant angles and fired with reduced charges to serve as large-caliber mortars.

Curt and his regimental staff were riding Chippie Number Six behind the Black Hawks and their birdbots in Chippie Five.

Curt didn't like not being first on the ground. Hettrick had had a long talk with him by tacomm during the extended transatlantic flight. Basically, it came down to her final words to him:

Colonel, you're a regimental commander. It is not your job now to be first in the fight. If you take a Golden BB when you come out of the Chippie, the regiment will be without its commander. So you've got to let your people do the job you've given them. They won't think less of you because you're not in front. A lieutenant leads a platoon, but a colonel commands a regiment. On occasion, a colonel may also lead. However, command comes first. You're a pro and you wouldn't be in charge of the Washington Greys if you hadn't shown command capabilities as well as leadership. If you intend to lead, it means that your Academy teachers, General Carlisle, General Bellamack, and I have failed. I don't believe I've failed, and I don't think the others have. However, you're the only one who can prove us right or wrong. I have other work to do now. Battleaxe out!

Curt knew that Gen. Belinda Hettrick had learned the hard way what she'd told him. There comes a time in the career of any officer worthy of promotion when it's a matter of learn and move up, leaving room below for others. Or the officer must get out of the way of those below him who will. So Curt did his job the way Belinda Hettrick expected him to.

But that didn't mean he liked it.

Or that the course of the campaign would always find him in the position of the commander on his horse atop the hill watching his troops fight in the fields below.

In his Chippie with his headquarters' contingent was Regimental Technical Sgt. Edie Sampson. She was working with the communications equipment inside the regimental OCV that filled a substantial part of the Chippie's cargo hold. *Time to let them know, Colonel?* she asked via tacomm.

Curt saw that Chippie Five was on the ground and that his own Chippie was over the airport fence and about to land. *Transmit Message Alpha!* he confirmed.

Edie sent a signal to the ECM center of Operation Bloodbath. It was in an Iron Fist Chippie still kilometers out over the ocean. From there, commands went to the Aerospace Force EW aircraft loitering offshore over the Atlantic and the orbiting satellites above. The VHF frequency channel of Dakar Tower suddenly became clear of jamming.

Dakar Tower, this is United States Army Chippewa Six over the fence to the west, her voice came through the tacomm channel as she read the prepared message verbally on the now-clear control tower frequency. *United States' armed forces are landing at Dakar on a mission of peace. Inform the Malitanian armed forces at the airport that any attempt to resist will be met with a like show of force. We regret the necessity to render unusable the Malitanian Air Force units at the airport. We require that the Malitanian Army and Air Force personnel remaining at the airport surrender. When they do so, they will be treated according to the Geneva conventions. Army Chippewa Six out!*

145

Well said, Sergeant! Curt told her.

Don't you mean, well read, sir? She relayed another signal to Bloodbath EW, and the jamming of the tower frequency resumed.

As Curt felt the Chippie's landing gear touch ground, a tacomm report filled his head. *Alleycat Leader, the Mustangs are taking incoming small arms fire from sentries on the perimeter fence and the guard contingent at the east gate! The targets are on the data bus!*

Alleycat Leader sees the target data, Mustang Leader! Puma Leader, take care of the east gate and any targets on the east perimeter fence. Cougar Leader, engage targets on the west side of the field! Then proceed with Phase Two of the operation! Jerry was in tight control of the situation.

Absolutely no incoming fire from the east side of the field where the military contingent was hit, Lew Pagan snapped. *What the hell? This isn't a fight! It's a walk-through!*

Don't anticipate, Puma Leader! It could get deadly. We don't know where all the Malitanian troops are! Jerry warned. Intelligence sources had reported that the airport was guarded although most of the Malitanian Army division was in downtown Dakar about fifteen klicks to the southeast on the tip of the peninsula. Jerry hadn't asked about the intelligence sources themselves; he had to presume they were reliable ones. A battalion commander doesn't inquire about such things because it isn't necessary that he know. Jerry still led at the FEBA; he could be captured with the information.

Alleycat Leader, this is Cougar Leader! Kitsy's thought voice broke through. *We've got a real furball going! The Stilettos are taking fire from some of the administrative buildings! The Panthers are facing a Malitanian squad of about twelve grunts driving civilians ahead of them as human shields! I can use some support to flank the bastards before they kill the hostages!*

Puma Leader, turn your front! Jerry ordered quickly. *Get back across the field and move around the south side of the passenger terminal!*

Sounds like the airport hassle in Yemen! Larry Hall remarked.

Alleycat Leader, I can't turn the whole company! I've got opposition from the remnants of the guard forces over on this side! Pagan pointed out.

Alleycat, Cougar Leader doesn't need the whole damned Puma outfit! Lew has his hands full, but Larry can help him lobbing some Saucy Cans' rounds where they'll discourage some Malitanians. I don't need a whole lot of help. I just need someone to sting this hostage-holding platoon on the south side to distract them! Kitsy interjected.

Puma Leader, Marauder Leader can turn about and get back there! We're all on trikes! That was Lieutenant Mickie Mikawa volunteering.

The Mustangs are also trike-mounted! Dyani Motega put in. *Lew, turn Mickie loose and I'll join her! We can do the terminal flanking maneuver together!*

Jerry hesitated. He was losing control of the fight. Curt had warned him about that possibility. But Jerry didn't like to lose control. He didn't yet know that a fight, once started and under way, takes on its own flow and velocity. The best that a small unit commander can do is trust his people and depend on their initiative. And to stand by in case the fight goes to slime, and he has to patch the hole in the shit can where it's all running out.

Okay, Marauder Leader and Mustang Leader! Puma Leader, Alleycat Leader has gotta detach the Marauders! Any heartburn?

Yeah, but I don't guess there's a damned thing I can do about it!

There is, Lew, but you'll have to be taking a whole hell of a lot more fire than you are at the moment! Jerry admitted. Suddenly, tacomm protocol had gone away. The fight was picking up momentum. In spite of intensive training and weeks of field exercises, Jerry knew by now that loss of tacomm protocol couldn't be corrected under such circumstances. Protocol took second place to winning. There had been times in field exercises when he'd maintained excellent tacomm protocol throughout . . . and lost as a result. So he let it go. *Mustang Leader, Marauder Leader, turn about. Shag ass and bypass! Give Cougar Leader some help! Hellcat Leader, join Puma Leader and give 'em hell!*

I was half expecting you to say, 'Double shot your guns, Bragg, and give 'em hell!' Larry Hall replied.

This is Dakar, not Chapultepec, Larry! was Kitsy's quick reply.

That was said by Zack Taylor at Saltillo, Kitsy! Jerry had an encyclopedic memory.

Dyani's RECONCO and her SCOUT platoon were short an NCO, but the Mustangs were in as good shape from a personnel standpoint as any other company in the Greys. When Mickie Mikawa and her three Sierra Charlies joined up on the ramp during the cross-airport sweep, Dyani's diversion group was almost as powerful as Kitsy's Cougars.

Coming around the mountain now! was the call from Harlie Saunders as he came around the south side of the terminal building in the lead. What he saw caused him to exclaim, *Holy shit! The Malitanians are about to cut the throats of those Senegambians!*

So shoot their goddammed nuts off! Dan Power replied, his excited tacomm voice indicating that he was hyped-up in his first shooting combat.

Easy, Dan, easy! Kitsy cautioned. *Dyani, can your Jeeps discriminate the targets well enough to take out the Malitanians instead of the Senegambians?*

We can! Mickie Mikawa responded at once. And immediately, her two Jeeps opened up. And so did she and her two NCOs. She didn't wait for the order. She saw what was necessary and did it before the Malitanians could start slitting throats.

The Sierra Charlies of the Mustangs and the Marauders did a better job of target discrimination than the Jeep and Mary Ann warbots, even if the human response wasn't quite as fast as that of the warbots.

The fire from two of the four Jeeps was off. The 7.62-millimeter rounds went over the heads of the Malitanians. One of the Mary Anns became confused and didn't fire at all.

Suddenly, small arms fire began to come from overhead. Kitsy looked up over the top of the ground fighting. She saw a uniformed body fall through the air from the control tower cab, its arms and legs flailing limply. It hit the concrete with a dull, wet thump. Then someone in the tower cab began firing into the Malitanians, too.

By the time the other Mary Anns of the Marauders got around the corner of the building, the fracas was all over.

The entire Malitanian unit was hit and down.

Unfortunately, three of the civilian hostages had been hit, too.

Dammit, Mickie, your Jeeps got the wrong targets! Adonica Sweet burst out.

I decline to accept the full blame! Someone in the control tower was firing at random into them! And the maintenance patches we tried to put on those Jeeps back at Huachuca probably went bad, the little officer replied. The excitement was gone from her voice now. She was as cool and concise as Dyani. *Sorry! There was no way to know. Or to control the fire from the tower! Medic! Medic! We've got wounded civilians here! Take them first. Forget those Malitanian barbarians until we get the civilians tended to . . .*

Going in now! came the call from Bio-tech Sgt. Ginny Bowles. *Only one of me here! Bio-tech Leader, we need some help!*

Coming out of Chippie Six! We see your beacon! Be there in thirty seconds!

In the meantime, where the hell's the fight? Lew Pagan wanted to know. *We're over here against the east perimeter fence. We've captured four Malitanians and shot about a dozen others. That's all we can find! Where the hell is the enemy?*

Mustang Leader, this is Alleycat Leader, Jerry called, resuming tacomm protocol. *Are your birdbots up yet? Got any make on Malitanians outside the perimeter fence? Or left on the field?*

Negatory from Mustang Leader!

Cougars and Pumas, spread out and send the Mary Anns along the perimeter fence. Activate Phase Two! Jerry snapped. *Grey Head, Alleycat Leader here! We've completed Phase One well ahead of schedule. Malitanian defenses were not as expected. I'm activating Phase Two now.*

Curt saw this on his helmet tac display as his OCV rolled across the ramp from Chippie Six toward the terminal building. The lack of intensive defense of the airport bothered him. An airport was always a prime target for any airborne assault force. Airports are easier to operate from than open fields. Airports also contain aviation support facilities — communications, fuels, and ground support equipment, for example. These make the conduct of an airborne operation much easier.

Why hadn't the Malitanians defended Dakar Airport better?

He didn't know at that point. But he would try to get some answers as quickly as he could. He needed to know so he could try to anticipate what the Malitanians might do next.

An airborne assault can be countered in any number of ways, but two of them have proved to be most effective.

First, any airborne assault is vulnerable in the first few minutes of the landing. The defending force must be aware of the pending attack or remain in a constant state of Red Alert. If an airborne assault can't be stopped as it's forming up on the ground, a huge defense must be on hand to counter-assault it immediately. Thus far, the Malitanians hadn't exercised this option. The initial resistance was minimal. Some of the operation's success could have been caused by the initial surprise air strike. Curt made a mental note to ask for as much continuing air support as he could get, especially to the east of Dakar. It was apparent that the Malitanian air defenses were weak, especially around the Dakar airport. If the Aerospace Force could gain air supremacy, it would make his job a lot easier.

A second tactic is Number Two Priority: Wait until the assault force is on the ground, withdraw the defending forces to conserve personnel, ammo, and equipment, and then pick a soft spot in the assaulting forces. Sometimes this tactic is useful to throw the assault force off guard and make them relax their vigilance. Number Two requires planning and outstanding C^3I. Curt didn't know how the Malitanians could pull it off. The heavy American ECM was disrupting all activity in the electromagnetic spectrum from the infrared to ELF. The only open frequencies were the narrow skip channels used by tacomm.

But Curt called in a second and third opinion before making his next important decision. *Grey Major, this is Grey Head! Will you give me your present operational assessment, please?*

Curt really didn't need to use formality when communicating with Regimental Master Sgt. Henry Kester.

Grey Head, I'd say we got off easy on this one unless Modibo has something very big hidden outside the perimeter fence. Even if he does, it may take those troops a few more minutes to put on their pants. Let's get on with this fracas so we can go home! We've got momentum, so we oughta keep it up. Henry Kester wasn't one to mince words. He didn't need to use formality. He was the top NCO in the Washington Greys. Everyone knew that Henry Kester's respect wasn't a measure of the language he used.

Grey Ops, what do you think? Curt addressed Russ Frazier.

Grey Head, we got off cheap! But the Brand X guys won't sit on their asses and wait for us to make the next move against them. They could be all over us like a rug in the next hour. And we sure as hell can't hold off the whole damned Malitanian Army. So I think it's time to bring in some backup according to plan. Russ was also somewhat coarse in his terminology, but he was only two steps below his CO on the TO&E. He was also the staff "expert" on operations. *Time for the cavalry to come over the hill!*

Alleycat Leader, Grey Head here! Jerry, is Dale up with his birdbots yet? Do we know what's outside the perimeter fence?

Wait one, Grey Head. I'm getting a report now from Mustang Leader.

Put it on the command channel.

Mustang Leader here! Black Hawk Leader reports nothing beyond the perimeter fence but a lot of houses. We see some people moving around in the streets because of all the ruckus we've made here at the airport, and . . . Stand by! We've got three armed civilians at the west gate!

Are they shooting?

Negatory!

Alleycat Leader, this is Grey Head. Have Mustang Leader check this out! Curt told his TACBATT commander.

A new voice came on the tacomm net. *Grey Head, this is Battleaxe! Check them out! Local partisans are supposed to contact us. Ask the following question, and make sure you ask it exactly this way: 'Dealer's choice. One-eyed queens or better to open.'*

Sixteen

Curt immediately knew that Hettrick had been plugged into intelligence data that he hadn't seen. The contact cliché had probably come down from somewhere on high, perhaps even the NIA, through Bellamack to Hettrick. Until this moment, it wasn't necessary that Curt or the Greys know about any possible contact with Senegambian partisans.

Jerry Allen didn't need to repeat it to the regimental S-2, Capt. Dyani Motega. She was listening and acting. Dyani messaged back to Jerry, *Mustang Leader is proceeding now to the west gate to make contact. Marauder Leader, if you're not too busy mopping up, would you please cover us?*

Roger, Mustang Leader. The Marauders are with you! Mickie Mikawa replied at once.

The Dakar Airport operation was growing more complex by the second. Curt had to divert his attention to it momentarily. *Grey Ops, this is Grey Head! Is Wolf over the fence yet?*

Russ was staying on top of all this. *On schedule, Grey Head. Grey Tech and I are proceeding up the Dakar Tower to coordinate from there.*

Be careful! Someone was shooting from up there! Curt warned.

Roger that! But it was friendly fire. I think. I hope. The body that tried to fly from the tower was a Malitanian corporal. Looks like the tower is occupied by the Senegambian air traffic control people. But I won't believe that until I see it. Grey Tech and I are both primed to shoot. Russ and Edie together made a good

153

combat team. Neither was hesitant to blow away anyone who gave them any grief in a combat situation such as this. *Elevator's out of commission! These damned stairs go on forever! No wonder air traffic controllers stay in good shape!*

Philip, continue present course. Proceed to the west side of the terminal building ahead. Curt flashed the neuroelectronic thought order to the Mod 7/11 artificial intelligence circuitry of his OCV's robotic driver, Philip.

Although Curt had complete combat information on the displays inside his OCV, he always needed to get the actual feel of the fight. So he stuck his helmeted head up through the top hatch of the OCV, keeping his eye on his helmet visor's tac display.

The sight that met his sweeping gaze was a combination of apparent confusion and obvious destruction.

It was a scene typical of a war environment.

Dawn had come, and the low sun cast long shadows. Smoke was rising from the military ramp complex on the east side of the field. The Chippies carrying the Sierra Charlies and warbots of the 27th Robot Infantry (Special Combat) Regiment, the Wolfhounds, were in the northwestern sky as they began to settle for landing. Some were on the ground disgorging troops and warbots.

The Chippies of Capt. Tim Timm's AIRLIFTCO were beginning to lift off. They were empty and light now. As a result, they appeared to jump into the air. They were on their way back to Praia in the Cape Verde Islands to pick up more troops and warbots. En route, they would be refuelled in the air by other Chippies serving as tankers.

Overhead, Cal Worsham and Paul Hands led their Harpies on tactical air cover.

But visually and on his tac display, Curt saw something new and unknown coming from the north. Those oncoming specks in the sky had to be the Malitanian warplanes from Saint Louis that had been reported. Quickly, he shifted tacomm frequencies to warn Cal. But Worsham

154

and his minions were already adequately warned by others.

Grey Warhawk Leader, this is Navy Black Ace Leader! Roger your last! Maintain your surveillance of the ground situation! We have the incoming bogeys! Intercept in twenty seconds! Fox Two! Fox Two!

Navy Black Ace Leader, if you don't mind, we'll keep an eye on the incoming bogeys, too! Cal responded. *Not that I don't trust you, mind you! But I don't like it worth a damn playing sitting duck while you cruise in to take the glory! Make goddamned sure you're squawking the right codes! We'll fucking blow the balls off anyone we see that isn't a friendly blip on the screen! We'll go Fox Three on the bastard!*

Trust us, Warhawk Leader!

Only if I cut the cards first, Navy!

Curt saw other AD-40s coming in on an intercept course. They were apparently aircraft of VF-41, the Black Aces, operating from the newly-commissioned U.S.S. *Gallery*, the last of the authorized carrier submarines. Under presidential instructions, the multi-billion-dollar *Gallery* was positioned out of immediate harm's way several hundred kilometers off the coast. This was far enough from Dakar and Saint Louis that any Malitanian aircraft or missiles could be spotted in time to intercept them. It was also just within the combat radius of Navy's AD-40Bs.

Operation Bloodbath was an incredibly complex mission, far different from most of the overseas deployments Curt and the Greys had participated in. This was a major surgical strike involving combined operations of all three armed services. It was a lot like Operation Steel Band on Trinidad but very different from the Sakhalin Police Detachment. Curt hoped that the present administration had the balls to stick with it and not go wimpy the first time something went wrong. The Greys were still suffering the aftereffects of the pull-out and retreat from Yemen when the current president changed the policy of his more hawklike predecessor.

And as typically true in any large combined arms operation, no one except those at the very top saw the complete scope of what was going on. However, down at the individual level of personal combat, the high brass couldn't know the details. In fact, they didn't need to know. Or want to know. But to the Sierra Charlies, it was the most important part of the operation. They were the ones taking the incoming and returning fire. They were the ones whose pink bodies were constantly at risk.

The high command might garner such decorations as the Distinguished Service Medal. But the Sierra Charlies were the ones who would qualify for the Purple Heart or the Bronze Star. Or even the Congressional Medal of Honor.

When Dyani, Lt. Harlan Saunders, and First Sgt. Tracy Dillon got to the east gate of the airport, they found no opposition. Apparently, the three Malitanian Army guards had been shot from outside the airport perimeter. The guard shack was full of bullet holes on its external walls. It had no glass left.

Harlan, Tracy, be careful! Dyani warned, perhaps unnecessarily. They were all wearing body armor that would stop anything less than a 9-millimeter Magnum. That didn't mean that they were going to walk blindly into any ambush.

Dyani, you be careful! Dillon told her. It was almost impossible for either Dillon or Saunders to maintain protocol with Dyani Motega. She'd once been an NCO who'd served with Dillon as one of his squad leaders. Her field commission had elevated her to officer status only on paper. Harlan Saunders, recently commissioned himself because of the losses sustained in Yemen, was beginning to learn about that, too. As for Tracy Dillon, he'd turned down a commission; like Henry Kester, he was an NCO down to his core. *That girl with the eye patch looks mean enough to whip her weight in infuriated wildcats! She may be a partisan, but I'll believe it when I see it!*

156

Dyani rode her M92 PTV in an erratic path over the last fifty meters down the paved highway to the guard gate. She dodged back and forth, trying to make a difficult moving target of herself. She rode rather than walked. A fast moving target on a Trike is harder to hit than someone on foot who moves more slowly. At the guard gate, she pulled up in defilade behind it and dismounted. Crazy Horse, her M33A2 Jeep, got out with her. It swung its 7.62-millimeter auto back and forth as it sought out and identified potential targets. It spotted the three partisans and stored their location coordinates— bearings and ranges—in its short-term memory. It could fire on those targets in less than a second if ordered to do so or if the targets opened fire on it.

Dillon and Saunders were behind her. They dismounted as well. They had one other Jeep with them, and it was ready for action. But they really didn't fully trust the Jeeps. At Huachuca, they'd had to make far too many quick fixes with surplus or commercial parts. So they shouldered their Novias J.I.C. The Novia is an accurate personal assault rifle. Look through the sight, put the red laser pip on the target, and then move the rifle until the cross hairs centered on the pip. The sight was laser-ranged. It also compensated for the external ballistics of the 7.62-millimeter caseless Novia rounds. Unless there was a hell of a cross wind, it was almost impossible to miss with a Novia at less than a hundred meters unless the trooper didn't aim it right in the first place.

The Sierra Charlies had always counted on this level of military technology to survive on the battlefield. Ordinary warbots didn't have to worry about survival. Sierra Charlies did. And it had been a long road to develop the sort of self-preservation programs needed for the Mod 7/11 AI in the Sierra Charlies' Jeeps and Mary Anns. Unlike the warbot brainies who were mostly technology twits enamored by the high tech of their weaponry, Sierra Charlies treated technology as a tool for survival and success.

One suspicious move from the three "partisans" standing on the road outside the gate, and they would never know what hit them. Dillon and Saunders had set up for three-round bursts if their fingers touched the triggers. The Jeeps were set to respond on the infrared or audio signal of someone firing toward them or their Sierra Charlies.

When Dyani was within earshot of the partisans, she called out, "Dealer's choice. One-eyed queens or better to open."

And she immediately understood the hidden meaning of the coded password. The slender young woman leading the partisan group had a black patch over her left eye.

The reply came at once. "There is no one-eyed queen in the deck!"

Dyani didn't have to relay the reply to Curt. Her helmet tacomm unit picked it up and transmitted it.

Ask her if there are any one-eyed queens in Senegambia, Curt instructed Dyani.

She voiced the question.

"Only in the fashion world!" was the response.

Bingo! Curt exclaimed as he heard it. *Her name should be Nyamia Lébou. Confirm it, Mustang Leader!*

Dyani did so.

Bring her to my OCV, Curt ordered, then toggled to division tacomm command channel. *Battleaxe, we have confirmed contact with Nyamia Lébou. She's being escorted to my OCV on the west side of the terminal.*

Roger from Battleaxe! We're just getting on the ground with the Wolfers, Hettrick's NE tacomm voice came back. *While I'm on my way to where you are, you can be studying Lébou's cee-vee and eye-dee. It's coming over the data link now. If anything doesn't match her appearance or mannerisms, put her in Delta Two physical security until I get there. She may be real, but she may also be acting under duress if the Malitanians captured her and managed to bring her out here on schedule.*

Curt knew exactly what she was talking about and

didn't really have to think about it. The ancient Chinese student of war, Sun Tsu, advised his readers, "All warfare is based on deception." One can't trust belief or hearsay. Sometimes, G-2 intelligence can't be trusted either. Sometimes the enemy has a lot of expertise in counter-intelligence.

He didn't think the Malitanians were that sophisticated, however. And nothing he'd seen thus far caused him to change his mind. Operation Bloodbath had caught Modibo and his minions completely off guard.

Curt knew this to be true right then because the initial recce reports from Dale Brown's birdbots confirmed the earlier satellite data: No Malitanian units were on their way to the Dakar airport from either the city of Dakar or from the east.

But he knew that the enemy could be wily and clever. So he quickly ducked back into the OCV when he heard the whine of the hard-copy printer there.

Curt had to admit that Nyamia Lébou was a stunning woman. But what was the eye patch that Dyani had reported? The photos of the Senegambian resistance leader showed no such thing. Why would a highly paid Dakar fashion model wear an eye patch that marred an otherwise lovely face?

He got his answer when Dyani showed up with Nyamia in tow.

Curt debouched from his OCV to meet her outside. No sense in revealing all the tactical data that was displayed in the command vehicle.

"I am Nyamia Lébou," the tall, slender, striking Senegalese woman said with confidence in her voice as she stepped up to Curt and offered her hand. Her accent was slightly French but also had the fascinating rhythm and intonation of West African English. It sounded like Hindu-accented English but far more like the unique accent that the Brunei Sultana Alzena occasionally lapsed into. "Where is General Bellamack?"

The eye patch didn't mar Nyamia's beauty. Instead of diminishing that, it served to enhance it. It made Nyamia Lébou more than just another beautiful woman. It made her unique and somehow drew attention to her other lovely features.

Curt introduced himself, being careful not to identify his regiment. As he had been taught to do by the Sultana Alzena, he greeted Nyamia in the continental manner by taking her right hand and kissing it.

Nyamia reacted with an immediate softening of her demeanor. *Here is a man,* she thought, *who isn't just another barbaric American. He knows how to treat women!*

"General Bellamack is quite busy. I've been asked to greet you. General Hettrick will join us shortly," Curt told her.

Dyani remained with Nyamia. As the regimental intelligence officer, she was expected to stay and collect whatever information this Senegambian beauty could provide. Dyani kept her Novia assault rifle slung over her shoulder in the quick reaction mode; she could swing it around and get off a burst within a second if necessary. Dyani remained suspicious of this woman. Her suspicion wasn't related to the gallant manner with which Curt greeted this stunning woman. Dyani expected that. Furthermore, Dyani wasn't a spiteful or suspicious woman when it came to her relationship with Curt. This wasn't off-duty socializing; this was the dangerous business of war, and Dyani was all business at that moment.

With her single eye, Nyamia took in the scene with all the Jeeps, Mary Anns, ACVs, Sierra Charlies in their battle gear, and Curt's hulking OCV behind him. "Frankly, I'm impressed with the sort of military effort that the United States has brought in to counter Modibo's butchers, Colonel. The Malitanians are slaughtering Senegambians. They've tried to kill me but didn't succeed."

"Your photos don't show you with an eye patch, ma'am," Curt pointed out. He wanted to find out why, so

160

he asked, "Is that injury quite recent?"

"A matter of days. A Malitanian soldier shot at me and missed," Nyamia explained, carefully keeping her FAMAS submachine gun slung behind her. "That was his mistake. He was killed very shortly thereafter. The bullet hit a tree, and one of the splinters hit my eye. I've lost the eye."

"You're in very good shape if you were wounded only since this Malitanian invasion began," Curt observed cautiously.

"It is still very painful. But I have work to do," Nyamia told him bluntly.

"Would you like to have our regimental surgeon look at it and maybe give you something to ease the pain?"

She shook her head. "We have very good doctors in the Garamandes' organization. The eye has been enucleated. The pain will go away."

"I'm sorry," Curt told her honestly. "That's likely to seriously affect your career as a fashion model . . ."

"Not at all! People will know how and why I lost my left eye as a patriot for Senegambia. The loss doesn't affect my ability to make a living. And the eye patch doesn't change my ability to display clothes or cosmetics." Nyamia suddenly began to project feminine allure. Curt had seen women do this before, especially those who had to convey allure through media such as television and photographs. What made Nyamia Lébou such a successful fashion model was her ability to reach through the technology of the camera and communicate the image of her beauty to both men and women. "The eye patch will become my trademark, Colonel! It serves the same purpose as a beauty mark. Although there is no queen of Senegambia, I will become the one-eyed queen of African fashion."

Curt knew what she meant. When he'd first encountered Adonica Sweet on Trinidad ten years before, her wholesome loveliness was marred by a large gap between her front teeth. In retrospect, that minor flaw served to amplify Adonica's natural beauty. Modern orthodontistry had corrected the gap, but, in the process of growing up with the flaw, Adonica had learned to emphasize her other beautiful features. The results had been startling. And still were.

Another OCV rumbled into the terminal parking lot. Maj. Gen. Belinda Hettrick got out, accompanied by her G-2 intelligence staffer, Lt. Col. Eleanor Aarts. The two of them joined Curt, Dyani, and Nyamia. Curt performed the introductions.

"General Hettrick, I was expecting General Bellamack," Nyamia told her.

Hettrick merely smiled. "Your message from General Al Murray may have indicated that, Miss Lébou. However, General Bellamack isn't here at the moment."

"I see," Nyamia remarked. "Wartime operations must always remain hidden. Very well. So be it. But the Garamandes cannot retake our country and oust the Malitanians alone. So I must cooperate with you. And I will. So you can open in the poker game. You've got a one-eyed queen, even though no deck of cards has a one-eyed queen. Will you allow my colleagues—my staff—to come in, please? They're waiting at the gate."

"Of course!" Hettrick replied and turned to Curt. "Make it so, Colonel."

Curt did. But Dyani stayed with the group. Others could carry out the duties of an escort for the other Garamandes.

But Nyamia didn't wait until they arrived. "General, we have good information that tells us Modibo may well be on his way to the airport at the moment. He headquarters in Dakar because it's a nicer place than Bamako. But he has to fly back to his capital city to take care of everyday matters. He was supposed to depart this morning for Bamako in his private military VIP transport."

"We've pretty much wiped out his personal airplane along with the rest of the Malitanian Air Force here at the airport," Curt pointed out.

"Modibo should be on the road to here by now," Nyamia insisted. "Our contacts in Dakar reported that he's left the Presidential Palace."

Black Hawk Leader, this is Grey Head, Curt tacommed to his birdbot officer. *Have you checked the road from Dakar to the airport? Any traffic on it headed this way?*

Negatory, Grey Head! I'm surprised we haven't seen Malitanian forces coming out of Dakar to counter our assault. Nothing from the east, either. If we spot anything, we'll let you know ASAP.

"General, my recce operation reports no activity on the Dakar road," Curt reported.

"Then where is Generalissimo Modibo?" Nyamia asked.

Seventeen

Generalissimo Modibo Ould Daddah Sidi Ahmed knew exactly where he was.

He and his East World military advisor, Col. Godavari Singh Pratihara, had ducked into an underground bunker just after the hypersonic overflights had put their kinetic energy weapons into the Malitanian Air Force at Dakar Airport.

It was a deep bunker. They had to descend a flight of steel stairs to get to the second security door at the bottom. As they reached it, it opened.

Four Malitanian pilots in flight gear accompanied by five ground crew technicians started to come out. They backed up quickly when they saw the Generalissimo and his advisor running down the steps.

"Get back inside!" Modibo snapped at them. "The ramp is under air attack! How secure is this bunker?"

The flight leader, obviously a Songhai because of his features, saluted and replied, "It may not be very secure, Generalissimo! The bomb impacts shook us up pretty badly. They must have been from thousand kilogram bombs. I never suspected that this bunker would be that vulnerable."

"They weren't bombs!" Pratihara told him. "They were hypersonic kinetic kill weapons."

"Oh," was the only response from the flight leader. "Who's attacking us? Shouldn't we get up to our aircraft and get airborne?"

"There's nothing left of your aircraft . . . or any other aircraft on the ramp," Modibo said in an irritated fashion. Then he went on in the flowery rhetoric of a typical Islamic fundamentalist zealot, although his language was French, not Arabic. "I do not know who the criminals are that attacked us. But they will pay dearly for this! I will see to it that their bodies are beheaded and laid as a carpet of blood for my Malitanian colonists to drive over. I will display their heads atop every pole and tower in the land! I will . . ."

Pratihara gently interrupted his temporary boss. He could do it and get away with it because he wasn't under Modibo's direct command. The worst that Modibo could do was to send him home. He was responsible to the government of India that had sent him to Malitania as a military advisor. And as someone who could keep Modibo and his people from killing themselves with the advanced East World weaponry that had been supplied to them. Pratihara was a Sikh and a professional military man. He tended to look upon this situation with a cool and professional demeanor. And he spoke in English rather than French because it was the only language that everyone in the bunker understood. Pilots everywhere speak English, and even Modibo himself had found it necessary to learn the international language of science, technology, politics, and diplomacy.

"Flight Captain, what is your situation here in this bunker?" Pratihara asked. "Are the bunker facilities operational? I see that you have electrical power. How about water? Communications? Weapons? Ammunition?"

The Malitanian flight leader suddenly became very military in his attitude and response. "Sir, I think we have water. I haven't checked. The electrical power is probably coming from the emergency fuel cells. I noticed the lights flicker. That means the bunker emergency power was probably switched on when the bombs cut off the mains. I have not tested the telephone. I think that the gun cabinet contains a dozen Durga assault rifles, some ammunition for them, and several bandoliers of fragmentation grenades . . ."

Modibo had calmed down now. He realized that he had to assume command of this situation at once. If he didn't, Pratihara might. Modibo didn't like the idea of having East World military advisors scattered throughout his armed forces. However, he had no choice. That was part of the deal with the East World alliance. The secret treaty gave Modibo the land and the loot. East World got exclusive trading rights for the natural resources. East World was also granted the right of a powerful military presence once Modibo's forces, with East World armaments and training occupied Senegambia and other West African countries on the list of conquest.

The Generalissimo had been surprised by the sudden, unheralded, and overpowering attack. He had trouble believing that the Americans had done it. Military intervention was completely against the publicly stated policies of their isolationist, pacifist President. Modibo thought he'd successfully conned the American President into believing that Modibo would not do what had been done in Senegambia. Modibo had gotten away with it in Mauritania two years before. The Americans had been outraged but had done nothing more than fuss and fume impotently in the United Nations Security Council and General Assembly.

So Modibo decided he would have to first find out what was going on now that he'd successfully saved his ass by ducking into the bunker and abandoning his wife and staff to the holocaust above.

Modibo drew himself up to his imposing two-meter height and once again assumed the appearance and attitude of a great leader. He remarked confidently and personally to the nine men of the Malitanian Air Force, "Flight Captain, you and your men will help me fight my way out of here! I promise you that you will become the nucleus of my new Presidential Guard when we get back to Dakar."

Then he snapped out a rapid-fire series of orders. "Pratihara, organize these nine men into a suitable ground fighting unit. They don't have any aircraft left to fly, so they might as well become my new bodyguard. See to it that they're armed with those Durga rifles. We may have to fight our way out of here. While you're doing that, I'll find out if the telephone works and get some help on its way."

He was greatly surprised when the telephone did work. He wasn't a technically-minded man. In fact, he was technically illiterate. He didn't care how anything worked, only that it worked right when he wanted it to. Thus, he didn't know that the Senegambians had installed a fiber optics telephone system around the airport and from there into the main exchange in Dakar. This had been done to ensure reliability and high data rate exchange between the two points. The bunker's telephone system was as far underground as the bunker and hadn't been touched by the KE weapons.

He didn't know how to dial a telephone. All of his telephone calls were placed for him by his subordinates. So he took a chance and pushed the button labelled "Operator."

It took nearly thirty seconds for a voice to answer. It wasn't a human being but a phone robot. The voice asked him pleasantly in French how it could be of service.

"This is Generalissimo Modibo! Connect me with the Presidential Palace immediately!" Modibo snapped, unaware that he was dealing with a machine. Thus, he expected a lot of acquiescing deference and subordination. He got neither. The robot continued in its pleasant female voice, "The Presidential Palace has many numbers. Do you have a specific office you wish to talk with?"

"Connect me to the Presidential Palace! I don't care which number or office!"

"If you can tell me to whom you wish to speak, or if you can state the sort of business you wish to discuss with someone there, I can be of greater assistance to you."

"I don't have to tell you who or why I wish to speak to anyone! I am Generalissimo Modibo! Do as you're told! Connect me to the Presidential Palace!"

The phone robot didn't take offense. It couldn't. It was a machine. It continued brightly and pleasantly, "Yes, sir!"

He found himself connected to the answering machine at the main switchboard. It was before normal business hours. The machine, another primitive robot, offered to record his name, the telephone number from which he was calling, and a message for anyone in the palace he wished to speak with later in the day.

Modibo found himself entangled in the confusion generated in the normal bureaucracy by his invasion of Senegambia. "This is an emergency! I want to speak to Colonel Kassem immediately!" Modibo bellowed at the machine.

"I will leave a priority message for Colonel Kassem, sir," the machine replied in pleasant and almost saccharine tones that further infuriated Modibo. "He will return your call as soon as he arrives at his office."

"Don't disconnect!" Modibo yelled, but it was too late. The machine severed the connection.

So he hung up and was forced to go through the whole procedure over again. This time he told the answering robot at the Presidential Palace, "This is an emergency! I wish to speak to anyone who's there!"

"Please press 'zero' on the touch tone pad, sir, and remain on the line until someone answers."

He did so and waited.

And waited.

And waited while a telephone somewhere in the Presidential Palace rang and rang and rang.

At long last, another voice came on, speaking in Bambara, "Presidential Palace. What do you want?" The tone was surly and sleepy.

"This is Generalissimo Modibo!"

"And I'm the King of Chad." The Malitanian Army corporal who had finally been awakened by the telephone was in no mood to play games with some nut who had the balls to call and interrupt a badly needed rest. The looting and pillaging party of the night before had gone on until just a few hours ago. Everyone in the palace knew that the Generalissimo had flown off to Bamako that morning. Some explosions had been heard in downtown Dakar a few minutes ago. However, explosions and rifle fire had become commonplace around Dakar recently. No one paid much attention any longer. The looting, pillaging, raping, and killing were too good and occupied the attention of the Malitanian Army. Everyone wanted to get as much loot and rape as many women as possible before it all went away and their lives returned to the normal situation of poverty, want, and shortages.

"This is indeed Generalissimo Modibo, and I'll have your head for this insubordination! Report at once to your superior officer under arrest!" Modibo snapped. "But find Colonel Kassem and put him on the phone first! I'm under attack at the airport!"

No one will ever know what caused this Malitanian corporal suddenly to change his mind. But he did. He replied, "Yes, Your Excellency!" He rang the telephone in Kassem's quarters. Then, instead of doing as he'd been ordered, he simply left the palace, shucked his uniform, blended into the population, and thus disappeared from history.

Col. Abdul Karim Kassem's sleepy voice finally came on the phone.

Modibo bellowed, "Kassem! Get your ass out of bed and get busy! We've been attacked at Dakar Airport! I'm in the ready alert bunker! Get an armored unit out here to pick me up! Sound Red Alert and bring all forces to a condition to repel a possible attack!"

"Generalissimo, please go over that again slowly and carefully, sir," Kassem replied, trying to make sense out of the shouted message. "Can you tell me what happened, sir?"

"As I arrived at the military ramp, we were heavily attacked with bombs and hypersonic kinetic kill weapons," Modibo told him. "I barely managed to get to the ready alert bunker with Pratihara!"

"What's the situation there, sir?"

"I don't know. I'm in the bunker. I've got nine Air Force men with me. We're armed. I've spent the last five minutes dealing with this stupid robotic telephone system which I am going to tear out and replace with people!"

"Sir, I'll have an armored unit on its way from M'bao at once! Can you send some of your men upstairs to find out what's going on? I need a report of the situation. Is the bombing over? Have there been any landings of troops?"

"M'bao is too far away! Send out one of the units from Dakar!"

"Yes, sir," Kassem replied, knowing full well that one did not argue with the Generalissimo when such an order was given. He would try to find a company or battalion in Dakar that was ready to move, but he doubted that he would be successful. The sacking of the city had put most Malitanian Army troops in a state of frenzy, and discipline had been extremely difficult to maintain. He'd ordered his commanders to shoot to maintain order, but he suspected that even the commanders were too busy collecting the spoils. "In the meantime, if your men could give us a situation report, it would help me take care of the matter."

"All right! Stay on the line, Kassem! It took too much effort to get you in the first place. Now that I have communications, I'm not about to lose them! Stand by! I'll have my Guard unit go up and have a look."

"Yes, Your Excellency!" Kassem had made the Great Journey with Modibo out of the Sahara Desert to capture Bamako. As such, he was one of Modibo's elite companions. But he also knew that Modibo could become irrational under pressure. Modibo knew how to shoot and had personally executed many of his followers who had also made the Great Journey. And Modibo had done it in full view of everyone else. No one had any doubts about who was boss. And no one dared attempt to form a cabal to shoot Modibo and take over in a coup. Modibo had too many people who would gladly snitch and thus gain a higher standing and greater rewards.

Modibo turned to Pratihara. "I want a reconnaissance force to go upstairs, go outside, and find out what's going on. I want them to report back here within fifteen minutes."

Pratihara suddenly discovered that he'd become Modibo's de facto chief of staff. In this situation, he had to accept. The Malitanian Air Force members whom he'd just armed were probably loyal to Modibo and wouldn't hesitate to shoot Pratihara with the Durga rifles he'd just given them. To be summarily shot by men he'd just trained to load and shoot the weapons was one hell of a way to go, he decided. And he definitely didn't want to be killed in such circumstances. If he was to be killed, he decided, he would die honorably in battle as a Sikh should.

"You and you!" Pratihara snapped, pointing at two of them. "You stay here and guard the lower door. You and you, come with me to the top of the stairs; you'll guard the upper door. I want the rest of you to go outside and see what's happening. I don't want you to go far. Just find out what the situation is and report back within ten minutes. I'll remain at the bottom of the surface ramp. Without something to cover my white turban, I'm a prime target if anyone is up there shooting."

The Air Force men hesitated. Modibo saw that. With the telephone handset in one hand, he stood up. With his free hand, he pulled his 9mm. Kufahl automatic pistol from his belt holster. He knew it didn't have a round chambered, but the Air Force men didn't. Modibo didn't have to say a word. The look in his eyes confirmed the rumors about the ruthless savagery of the Savior of the Sahel that had circulated among his troops.

"Let's go!" the flight captain urged. "Follow me!"

When they opened the blast door at the top of the stairs, the firecracker-like sound of small arms fire could be heard. They also heard the whine and rumble of military vehicles and the thundering blast of aerodynes.

"I think," the flight leader said in a quick assessment of the situation, "that we'd better go up the ramp very carefully. Someone is fighting at the airport. Kori, let's go. The rest of you stay here until we see what's happening."

It was a high pucker factor operation at this point. The pilot and his ground crewman slowly and carefully went up the ramp. Then they poked their heads carefully over the edge at ground level.

It took them five seconds to see what they needed to see. Quickly, they ran back down the ramp. "Back! Inside! Close the door!" the pilot urged them.

The group needed no more incentive than that.

"Well?" Pratihara asked once they were inside the heavy blast door.

"Americans," the pilot said tersely. "American Thunder Devil tactical assault aerodynes patrolling the sky. Chippewa aerodynes landing in great numbers."

"I saw many American war robots," the crewman added. "They are everywhere and more coming out of the aerodynes."

"How many?" Pratihara wanted to know.

The pilot guessed. He wasn't an expert on the size of units in the United States Army. "A whole division!" he exaggerated.

Pratihara knew that the man was exaggerating, so he cut the estimate in half. Then he halved it again. He knew that Modibo wouldn't believe that a brigade of American warbot troops had landed at Dakar Airport in the short time since the bombs had fallen.

"Where are they?"

"Everywhere I could see!"

"What's left of our Air Force?"

"Nothing! Nothing!" The pilot almost had tears in his eyes. He'd seen his beloved Shenyang J-22 interceptor, the machine that helped him assert his manhood, the device that allowed him to soar far above his fellow Malitanians. It was now a fiery pile of junk on the ramp. "The American bombing raid destroyed them all! Every airplane!"

"And the Generalissimo's limousine? The other vehicles that were in our convoy? What of them?"

"Gone! Gone!"

"Did you see any Malitanian troops up there? Were they fighting?"

"I saw only American war robots and some of their soldiers."

This caused Pratihara some real concern. He wasn't too much worried about American warbots; those could be easily handled by human wave attacks that overwhelmed their targeting capability. He'd studied the intelligence reports from Zahedan, Trinidad, and Iraq. Pratihara had also kept current on recent American developments in tactics and combat. He read American publications such as *The Infantry Journal.*

From the report of the pilot and his crewmen, plus his own studies of the American military machine, Pratihara knew that the American government had sent in their picked assault troops, the ones that would give the Malitanian Army a real fight.

The Sierra Charlies had come.

He didn't relish having to report this to Generalissimo Modibo. He would also have to explain it. The Sierra Charlies were difficult for him to accept because of their legendary combat prowess. It was going to be even more difficult to explain to Modibo that it wasn't going to be a conventional war now, that the Malitanians were up against the best twenty-first century fighting machine in the world.

Eighteen

When Nyamia told them that no one knew where Modibo was, Col. Curt Carson reacted at once. Both via NE tacomm and verbally so Nyamia could hear, he gave the order, "Wolf Head, this is Grey Head! Do you read?" Then he toggled his external helmet speaker so the replies could be heard by others.

"Wolf Head here! Go ahead, Grey Head!" came the reply from Col. Rick Salley of the Wolfhounds.

"Malefactor may be at the airport somewhere," Curt told his counterpart in the other regiment that had just landed. Curt used Modibo's code name. "Keep an eye out for evidence of this. In the meantime, I'm going to have my ASSAULTCO Bravo over on the east side of the field start some detailed recce. Can you get one of your ASSAULTCOs over to the east gate to cover for me?"

"Happy to oblige, Grey Head, especially since the Greys silenced most of the hostile fire," Salley replied easily. "That will give us something to do . . ."

"Wolf Head, this is Battleaxe," Hettrick chimed in. "Don't deviate too much from the ops plan! Just because we've creamed the opposition in the first fracas doesn't mean we can sit on our asses here. I want to move the next phase along ahead of schedule. So shag ass and bypass if you have to!"

"Roger that, Battleaxe! We're moving!"

"Alleycat Leader, this is Grey Head," Curt fired at Jerry Allen. "Wolf Head is going to cover for Puma

Leader on the east gate detail. I need maximum search capability concentrated on the east side of the airport. Malefactor reportedly left Dakar for the airport but isn't on the road. He may have gotten to the airport before we landed! Have the Black Hawk birdbots sweep the field at high resolution before you send them off on Phase Three. Then see if you can identify Malefactor among the bodies on the military ramp."

"Grey Head, when we went through the military ramp area where the KE weapons impacted on our way to the east gate, we saw only a lot of dead meat and spoiling food," Jerry reported.

"Go back and check it again! You were in a hurry the first time," Curt reminded him.

"Yes, sir. You're right. We were in a hurry. Someone was shooting at us then," Jerry remarked. "Okay, here come the Wolfers. We're on our way back."

Alleycat Leader, this is Mustang Leader, Dyani reported. She was standing right next to Curt, but she was using the tacomm in NE mode. *Black Hawk Leader reports negative on the recce sweep of the military ramp. I've told him to get out of the airport area and begin his sweeps looking for Malitanian forces heading this way.*

Over on the east side of the airport, Jerry merged his beacon with that of Lew Pagan on the plot. *Okay, Lew,* he told Pagan on his down-command channel although he was standing right next to the company commander, *I want a thorough search of this side of the airport.*

Christ, Colonel I've got only one platoon! Pagan fired back. *The Marauders went over to the west side of the field when Cougar Leader called for help.*

Alleycat Major and I will help, Jerry offered. *We've got our Jeep, so you'll only be short one sergeant. The Wolfers will cover our minus-x. They're scheduled to move out to Dakar in Phase Three anyway.*

Yeah, and I'm perfectly happy to let the Wolfers do that, Alleycat Leader! Pagan admitted. *We did the open field running here at the airport. I don't exactly like the idea of forging on to Dakar through all the houses and hovels out beyond the gate. A hell of a lot of Malitanians could be hiding out there!*

For once, we got the easy job, Jerry agreed, but he had a slight touch of sarcasm in his voice that managed to make it through the NE circuitry. *All we had to do was make an airborne landing at an airport in the dark with unknown forces waiting for us on the ground! Okay, spread out as skirmishers. Let the bots take the lead so they take any unfriendly fire that may be left. We'll move behind them for visual search and scan.*

I was wondering when you were going to order the bots out front, Major, Battalion Sgt. Maj. Nick Gerard put in as the rump company, the remaining Sierra Charlies and warbots of Pagan's Pumas began forming up and moving back toward the military hangars and flight line. *They can give us fire cover when we have to go into what's left of them buildings to search. Lowers the pucker factor a lot.*

You get that sensor glitch out of Garfield? Jerry asked, referring to a problem he'd had a few minutes ago with the Jeep.

It must have been a transient, Major. It ain't there now. Everything's tickety-boo with Garfield, Nick reported.

Alleycat Leader, who are we looking for? Hassan wanted to know as they started back toward the demolished hangar.

Malefactor. Generalissimo Modibo. He may have been on the military ramp when the Aerospace Farce hit it. Jerry explained.

If that's the case, he's dead meat, Hassan observed as he and his Assassins got to the hangar area and began to search.

Not necessarily, sir, was the comment from Master Sgt. Robert Lee Garrison. *I've seen people survive bombing in ways I wouldn't believe possible.*

Well, I'm sure as hell not seeing anyone who survived, Sarge, Hassan told him as he rolled a dead body over with his boot. ·

Check every body you come to, Lew Pagan ordered, being his usual thorough, professional self. *I don't want one of them rising up in our minus-x and plugging one of us in the back, body armor or not!*

Sergeant Lunalillo, I want you to stick with Bio-tech Metford and cover her, Hassan snapped out an order. *Let the rest of us do the dirty work here.*

Excuse me Captain, but I thought this was an equal opportunity army, came the reply from Sgt. Maria Lunalillo, a short, round-faced, pretty Hispanic-American from Santa Fe who was one of the new NCOs.

Equal opportunity to get your ass shot off, said her platoon sergeant, Isadore Beau Greenwald. *Maria, shut up and soldier! You'll get a lot of opportunities to exhibit female equality! A hell of a lot of bullets out in the world that ain't been shot yet, and you can count on some of them coming your way eventually.*

As long as they don't have my name on them, I'll let them come, she replied. *Okay, Sarge, I'll soldier. Marla isn't armed. And you're right. She's going to need some cover when she starts working on any wounded. By the way, have you found any live ones yet?*

Negatory! Can the chatter! Jerry reminded them. The line of skirmishers was approaching one of the demolished military hangars. Fire still crackled among the wooden beams and studs. Most of the masonry structure was flattened to rubble. However, interior portions of the cavernous building remained erect and capable of hiding survivors.

The Jeeps and Mary Anns crawled over the debris. Their sensors were live and looking for warm bodies. Their 7.62mm and 25mm guns were armed and carried at the ready to cover the eight Sierra Charlies. Hassan's platoon and Garrison split into two two-person teams. They began working each of the enclosed rooms and spaces as they came to them. This was standard, classic room-to-room searching. With a Jeep or Mary Ann standing back, one Sierra Charlie would stand to one side while the other kicked the door open or otherwise created an opening. Then one of them would burst through and check the room, Novia ready and set to full auto. In spite of the firepower of the warbots and the state of demolition of the hangar, it was still an operation with a very high pucker factor. One or more Malitanians could be huddled inside, armed and ready to shoot to kill. Pagan's Pumas had been well-trained for this sort of mission, however. They knew what to do.

And most of them made their own personal evaluation of the possibilities that anyone could survive the sort of pounding and destruction the hangar had taken. It was almost inconceivable that any human was left alive inside.

But there was always the chance. And that one chance might mean being shot by someone. Even with the protection of the Krisflex body armor worn by each Sierra Charlie, taking a small arms round at close range not only hurt like hell but might mean being put out of action for several days because of subcutaneous trauma. Then there was also the chance of the Golden BB, the round that hit where body armor didn't protect, like the face or the hands. Or even the chance that a grenade or Limpet mine would catch them. Body armor would protect against bullet and shrapnel penetration, but it wasn't much protection against high explosive blasts.

Jerry and Nick made a thorough search around the outside of the hangar. They found nothing but dead bodies, all of them showing lethal concussion trauma— bleeding from the nose, ears, and mouth being the most common sign. Some had been partially dismembered by the force of the explosions or from being tossed about and hitting sharp corners. Others had been crushed by falling masonry or rolling vehicles.

It wasn't pretty, but the results of combat rarely were.

Two Chinese-made copies of the Japanese Type 173 Armored Personnel Carrier were parked on the east side of the ruined hangar. The building had shielded them from the blast waves of the KE weapons and bombs that had hit the ramp. They were apparently in operating condition, but both were empty. So Jerry and Nick moved around the hangar with their Jeep.

Nick made a discovery as he and Jerry were checking the west side of the hangar facing the ramp and runway.

Major, here's a couple of vehicles that aren't military trucks or utility cars, Nick called out. *Over here! Looks like a couple of big Mercedes limousines. One of them's rolled into a ball, but the other one is just smashed up.*

Jerry quickly joined his battalion sergeant major and saw for himself. *Good show, Nick! You're right! Let's check it out. Could be Malefactor's cars. Maybe he was indeed on the ramp when the Aerospace Force strike hit. If so, he's got to be around here somewhere!*

Him or his body, Nick muttered. *Jeez, blood and body parts all over the place. Don't slip, Major!*

Grady, this is Alleycat Leader, Jerry called on tacomm to the regimental computer housed in Curt's OCV on the other side of the field. *Display a recent photograph of Generalissimo Modibo.* Jerry had a general idea what the man looked like, but he wanted to have a visual displayed on his helmet visor. He needed it so positive identification could be made if they happened to find a dead body that might be Modibo.

Roger, Alleycat Leader. The visual is on your data bus now. The computer was a small and relatively stupid one, certainly nothing like the megacomputer with the power and speed of Georgie. But Georgie was so big and so tender that it had to stay underground back in Arizona; Grady was smaller and more rugged so the Greys would have some computer capability if they should happen to become isolated from Georgie. And this had happened in the past.

Jerry saw the photo of the long, lean Berber features of Modibo. If anything was left of Modibo's body, especially the man's face, he wouldn't be difficult to identify.

Okay, Nick, I've got a photo of Modibo on my data bus now. Transferring it to you for your download. Put it up on your visor display, Jerry told his top kick. *Let's check the interior of these limos and see if they contain any bodies. Then I want us to check every body we can find on this ramp. If Modibo is among them,*

179

I want to find him, identify his remains, and get a photo team over here ASAP.

Read you loud and clear, Major! If Modibo bought the farm on the first assault, this operation may be over in time for stand-to. It means we got the brains and left the body to thrash around without direction, Nick observed as he began to check into the interior of the Mercedes that was rolled up into a ball.

Okay, Nick, you check that limo, and I'll have a look at the other one. Not much left, but maybe we can make an i-d. And you're right, his batt commander agreed. *Modibo has been the grand and glorious leader of this whole Malitanian episode. He's shot anyone who could possibly become a contender, much less oppose him. Under those conditions when the leader is checked out of the game, his armed forces usually fall apart pretty damned quick.*

Uk! Major, there ain't anything left in this limo but something that looks like tomato aspic and probably was the driver. But it sure as hell ain't Modibo. Wrong color, Nick reported with distaste. The man had seen a lot of combat action and a lot of dead bodies. But when Nick Gerard reacted that way to what was left of a human being, Jerry knew that it had to be pretty gruesome.

And I wouldn't be too upset if this whole furball was over today so we could go home, Jerry admitted. Then he got far enough into the wreckage of the second limo to see what was left of its driver. And he backed out in a hurry. The body inside had been torn up badly by being thrown around with violence inside the limo when it hit and demolished the wall against whose rubble it now rested. In addition, blast and concussion had torn it up as well. *And Modibo isn't in the wreckage of this one, either. This is a pile of hamburger wearing a lance corporal's uniform. And I'm sure Modibo didn't travel in NCO's clothing.*

Okay, Major, I've started checking some of these bodies on the ramp. . . . Oh, my God, this one's a woman. Or was. Dressed like one. Jesus, must have been real young and pretty, too!

Modibo has several wives, Jerry recalled from his encyclopedic memory. *How about that body? Match the specs?*

Come have a look, Major. Obviously, Modibo doesn't have anything like our Rule Ten. This chick was a teen-ager. Probably one of his harem girls.

Berbers don't have harems, Nick.

Hell, they're Muslims, ain't they?

Yeah, but the Berbers never had enough women to go around anyway, so they never adopted harems in spite of the Koran's permission to have up to four wives. Jerry went to where Nick was standing over a heap of something on the ground.

Nick was right. The girl had been young and pretty. The corpse hadn't been badly busted up, but it had been burned by the fires that had raged in this area of the military ramp as a result of fuel spills from the destroyed aircraft.

The awful carnage of war suddenly got to Jerry. He was an experienced Sierra Charlie and had seen a lot of death and destruction during his ten years of service. But he'd never had the gory task of checking dead bodies and trying to identify them. That was a job for Graves Registration insofar as he was concerned. West Point and the Washington Greys hadn't prepared him for it.

But now he was ten years older than the raw brown-bar second lieutenant who'd graduated from West Point. He couldn't look at combat the same way now that he'd done then. He had far greater responsibilities, including that of sending his friends, colleagues, and lover into deadly combat where they might be killed or maimed.

Jerry had killed many people in combat. He'd seen men die. He'd never been up against female troops, so he'd never shot an enemy woman in combat. He didn't know whether he could if he thought about it. But, knowing combat as he did, he didn't worry. When the time came to either shoot or be shot, he knew what he would do without thinking very much about it.

But what bothered him about what he was now doing wasn't the killing. A soldier expects to have to kill. He realized that the bloody bodies on the airport ramp had been killed by Aerospace Force pilots who hadn't seen

181

their victims. And among those victims had been the pretty young girl. Was it really necessary to kill her to achieve what the diplomats had been unable to accomplish? He didn't know.

Well, he told himself, she'd had the misfortune to be in the way when it happened. If you weren't a combatant, the only sure way to keep from being hurt or killed in combat was to be where it ain't, as Regimental Sgt. Maj. Henry Kester often advised young Washington Greys . . . and older ones, too.

Jerry straightened up and took several deep breaths. He saw that Dakar Airport had been transformed from a sleepy international airport with perhaps a dozen commercial flights per day into a military operational base. Chippewa aerodynes were landing one after the other. They disgorged troops and warbots. Then they were in the air again, heading westward toward the staging base on the Cape Verde Islands. Overhead, he could see the Harpy tacair support aerodynes circling and hovering, ready to move in on any Malitanian forces attempting to retake the airport. On the ground, an increasing force of Sierra Charlies and warbots was gathering. He knew from the ops plan that the Wolfhounds had the task of moving south to pacify the city of Dakar proper. When the Cottonbalers landed and grouped, they would move to the southern side of the peninsula to cut the railroad. Once that phase of the operation commenced, the Washington Greys would move to new positions on the north beaches of the peninsula.

Everything looked like it was moving precisely according to plan.

So he got back to the grisly task at hand.

Puma Leader, this is Alleycat Leader, he flashed via NE tacomm to Lew Pagan. *How's it coming?*

We've just about got this hangar checked out, Alleycat Leader. No one here that could be identified as Modibo. Mostly Malitanian Air Force mechanics and some pilots who were caught inside when the strike hit. Some of them were quartered in the hangar and never even had the chance to get out of bed.

Okay, when you've finished the job, move the Pumas to the south hangar and check it out, Jerry told him. *It wasn't hit so badly. Likely to be survivors in there. Be careful when you get in there. But I don't need to tell that. You've got on-the-job experience now.*

We're on our way now.

Nick and I will follow you. We've just about finished checking the bodies on the ramp in front of the hangar.

Any luck?

Probably found what's left of his mistress of the day. But no Modibo. He was apparently here. So keep an eagle-type eyeball peeled. He could be around here somewhere with any of the troops that survived the strike, Jerry warned.

He might be in the other hangar, Pagan speculated.

So play it cool, Lew. I'll get some backup for us J-I-C. Jerry togged over to the batt channel. *Cougar Leader, this is Alleycat Leader.*

Cougar Leader here! Kitsy's voice snapped back.

If you've got the situation under control over on the west side, I want you to bring the Stilettos and the Panthers back over here to the military ramp. I suspect that some of the Malitanian survivors may have holed up in the south hangar that's still standing. I may need additional strength and firepower if that's the case.

Alleycat Leader, this is Grey Head. Have you found any trace of Modibo? Curt broke in.

Negatory, Grey Head. We found what was apparently the remains of his two Mercedes limos and the body of a woman who may have been one of his wives or doxies. But we haven't found Modibo's body yet. If he's alive, he may be with whatever troops survived, and he may be holed up in that hangar. That's why I called for the Cougars to rejoin me.

Very well, Alleycat Leader. Keep me advised.

As always, Grey Head!

Jerry noticed that the Pumas were proceeding south-bound on the ramp now, heading toward the south hangar. As they went past him, he tacommed to Pagan, *Puma Leader, don't bunch up on the ramp. Move south as skir-*

mishers. If anyone's getting ready to pop you from the south hangar, you make damned good targets all strung out with such precision on the ramp and no place to hide. Unless you're real good at digging foxholes in concrete.

Roger, Alleycat Leader. I was just waiting until we cleared this concrete entrance of an underground bunker of some sort. Just checked it out. Looks like an old ammo storage area. Heavy blast door at the bottom that's all rusted. Looks like it's abandoned.

Any indication of recent human activity there? Jerry asked, checking and double-checking the company commander.

Chem sensor on Jeep is out. We couldn't find a replacement in the boneyard before we deployed, Pagan reminded him.

Alleycat Leader, I think we're through here, sir. Nick reported. *We've checked all the meat. It's all dead. And none of it is Modibo.*

Okay, Nick, let's follow the Pumas. Garfield, maintain a position between me and Sergeant Gerard, Jerry gave orders to his first sergeant and his Jeep. Since there were no live and shooting Malitanians in the demolished hangar area, Jerry didn't want to waste his Jeep's sensor power.

The M33A2 Jeep affectionately named "Garfield" by Jerry obediently rolled into a position between them. They started across the fifty meters separating the two hangars, following the Puma's skirmisher formation.

Jerry took a quick look down the concrete slope of the bunker entrance as he went past. Pagan's assessment had apparently been correct. The heavy steel door at the bottom was covered with a layer of rust and hadn't been painted for years. Obviously, it was abandoned or out of use.

Five meters past that point, Jerry was momentarily deafened by the roar of two Harpy aerodynes passing about fifty meters overhead.

He didn't hear the squealing of rusty hinges on a rusty steel door.

His peripheral vision detected a fragmentation grenade rolling a meter away from him on the left.

Jerry never heard it explode.

184

Nineteen

The grenade exploded between Jerry and the warbot Jeep, Garfield. Thus, the bulk of Garfield's armored form shielded Nick from the fragments. But the concussion wave blew off his helmet, stripping the NE sensors from his neck and head. This caused him to scream in pain because those sensors had been attached with tempo-gel to provide a better contact. Usually, one removed such cemented sensors with great care in the post-combat period when the helmet was no longer required.

Then Nick was bowled over by the weight of Garfield's bulk as the warbot, blown off its running gear by the explosion, nearly rolled over him.

Sgt. Maria Lunalillo was closest to the scene because she was trailing the Assassins with Bio-tech Sgt. Marla Metford. But by the time she turned, whoever had thrown the grenade was no longer visible. But she saw what had happened to Jerry.

And she wasted no time. *Marla! Major Allen's hit! Must have been a frag mine!*

Metford then saw it, too. She didn't hesitate to act. Within seconds, she was at Jerry's side. *Maria, check Sergeant Gerard!*

"I'm okay! I'm okay!" Nick practically yelled because his tacomm was gone with his helmet. "Just rapid sensor strip!" He was busy trying to recover his helmet.

Lunalillo saw that he was all right so she brought her Novia to her hip, ready to cover for Marla Metford who was kneeling beside an unconscious Maj. Jerry Allen.

The bio-tech didn't like what she saw. Jerry's left arm had taken several large fragments. So had his left leg. The fragments had ripped and torn the tough Krisflex fabric of his body armor. What those fragments had done once they'd gotten inside the armor was even worse. The holes were gaping, showing red muscle and white bone as she tried to staunch the flow of blood by using pressure points because she couldn't get through the armor fabric. Jerry's arm and shoulder were being held together only by the remaining filaments of the body armor. There was so much blood that she couldn't accurately assess the damage to his leg. All she could do was to attempt to control the bleeding. So she called on tacomm, *Bio-tech Leader, this is Puma Bio-tech! I need help and wounded recovery and evac! Alleycat Leader has taken a frag mine! I can't tell much because of his body armor, but his left side is a mess! Either get a Chippie over us or bring an ACV ASAP! And I do mean quick! Major Allen is going to need serious medic-plus help stat! This is a major injury, and I'm not trying to be funny!*

Back on the west side of the field, Maj. Russ Frazier heard Metford's tacomm call to the regiment's bio-tech unit. He had a sudden sick feeling because one of his closest friends had been hit. Then he pulled himself together. TACBATT was without a commanding officer. As S-3 Operations staffer, Russ was in charge of the overall details of the mission. So he did what he had to do. *Grey Head, this is Grey Ops! Alleycat Leader has been reported wounded. No details other than it was possibly caused by a mine. I'm shifting some command responsibilities. Cougar Leader will assume TACBATT command. Stiletto Leader will assume AS-SAULTCO command. Any heartburn?*

Alleycat Leader is down? came Curt's concerned response. He knew it might happen some day. The chances of a Sierra Charlie coming through years of combat without a scratch were remote. In fact, Jerry had his Purple Heart from the Zahedan mission ten years before. It reminded Curt that this wasn't a maneuver, but deadly serious combat. And he couldn't afford to get emotional about it. He was responsible for too many other people. It might have been different if he had still been Jerry's company commander working on a much lower level in the regimental hierarchy.

Affirmative! Puma Bio-tech has called for immediate Bio-tech response and pickup!

Shift batt command as you see fit, Russ! Does Pagan need reinforcements over there?

I suggest that the Marauders be sent back to the east side. This might have been a frag mine. Or he might have taken a grenade.

Make it so!

Puma Leader, this is Grey Ops! Are you under fire?

Negatory, Grey Ops! But Alleycat Leader looks like he's out of it!

I'm sending Kitsy over to take command. She's bringing the Marauders!

Roger, Grey Ops! We can handle the situation, but it would make me feel a little better to have some additional help!

Cougar Leader, this is Grey Ops!

Cougar Leader here! I heard, Russ! Kitsy replied seriously.

Get over there and take charge, Cougar Leader. Your tacomm call is now TACBATT Leader!

That was standard procedure for changing code calls in combat. The new commander never assumed the code call of the replaced officer.

Roger! TACBATT Leader is on the way! Marauder Leader, follow me! Stiletto Leader, assume command of ASSAULTCO Alpha!

Stiletto Leader has ASSAULTCO Alpha! Adonica's tacomm voice came back with surprising calm. Then she asked, *Puma Leader, how bad was Alleycat Leader hit?*

Stiletto Leader, I don't know. I'm not there and I'm not a bio-tech! And I've got my hands full at the moment. You'll have to ask Ruth when she gets him back to her, Lew replied briefly.

This was something that Curt had worried about for years. Jerry Allen and Adonica Sweet were deeply in love with one another. He always wondered how either one of them would handle it when the other was badly hurt or even killed. Now he was going to find out. Curt was ready to step in and relieve Adonica of her responsibilities if necessary. No need to have a distraught officer trying to command troops under that sort of emotional pressure.

But Adonica surprised him. *Thank you, Puma Leader! I'll do that when the time is appropriate. He's in good hands. And I've got a job to do here.* She sounded strangely like her best friend in the regiment, Capt. Dyani Motega.

Curt suddenly saw that the two young women had learned much from one another. Adonica had helped Dyani loosen up and project her natural beauty while Dyani had taught Adonica about self-discipline in highly emotional situations.

In Adonica's cool, dispassionate reply, Curt also caught a hint of what Jerry and Adonica had repeatedly told him, that they'd worked through the various scenarios and knew what each would do in a variety of circumstances.

Curt felt relieved at that but deeply worried about what had happened to his oldest and most trusted subordinate. And his friend.

But he was the regimental commander. He had too many people depending on him. He couldn't take the luxury of spending too much time thinking about Jerry. To many people who might not have any military or command experience, it might appear that Curt was being cold-hearted. But he knew that he was just burying the worry down deep inside at the moment. It would eventually come to the surface. And he knew how to handle it when it did.

The cold-hearted man was down in the bunker. Generalissimo Modibo wasn't happy. It would take nearly an hour for Kassem to mobilize a Malitanian warbot infantry regiment and two armored regiments for the relief of Dakar Airport. Modibo thought that three regiments would be enough to do the job. Colonel Pratihara, his

East World military advisor, didn't believe three regiments were enough. But Modibo overruled him. The Generalissimo wanted to keep his Tenth Division in Dakar proper in case someone tried an amphibious landing. Modibo believed that the activity at Dakar Airport probably involved no more than three Sierra Charlie regiments. He also told himself it was a diversion for a bigger assault that would probably come either on the north beaches of the peninsula or through Dakar harbor. So he wanted to withold some of his forces until he saw how the assault was developing.

Of course, Modibo was wrong. He had practically no intelligence data. And he wasn't really a professional military man. He operated on the basis of the high-mobility tactics of a Berber nomad, which is all he knew. Thus, he tended to operate as many government and corporate leaders did: By instinctual "gut feelings." He was wrong.

But Pratihara knew from experience he couldn't tell the Generalissimo that. He'd seen Modibo shoot people who disagreed with him. The Malitanian dictator probably wouldn't shoot Pratihara because of the hassle that would cause among his East World supporters. But Pratihara certainly didn't want to be shipped home, labelled as a failure.

Kori, the Malitanian NCO aircrew chief, came back into the bunker. He had a quick word with the flight leader who was his immediate superior. Then he came over to where Modibo was sitting with the telephone handset to his ear. "Your Excellency, I've just made a recon at the surface. The Americans have their warbots and field soldiers all over the field. A group of them went past the bunker entrance. I was able to throw a grenade that killed two of them and damaged a warbot."

"You did *what?*" Modibo exploded.

"I killed at least two of them and probably damaged a warbot."

"*You idiot!*" Modibo was livid. "You gave away the fact that we're in this bunker!"

"Sir, I was only trying to do my job. I saw the opportunity to kill some of the enemy," the crew chief replied, suddenly very frightened. "They didn't see me!"

"They have ways of seeing other than their eyes! They have radar and lasers!" Modibo roared. Without hesitation, he pulled the Kufahl 9mm. pistol from its holster and fired point-blank at the man's chest.

The pistol's report was deafening. The impact blew the Malitanian Air Force crew chief backwards and slammed him against the wall. He looked very surprised and then pained as he slid down the wall to the floor. He was already dead. Nothing much remained of his chest except a gaping crimson hole. Modibo preferred using hollow soft point ammo; it was more effective. The Generalissimo didn't give a damn about the Geneva conventions.

Sliding the Kufahl back into its holster, Modibo looked at the shocked faces around the bunker. In a low and threatening voice, he told them, "All of you will do as you're told!" It didn't occur to him that the dead crew chief hadn't been told anything.

"Flight Captain, you're an officer. I'm going to trust you to go up and securely bar the upper door to the bunker. Then bar the secondary door here when you come back," Modibo continued, giving specific instructions. "If those doors aren't secured so that nothing short of a couple of kilos of high explosive can blow them in, the chambered round in my pistol is for you. Move! It may already be too late!"

"May I take three armed men along with me just in case?" the pilot wanted to know.

"No! Do the job yourself! If the Americans have already started to break in, I don't want to lose any more men than I have to. I'll need everyone for the defense of the bunker until Kassem arrives with help to get us out of here!"

Pratihara was getting very skittish around this man. Modibo was strong, ruthless, and aggressive. But, if Pratihara was correct in his professional assessment of

190

Modibo's capabilities, he strongly suspected that Modibo had a streak of insanity in him that could be triggered by small incidents such as this. Modibo certainly didn't appear to be the calm, cool, and collected sort of a person who turns out to be a great leader. Anyone can lead when the going is easy. Pratihara knew from his own military education and experience that the famous and heroic commanders were the ones who could prevail in adversity as well as in a winning situation.

"Generalissimo, what are your plans for the defense of the bunker?" Pratihara asked carefully. He was trying to get the man to think straight and to give some orders that could be obeyed. Otherwise, everyone in the bunker would spend too much time worrying about what he did or didn't do to incur the Generalissimo's displeasure. No one wanted to get a bullet in the back. Pratihara remembered what he'd learned about leaders in bunkers, men such as Adolph Hitler and Saddam Hussein, when the pressures on them got high.

"We will remain quiet and not attract attention to ourselves," Modibo explained. "We may have already failed to do that because of the stupid actions of the man I just eliminated. He won't be able to repeat his idiotic attack. He was only trying to assert his manhood! We will sit in this bunker and wait to be rescued by Colonel Kassem and his troops. I have telephone communications with him. We will be rescued."

"Very well, sir." Pratihara wasn't sure. It would take an aggressive counterattack to move onto the airport and get to the bunker entrance. He knew that Modibo was counting on Kassem's relief force to overwhelm the Americans.

Colonel Pratihara didn't think that would be possible. He knew how the Americans operated. While they practiced the principle of economy of force, they were so rich and powerful that economy to them was overwhelming force to nearly everyone except perhaps the Chinese. The Americans had gone through a period of trying to do the impossibly big operations with impossibly small forces. Pratihara wasn't about to assume that this was another one of those. He didn't like to err on the side of weakness. He knew all too well that the Americans could and often had over-reacted on many occasions. Trinidad was a recent example. And this could be one of those in spite of a pacifist, anti-military president sitting in the White House. Several peace-loving American presidents, Woodrow Wilson and Jimmy Carter being among them, had toggled over when the situations clearly demanded military action. Some had turned out to be commanders-in-chief of extremely effective American forces. Some hadn't. Pratihara didn't know enough about the current American president to be able to make a professional evaluation about him. The fact that the Americans had struck without warning this morning told the East World military advisor that perhaps the world had underestimated the man in the Oval Office.

"Generalissimo, all great military commanders develop a contingency plan," Pratihara remarked smoothly, laying on the snake oil in a professional manner to keep this man in the real world. "I presume you have Plan B. Suppose Colonel Kassem's forces can't break through to us? Can you run the defense of your Senegambian province from here?"

"A good commander can lead very well from a bunker if communications can be maintained and good intelligence is available," Modibo pointed out. "We are in the middle of the enemy, and the enemy doesn't know we're here. And there are many Senegambian civilians working at this airport. I will send these men outside on reconaissance sweeps. They will appear to be civilian. Therefore, I will be able to find out exactly what the Americans are doing, make plans, and direct Kassem's counterattack. I will lead from here until the Americans are defeated. The fact that I can do this will make me an even greater leader!"

"Generalissimo, we're cut off from the world except for

communications. How long can we hold out here with limited supplies of food and water? And electric power? And suppose their signals technicians discover the fiber optics communication cable? What then? All contingencies must be considered, sir," Pratihara pressed carefully.

"If Kassem cannot break through," Modibo decided, "I will have him create a diversion to distract the Americans. Then we will come out of the bunker and make our way to friendly forces." Modibo paused and began to think. His military thinking was based exclusively on his own experiences, not those of others recorded in the history books and studied by nearly every other military commander in the world. Finally, he told his military advisor, "In the unlikely event that Kassem can't break through and we begin to run out of food and water in this bunker, I will get out under cover of night and deception. These men here may be from my Air Force, but they're also warriors of Malitania. All of us come from warrior background! We know how to fight no matter where. Warriors can fight anywhere. These men of my armed services can fight on the ground as well as in the air. They will be my covering force."

Pratihara couldn't say much in reply. He knew that he was going to be forced by circumstances to organize the escape operation on the sly in the bunker. The only feasible outcome appeared to be the one where Kassem conducted an assault on the airport or elsewhere to divert American forces and attention. Then the bunker inhabitants would have to sneak out.

His own ass was bared to the breeze here. He would have to take care of the military side of the equation without letting Modibo know it. Modibo was no military genius. Pratihara didn't trust the Malitanian dictator to organize and lead an effective breakout from the bunker. On the other hand, Pratihara knew something about war and fighting as it's done elsewhere than the Sahara and Sahel where armed forces are basically tribal in background. Over the past two hundred years, tribal armies

193

hadn't fared well against those from countries with more modern and efficient forms of organization. The Zulus had given the British a run for it, but the British had prevailed in the war. If the Brits hadn't withdrawn from their empire because they'd been bled to death by two major European wars, the Zulus would have been permanently crushed.

"If the escape is planned and carried out properly, we will be able to do it without having to fight our way out. I am an expert on stealthy movement and trickery, Pratihara. I would not have conquered Mali, Mauritania, and now Senegambia if I hadn't been," Modibo boasted. Then he added, "We can remain here undetected if we behave like jackals avoiding the hunters. Kassem will attack and rescue us by this evening. If he can't, then we can get out of here at night under cover of a diversionary attack. After all, the Americans aren't all-seeing and all-knowing!"

What he didn't know was that, in comparison to the primitive means of intelligence gathering that he'd had to use against armies in the Sahel and Senegambia, the Americans were indeed all-seeing and all-knowing.

Twenty

Modibo isn't at the airport? Curt could hardly believe the report from his new tac batt commander, Maj. Kitsy Clinton.

Grey Head, TACBATT Leader says again: Malefactor has not been found or identified. All buildings and debris on the east side of the airport have been searched. All bodies have been examined. Uh, can we please get some of the Malitanian POWs over here to take care of these dead bodies before they start to stink, sir? The Aerospace Force strike had left a very messy ramp. Kitsy had cleaned up a battlefield once before in Yemen. But, like the other Greys, she wasn't used to examining closely the victims of war.

Curt sighed. He'd thought for a moment there that this might be a quickie mission. If Modibo had indeed been killed during the air strike, it would have left the Malitanians without leadership. In turn, that might cause the Malitanians to fight less efficiently or their unit commanders to surrender.

From what Curt had picked up during the pre-strike intelligence briefings, Modibo had established the usual sort of linear command structure of a dictatorship. Orders came down from the top, and reports went back up to the top where all the decisions were made. Linear command doctrine certainly worked to keep subordinates from staging a coup or even a mutiny against a dictator or totalitarian regime. But it could slow up the whole process of command and control. Slow C^3I usually meant defeat on the modern high-mobility battlefield.

In addition to better weapons technology, this was where the military services of the West World—North America and Europe—had a definite edge. Soldiers the world over were trained to follow orders. However, Americans were also taught to take the initiative when the chain of command was broken in the heat of battle or when it became obvious that blind obedience to orders would result in failure of the operation. This personal initiative policy didn't relieve the commander at any level of personal responsibility for the consequences of such independent action.

In other words, if you stick out your neck and you're wrong, be prepared for it to be shaved or, at the worst, cut off.

TACBATT Leader, this is Grey Head. Roger your last. Regroup and reconfigure. Proceed with the operation as planned, Curt told her. *Secure the east airport perimeter and stand for Wolf to pass through followed by First Cav.*

Yessir!

And I'll get you a POW detail to take care of the meat.

Thank you, sir.

Curt switched to the division command channel. *Battleaxe, this is Grey Head.*

This is Battleaxe. Go, Grey Head.

Negatory on Malefactor. I say again: Negatory on Malefactor. I don't know where the hell he is. We found his limo and his mistress. They both were totalled. No i-d on any of the bodies, but their appearance doesn't match Malefactor's. I don't know what happened, Curt reported to Kettrick.

We haven't got time to screw around with it any longer, Grey Head. Malefactor will have to show his head sooner or later if he's hiding somewhere at the airport. We'll have to keep an eagle-type eyeball peeled for him. So proceed with the operation as planned.

That's what I've done, Battleaxe.

I thought you would.

Grey Head, Mustang Leader here! Dyani's NE tacomm "voice" demanded his attention as she overrode his helmet switching. She'd jumped a level of command, but she could do that because she was Curt's S-2 staffer as well as

196

the RECONCO company commander. *Black Hawk Leader reports that the Black Hawks have spotted two Malitanian armored columns headed toward the airport. Data on the bus now!*

Any make on the equipment? Tanks? Or warbots?

Preliminary analysis indicates Red Hammer warbots.

Those were literally Chinese copies of the old, obsolete American Hairy Fox warbots. In the early years of developing the Sierra Charlie doctrine, the Washington Greys had worked with whatever warbots were available from the regular Robot Infantry. In the current situation of anti-militarism in the White House, they still had to do that. Warbots are expensive to develop and put into production.

But the old Heavy Fire Support Warbots—tagged Hairy Foxes by the Greys—were too big, slow, klutzy, over-gunned, and over-powered for the highly mobile strike tactics the Greys had developed. Operation High Dragon on Kerguelen Island was the last time the Hairy Foxes had been used. That had been a very black mission. Circumstances had forced the Greys to abandon most of their Hairy Foxes on a Kerguelen Island glacier. When American warbot recovery teams went in later to recover those abandoned warbots, they discovered the area had been picked clean by someone else. Both the Soviets and the Chinese were suspect.

Indeed, the Soviet Silver Pilgrim warbots first used on Sakhalin resembled the Hairy Foxes. Silver Pilgrims were remotely-controlled lash-up mods of Soviet light airborne tanks without NE linkage. A Chinese version of the Hairy Foxes had been encountered when the Greys tangled with East World forces in Yemen. Red Hammer warbots had been captured there and shipped to Aberdeen Proving Ground and McCarthy Proving Ground. After they'd been carefully tested and analyzed there, the intelligence information had been passed to the regiments of the Iron Fist Division. Like the Soviet Silver Pilgrims, the Red Hammers didn't use classified NE linkage. So Curt knew what the Greys were be up against here in Senegambia.

Curt checked the tactical display in the holo tank of his OCV. One Malitanian armored column was moving westward toward the airport along Route de Rufisque from Pikine. *Grady, this is Grey Head. Show me the estimated position of the armored column I am indicating on the tactical display,* Curt instructed his regimental computer, Grady.

The computer was a small one designed and programmed for tactical support. Grady didn't have the immense power of Georgie, the Iron Fist divisional computer tucked safely away underground in far-off Arizona. So Grady required a few hundred milliseconds to check movement rates of the incoming armored column, determine the most probable road routing, and present its results to Curt on the tac display.

"Two hours," Curt mused to himself *sotto voce.* "We've got time to deploy against them if necessary."

He saw the position of the other armored column coming out of the university area on the west side of Dakar. So he directed a similar question to Grady who fired back another answer. Grady was slow. However, insofar as Curt was concerned, Grady's time delay was inconsequential. Georgie might take a few milliseconds compared to a couple of hundred milliseconds for Grady. To Curt's slower colloidal jellyware up in his head, a few hundred milliseconds was instantaneous. Good enough is the enemy of the best, he decided.

"They're coming out of Dakar! Good!" he said verbally to Joan Ward. "I'd rather have them come out of the city and fight us in the suburbs."

His chief of staff nodded. "Urban street fighting in a highrise area like downtown Dakar isn't the sort of fracas I like," Joan admitted. She'd been through several urban fights with the Greys. "Sierra Charlies can fight better in an urban environment than warbot brainies, but I'd rather have the additional mobility. Building-to-building and room-to-room combat is slow and deadly."

"That plus we should try to keep collateral damage to a minimum," Curt added. "A lot of noncombatant civilians could get hurt. And Dakar shouldn't be destroyed."

"The Paris of West Africa," Joan reminded him. "By rights, it should be an open city."

"Modibo won't make that declaration," her regimental commander speculated. "Dakar as a civic and cultural center doesn't cut it with him. He's the sort of military strong man who believes cities are meant for looting and pillaging. Which is another reason why we've got to draw his forces out of there to fight us on our chosen ground."

"Part of the ops plan," Joan reminded him.

"Yeah. I know. Okay, so we've taken Dakar Airport. First objective completed. I need an update on the rest of the incoming forces," Curt shifted gears. The Malitanians wouldn't be at the airport for another hour or so at their present rate of movement. And the Greys wouldn't have to defend the airport as the first line of troops at that point. The Cottonbalers were tasked with moving southward to draw Malitanian forces out of Dakar. The Wolfhounds were already moving southeastward toward Hann Plage to seal off the eastern routes out of the downtown area. The First Cavalry Division would be the ones moving eastward to seal off the entire Cape Verde peninsula from Malitanian attempts to bring additional forces into the area.

Operation Bloodbath, as it had been finalized and signed-off, was simply to take and hold Dakar and the airport, prevent the Malitanians from destroying the city, and provide security for the evacuation of foreign nationals in Dakar.

"How's the rest of Bloodbath proceeding?" Curt wanted to know.

Joan spread her hands over the tac display. "Nominal," she replied briefly, that one word signifying the general state of affairs.

It had been a little over an hour since the assault had touched down. The Bloodbath forces had the airport secured. Aerodynes were roaring in constantly, then lifting off to return to Praia for refueling and another load. Hettrick had her people up in the control tower directing the flow of inbound and outbound traffic. Curt didn't like the feel of the situation. "Too easy," he suddenly remarked, voicing his thoughts.

"Pardon?"

"Joan, it's been too easy," he told her. "I anticipated far more Malitanian opposition than we've actually encountered."

"Our losses have already been too high," she reminded him without referring directly to Jerry.

Curt just nodded. He didn't want to think about Jerry right then. He had other responsibilities, and he could not allow emotional factors to interfere. Jerry was in the best possible hands right then, and there was nothing further that Curt could do.

He had to make sure the airport was secured, and he also had to be prepared for the contingency that the Malitanians might come knocking at the door. Two columns were converging on the airport. Maybe the Cottonbalers or the Wolfhounds would tangle with them first. Or maybe even the warbotic First Cav might make contact first. However, Curt had to prepare for the possibility that the Malitanians might get as far as the airport.

He'd thought about this on the flight over. Any good commander always tried to have Plan B. And Plan C. And even more plans. Good commanders played the game of JIC (Just In Case). Curt was a good commander. Furthermore, Hettrick was counting on him to handle the tactical situation if conditions went to slime. She didn't tell him that. She didn't need to. That's why the Greys had been chosen to make the initial assault and hold the airport, much to their chagrin. If it had been up to Russ, Kitsy, and Lew, the Greys would be off on a grand cross-country chase right then. But the Third Herd would take the initial fire, then stand by to serve as a mobile reserve force.

Curt had learned over the years a series of unwritten principles that not only served the leadership requirements of the Greys but helped make operations with other regiments and divisions a lot easier: *Don't try to win the furball yourself. Always leave room for someone else to shine. There's plenty of "glory" for everyone.*

"Where are the engineers?" he suddenly asked, referring to the 132nd Engineering Battalion that had been attached to the Operation Bloodbath forces. The primary mission of the 132nd was to establish proper defensive facilities across the narrow neck of the peninsula. Curt had other jobs in mind for them right then.

Joan pointed at the tact display. "On the ground."

Curt toggled his tacomm. *Battleaxe, this is Grey Head.*

Grey Head, this is Iron Fist ops. Battleaxe is unavailable. The "voice" was familiar to Curt. It was that of Col. Hensley Atkinson, formerly S-3 of the Greys. In the aftermath of the Yemen debacle, heavy losses had caused the whole division to undergo a drastic reorganization. Curt had lost Hensley to the division staff. He had no heartburn about that. In fact, he was pleased that people in the Greys had opportunities for such upward mobility. And proud that two of his staffers from the Greys had been chosen by Hettrick.

Okay, Hensley, I've got a snivel and you can do something about it. Please detach a platoon from the One-thirty-second. We've got some A-P mines at the airport. If we're going to hold on here, we can't be worried about stepping on a mine. I'd like the engineers to do a little mine sweeping and clearance before I lose someone else.

You've lost someone?

Major Allen has been wounded.

There was a long pause while Atkinson reacted to the news. As a former Grey, she had known Jerry well. Everyone in a combat outfit gets to know one another almost like family. In fact, the Washington Greys were really the only family most of them had. But she replied calmly, *Yes, sir! I'll get the One-thirty-second on the job.*

Because the Greys were tasked with holding the airport during the tactical deployment phase, Curt went on, *In addition, I'd like to have the engineers available, They can string a little concertina wire and plant other nasty little antipersonnel and anti-armor defenses. I want to channel any potential Malitanian counterattack into areas where we can cream them with firepower while we move to cut them off. Please ask their battalion commander to drop over to my OCV. I need to find out what they brought along and can do with it.*

Yes, sir!

Edie Sampson had been monitoring tac displays in gen-

201

eral, and she'd set up the screens so they would show when Curt wanted and needed to see. So much combat information flowed in that she had to be selective. Otherwise, all of them would have been overwhelmed. On the twenty-first century battlefield, combat information wasn't a matter of not having enough. That was the historic situation. They now had too much. Selective control of data was important. So Edie had patched up automatic alerts. They caused the computer to do a "hey-boss" when something unusual showed up.

"Colonel, I've got some bogies here," she suddenly remarked.

Curt didn't want to be distracted with outside issues, but he trusted Edie not to joggle his elbow unnecessarily. Both Curt and Henry turned to look at her display.

At first glance, it was a madhouse squared because of all the units, aerodynes, and military factors on the display. And it wasn't static. The beacon pips moved as he watched.

"What have you got?" Curt asked.

Edie pointed to a cluster of beacon pips. "Bearing zero-one-zero. Range thirty klicks and closing. Projection of the plot indicates destination is Dakar Airport," she replied.

"Couldn't be more Malitanian Juliet-two-twos," Kester opined. "Not unless they moved more than one squadron to Saint Louis."

"They're not Juliet-two-twos," Edie insisted. "The radar signature of each blip matches that of a large transport aerodyne."

"Could be Malitanian reinforcements," Henry guessed, then corrected himself. "But the Malitanian Army isn't air-transportable. They move on the ground."

"Do they have a parachute regiment?" Edie asked.

"Negatory," Curt replied, shaking his head. "Not according to the latest force updates."

Kester looked again. "Pretty big primary return for a nonstealthed 'dyne."

"Secondary radar. They're squawking," Edie told him, indicating that the incoming aerodynes had regular radar transponders. Furthermore, these were turned on and replying."

"What the hell? No stealth? Transponders on? By God, if it's a commercial operation, they'd better be warned off!" Curt said.

"Unless they're incoming friendlies and want to make damned sure we realize it, Colonel," Henry Kester observed, calling on his years of combat-honed wisdom.

"Friendlies? Who?" Curt wondered aloud.

"Colonel, who else has embassies and personnel in Dakar?" Henry responded.

"Could be any one of a hundred nations," Curt decided. This needed to be reported to Iron Fist Command. Maybe they hadn't spotted it among all the confusion and clutter on the screens. It was certainly unanticipated. At least to the Third Herd.

Iron Fist this is Grey Head, Curt called Col. Hensley Atkinson back. *We are receiving secondary radar returns from a gaggle of transport aerodynes, number unknown, bearing zero-one-zero, range two-five klicks and closing, estimate course projection indicates Dakar Airport. Don't tell me it's a flock of seagulls! The radar sig says aerodynes! And seagulls don't carry radar transponders! Know anything about this?*

Stand by, Grey Head, Hensley told him. It was apparent that she'd been caught with her screens down. *Roger we see them! Uh, no, we don't have the foggiest who or what they are! Come to Alpha Red Condition!*

"All right, everyone! Red alert! Possible air strike inbound!" Curt snapped to his staff inside the OCV.

The call went out on tacomm from the S-3, Russ Frazier, in a calm and collected "tone of voice" for everyone to hear: *Greys all, this is Grey Ops! Come at once to Alpha Red! I say again: Come at once to Alpha Red! Multiple unknown targets, bearing zero-one-zero, range two-three klicks, estimated altitude one-triple-zero meters, speed three-zero-zero klicks, course inbound. Load, lock, and track. Mary Anns, Jeeps, Novias, and Smart Farts will be primary. Saucy Cans load alpha-alpha smart rounds. Hold fire until advised. Do it!*

Grey Ops, Warhawk Leader! We can intercept the fuckers! Looks like a merged plot in about forty seconds! That was classic Cal Worsham.

Roger, Warhawk Leader, Perform a cold Fox Six visual intercept. Report results. Russ didn't need to ask Curt. Curt had trained him.

Which gave Curt the feeling that he was sort of a supernumerary in the operation. But, he reminded himself, that's what a true commander is supposed to feel like.

How's your fuel state, Warhawk Leader? Russ asked solicitously. The Harpies had been over the airport for almost an hour now. They'd had a midair drink from a tanker on the way in. That should give them about another thirty minutes, Russ had figured. He made a mental note to call for tankers once the intercept was complete and the problem resolved. But he saw from the display that Bloodbath CINC had apparently ordered the tankers withdrawn offshore until this was over. Those radar beacon blips were moving westward.

Nowhere near bingo, and if I have to I'll squat at Dakar. Got any fuel for us there yet?

Not for three-zero minutes max unless the airport fueling system is operative.

We brought mil-com adapters for our single point systems, Worsham reminded the operations staffer. Military aircraft used a slightly different system for attaching fueling hoses to their single-point refueling systems. What worked for commercial aircraft didn't really work for military craft whose fittings had to be designed and built to keep out a lot more sand and dirt. Military aircraft operated under somewhat primitive basing conditions sometimes.

In the meantime, deconflict those goddamned Chippies inbound! I don't want them to be a column of ducks if the inbounds turn out to be Brand X! Worsham continued.

He was interrupted. *This is Harrier Leader! Tally ho! Tally ho! Two o'clock low, two klicks! A formation of ten. . . . twenty! I'll be go to hell! They're Delauny Eperviers! They're carrying French markings!*

Twenty-one

Battleaxe, the incoming bogeys have been visually identified as French military! Curt passed the information along to the commanding general of the 17th Iron Fist Division.

French? What the hell? was the sudden and surprised reply.

We weren't informed that the French were part of Operation Bloodbath, Curt reminded her.

Maj. Gen. Belinda Hettrick was in her battle management mode, ensconced in her OCV with the top members of her staff. Hers was a job that required outstanding communications. So most of the OCV was filled with high-tech comm gear. Quickly, she responded to her subordinate, *Stand by. Tell that squadron commander of yours to formate in scat mode with them.*

She switched to the Bloodbath CINC channel. *Bloodbath, Battleaxe. Grey air support has intercepted and made visual on the incoming aerodyne bogeys. They are French military. When the hell did the French get involved in this?*

From the Operation Bloodbath command center in Praia, Col. Rhett Rathbone replied, *Battleaxe, Bloodbath Ops here! We have no indication of operational support from any Nation X. Stand by for Bloodbath Star.*

Lt. Gen. William Bellamack came on the channel almost at once. *Belinda, did you say French aerodynes?*

Affirmative! French aerodynes! Data bus indicates Delauny Sparrowhawks, standard French army airlifters. What the hell are the French doing here, Bill? At this level of command, tacomm protocol and procedures were not followed on many occasions.

205

General officers knew one another very well. As a result, their communications were far more personal.

Roger your last, Belinda. Hell, I don't know what the French are doing here! Let me run this back through DCSOP and see if they have any answers. You get the French on the ground and out of the way of our airlift corridor. If they shoot, shoot back. Wild Bill Bellamack was wondering what the hell had come unbonded here. Pickens hadn't told him anything about this. Was Pickens out to screw him up? Bellamack immediately put that paranoid idea out of his mind. It smacked too much of Soviet-style thinking, and he'd been screwed by that already in his career. It wasn't totally illogical that the French might react militarily to Modibo's invasion of their former African colony. Or that the French might attempt to come in to rescue their legation and citizens from Modibo's bloodbath. It was consistent with French behavior patterns.

Belinda, you speak French, right? Bellamack asked as an addendum.

Poorly, Bill. It's been years.

Looks like you're going to get some practice! Whoever the French commander is, stroke the hell out of him until I can get a reading from topside.

Roger that! Maybe the question will be who's stroking who.

In case, I don't have to worry. And I'll leave you to figure that out on your own.

When Bellamack broke off, Hettrick turned to her G-2, Col. Ellie Aarts. In verbose mode, she ordered, "Have the tower attempt to raise the French flight leader on the CTAF. Get them on the ground and out of this fly swarm of Bloodbath air traffic. Pick a landing spot for their aerodynes over on any clear part of the commercial ramp. Keep them the hell and gone away from our logair operation."

Aarts nodded and got busy.

To her chief of staff, Hettrick said, "Joanne, hold down the headquarters. I'm going out to meet whoever is in charge of this French incursion. I'll be on Channel Niner Tango."

"Yes, ma'am!" Wilkinson popped.

"Come on, Jim, I need you to cover my minus-x!" Hettrick told her Operations staffer, Col. Jim Ricketts. She grabbed her combat helmet with all its built-in comm gear and headed out the door.

Good people, she reflected. Joanne Wilkinson, along with Ellie Aarts and Hensley Atkinson, had been staffers in the Greys. They were good and they'd been blooded in combat. All of them had finally decided they'd had enough of actual combat. They'd requested early retirement after the debacle of Yemen. Hettrick didn't blame them, but she also didn't believe in wasting good people. So when she had to rebuild her division staff after Yemen, she'd convinced them to join her instead of retiring. They were all still young in mind, and being Sierra Charlies had required them to remain in top physical condition. Retirement for women like them often meant years of boredom and loneliness unless they took civil service positions doing the same jobs they'd done in the Army but without the military perks.

On the other hand, Col. Jim Ricketts had been left without a regimental command when the Regulars were deactivated after Yemen. So she brought him aboard as her operations staffer.

The only hold-over from her pre-Yemen staff was her logistics specialist, Col. Adrian Kleperas, a solid and reliable legacy from Jacob Carlisle's days of division command.

Some indictments of the Army's "Old Comrades' Network" may have validity. But no more so than in any comparable non-military organization or corporation. Leaders and managers prefer to work with subordinates they've trained, worked with before, and grown to trust. Familiarity breeds confidence. And the real measure of worth is performance, not just friendship.

She could see the French aerodynes coming to hover over the field. They had no tactical air cover. She considered it damned stupid to mount an air assault without air cover. But the French sometimes carried out strange operations.

Her experience in handling international military operations—and this appeared suddenly to have turned into one—told her she'd better take command of the situation from the moment of first contact. It had been years since she'd used her knowledge of the French language, and French military officers often got upset if another officer misused the language. Hettrick looked around. *Grey Head, this is Battleaxe. I'd appreciate some backup here in the form of a platoon and some Jeeps. Do you have anyone who can speak French?*

Affirmative! Lieutenant Dan Power. Came on board recently. I'll assign him and his Panthers. Want me along?

Negatory! Command your regiment, Grey Head!

Battleax, doesn't look like there's anyone left here who wants to fight, Curt complained.

Are you bragging or complaining? Stand by because these French troops may not be exactly friendly. Granted, they always have been, but the world is full of surprises.

A young second lieutenant stepped up to her and saluted. "Lieutenant Dan Powers reporting as ordered, General! The Panthers are at your service, ma'am!" He was a strapping young officer with a determined expression on his handsome face. From his attitude and bearing, Hettrick knew at once the boy was recently graduated from West Point. It stuck out all over him. Behind him was his platoon sergeant, an NCO who was well known to Hettrick. Betty Jo Trumble had been in the Greys since Namibia. But Hettrick didn't recognize the new sergeant, Denny Dent. A Jeep and eight Mary Anns accompanied the Sierra Charlies.

Hettrick returned his salute and nodded in recognition to BeeJay Trumble. "You and your platoon will be my military escort, Lieutenant. I want you and your platoon to accompany me to my meeting with whoever's in charge of this French intrusive force. How's your French?"

"Not very good on NE tacomm, General. I don't think in the language very well, but I'm otherwise fluent, ma'am," Powers admitted.

"Well, we don't have the French NE tacomm channel specs anyway, so we'll stay verbose. My French is rusty, so I'd like you to keep me from making a damned fool of myself. And have your platoon watch minus-x. Switch now to NE tacomm Channel Niner Tango. Let's go!"

Yes, ma'am! Uh, General, what the hell are the French doing here?

That's what we're going to find out, Lieutenant! Iron Fist Spook, have the tower relay these instructions to the French: Ask them to re-main inside their aircraft. I'm coming out to see them, and I request a conference with their commander! Which 'dyne is their boss man riding in?

Roger, Battleaxe! Done! The French commander will meet you at the aerodyne numbered Foxtrot Two Three.

It was difficult to read the low-contrast markings on the French aerodynes. The aircraft were painted in European gray-green colors. This told Hettrick that the French operation had been laid on in a hurry. But she saw the F.23 designation on one of them and headed toward it.

As she approached with her escort, the aerodyne cargo doors opened and four men in desert cammies came out. They were all armed with the new FAMAC assault carbine issued to the French parachute regiments. Hettrick knew from her reading of the professional literature that these units were the closest the French had to the American Sierra Charlies.

But she was surprised when the tall man in the lead who was wearing the muted epaulets of a French colonel introduced himself in English.

"Madame General, I am Colonel Robert Debas, commanding officer of Deuxième Regiment Entranger de Parachutistes, Legion Etranger," the tall officer said with his right hand in the stiff French salute. "I am also in command of Mission Épée Vert. I am very surprised to find the American armed forces here."

"Major General Belinda Hettrick, commanding officer of the Seventeenth Division, Army of the United States," she replied with a much softer salute. "We didn't know you were coming, sir. Why didn't your government let my government know?"

"It was a secret mission, madame. I did not know of your presence until we were intercepted by your aerodynes and contacted the control tower."

"Well, Operation Green Sword is no longer a secret! What's your objective, Colonel?" Hettrick wanted to know. The colonel was a dashing Frenchman who appeared gallant and cultured. But he had behind him one of the most legendary of the regiments of the French Foreign Legion. The Second Parachute Regiment was no group of wimps. The situation could become very confused if this French commander turned out to be as tiresome as some of the Gallic officers with whom she'd tried to work in the past. Hettrick remembered Operation Diamond Skeleton in Namibia. There an aged French general decided to grab the glory and protect the honor of the French nation by totally fucking up the whole plan. The Washington Greys had saved it.

"We are here to liberate our diplomatic delegation and to assist in the evacuation of French citizens from Senegambia!" Debas announced imperiously.

"I thought as much. That's our general objective as well."

"Why is it that I was not told of your operation here?" Debas asked.

Hettrick gave a little shrug of her shoulders. "Damned if I know, Colonel. Sometimes our respective governments don't tell us military people everything we need to know. However, you're here now, and I welcome you to Operation Bloodbath. Your command will be a valuable addition to the three United States Army divisions already involved," Hettrick told him impassionately, knowing full well that a single regiment stood zilch chance of carrying out such a mission alone. She'd studied the intelligence reports about Malitanian forces in the area. "If you and your staff will join me and my staff in my command vehicle, we can talk to the overall operational commander in the Cape Verde Islands. A regiment of crack Foreign Legion troops will be most welcome in this effort, I assure you."

Debas replied with Gallic charm and gallantry although his tone was cool, "General, I have my orders. I intend to carry out my mission. I am not authorized to place my regiment under the command of a foreign power."

Hettrick sighed. This was going to be another tough one. This colonel showed signs of becoming wearisome.

She stopped for a moment to think. To her surprise, Lt. Dan Power spoke up in fluent French, "Colonel, we know that the glory of France and the honor of your regiment are involved here. We respect that. Our countries have fought together in many places around the world. We Americans have never forgotten the great debt we owe to France for Lafayette and the French forces under General Rochambeau at Yorktown. We have won before by working together. We can and will win again if we continue our historic tradition of mutual trust and respect for one another's honor."

This young man deserves watching! Hettrick told herself, being careful to keep her thoughts out of the tacomm channel. He'd apparently come out of nowhere, but she knew he was recently graduated from West Point. He'd taken the initiative and, with grace and charm of his own, voluntarily interjected himself into the conversation in a way that could break a deadlock.

Deep in her memory, she remembered another young brown-bar lieutenant fresh from the United States Military Academy who had joined Hettrick's Hellcats. He was now the commander of the Washington Greys. Curt Carson had behaved in a similar manner in the past.

Debas was impressed, too. He wasn't stupid. Any man who can rise to the command of the 2nd Parachute Regiment of the French Foreign Legion is no fool. A graduate of the French military academy at St. Cyr, Debas began to see that careful and studied cooperation with a much superior American force in Senegambia could result in fewer losses and a quicker end to this operation. No rational military leader, regardless of national background and characteristics, wants combat that destroys the officer's command, causes terrible casualties, and expends valuable arms and supplies. And there's always the chance that the operation won't go well. Friendly forces nearby are helpful if a call for help is necessary. Combat always contains the possibility that it won't go well because it never goes as planned. Debas saw that the situation had changed from the time he'd received his orders and briefed his regiment at Aubagne in southern France last night. Therefore his plan had to change.

Debas replied in French, "Lieutenant, you have rejuvenated my belief in the civility and sensitivity of American Army officers. We may have a basis for understanding after all."

As a result of this exchange in French, Hettrick replied in the same language, "Colonel Debas, let us adjourn to my command vehicle while your regiment is unloading from the aerodynes. We have secured the airport. Your men will not be required to come out shooting. Therefore, while they are getting organized on the ground, we can be working out a joint operation that will allow the Second Parachute Regiment to add yet another battle streamer to your colors."

Perhaps these Yanks weren't such barbarians after all, Debas decided. Certainly this woman general officer acted cultured but definitely was not one who would suffer fools. But he also didn't want to concede anything to them. Not yet, in any event. Hettrick had spoken about a higher command with which they would be talking. Debas wasn't about to go charging into Dakar at this point without finding out something of the American operations plan. If he couldn't arrange to become a major part of that plan and at the same time carry out his orders, then was the time to see what he could do independently. But not until he knew what the Americans were up to. Their warbot forces were too powerful, and their new Sierra Charlies were incredibly versatile (but not as much as his own 2e Regiment de Parachutistes, of course).

Once he was in the loop, he could communicate with Legion headquarters and present a decent report about what was going on here.

"Very well, Madame General!" Debas said, continuing to use French. It made him feel that he was one-up on these Americans to have them speaking to him in his language. It didn't occur to him that Hettrick was playing him on the line by doing so. "But first allow me to rectify my error. I did not introduce you to my staff . . ."

"And I didn't introduce you to my escort officer, Colonel, so we're even on that score . . ."

Twenty-two

Maj. Kitsy Clinton had her hands full.

Like everyone in the Washington Greys, she'd been cross-trained to fill a variety of positions in the regimental chain of command. Col. Curt Carson had insisted on this. The Greys had to be able to continue to function in an emergency.

This cross-training policy was predicated on the assumption that every individual was expendable. At first, some people took this as a mild affront. The military black humor of the Greys tended to ease this somewhat; the cross-training activity was known as "Karson's Kollege of Kannon-fodder Knowledge" or "K-4."

Its saving grace was the demonstrable fact that it worked. And it assured people that when they proceeded up the ladder of promotion and command, they would be better prepared for what they were getting into.

Kitsy had served several stints as temporary regimental commander in non-combat status at Fort Huachuca when Curt was on TDY or leave. As with many other junior officers who'd lusted for higher command, it brought her to the realization that even in peacetime a regiment was more than she could handle yet. But she'd been trained to command a battalion under all circumstances. And she could do it and liked it.

However, when she suddenly found herself commanding Maj. Jerry Allen's battalion in a combat situation, it was somewhat daunting. But it wasn't Kitsy's style to be daunted. So she plunged ahead.

Grey Ops, this is TACBATT Leader. I've been checking out TACBATT. This situation is a real sheep screw! We've been on the ground here only three hours, and the plan has already been shot to hell, she remarked to Russ Frazier.

What's your snivel, Kitsy? Russ wanted to know. He'd seen what Kitsy had reported, but he knew that a regimental commander, an S-3 staffer, and the tactical battalion commander had to remain flexible. No plan really survives the first contact. TACBATT was spread all over the Dakar airport. Various companies were engaged in little pissy-ass tasks that were far from the grand and sweeping assignments handed out in Praia.

What the hell are we supposed to do with these Frenchmen who just showed up? Kitsy wanted to know. She'd seen the French aerodynes land, and she didn't remember that the French were included in the Operation Bloodbath plan.

Let them unload. They're Foreign Legionnaires.

They are? Oh, my! Yes! Thank you! I don't want to argue with those troopers! In fact, I don't think I want to tangle with them in addition to the Malitanians! How come we weren't told about them?

No one in Operation Bloodbath knew about them, Russ admitted. *Being French, they probably dropped in with the idea they were going to pull it off on their own for their national honor or something. But they're here. We'll have to work them into the plan. So I'm about to get into a meeting with their commander and his staff now. Battleaxe will try to get them to cooperate. We can use the extra cannon fodder. The ops plan was a little thin to begin with.*

What's left of it, you mean. Okay, I figure it's out of my league. However, what the hell do I do with the Senegambian civilians here who were on the night shift and want to go home? Do I let them off the airport? And how about the civilians on the day shift? Do I let them in the gate? Do we need them to operate the critical airport facilities? Please advise.

Keep the civilian night shift on the job. The rest of the silly servants can take the day off and go to the beach. Wish to hell I could. Looks like some pretty nice beaches to the north of the airport, Russ remarked. He was behaving like any S-3 in a combat

214

situation: he was making it up as he went along. At that point, he didn't know what else to do. The operation was running according to schedule insofar as the airlift was concerned. Keeping that airlift moving along smoothly was of critical importance right then. What happened next depended on the results of the new Papa briefing with the French. *Once we get all the tactical forces on the ground here, we'll start bringing in the support units. The civilians will have to continue to do their jobs until the support people can take over.*

Is that part of the plan still good to go?

Affirmative! Don't you see all the 'dynes coming in?

Yeah, but I've been sort of busy myself. Uh, any report on Alley-cat Leader?

Negatory! He's in surgery and Major Ruth is too busy to chat about it. Let me ask you a collateral question: How's Adonica?

Solid as a rock so far. I'm trying to watch her out of the corner of my eye. I'm giving her tasks to keep the Stilettos busy.

Keep it up. And I'll keep you advised. You do the same.

That's what tacomm is for. Any other instructions, Grey Ops?

Run your show. I'm up here without Sampson in the control tower trying to bring order out of chaos at the airport until the Aerospace Farce support units get here with some air traffic controllers. Grey Ops out!

Suddenly, Kitsy realized that she was in charge. Curt, Joan, and Russ were involved with Hettrick because of the new situation created by the unheralded arrival of the French Foreign Legion. Jerry was definitely out of it. The combat involvement of the Greys in Operation Bloodbath was, for the moment, in Kitsy's lap.

Kitsy decided she had a tiger by the tail. And she also decided that the only thing to do was to swarm aboard and ride the hell out of that tiger. So that's what she did.

Mustang Leader, this is TACBATT Leader! Can you give me the latest poop on those Malitanian forces moving toward the airport?

They're on the data bus, TACBATT Leader.

I don't have access to that data bus. I'm new on the job here, and the reassignment didn't include an equipment upgrade. So I'm relo-

cating to Grey Can where I've got better tac displays. In the mean-time, Grey Tech, can you throw a patch to put me on the big data bus? Kitsy messaged to Master Sgt. Edie Sampson.

TACBATT Leader, this is Grey Tech, Edie's tacomm voice replied coolly from her post running the regiment's com-munications and displays in Curt's OCV. *You don't have to return to Grey Can. Tell me what you want to see, and I'll squirt it to you. Set your tacomm data bus unit to multiplex-receive so I've got enough bandwidth to work with. When I've got time to scratch, Major, I'll send a Jeep out to you with a batt commander's helmet and backpack unit. Then I won't have to multiplex. You'll get cleaner and faster data without snow.*

Is snow what I'm seeing now? Kitsy wanted to know.

Affirmative, TACBATT Leader!

Okay, it's snowy but readable. I'll with what I've got for right now. I see the input for the Malitanian forces. Looks like the east element will get here first. Can you give me any better discrimina-tion on those targets?

Negatory, TACBATT Leader! Unless you have a batt com-mander's helmet that will accept a better quality data stream . . .

Okay, Grey Tech, please send it out!

On its way. TACBATT Leader!

Kitsy decided she would have to put something on or over those oncoming Malitanians to slow them down a bit and cut them down to size. The target was nothing but a big blob of a return on her company commander's display.

Hellcat Leader, this is TACBATT Leader. I want you to target the Malitanian column coming in from the east. Get the best target coordinates possible from the Black Hawk birdbots. First objective is to take out their Red Hammers. Once we get rid of the hard-shelled stuff, we'll take care of the soft, walking non-warbots. So load SADARM rounds.

"Sense and Destroy Armor" rounds weren't new. How-ever, U.S. Army Ordnance had squeezed them down to 75-millimeter size suitable for the Saucy Cans guns. Kitsy knew from Yemen that these were particularly effective against the Red Hammers, which were lightly armored on top.

216

A SADARM round airbursts over the target area, dispensing several high-drag submunitions. These were equipped with simple sensors that look for the infra-red emissions of operating vehicles. If a submunition sees such a target, it detonates an explosive charge in midair. This charge not only forms a penetrating projectile by explosive-forming techniques but accelerates the resulting penetrator toward the target at high velocity. The projectile hits the top of the vehicle where armor is likely to be thin. If a SADARM submunition doesn't see a target, it falls to the ground where it becomes an anti-vehicle and anti-personnel mine.

Roger, TACBATT Leader, wilco. But I'd like to get rid of some of these seeker warbot rounds, Capt. Larry Hall replied. He was referring to another munition that could be fired by the 75-millimeter Saucy Cans guns. This had a warhead that landed without an explosion, erected itself on three extendable legs, looked around with sensors, then fired at any target radiating an infrared signature. In essence, it was a gun-delivered stupid destroyer warbot. Some of the rounds were AT and others AP.

You're god-awful short on manpower, so don't overload your people running the LAMVAs. And don't waste anti-tank rounds on personnel, and vice-versa, Larry, Kitsy told him. She knew all too well that Hall's Hellcats had only about two-thirds of authorized manpower. This meant that Larry Hall's people were running several warbots more than normal. This in turn was spreading them more than just a little thin. And regimental artillery support could be vital in the coming fracas. GUNCO's smart Saucy Cans ammo such as the SADARM rounds helped to offset their manpower shortage. *Keep the warbots seeker rounds handy J-I-C. When we get a good make on Malitanian soldiers out in the open, you can figure on using the AP rounds along with ordinary airbursters.*

She wished this was over. Some of the materiel that the Sierra Charlies had dreamed up and cobbled together in the face of reduced budgets was getting very lethal. The partial reversion of the United States Army to Sierra

Charlie doctrine—at least in one division—and the shortage of R&D funds to develop even higher tech weapons had stimulated the bright techie people to apply twenty-first century technology as they hadn't done before with the regular warbot operations. They'd not only come up with new ways to kill people but also to destroy warbots. And they'd dusted off a lot of old technology from the nineteenth and twentieth centuries. In some cases, they'd taken it off the shelf where it had lain unneeded and unwanted for fifty years. This old equipment, rejuvenated with modern technology, became outstanding new weapons with enhanced kill capabilities. Other countries would pick up these new weapon concepts as quickly as their technical and industrial base could embrace them. These nations were still playing catch-up because the last hundred years had proved that the United States was unbeatable when it came to technological warfare.

It was a deadly situation that wasn't being helped by the administration's anti-military policy. That was also tough on people who had dedicated their careers and lives to the defense of the United States. The official government policy changed from support to neglect and back again, often on a four-year time cycle. It was like riding a yo-yo. Dedication plus the maintenance of the warrior tradition were among the factors that kept people like Kitsy and the other Greys in the business. They knew the warriors were still needed, even when other people didn't believe they were.

An M33 Jeep rolled up with a battalion commander's combat helmet and backpack in two of its arm-and-claw effectors. So Kitsy momentarily went out of tacomm linkage to shuck the old helmet and backpack and don the new one. The Jeep collected her old equipment—no sense in leaving it out where it could be picked up by an enemy, and no sense in wasting equipment when they were short of everything except enemy—and rolled back to the regimental OCV.

When Kitsy slipped into the helmet, she knew from experience and cross-training that the batt commander's equipment would give her a better tactical view, but it still surprised her.

Almost at once, she saw something on her new helmet's tac display that hadn't been visible on the old one.

Mustang Leader, this is TACBATT Leader! Do you and your birdbotters confirm what I'm seeing on the data bus? Looks like there's a hell of a lot of Red Hammers incoming from the east!

TACBATT Leader, Mustang Leader confirms your evaluation! Black Hawk Leader reports about a hundred Red Hammers! Dyani reported.

Where are their human troops?

We don't see any on the east side of the airport. The units moving up the west side of the peninsula from Dakar along Rue de Ouakam appear to be motorized infantry riding open-topped trucks.

Is the First Cav on the ground yet?

Affirmative! Rolling out the west gate!

Kitsy knew that the light armored warbot forces of the 1st Cavalry Division would be able to handle the Malitanian motorized infantry units coming up from the southwest. That meant she could concentrate on the eastern front.

Grey Ops, this is TACBATT Leader! I need to get some information to Battleaxe! Kitsy flashed to Russ Frazier up in the airport control tower.

Battleaxe is tangling with the French at the moment.

Then get me a line to Hensley Atkinson or Joan Ward! I've got to coordinate some tactical movements with Wolfer and Cotton! Kitsy had seen that the Malitanian advance on the airport was something more than the Greys could handle alone. Furthermore, if the heavy Malitanian Red Hammer forces continued along their present route, they would cut off the Wolfhounds. Kitsy wanted to swing the Wolfhounds to the left to hit the Red Hammers from the southern flank while the Cottonbalers moved around the enemy's left flank and took them from behind. Kitsy estimated that a hundred Red Hammer warbots might be a sizeable portion of the Malitanian heavy warbot forces, and she wanted to get rid of them if she was presented with the chance. And she thought she was.

Furthermore, since she'd heard nothing on the command nets, she surmised that perhaps the other regiments hadn't seen the massive Red Hammer force or had dismissed it as being trivial.

But Kitsy had surmised incorrectly. She hadn't been plugged into the higher command net before she'd donned the batt commander's helmet. Almost as quickly as she thought a call to Col. Joan Ward, the chief of staff of the Washington Greys contacted her.

TACBATT Leader, this is Grey Chief! Move to the east perimeter with the Mary Anns and Jeeps! Keep the Saucy Cans where they are and continue with your plan to use SADARM and seeker bot rounds! But the Wolfers are going to be in close by the time we engage the Red Hammers! So work from the best target information the birdbots can provide!

I was hoping that someone else besides me had seen those Red Hammers! Roger, Grey Chief, TACBATT Leader understands! Kitsy flashed back with some relief. Russ might be engaged in handling the air ops support, but Joan was still on deck as the regimental second-in-command. Kitsy had staff backup to keep watch on her minus-x. Furthermore, she really hadn't relished the thought that she would have to run the Grey's defense of the airport on her own. It might have meant a gold star on her eval rep if she had, but it might have been a black star too if she'd botched it. And she wasn't about to screw up anything this early in her career. Thus, she was somewhat relieved to be handling something she felt comfortable doing.

Mustang Leader, I want you to continue to provide security on the west side of the runway around the Battleaxe area, Kitsy told the RECONCO commander. *I know that's not your job, but I'm thin on forces to man the east perimeter. ASSAULTCO Alpha Leader, move your unit across the airport and to positions along the east perimeter fence to help handle airport security there. We can't take on a Red Hammer unit unless we kick the hell out of them first with as much firepower as we can put into them. So that's what we'll do!*

Kitsy assumed, of course, that the airport itself had been secured and that no Malitanian elements were left on the field.

In combat, a commander can't assume anything.

And, since she was only an infantry assault company commander not used to handling a full battalion and arranging for tacair cover, she'd forgotten to coordinate the activities of the Harpies swarming over the area.

Twenty-three

"I am sorry, but I cannot immediately conform to your operational plan, General Hettrick." Col. Robert Debas was polite but obstinately firm. "I have my orders from the Ministry of Defense. The Deuxième Regiment de Parachutistes of the Legion Etranger is to proceed into Dakar, liberate anyone in the French embassy, and provide security for them while the Armée de l'Air evacuates them from the Aéroport Dakar."

Maj. Gen. Belinda Hettrick replied to him in English. Colonel Debas had reluctantly agreed to this since the other Operation Bloodbath officers in Hettrick's OCV spoke English better than French. "Colonel, I understand your situation. Orders must be obeyed. But your arrival was unexpected. Welcomed but unexpected. I believe that our two nations can quickly agree to modify your original operations plan."

"Colonel Debas, I've already contacted my superiors in the Pentagon, and the Department of State is already involved," Lt. Gen. Bill Bellamack put in via satellite comm link from his headquarters in Praia on the Cape Verde Islands. "We are quite agreeable to working side by side with you, and I'm sure that your government will agree. May I ask that you instigate a contact with Paris and request the same?"

"I can do that," Debas admitted. "But I do not know if I will. I must make sure that your operations plan is in-

222

deed aimed at freeing foreign nationals from the clutches of the madman Modibo."

"It is," Hettrick assured him.

"Is there no hidden agenda? You appear to have mounted an assault with three entire divisions of troops and warbots," Debas pointed out.

"Hidden agenda? What do you mean, Colonel?" Hettrick wanted to know.

Colonel Debas paused for a moment. He'd worked with the Americans before in western Europe. They were unlike the British who tended to be very polite and affable while keeping their basic ruthless traits under control. Or the Germans who were pedantic to the point of being tiresome and acted like they were the only ones who really understood everything. The Americans always seemed overly friendly in a disengaging sort of way. But Americans also struck Debas as somewhat bumbling adolescents with their youthful enthusiasm, positive outlook on the future, and eagerness to accommodate. Therefore, he hoped he could get away with being frank with them as he had in the past.

"Do you also have a secret plan to oust Modibo from power in Malitania? To place a holding force in Dakar because of its strategic position? In France, we are fully aware of the importance of West Africa. France has maintained a presence here in one manner or another for more than two hundred years. France has an interest still in West Africa. Apparently, so does the United States," Debas went on, trying to choose his words carefully. As with most modern twenty-first century Frenchmen, English was a second language that was part of his elementary education. Because of the Trans-Channel Tunnel, English was spoken in France almost as much as German or Italian. In fact, most educated French people weren't just bilingual; they were multilingual. Most Frenchmen didn't exactly like this. French had once been the universal language of international affairs, but that ended a hundred years before. And the French had missed out on having their tongue accepted as the world language of aerospace. Now Debas found himself in a situation where France had been anticipated again, forcing him to accommodate. "Your military presence here is quite a surprise. I must compliment you on the high level of security and secrecy you have maintained while carrying out the operation. But quite frankly, the strength of armed forces you have introduced into the Dakar area today is a gross overkill. We have determined that a single Regiment de Parachutistes of the Legion Etranger would be sufficient to do the same job."

As her fluency in French slowly returned to her, Hettrick spotted this bit of ego puffery at once. It was very French. But she was going to have to work with this man. And he did indeed command an outstanding fighting force of by-God *regular infantry* supported only by small, light, maneuverable French warbots. She knew Operation Bloodbath might need all the help it could get if the situation really went to slime. So she didn't want to prick the Frenchman's balloon. "A tribute to the gallantry, valor, and fighting ability of the Legion Etranger, Colonel! Now: Concerning hidden agendas, let's dismiss your concern at once. I can speak only from the viewpoint of my orders. The Seventeenth Iron Fist Division is scheduled to ship out of here once the First Cavalry has secured Dakar and the Fiftieth R.U.R. Robot Infantry Division comes ashore. Like your regiment, my division is a highly mobile outfit trained as a shock or assault force. I can't speak for the long-term plans of my government, but we're outta here as quickly as we get our part of the job done."

"And I can speak for the entire Operation Bloodbath," General Bellamack interrupted from his image in the holotank. "My orders are simple: Hold Dakar until diplomatic efforts can reinstate the legitimate government of Senegambia."

"Ah, but that is the plan now!" Debas pointed out. "How can we be certain that it will remain in force?"

"We can't, Colonel," Bellamack stated flatly. He looked like he was right there in the OCV with them. Holographic teleconferencing was so commonplace in the business world that the armed services were able to buy off-the-shelf systems for military use. "Like you, we take the orders given to us by politicians. I can't be certain that the French government will require you to withdraw from Dakar, either."

"Sir! Our national honor is at stake here!"

"I'm well aware of that, Colonel," Curt Carson broke in. He had an idea that might break this log jam that was not only semantic but the result of some basic cultural differences and perceptions. "However, as one regimental commander to another and as a graduate of one national military academy to a graduate of a sister academy in another country, let's be practical about this."

"Ah, practicality! You Americans are certainly practical people!"

"Thank you, sir! You're here. We're here. We have similar if not identical military goals. Therefore, we can either get in each other's way and perhaps even fail to do what we were sent here to do. Or we can work together." Curt paused. "You're familiar with what we Americans call a pie? A sort of bakery item with a crust and a filling?"

Debas nodded. "I greatly enjoy apple pie!"

"So do I," Curt admitted, thinking that one of the shibboleths about the United States was to be "as American as apple pie." "If you have some way to heat pastries, I'll send over some apple pies from our stores. However, do you understand our saying about getting an equal piece of the pie?"

"Of course! I've served alongside American troops in Europe."

"Very well, we have no intention of hogging the whole pie to ourselves here in Dakar. There will be glory enough for everyone if we cooperate and carry out our missions. The pie is big enough for everyone. Let's cooperate as our countries did in Iraq but not as we did not in Namibia," Curt said, trying to put it in simple and familiar terms. "We have only one outfit going into Dakar. The First Cavalry will be moving down the west side of the city because that's the best and quickest route to beautiful downtown Dakar where the government and diplomatic buildings are located. As mobile as you are, if you can move down the east side of the peninsula, we both have a much better chance of forcing the surrender of the Malitanian divisions in the city. And we can do our job with the minimum casualties on both sides."

"What American unit will have the honor of capturing Generalissimo Modibo?"

Curt shrugged. "That doesn't make any difference to us. Modibo isn't our objective. If we could find and capture him, I think we might have cut off the brain from the body. But that isn't necessary to win. He was reported to have come to the airport just about the time our Aerospace Force made its initial strike. But no one can find him or his remains. So we'll proceed with the operational plan. If he shows up, and if we can capture him, we'll do it. Or if you can find him, be our guests and capture him!"

"Will the Deuxième Regiment de Parachutistes be fighting alongside your Washington Greys?"

Curt shook his head. "We have the assignment of sealing off the peninsula to the east to prevent the Malitanians from bringing in reinforcements. You'll be fighting alongside the First Cavalry."

"The First Cavalry Regiment?"

Curt shook his head and continued to stroke the French colonel. Curt didn't give a damn who got the glory. He'd had enough of glory. He just wanted to get the damned job done and take his regiment home. He may have lost Jerry Allen on this one. If so, that was too high a price to pay. If the Greys lost other people, it would just make a bad situation even worse. Curt wasn't afraid to fight any more than Colonel Debas, Rick Salley,

226

Maxie Cashier, or Belinda Hettrick. But he also knew that the first goal of any fighting force is to win with minimum losses. The real and professional objective of armed conflict is to get the other side to quit fighting and do what you want. The days of squalid butchery belonged to the Dark Ages. However, some countries of the world still operated with the kill-em-all Mongolian doctrine. So Curt explained, "No, the First Cavalry Division. As you pointed out a few minutes ago, your regiment of Legionnaires is fully equivalent in fighting power to one of our divisions. Now you will have the opportunity to show that to the world."

Debas looked around, then said, "General Bellamack and General Hettrick, if you agree with Colonel Carson, I believe we have a basis for the closest cooperation. My orders were straightforward. However, I can continue to follow those orders even if I modify my operational plan. My government does not micromanage its field commanders any more than your government does. We learned a great deal from your Viet Nam experience. And we saw how well Desert Storm worked because we were part of it.

"I will contact my minister of defense and inform him that we will be carrying out orders and cooperating with the American forces of Operation Bloodbath. My staff will immediately begin to work with your staff, General. Time is short, and we happen to have gained the initiative by surprise. We cannot afford to lose that advantage by bickering among ourselves. I, too, wish to return to Aubagne as soon as possible. We have enough good wine to last for several days. I hope to complete this mission before we run out because the Senegambian wines are pretentious!"

"Spoken like a loyal French officer, sir!" Curt said with a grin. "We'll run out of hamburgers and beer in a few days ourselves. And if the American fast food franchises in Europe are typical, the ones we find in Dakar won't be any better than you believe their wine to be!"

As the joint Franco-American cooperation meeting moved into a highly cooperative phase, another meeting was taking place at Dakar Airport. This one was deep underground. It wasn't as cooperative as the other one.

"Generalissimo, I've mounted the major attack on the east side of the airport," Colonel Kassem reported. "More than one hundred Red Hammer warbots will strike the perimeter. They will seek a weak spot. Once the warbots have broken through, they will be immediately followed by crack assault troops of your personal Republican Guard. The Guard's primary objective will be to liberate you from the bunker."

"What is your timing, Kassem? When will you be here?" Modibo demanded to know.

"By sunset."

"That's almost nine hours from now! You must accelerate the assault. We could be discovered at any moment. Each minute that goes by increases the probability that some American soldier will stumble onto this bunker," Modibo snapped with irritation. He was still livid over the fact that the Malitanian crew chief had lobbed a frag grenade at some American troops and warbots. That might have compromised the whole situation. Modibo was very much on edge because of that.

"Generalissimo, we cannot proceed rapidly because we have no reconnaissance," Kassem admitted nervously. We don't know where the American forces are located. We don't know their movements. We're fighting blind. So we have to move with caution. Otherwise, the Americans could ambush us. Or outflank us."

"My Air Force has perfectly suitable reconnaissance aircraft! Use them!" Modibo stated.

"Generalissimo, the Americans have achieved air superiority over Dakar. I don't think we could get a reconnaissance aircraft in there without having it intercepted and shot down," Modibo's chief military commander reported with a great deal of hesitation. "We need eyes inside the airport, Your Excellency. We need to have some scouting parties go out from the bunker, find where the Americans are, and report their movements."

Modibo looked around. The five pilots and flight crew members were waiting around the bunker room. They'd armed themselves with rifles and grenades. "I want to retain my men here as my personal guard. If they go to the surface, they'll be spotted immediately! If they're captured, they could reveal my whereabouts when the Americans torture them."

"Americans don't torture prisoners, Generalissimo," said Colonel Pratihara, his East World military advisor who was by his side. "They feed them and give them first-class accommodations instead. This not only makes the Americans feel good about following the Geneva conventions, but it sometimes makes prisoners talk voluntarily because of the good treatment."

"Generalissimo, I desperately need good intelligence data," Kassem continued. "The Air Force people who happened to be in the bunker could pass as Senegalese civilian airport employees and workers. Several hundred of those remain at the airport. They were night shift personnel whose jobs included refuelling aircraft, baggage handling, maintenance activities, and service. I urge you to use them in reconnaissance teams, sir!"

"I don't want them coming and going from the bunker!"

"Your Excellency, most of the telephone service at the airport remains useable. It was installed by American Telephone and Telegraph under contract to the Senegalese government. This system is top of the line equipment," Kassem informed his dictator, who was unaware of most technological factors. He left the details up to people who had been trained in the United States and Europe. Kassem went on to explain what he'd been told by these foreign specialists. "Most of the system uses fiber optic cables. These are buried. The Americans have made no move yet to trace and cut these optical cables."

"So? Explain to me what this technical talk about the

telephone system means!"

"Your reconnaissance teams on the surface can report back to you using any telephone at the airport. You can continue to monitor the reports and pass the information along to me by telephone."

"I see. But can they operate the telephone system?" Modibo recalled the difficulty he'd experienced with the robot telephone system in Dakar when he'd tried to make contact with Kassem a short while before.

"Of course! Your Air Force troops are highly trained and technically literate! If they can fly supersonic Juliet-two-twos, they should be able to operate a telephone, Your Excellency." Kassem recalled that Modibo's experience with soldiers tended to be limited to those he'd brought out of the Sahara with him. Those were technically illiterate Berber tribesmen who could fight like devils but had trouble handling the technology of a knife and fork.

"So you really need the reconnaissance information we could provide from inside the airport?" Modibo asked again, wanting to pin down his military commander.

"Yes, Your Excellency! And the sooner the better! Our Red Hammers are within ten kilometers of the airport at this time!"

"Very well, I'll get reconnaissance teams up on the surface. Stand by. Do not hang up. If we lose this connection, we may not be able to make it again!"

Kassem said nothing. He now had the telephone number for the bunker. The phone was a direct line to the Senegalese Ministry of Transport in downtown Dakar. He could reach Modibo at any time if the fiber optics cable wasn't discovered and severed by the Americans. However, from what he knew right then, the Americans had concentrated on electronic warfare, blocking all the radio frequencies. They hadn't gotten around yet to killing the telephones.

Modibo turned to the Malitanian pilot. "Flight Captain, I want two teams of two men each to get out of uniform, take off all your military identification, find some civilian clothes if you can, and operate up on the ground as scouts. I want you to use the airport telephone system to report back to me. We need to know where the Americans are. We need to know their movements. We must know what kind of equipment they have and how much of it is available to them. Flight Captain, you're in charge of one team. Pick two more men as your second team. Then go do it immediately!"

The flight captain hesitated. A military person operating as a civilian noncombatant out of uniform without identification was a spy. The Geneva conventions said that spies could be shot. The pilot worried about being caught.

But he was far more worried at that point because Modibo had shown no mercy in shooting any dissident in cold blood right there in the bunker.

The pilot was a military man, an aerial warrior who'd been trained in Thailand. He'd been given an order. His personal honor required that he carry it out to the best of his abilities. He had absolutely no thought of getting out the bunker in the guise of a civilian, then simply disappearing and leaving his glorious leader's service. So he saluted smartly and said, "Yes, sir! Right away, sir!"

But he would keep his dog tags in his pocket.

Twenty-four

"I think we of the Garamandes must have something to say about this military plan," Nyamia Lébou suddenly put in. "Unless, of course, you wish to fight the Garamandes as well."

Curt was surprised at this sudden interruption. However, he was immediately aware that the beautiful Nyamia and her Garamandes' partisan organization had been ignored thus far. In the face of an overwhelming foreign military presence, Nyamia's patriotic concerns were certainly understandable. Furthermore, she'd brought them forth in no uncertain words.

"We don't wish to fight you, Nyamia," Hettrick told her. The CO of the 17th Robot Infantry (Special Combat) Regiment was also rather chagrined at having forgotten the stunning Garamandes' leader. Her group of Garamandes partisans would certainly help an otherwise somewhat short manpower situation. Hettrick mentally kicked herself for allowing the military considerations of the moment to overshadow the basic reason why the troops of Operation Bloodbath were in Senegambia. So she replied in a conciliatory manner without being condescending, "You've heard our plan. We're here to get foreign nationals out of Senegambia. We also want to see the legitimate government reinstated. I presumed you shared this goal with us. And that you would work the Garamandes into the plan as you saw fit. In view of your expressed concern, what do you see as your part in this?"

232

"Nothing! I see that you are in our country and intend to save us your way!" Nyamia retorted bluntly. "General, we welcome your help. But we have no intention of standing meekly on the sidelines and allowing foreigners to do the job that we could and should be doing for ourselves!"

"Madame Lébou, may I ask exactly how the Garamandes plan to liberate Senegambia all by themselves?" Bill Bellamack's holotank image wanted to know. He said it in a gentle way that was far from the brusque approach of a military officer. He was somewhat thrown off-balance by the sheer feminine beauty of Nyamia.

"We are prepared to harass the Malitanians until they are forced to retreat!" Nyamia replied proudly.

Bellamack and every other military person in the room knew at once that she might be a valiant warrior. But it was also apparent that she didn't know a damned thing about how to use controlled force and violence in the most effective manner to gain militarily what was impossible diplomatically. Bellamack, Hettrick, Curt, and others had run into other people like her among the Kurds of northern Iraq.

So Bellamack again told her gently, "I have the latest intelligence reports about the size and strength of the Garamandes. Our experts on partisan warfare say you might be able to run the Malitanians out of Senegambia in about six years. Providing, of course, you're not killed or captured."

"We will fight forever if that becomes necessary!"

"Proud words, Nyamia, but are they realistic?" Hettrick posed the question to her. Hettrick knew that the beautiful woman's enthusiasm had outrun her thinking. That wasn't unusual or unwanted in a follower of a cause. But it could be dangerous to the cause if its leaders such as Nyamia weren't thinking any deeper than that. "What will be left of Senegambia in six years? Based on what I've seen in other parts of the world, it'll be overpopulated by Malitanians who've had plenty of time to raise

233

hell. They'll demolish your culture, decimate your Paris of Africa, and complete their genocidal plan."

"And what do you think you can do with foreign military intervention?"

"First, deny Dakar to the enemy, Generalissimo Modibo. That's a prize he desperately wants. Second, draw his army into combat on our terms and then render his military might ineffectual. Third, force him to withdraw from Senegambia because it's too expensive for the East World to continue to subsidize him. We can do that, and we're implementing a UN resolution that your government asked for. We're here and we'll finish what we're ordered to do. What happens after that is up to the United Nations, not us," Bellamack explained patiently. He didn't want to lose the support of the Garamandes. Operation Bloodbath needed the Garamandes as they needed the American and French forces.

"We believe the Garamandes can help," Hettrick added. She wanted to come over a little bit softer and more feminine than Bellamack, who was trying hard. But Hettrick knew they were talking with another woman warrior who might perhaps have hangups. The warrior class in this part of the world was still very male-dominated. On the other hand, Hettrick wanted to project the image that the Americans indeed respected the woman warrior. She wanted to show there was no need for Nyamia to behave so strongly and with such a stubborn and defensive attitude. "The Garamandes can provide us with expert guidance. You know where everything is. You know what's important or trivial. As for us, we have the necessary armed force to put down this bully. I don't think you stand much of a chance of doing it all by yourselves. At the moment, I believe it is in your best interests to cooperate with us. You'll have the final victory, not us. We're going home when this is over. Nyamia, I'm not trying to lecture you. I'm leading up to the crucial question that you must answer:

"What do you bring to the table? What do you throw

in the pot? *Tell us your perceived role here!* And please be realistic about it."

Nyamia's empty left eye socket was hurting terribly just then. It distracted her from the important matter at hand, the confrontation and the need to maintain the rights of the Garamandes. She really wanted the pain to go away. Actually, her eye socket wasn't hurting at all. She was feeling phantom pain in her mind.

With resignation, she sighed and admitted, "The Garamandes will cooperate with your plan . . . for now. I'll arrange for you to be told what forces we have and where they are. But we want to be in the vanguard of the force that liberates Dakar."

"We're on our way already," Hettrick admitted. "The Garamandes really shouldn't be involved in that sort of lethal operation anyway. Urban fighting is nasty. It could wipe out your partisan forces. The Garamandes are far more valuable to the operation as intelligence sources. If you want to fight the Malitanians, the way to do it effectively without incurring unacceptable losses is to bushwack the invaders out in the field."

"Bushwack? What's that?"

"American term. Means ambushing," Curt explained. "We learned a lot about that in the Viet Nam War. We were on the receiving end of it during that fracas. We forgot what we'd learned during the Indian Wars."

"We need to know now, Nyamia. We have units deploying. We have units about to be engaged by Malitanian forces. What is your answer? We don't want to fight the Garamandes, too. We're not here to do that," Hettrick said firmly, basically asking for a go-no-go.

Nyamia looked at her companions who'd remained quiet during the briefing and her confrontation with the Americans. Nyamia was the leader. The Garamandes met to decide strategies, but she was the one who fronted for the partisan organization. This leadership management method was common among people who had little experience running large groups. Léon Keita, Georges Damas, and Sundiata Linguére sent subtle body language messages of agreement.

Dyani read that language, and she communicated her assessment silently with her eyes to Curt. So it was no surprise to him when Nyamia replied, "We'll need communications with you so such operations can be coordinated."

Tacomms were supposedly classified. But the Greys had given them to partisan helpers before. Some of the tacomm bricks hadn't come back. Harriet Dearborn had dutifully marked them as "expended in combat." Knowing how the frequency-hop tacomms worked and how to make them were two different problems. No one had yet managed to duplicate the incredibly complex system of interlinked hardware and software inside a tacomm.

"No problem," Hettrick responded.

"And we will want to be represented at all times in your headquarters operation."

"Again, no problem," Hettrick admitted. "We'll want you and your top people working directly with our top people all the time."

"Very well, let's stop talking and run those Malitanian butchers out of our country!" Nyamia said viciously. There was no doubt in anyone's mind that she intended to make someone atone for the loss of her eye, even though her eye patch would make her absolutely unmistakable in the fashion world when this war was over.

Hettrick extended her hand to Nyamia who took it. "Done!" Hettrick exclaimed, then added, "And I want our bio-techs to look at your eye wound, Nyamia."

"Our Garamandes' medical chief, Doctor Mermoz, has taken care of it," Nyamia replied.

"That's good, but we have trauma specialists in our bio-tech units. They can help you, because I suspect it's painful."

This took Nyamia aback. "How did you know?"

"My dear, I have fought with and led gallant young men and lovely young ladies during my military career,"

Hettrick explained. "I've seen them severely wounded. I've been wounded myself. It hurts like hell. It always does, no matter how good modern medicine may be. And it affects one's personality and approach to problem-solving. Even a minor wound will do that. Please let my doctors have a look at it."

Nyamia suddenly softened. Curt noticed it first. He'd always been attracted by beautiful ladies, and Nyamia was certainly one of those. Nyamia relaxed from her hard, unyielding, formal, and adversarial attitude, one which she obviously believed was expected of a resistance leader. She'd read the books about the French *Maquis* of World War II, and they had unconsciously colored her expectations and responses. "It does hurt, but a leader isn't supposed to be affected by it."

"Merde!" Hettrick said softly. "It hurts. It hurts badly enough to fill your whole universe. You can think of nothing else. Even men cry when they're wounded. The idea that women can bear pain better than men is another pile of *merde*. Colonel Carson, will you ask one of your staff to take Nyamia to the Grey's bio-tech van, please? Doctor Gydesen is probably the best trauma surgeon we've got . . ."

"I'll be honored to do it myself, General," Curt volunteered. "I want to talk to Doctor Ruth about Jerry Allen anyway."

"Give whatever orders you need to issue, Nyamia, and my people will work closely with yours," Hettrick assured her.

The partisan leader revealed that she and her associates weren't totally unprepared for the job ahead of them when she replied, "That's not necessary. The mechanisms are already in place. The Garamandes know what to do. We have worked through several scenarios. We're prepared to handle any of them, but I'm pleased that we will work with a positive one."

As Curt left Hettrick's divisional OCV with Nyamia, he found himself accompanied by Capt. Dyani Motega and the chaplain of the Washington Greys, Maj. Nelson Crile. The sun was rising higher in the sky now, and the temperature and humidity were rising with it. However, situated as it was on the Cape Verde Peninsula, Dakar was favored by fresh breezes which moderated the tropical heat.

"You sure the Mustangs don't require your attention, Captain?" Curt asked Dyani. He wasn't worried that she might be tagging along because Nyamia was such an attractive woman. Dyani didn't have to worry on that score, and she treated competition quite differently than many other women. She and Curt were a pair. They both knew it. She didn't have to walk with the group in the open from the divisional OCV to the Greys' bio-tech vehicles. So Curt really had her welfare in mind when he went on with the observation, "I really don't require an escort."

Dyani merely touched the barrel of the Novia assault rifle she carried. "The airport isn't secure yet, Colonel. We're still encountering a few snipers. And in this sort of combat environment, firepower can be helpful in the crunch."

Nyamia looked closely at Dyani with her good right eye and remarked, "Captain, you don't look like a typical American."

Dyani returned her look and replied, "I don't know what a typical American looks like, but I'm more than typical. My ancestors were original Americans."

"Oh," was all that Nyamia could say. She didn't know whether the subject of race was as sensitive in America now as it still was in parts of Senegambia, and she didn't want to touch any raw cultural nerves.

It was Maj. Nellie Crile who stepped into the situation at this point by observing, "We're a very diverse people, Madame Lébou. Even Dyani's remote ancestors came from somewhere else, perhaps from Asia across the Bering Strait in the dawn of time. Most of the rest of us came westward across the ocean from Europe and this part of Africa. We're a nation of different people. However, we've learned how to appreciate people for their differences in appearance and even their religions."

"God, what a great ideal! And we were almost there before Modibo wrenched us back to the old days!" Nyamia said with more than a touch of sadness in her voice.

"You mentioned the Deity but not in the Muslim manner," Crile noted as they walked. He was trying to make conversation, hoping to take Nyamia's mind off her injury. "It is my understanding that most Senegambians are Muslim."

Nyamia didn't shake her head. That hurt when she did it. "I grew up in Dakar in the artistic community. I was educated in Paris. I converted to Catholicism in a cathedral no less grand than Notre Dame itself!"

"Well, then perhaps I can be of help and solace to you," Crile told her. "I graduated from Notre Dame, but that's a university in America! I'm prepared to serve the spiritual needs of the regiment. I can even act as an imam if necessary, although I've not been called upon to serve as such."

Nyamia turned to look at Crile with her good eye as the group walked. It was apparent that she was greatly relieved for some reason. She suddenly asked, "Father, when the American army doctors have looked at me, would you hear my confession, please? It has been a long time. Many things have happened. I have had no opportunity lately. And I'm very concerned about facing death without having confessed my sins recently."

"I am available to you at your convenience, Madame," Crile told her.

Curt decided that this beautiful woman was very complex indeed. But he had discovered that the world was full of interesting and complex people.

Capt. Denise Logan and Lt. Bill Molde took Nyamia into one of the M660E Bio-tech Support Vehicles to look at her wound. Nellie Crile went with her. Curt and

Dyani went looking for Maj. Ruth Gydesen. They didn't find her. Instead, they found Capt. Helen Devlin, the chief nurse, as she stepped out of one of the vehicles. Helen stripped off her surgical mask as she stretched. When she saw Curt and Dyani, she walked over to them. It was obvious from her expression that she wasn't happy.

"Colonel, I know you're probably here to ask about Major Allen," Helen said as she walked up to them.

Curt didn't waste any time. "How is he?"

Devlin shook her head. She knew that Maj. Jerry Allen was a close friend and Curt's protégé and she didn't like what she had to tell him. "He'll live, Colonel. We got him stabilized, thanks to the quick response of that new bio-tech, Marla Metford. We're still taking shrapnel out of him." She hesitated.

"How bad?" Curt asked the next question, fearing the answer.

"We'll save his left leg. It's torn up, but it can be rebuilt. The shards went right through his body armor . . ." Helen had been one of the nurses who'd prepped the wounded man. She was an experienced bio-tech, one of the first to have made the conversion from helping warbot brainies go in and out of linkage to a full-fledged registered nurse capable of handling the sort of combat wounds experienced by Sierra Charlies. The Washington Greys had not only written the book on how to put human infantry troops back in the field alongside warbots. In the process, they'd also rediscovered combat medicine and applied modern biotechnology to it. Warbot brainies of the Robot Infantry rarely were wounded; Sierra Charlies could and had been badly wounded or killed.

Curt detected Helen's hesitation. "And . . . ?" He pressed her.

"We may not be able to save his left arm," Helen blurted out suddenly in a burst of emotion uncharacteristic of a nurse.

"What? Can you explain?"

240

"The force of the mine explosion and the violence of the fragment impacts must have been enormous . . . His left arm would have been blown off if it hadn't been held on by his body armor. We can try—and we are trying—to save it. Normally, we could reattach a severed limb; that's a routine procedure. But the arm was badly broken up." Helen sighed. "Colonel, we're doing our best."

"I know you are," Curt told her.

"We need to get Major Allen out of here on the next available aerodyne. This is clearly beyond our regimental field bio-tech capabilities," Helen went on.

"I'll have Russ hold an outbound aerodyne," Curt assured her, sick at heart to hear this news. "Tell Major Gydesen to contact Russ directly to arrange for the transfer. Will she want anyone to go with him?"

"Yes. I'd recommend Shelley Hale from GUNCO. We can't afford to strip personnel out of our field unit here, and either Ginny Bowles or Marla Metford can cover for her." Helen tried to change the subject. "I hope you've got those engineers looking for more of those AP mines . . ."

"They haven't found any yet," Dyani revealed. "You might let me know when you can release the fragments to Major Hermann. His engineering ordnance experts may be able to look at them and identify the type of mine they came from. It would give us all a better idea of what to look out for."

"I'll do that. Right now, I've had my breath of fresh air and life. Got to go back. The doctors need all the help they can get right now," the chief nurse said as she pulled her surgical mask over her lower face. She didn't touch either of them; she was maintaining sterility protocol. She turned, slipped her elbow into the door latch, rolled it open, and disappeared into the bio-tech van.

Curt looked down at Dyani. He knew why she had come along. She and Adonica Sweet were "sisters" in the regiment. In spite of the gender equality of the twenty-first century U.S. Army, male bonding of "buddies" and

241

female bonding of "sisters" took place in addition to mixed gender bonding such as existed between Curt and Dyani. "Are you going to tell Adonica?"

Dyani shook her head. "At the right time. A scout always reports truthfully. But it's not necessary for a scout to report everything. Especially that information which isn't important at the moment."

"Are you afraid Adonica will go ballistic?"

"Would you? Have you?"

"If it were you instead of Jerry, I think I know what I'd do. We spent a lot of time working on that problem, didn't we?" Curt recalled. "But maybe I'll never know until it happens, and I don't want it to happen. As for Adonica, she's strong. But is she strong enough?"

Dyani nodded. "Adonica and I have learned a lot from each other. When she's told, I think she'll take a few minutes of private time. Then she'll go ahead and do her job. But how about you, Colonel?" She looked up at him and didn't need to say anything more. Dyani talked with her eyes.

"I . . . I'll take a few minutes of private time right now, then I'll go ahead and do my job," he admitted, his voice husky with emotion.

"I'm here if you need me," Dyani told him. "And we may have only a few minutes."

Curt didn't get even a few minutes.

Col. Joan Ward's tacomm voice sounded inside his head, *Grey Head. this is Grey Chief! We've got a major Malitanian assault shaping right now in the east as well as on the northeast side of the airport!*

Twenty-five

Curt switched at once to neuroelectronic tacomm because it was a faster way to communicate. *Grey Chief, this is Grey Head! Give me a sit-rep!* He took off at a run for his regimental OCV parked to the north of the terminal building.

It wasn't necessary for him to tell Dyani what to do. She already knew. It was her job to hold the unattacked west gate using her SCOUT platoon under Lt. Harlan Saunders while coordinating the reconnaissance activities being carried out aloft by Dale Brown's birdbot platoon.

Looks like the Malitanians are trying to pin us down with concentrated Red Hammer fire around the east gate while they bring their foot infantry in from the northeast. Joan Ward replied. *The sit is on the bus.*

I see it! How's Kitsy handling it?

She's called in the Saucy Cans for support against the Red Hammers. Seventy-five mike-mikes do a better job with less fuss than the five-three mike-mikes on the Red Hammers. The SADARM rounds are working great! Problem is to find targets. The Red Hammers are belching smoke.

So?

It's infrared blocking smoke! Also blocking laser.

Aha! Leave it to the Chinese to come up with interesting pyrotechnics! Millimeter radars working?

Affirmative! But we haven't got a lot of them! The Jeeps are doing the best job of penetrating the smoke with their radar.

Grey Ops, this is Grey Head! Can you see any better up there?

Curt asked his S-3 operations staffer who was still in the Dakar air traffic control tower.

Negatory! Smoke is drifting this way. And it stinks! No windows left in the tower, by the way, Russ Frazier reported.

Roger! Grey Ops, get out of there and return to the OCV! You're a target where you are! Grey Chief, have Grey Tech patch best quality data stream over to me. Activate Bucephalus and my trike. Kitsy may need some help. Curt was using that as an excuse. He wanted to be where the action was. He never was a commander who liked to sit on top of the hill and issue orders to his troops in the battle below. Furthermore, with Jerry now out of this fight—and maybe future ones as well if his arm couldn't be saved—he didn't want Kitsy to buy the farm either. And she would need a lot of help from now on because his competition for the next regimental commander was over. At least for right now.

As he double-timed toward the OCV, his fleeting thought involved the possibility of trying to groom Russ Frazier as well. He had learned the hard way to "always have Plan B," even if he never intended to use it. He knew that Russ would have some real problems becoming a regimental commander. The man had neither the education or background for it. It would be an uphill fight for Russ all the way.

Waiting for Curt at his OCV was the M33 Jeep, code-named Bucephalus after Alexander the Great's horse. That was no accident because the Jeep occasionally was about as bullheaded as the Macedonian steed's name implied. Edie had tinkered with the circuit cubes to get the Jeep to follow some of Curt's commands as well as following him physically on the battlefield. Jeeps normally lead the way because of the Sierra Charlie doctrine in which warbots precede humans in the assault.

Bucephalus was mounted up in the PTV's sidecar.

Without hesitation, Curt cranked up the trike and took off across the runway area. He checked for runway crossing clearance with the air ops control people the Aerospace Force had finally gotten on the ground.

He encountered two civilians making their way on foot westward across the field. He stopped the trike in front of them. "What were you doing on the east side of the field?" Curt wanted to know.

"Colonel, we were trapped in the hangar," one of them told him in strangely accented but good English. "We were told by an American sergeant to go to the west side of the field, sir!"

"Take off! Get out of here! And keep your heads down! Get under cover and out of the way! We're still fighting for this airport!" Curt told them with a wave of his hand toward the terminal building.

"Yes, Colonel!"

More Senegambian civilians caught in the melee of war, Curt told himself. Kitsy must have found them and sent them to an area that would be safe for noncombatants. He dismissed them from his mind because of something he saw on the military ramp ahead of him.

A major ground action was taking place on the east side of the airport. However, six AC-40C Harpies of Cal Worsham's TACAIR squadron were sitting on the ground.

Grey Air, this is Grey Head!

Grey Air here! Go! Cal Worsham's tacomm voice replied. It lacked some of the gravel-like quality of Worsham's verbal voice, but even the man's neuroelectronic messages "sounded" like him.

Are you out of fuel? Why are your Harpies on the ground?

No call for tacair support. The furball quieted down, so we squatted here, got refueled, and are standing ready to lift when TACBATT Leader calls for us to expend ordnance on someone!

TACBATT Leader hasn't called for tacair yet? Curt could hardly believe it. According to his helmet tac display and what he actually heard from the east side of the field about five hundred meters away, a raging battle was in progress.

That's an affirmative, Grey Head!

Hell, Cal, can't you hear the goddamned battle?

Damned right! But I ain't putting my Harpies up there where

245

they can take the Golden BB from a brush fire fight if Kitsy doesn't call for support!

Spool up and stand by! Curt told him, jumping several levels of command. Then he called, *TACBATT Leader, this is Grey Head!*

TACBATT Leader here! Go ahead!

How goes the fight? Give me a sit rep, please.

The Hellcats and the Puma Mary Anns are holding them around the gate area. We're on the left flank with all the rest of the available Mary Anns and all the Jeeps. The left flank operation hasn't opened fire yet. We're taking incoming small arms, but I'd rather they waste their ammo at long range. We'll commence firing when they're within five hundred meters, Kitsy replied, even her tacomm "voice" reflecting the excitement and adrenalin flow of combat.

TACBATT Leader, this is Grey Head. I thought you believed in the doctrine that anything worth doing is worth overdoing.

Sir? It is! I think! What am I not doing that I should be overdoing?

You've got six flying pillboxes sitting on the ramp here with six hot Harpy pilots eager to expend ordnance. Are you holding them in reserve for some reason?

Curt's question was answered by five seconds of silence, then: *Oh shit! Pardon me, Colonel, but I flat forgot about tacair!*

Why? Curt wanted to know.

Because we went through such a flap in the Papa and Oscar briefs about air cover, 'dyne combat radiuses, and that sort of thing. I guess I unconsciously wrote off air support as being unavailable! Call it heat of battle, I guess! Kitsy sounded contrite. *Forgot part of my force. Just like McClellan at Antietam! Colonel, do you want me to step down from command because I'm incompetent?*

Negatory! Negatory! Every commander in history has had a bad day from time to time. Others have forgotten things. So get your sweet ass in gear, Major, and correct the mistake as quickly as you can! Curt advised her. He could have done it easily. It was only a tacomm call to Cal Worsham. But Curt wanted Kitsy to do it. His role was one of back-stopping

246

her by coordinating with the other regiments and with Hettrick. And keeping her from making too many mistakes.

Kitsy didn't waste time. *Grey Air this is TACBATT Leader! How many Harpies can you get up. I need tacair on the east and northeast sides of the airport!*

Wondered when your call would come, TACBATT Leader! I've got six Harpies and can arrange for ten more from my compatriots in the Wolfhowls and Cottonballs.

I need them all! I want to bust the back of this Malitanian two-pronged assault. You see it on your tac display?

Affirmative!

Take out the Red Hammers at the gate first! Watch out for Calcutta Cutters!

Rog! Anyone stupid enough to shoot one at us ain't gonna live very much longer! Red Hammers are easy. You want us to go after the target-rich environment on the left flank next?

Affirmative! Those are very soft targets, Grey Air.

Best kind!

Curt checked his tac display again. The Harpies were spooling up for lift behind him. He could hear the firing on the left where the Mary Anns, Jeeps, and Sierra Charlies were firing from behind the perimeter fence. The fence made a perfect tactical barrier against assaulting infantry. At the east gate, the Red Hammers were themselves being hammered by the SADARM rounds from the Saucy Cans plus anti-armor rounds from the Mary Anns.

It was a prolonged fight. Curt was surprised. He watched the ebb and flow of enemy forces. Something didn't seem right.

Damn, he didn't like being in the defensive mode. But the Greys had led the assault at dawn. Modern combat is intense and highly stressful. It can wear out a unit in a few hours. So now the Greys needed to stand aside and let the fresher troops of the Wolfhounds and Cottonbalers carry out the next phase of Operation Bloodbath.

He could find no enemy recce. Yet the Malitanians looked like they were operating as if they had excellent intelligence data on where the various elements of the Washington Greys were located. The enemy moved in quick response to probes against the defenses of the Washington Greys. It also appeared that the Malitanians in the airport fracas were well aware of other Bloodbath tactical elements both at Dakar Airport itself and on the road to Dakar.

New Malitanian units were joining the fight from the east, threatening to take the Wolfhounds on the right flank. But the Malitanian forces maneuvering with the Wolfhounds behaved differently. They were probing the Wolfhound deployment, unsure of what was where. Meanwhile, the Wolfhounds moved with the confidence of a regimental commander who has birdbots aloft and a good SCOUT unit on the ground. Rick Salley's Wolfhounds were outmaneuvering the Malitanians.

So were Maxie Cashier's Cottonbalers. In fact, even without plugging into the inter-regimental tacomm net, Curt could see from the tac display that Rick and Maxie were coordinating their efforts so they could take on the Malitanians in the Pinkine area on their own terms, not those of the enemy.

The Malitanians at the airport, however, were apparently ignoring their minus-x. Their assault could be cut off from the northeast along the north shore of the peninsula once the Wolfhounds and Cottonbalers dispatched their opponents and swung left. The Malitanians didn't seem to care. They moved against Curt and his regiment with uncanny skill.

It could only mean that Curt was up against an enemy with outstanding recce.

But where the hell were they getting their inside information?

The Malitanians had no birdbots up. They had no scouting parties probing here and there, only strike forces. Those strike forces were mobile and moving. They were trying to maneuver and find a soft spot while their Red Hammers held down part of the Grey forces.

That sort of recce could come only from an inside

source in Curt's minus-x on the airport, he decided.

How?

Who?

Where were they?

How had the Greys missed them?

Grey Tech, this is Grey Head! Edie, do you detect any enemy activity in the e-m spectrum?

Negatory, Grey Head. We've got ECM all over them like a wet blanket. We're opening time-phased holes only for tacomm, and those are millisecond holes that don't last long enough for them to do anything with them!

An assumption! Check those holes when we're not in them.

Yessir! A pause, then: *Negatory!*

What the hell? Are the Malitanians using carrier pigeons like we had to in Trinidad? Curt wondered and allowed his thought to get into the tacomm net.

Edie picked up on it. *Negatory, Grey Head, or we'd see them on millimeter radar!*

Runners, then?

What's the technical problem, Grey Head? Maybe I can look for the signature if I know who's doing what. Master Sgt. Edie Sampson had been with Curt and the Greys for a long time. Sometimes she could almost read her regimental commander's mind. This was one of these times, but she had the good sense not to out-guess him.

The Malitanian force on the east side of the airport acts like it's operating with outstanding recce. They don't have birdbots. I don't see recce teams on the ground. We've air supremacy, so it isn't coming from a high-flying RPV. So it's coming from inside the airport itself. If so where the hell are they? And how are they getting the information out?

We've ruled out radio or tacomm. I don't see the side lobes of any satellite dishes on the airport; those sets are down. There's enough smoke and haze that we'd see the beams from lasercomm. We've eliminated carrier pigeons and runners. Edie stopped for a moment, then observed, *Colonel, we're missing something.*

Telephones?

No chance. The gear I've got here will pick the radiation from a twisted pair or a cable. I'm getting nothing there,

Edie reported.

Curt allowed his thoughts to get onto the tacomm channel with Edie. The free flow of information between him and his chief techie was important at this point. It could turn up an answer. *When you've eliminated everything that you think is possible, and if the problem is still there, it means you've overlooked something obvious . . .*

Speak for yourself, Colonel . . .

I am. What are we overlooking? And let's not take forever to answer that question!

Maybe we should ask ourselves who is doing it. That might lead to how they're doing it.

Curt had a flash of inspiration. *Grey Person, this is Grey Head!* he called to Maj. Pappy Gratton, the regimental adjutant.

Grey Person here. G-A, Grey Head!

You're keeping track of all the Senegambian civilians at the airport plus the few Malitianian prisoners we took, right?

Affirmative! That's my job! I've set up a data base in Grady. They've all shown me their i-d cards or drivers' licenses. This was a standard procedure now when the Greys occupied an area in which civilians were present. Too many times in the past, governments had complained after the war that civilians had been brutalized, tortured, slain, or otherwise treated with disregard for the Geneva conventions. In the twenty-first century army, the task of keeping close track of noncombatants and prisoners alike had been given to the unit adjutant who already had a personnel data base up and running.

What are they doing? Where are they?

Doing their jobs or hunkering down in the terminal waiting to be let off the airport so they can go home. Most of them are scared shitless because of fire fight going on over where you are.

Check everyone out! One of them may be spooking on us, Curt told him, then checked back with Sampson. *Edie, any of the SERVEBATT people on the ground here yet?*

Negatory! What do you need, Colonel?

Someone to make sure the airport telephone system is disabled. We could have missed something. Hell, I'm sure we did miss something!

I can do it!

No, you're up to your armpits in alligators already! Whose available who knows a telephone line from a sewer pipe?

No one! We're spread as thin as meat in a BX hamburger!

You're right! Okay, we'll have to leave it to Pappy, Curt decided. There wasn't time, and he didn't have enough people. This seemed to be the story of his life when it came to running a regiment in combat. *Grey Person, this is Grey Head! As you're checking out the civilians, see if you can find the main telephone system equipment room. You ought to be able to tell from status lights and other indicators there if the system is in use. Can you hack it?*

Grey Head, Grey Person is no tech nerd. But I've debugged enough networks in my time to be reasonably familiar with telephone systems, Pappy Gratton admitted.

Do it and report to me when you've done it. I've got to get back to business here. I've got a battle to supervise. And according to Army policy, every job needs a supervisor! Curt turned his attention again to the combat situation.

In the few seconds it had taken to carry on the tacomm conversation with Edie and Pappy, Curt hadn't lost situational awareness. He saw that the Malitanian infantry was still probing for weak points in the perimeter. Kitsy wasn't giving them any slack. Mikawa and Power were providing Sierra Charlie cover for Hall's Hellcats. The Stilettos and the Assassins were holding the perimeter line. It looked like a turkey shoot because the Malitanians were taking equipment losses and casualties. But they had reserves. They could bring up more Red Hammers and more infantry cannon fodder. Curt was stuck with what he had on the ground, and he'd been short-handed and short-botted to start with.

Furthermore, the Greys were in a defensive mode, and Curt didn't like to be on the defensive. The Washington Greys were an aggressive outfit, trained and experienced in offensive operations.

He wanted to see if it might be possible to break out.

TACBATT Leader, this is Grey Head! Any chance that either

the Pumas or the Cougars could find a weak point and start cutting the Malitanians?

Grey Head, I'm looking for such a soft spot. I haven't found it yet! Tacair is helping a lot. But I've just got to let these Malitanian bastards wear themselves out against our defenses. Once we've let them take losses attacking, I can convert this tactical defensive into a strategic offense like Moltke did. But we aren't at that point yet!

Kitsy had indeed been studying military history, Curt decided. He'd gently scolded her in Yemen about that. Jerry Allen had been a wiz at it with his encyclopedic memory—Damn! Why did Jerry have to go get wounded?—but Kitsy was a little slower to appreciate the perspective and insights offered by military history. Once he'd suggested she study a little bit, Kitsy attacked it with her usual dauntless energy.

Our losses are mostly equipment thus far, Kitsy went on. *We can let the Malitanians bust their asses against us for a long time yet.*

I don't want to wait long before going on the offensive, TAC-BATT Leader, Curt advised her. *Offensive action is essential to positive combat results! In the War for Southern Independence, as you like to call it, the Confederacy never broke out of its basic defensive posture. I didn't think you inherited that tendency, TAC-BATT Leader!*

No, suh! Ah didn't! Mah grandma was a damn Yankee, remember? she replied in a mock Southern drawl. Kitsy might be in the heat of battle, but she hadn't lost her sense of humor or the perspective that came with it.

Then she suddenly exclaimed, *Yeah! Yeah! Great! Grey Head, we've got help outside the perimeter fence! Look at what's started to happen on the enemy right flank!*

Twenty-six

The new spots on Curt's helmet tac display weren't beacon returns. They were smudges. That's the way Grady and Georgie interpreted non-beacon radar, lidar, i-r, or chemical signatures that hadn't been assigned tags by regimental or division ops.

Any make on those new elements, TACBATT Leader? Curt quickly asked. *Who the hell are they?*

Some of Sierra Charlies have visuals only on them. Reported to be irregulars. Partisans. Non-uniformed.

Garamandes! Curt guessed.

Who?

Senegambian partisans, Curt explained. *Do not fire into them. Repeat: Do not fire into them. Let me get a clarification from Battleaxe.*

He quickly toggled over to the Iron Fist channel. *Battleaxe, Grey Head. What are those targets on our left flank, bearing zero-two-zero, range about three hundred meters? No beacons showing. Looks like something Georgie just put up. Who are they? What are they? Do you know their intentions?*

Grey Head, Iron Fist Ops. The new targets are Garamandes. They decided to take on the Malitanians on your left flank, was the reply from Col. Hensley Atkinson.

That's what I thought! Why wasn't I informed?

Because we were just informed on tacomm the one-eyed queen's military commander, Fulani.

They've got to do better than that next time! If the furball gets hot and confused, they could be greased by friendly fire!

253

Grey Head, bitch to Battleaxe. Or to Bloodbath. The partisans are not under our direct command. You were there. They're pretty damned independent, and this is their country!

Yeah, but it's our blood. I thought I left the one-eyed queen with Grey Bio . . .

You did. But she's in tacomm contact with her forces from there.

Okay, never mind. We'll work with them. We'll have to. Grey Head out! He switched channels and told Kitsy.

Grey Head, I acted on your hunch, Kitsy reported. *We're turning the Malitanians! Can we get the engineers up here to blow a hole in the perimeter fence real quick like? I want to stay hot on the tails of the Malitanians once they start to run.*

Roger, I'll alert the engineers now. But I want you to turn right in a wheeling maneuver. Then you can hit the left flank of the Malitanian warbot force being pinned down at the east gate. Let the Garamandes chase the Malitanian force. The partisans know the neighborhood. We don't. And I don't want us to get caught up in the nooks and crannies of the suburban jumble out there. My prime short-term goal is to clear this airport furball once and for all. And quickly. We've got to move to the north beaches where we're supposed to be. We've got to seal off Dakar and keep more Malitanians from pouring in on us. Curt didn't want half his regiment to go charging off into the suburban environment east of the airport. He didn't want to split his meager forces. He couldn't afford to. He knew how desperately short of people and warbots they were until the First Cav and the Foreign Legion took Dakar. Then those units could move out to the neck of the peninsula to add to the defensive wall and secure Dakar harbor. Once the 50th RI showed up, the job of the Greys was over. Curt would be happy to let someone else stand guard on the free world for a change.

He put in a call to Iron Fist and requested a demolition company from the 132nd Engineers to come forward. They were needed to take down thirty meters of the stout perimeter security fence with high explosives so Kitsy's forces could go through.

As he finished making that request, two tacomm calls came through to him simultaneously. Bedlam raged in his head as two tacomm voices spoke at once.

Calling Grey Head: one at a time! Tacomm protocol, please! You're stepping all over each other! he blasted out when the two call-ins stopped talking.

Grey Head, Grey Person here! It was Maj. Pappy Gratton, the regimental adjutant.

Grey Head. Grey Bio here! Maj. Ruth Gydesen identified herself.

Curt made the priority decision. *Grey Bio, stand by. Grey Person, go ahead!*

I found the main airport telephone equipment room in the basement of the terminal, Gratton told him dispassionately. *Wasn't hard. Kept following the signs even though I don't read French worth a damn. I'm in the terminal room now. And I've got some interesting news.*

Tell me, Grey Person.

This is good old Phillips-Siemens gear. I had to use the same sort of equipment to network our computers in Europe while we were there. Some places at the airport are linked with an internal set of fiber optics cables . . .

"So that's why Edie couldn't pick up any electromagnetic radiation from telephone lines or cables!" Curt said to himself, keeping it off the tacomm. Both Edie and he had completely neglected to think of the old low-tech fiber optics that had tied together many telephones over the last fifty years. In the heat and confusion of combat, they'd thought only of the obvious: telephone wires. Their high-tech, twenty-first century orientation had caused them to forget about fiber optics.

Pappy went on as he examined the terminal room, *I see a fiber optics circuit that's hot from the terminal to the east side of the field. The phone in use here is a public one on the observation desk on the north side of the terminal. I think I'll go and check it out. And there's another active fiber optics cable outbound from the airport to Dakar. The indicators tell me that someone or something is talking on it to Dakar.*

Can you find out who's saying what to whom? Curt asked.

Negatory, Grey Head. I don't have any telephone test equipment here to find out who's saying what to whom.

Can you disable them?

Are you sure that's what you want. Grey Head? I wouldn't want to screw this up by cutting them off. That might give away the fact that we're now on to whatever they're doing. Which appears to be simple. Someone here is doing visual recce from the terminal, then reporting it to some other higher command here on the field. That someone else probably survived the air strike.

It was all making some sense at last to Curt. He speculated to Pappy, *Could be Malefactor himself. If so, he's relaying the information to Dakar. It's coming back up the line to the Malitanian troops outside the airport. So their commander is playing games with us because he's got combat intelligence we didn't know about. Sounds like you've got a winner, Grey Person!*

Grey Head, after a dozen years or more, I've learned something about combat myself! I suggest TACBATT Leader start looking for something over on the east side of the airport where someone could be hiding. I'll check out the terminal here. I may need help.

Call when you do. I'll get on the other matter. That matter attended to, Curt cleared the air and announced, *Okay, Grey Head is clear of Grey Person! Who else was calling Grey Head?*

Grey Head, Grey Bio here! It was Dr. Ruth Gydesen.

How's Alleycat Leader? Curt was very concerned about Jerry, but he hadn't had a lot of time to think about his junior officer in the past few minutes.

He'll live, and I'll talk to you about that later, the regimental medical officer replied. *Another matter here that you should know of immediately. The metal we took out of Alleycat Leader had embossed markings on some of the pieces. And it looked like they'd shattered in a distinct pattern along definite break lines. The pieces also have a sharp curve to them. I've never seen shrapnel like this before.*

What the hell are they? Have you shown them to an ordnance expert?

I try to anticipate what my regimental commander wants, Grey

Head. I called Major Hermann of the engineer battalion. He dropped by the van to have a look at them. He just left in a hurry to take care of some work for you. But he got enough of a look to identify the pieces. He tells me they didn't come from any East World mine he knows about. And he's an expert in this area. He has to find and blow up enemy mines. And handle other kinds of unexploded ordnance that didn't go bang and hurt people. He says the pieces came from a Chinese Mark Nine fragmentation grenade!

More pieces of the puzzle suddenly began to fall into place for Curt. *Thank you, Grey Bio! Your information is very important! Now, how's Alleycat Leader?*

Too early yet to tell. He's stable. He'll live. I think he'll walk on his leg again. But he may lose the arm. I can't tell at this point. He needs immediate high speed evac to a stateside hospital. But he's out of this fracas for sure.

She really didn't want to tell him more than that at this time. She wasn't an expert in some areas of reconstructive biotechnology. So she hesitated to speculate and thus raise Curt's hopes. She knew her regimental commander well. She didn't want to create any emotional baggage that might interfere with his ability to fight the regiment in this present difficult tactical situation.

I was afraid that's what you'd tell me, Grey Bio. And that you might not tell me everything you think. But we'll talk about that later. Thanks for your efforts. And thanks for trying to do what would keep me tactially high and tight. Grey Head out! He, too, knew Ruth Gydesen and the way she behaved. It was difficult to keep personal secrets from one another in the Washington Greys. And it was even more difficult to do so when a doctor-patient relationship existed. Ruth looked upon all the Greys as her patients. She had their physical records and gave them their regular physical checks. From time to time she'd had them under her care for sickness and injuries.

Curt jumped levels of command because of the situation. He needed an answer to a question. *Grey Head direct to Bio-tech Sgt. Marla Metford. Acknowledge!*

Sergeant Metford here!

Sergeant, do you remember the exact location where Alleycat Leader was wounded?

Affirmative, sir! Between the two hangars!

Could you lead someone back to that spot?

Affirmative!

TACBATT Leader, Grey Head here!

G-A. Grey Head! Kitsy shot back. *You on to something, I hope?*

I've got a hunch we've been blindsided, Curt informed her and went on to explain, *Can you detach a couple of Sierra Charlies and Jeeps from the east gate area? Turn about their front, and send them back with Bio-tech Metford to the spot where Alleycat Leader was whanged. Have them check for hidey holes around there. Maybe a bunker. Be prepared to encounter Malefactor.*

You've found him?

No, but you may. That's what I want your detachment to do: Look for him. Gratton just found a fiber optics link between the terminal to someplace on the field, and another outbound fiber optics cable to Dakar that's active. At the moment, he's looking for a couple of Malitanians in the terminal.

I'll detach the Stilettos for the job on the east side.

Give Adonica specific orders. If she encounters Malefactor, she is not, repeat not, to kill him in spite of what happened.

I'll do that, Grey Head.

Events were rapidly coming to a head here because Gratton suddenly called in, *Grey Head, Grey Person! Need help! Need help now!*

Okay, Pappy, Grey Head here. Say where, and how much!

Grey Person found two civilians, one on a public telephone near the terminal observation deck, the other on the deck observing. They ran when I approached to ask for i-d! I've got them trapped on the north wing roof. Need assistance to detain them.

Pappy Gratton knew he wasn't in any dire difficulty. At least not at the moment. But he could be. He was armed with a Novia, as were all Greys. However, the adjutant didn't have an RPC 11E as a combat Sierra Charlie.

He'd fought in the past, and would do so when the occasion demanded it. Like right then. But he apparently didn't want to shoot the two civilians he'd apprehended.

And he wasn't sure they were Senegambians like all the other civilians that had the misfortune to be at work at the airport when Operation Bloodbath landed. This part of Africa had a mixture of racial types. They ranged from negroes to Berbers with all skin colors and physical features in between. It was difficult to tell a Senegambian from a Malitanian without some sort of identification document.

Curt didn't want to distract Kitsy from the intense furball she was involved in. Kitsy was making progress. She was winning. So he decided to jump command structure again. He quickly tacommed back, *Roger! Pappy, keep them covered but don't shoot to kill. Whoever those two are, maybe they'll talk if they're alive when we take them. Mustang Leader, answer Grey Head!*

Mustang Leader here! You want me to help Pappy? Dyani replied.

Affirmative!

Roger! Pappy, I'm coming up with Sid Johnnie. Scout Leader, take over on the west gate, Dyani snapped a series of replies and orders.

Make it so, Deer Arrow! Curt told her.

That's what we're doing!

Curt decided that Kitsy had the tactical picture well enough in hand that he could swing south on his trike and join up with Sweet's Stilettos. He intercepted them as they were proceeding westbound toward the hangar line.

Stiletto Leader, Grey Head coming with you. Just in case you need another pair of eyes, Curt told her.

Thank you, Grey Head. Any help is welcome on a search and destroy mission, Adonica Sweet's tacomm voice replied.

Curt was glad he'd made that decision. *Captain Sweet, your mission is to seek and find. You will not destroy. If we run into Malefactor, we'll try to take him alive. Is that fully understood?*

Adonica didn't immediately reply.

Adonica, Curt told her in a personal manner, *we don't know whether or not it was Malefactor who tossed the frag grenade at Jerry.*

Is that what it was? A frag?

Doctor Ruth told me that the engineer boss identified the fragments as coming from such.

Oh.

And we don't know that Malefactor is here at all. Just speculation. Could just be some Malitanian soldiers who got trapped here during the air strike.

If they're military and if they shoot at us, they're fair game, Colonel.

That may be true. But in any event, the orders are to take Malefactor alive if he's around, Curt reminded her. *Understood?*

Affirmative! Understood! What do we look for?

Someplace that someone could be hiding. Like an underground bunker. I suspect that's the case because I also suspect that the two Malitanians discovered by Pappy in the terminal were reporting by telephone to someone over here who can't see out. That someone was then reporting our movements to someone else in Dakar who was in turn passing the information along to the forces on the east side of the airport, Curt tried to reconstruct what he thought had been taking place.

There's Metford! Adonica pointed out. *Damned brave to be standing out there with the chance that a metal jacket could come buzzing her way.*

Brave like a puppy, was Curt's appraisal. Some new medics thought that the red cross on the white tabard was automatic protection against being shot at. But Curt knew from experience that some enemy armies used the red cross on the tabard as an aiming point. He made a mental note to have a chat with Ruth and maybe with Metford about that.

Stiletto Leader, this is Puma Bio-tech. Metford made contact. *I just got here, and I don't see structure left above ground within range of someone throwing a frag grenade. But I do see what appears to be an old ammo bunker of some sort with a ramp leading into it.*

As Adonica, Platoon Sgt. Charley Koslowski, and Sgt. Paul Tullis joined her, Medford went on, *I'm standing just about where Alleycat Leader was when I found him. That ramp over there is only about seven meters away. It's well within throwing range.*

Curt and Bucephalus joined the group which also included two Jeeps. Adonica had left her Mary Anns at the northeast fight where their firepower was needed. *Don't bunch up,* he warned.

We won't. Who wants to volunteer to go down that ramp and try that rusty old door at the bottom? Adonica asked her platoon members.

Dammit, Adonica, take a few precautions first! Curt admonished her. *If it's a bunker, it has to have ventilation. Let's find the ventilators. And anywhere that utility services could come into it.*

If someone is down in the bunker, we need to go in there and get him out, she replied firmly.

No, only as a last resort! First let's see if we can do something to drive him out into the open. Don't try to go down in that rabbit hole first. He may have deadly defenses set up. Make him come out, Curt advised.

Got any ideas? Adonica wanted to know.

Her NCOs did.

Find a vent and drop a frag down it. Charley Koslowski suggested.

Tullis took a small canister off his equipment belt. *Druther drop a smoker down there instead. Or fire a Smart Fart down there and hope it rattles around inside a bit before it bangs.*

Find some above ground vents or other facilities. I'll station my Jeep to watch the entrance ramp, Adonica ordered.

Curt was relieved. Adonica was thinking straight again. At least for the moment. He knew she was a very complex person. For some reason, she was a vicious warrior. Her wholesome beauty caused many people to overlook that. He didn't know what had triggered in her mind now that Jerry had been so badly wounded. He suspected that she would be very vindictive. On the other hand, he wasn't at all certain what Dyani had taught her about self-control. Certainly, Adonica had managed to toggle very quickly right then from action orientation to a condition of searching for non-lethal alternatives.

For almost ten minutes, the group poked around the area of the bunker ramp. It was an old bunker, perhaps dating back to the days of World War II when Dakar was a primary strategic spot, as it still was. Some of the Stilettos were familiar with the ancient facilities and fixtures that were similar to many they'd encountered around an even older military installation, the regiment's home at Fort Huachuca in Arizona.

We do have a ventilation shaft here, Koslowski finally reported. *The chem sensors on my Jeep are detecting human smells.*

Are they new smells? Adonica asked.

Yeah. Not essence de la locker room stuff. Unwashed armpits. Fear stink. Farts. And a decaying body. Koslowski didn't mince his words.

Can you get a smoke grenade down the pipe to the bottom?

I just got the rain hood off and I'm checking . . . sorta carefully, I might add. I don't want to get a face full of metal jackets. Could ruin my whole day. Okay, I can see about thirty meters straight down to a metal grill that appears to be in the ceiling of a room. Maybe I drop a fragger down first to take out the grill, then follow it with a smoker.

Any other vents?

Yes, ma'am. Over here. Another one. Can't see the bottom. But it's probably an air intake. Seems to be sucking air, was the report from Tullis.

Roger! Okay, on my command, Paul, you drop a fragger down the intake and follow it with a smoker, Adonica told him. *Charley, you stand by to do the same thing when Paul's fragger takes out the intake fan on his vent. I don't want your smoke to come back up an exhaust vent to haunt us without doing a job down there inside first. In the meantime, let's deploy our Jeeps to cover the ramp. Colonel, I can indeed use your help on the ramp.*

I'm right with you, Adonica, Curt told her. He began to move with Bucephalus to the head of the bunker's sloping entrance ramp.

But they didn't get the chance to carry out the tactical action against whoever was in the bunker.

All hell broke loose to the east of them.

Twenty-seven

TACBATT Leader, Puma Leader here! I can't hold my position! We're taking incredible incoming! came the tacomm voice of Capt. Lew Pagan. *Looks like a Malitanian regiment of battle tanks hitting the east gate! Kitsy, for God's sake swing south and give us some help!*

Curt saw it too. The new Malitanian force on his tac display was still untagged because it hadn't been identified yet. When he dropped his gaze from the visor display, he could also see the new battle development with his eyes.

Four hundred meters east at the gate, multiple hulking targets appeared through the clouds of smoke and dust kicked up by combat.

They were indeed main battle tanks. It didn't make any difference whether they were manned or robotic. Curt didn't care. They were large, heavily armored, and heavily gunned. And they were attacking. That's what mattered.

As Curt watched, one of the Pumas launched an M100A Smart Fart rocket at the nearest tank. It hit the armored glacis with the dull explosion of its penetrating warhead. But instead of the shaped charge blowing a hole through which the secondary penetrator projectile could enter, the explosive force of the warhead was somehow absorbed or dissipated by the tank's armor.

The oncoming tracked vehicle didn't even hesitate.

Its turret cannon—it looked like a long-barrel 125 millimeter gun—erupted flame. A Puma Mary Ann ceased to exist in a flaring cloud of smoke and fire.

It ran over a SADARM mine which jolted it but didn't stop its oncoming grinding progress.

Main battle tanks? What the hell? A battle tank is a museum piece! Kitsy reacted.

No! The Chinese still build them! These are Type Six-Forties! They're supposed to be the latest! Capt. Hassan Ben Mahmud put in quickly. He was a student of armaments, and he had a memory that wouldn't quit.

How the hell did the Malitanians get them? was Kitsy's amazed response.

I'm just a Sierra Charlie, not a spook! Ask me a question I might be able to answer! Hassan replied, obviously under a lot of pressure from the sudden onslaught. *Hey, look, don't waste any more Smart Farts on them! They can't be stopped from the front with the Em-one-hundred's penetration capability! And they're top armored. A SADARM will stop one only if the penetrator goes through an engine intake! Larry, you might try armor-piercing seven-five mike-mike rounds into them.*

Hell, Hassan, they've just taken out two of my Saucy Cans on the first salvo! We fire and they counter fire on us. But here goes!

Why the hell are the Malitanians mounting such a strong assault against the airport all of a sudden? Lew Pagan asked rhetorically.

I don't know, Curt responded. But in the back of his mind he suspected that it might be a Modibo rescue mission. The dictator might be in the bunker the Stilettos had been about to flush. It looked like that operation would have to be suspended. The Chinese armor was coming forward quickly.

He and the Stilettos would have to get the hell out of there fast.

In fact, he knew he would have to put the Greys into

a resilient defense mode. If the Greys and their warbots tried to hold firm, the Malitanian main battle tank assault would shatter them like brittle glass. If the Greys responded with elasticity and let the tank force go through them, they would have the chance to remain effective and counterattack from the flanks of the salient.

Curt knew that the resilient defense was the only tactical move possible when he saw a Saucy Cans AT round bounce off the front of another Chinese tank.

The heaviest guns of the Washington Greys were ineffective against the frontal armor of the Type 640s.

The NIA, DIA, and Iron Fist G-2 would have to reevaluate their intelligence data about the Type 640. But that was for the next conflict. These Type 640s were at his throat. He had to work with what he had.

Which meant that he'd have to take tactical command immediately. Kitsy was two kilometers to the north. Lew Pagan might not be able to hack it alone. The staff was on the other side of the airport. Curt was on the spot. He had to act.

So he snapped, *Puma Leader, reverse your front and back off to your right! Let the Malitanian tanks through! Attack them from the side and rear. Try for their running gear rather than their frontal armor. And keep the Red Hammers engaged! The Red Hammers are thin-skinned. But back off NOW!*

Retreat, hell!

Pagan, you'd damned well better retreat as I ordered you. If you don't, you'll get creamed! And if you survive without pulling back because of some miracle, better count on another miracle later because you'll need both. You'll have to deal with me after this is over! Go to the resilient tactical defense! Get the hell out of the way of those tanks! You can't stop them in a frontal assault! Try to take them from the sides or rear! Dammit, don't waste yourself or anyone else! We've already had too much wasted! Curt was sharp and quick with his response. He usually didn't talk to his subordinates that way. But this was tight combat. He didn't have time to play Colonel

Nice Guy. And he knew Lew Pagan's penchant for the assault rather than a fall-back withdrawal.

Trying to stand and fight against this sudden heavy armored attack was suicidal. Maybe the First Cav could handle it. The First Cav was elsewhere right then. As a Sierra Charlie outfit primarily trained for maximum mobility and shock, the Greys weren't prepared to come up against heavy armor.

Somehow, the Malitanians knew that. Curt suspected that the man in the bunker, probably Modibo, knew that. If Modibo wasn't running the military operation from the bunker, then perhaps one of his military advisors who might be with him was calling the shots. Modibo wasn't renowned for his military brilliance or knowledge of military equipment. He was a nomad whose approach to war was one of fitting modern weapons into the ancient niches reserved for horses, chariots, lances, pikes, arrows, and swords. Sometimes that worked, but not against a modern warbot or Sierra Charlie adversary.

Curt needed to conserve his forces and create mass and facilitate mobility. If the Greys couldn't stand up against heavy armor, they could go around it and cut it off. Or let it go by and then take it from the flank. The old verity of combat was still valid: "Seek the flanks!"

TACBATT Leader, Grey Head! Can you disengage and let the Garamandes handle the Malitanian infantry up there? Curt asked, realizing that he would have to move some units around fast to counter this strange new threat at the east gate.

TACBATT Leader here! What's going on down there by the east gate? Kitsy broke in.

Armor assault, heavy tanks! Answer my first question!

We can break it off here! The engineers haven't done their job on the fence yet!

Are the engineers there?

Affirmative!

Bring them with you! They may get the chance to kill some tanks with HE. Shag down here and position yourself on the north flank of the Malitanian attack salient! We're going to let the Malitanians in! Then we'll try to cut them off and force them to fight going out, too! How are you fixed for Smart Farts?

We have some!

Good! Be prepared to use them, but not straight against the armor on the glacis plate. Go for the running gear or sensor mounts! Curt instructed her, then warned, *And don't fire into the Pumas. They're on the south side of the salient!*

We're on our way. ETA three minutes!

Curt then called for his air support, *Grey Air, Grey Head! Are you upstairs?*

Roger! We're here!

Can you hit these tanks coming through the east gate?

Yeah, but we got only Smart Farts and two-five mike-mikes! If a seven-five mike-mike won't scratch them, the best we can do is worry them! Or make them mad at us, Cal Worsham admitted. *I'd rather go for the tail. They're trailing some armored personnel carriers and . . . Oh, shit! They've got quad fifties! Harriers, Grey Air here! Paul, keep your Harpies the hell and gone clear of those quad fifties!*

Roger! We see that! Let's spook them with weasel tactics!

Cal, what the hell are you seeing? Curt wanted to know.

Behind the Six-Forties are some Hindustani quad fifty forward air defense guns mounted in light armored vehicles! Those suckers can hurt us real bad out to two thousand meters! We've got to stand back out of their range and hack at them with Smart Farts!

The Hellcats will lay Saucy Cans on them! Larry Hall volunteered. *If we can't hurt the Six-forties, we can sure as hell make life miserable for the lighter stuff that could give you heartburn, Grey Air! Can you play FAC and give me a target designation on the quad fifties, please?*

Curt was more than a little concerned by the abrupt

change in the situation. Why had the intelligence people fucked up so badly?

Neither Bloodbath or Iron Fist G-2 had indicated that the Malitanians had Chinese Type 640 tanks. Maybe they didn't have many of them. Maybe Curt was seeing nearly all they had. That made little difference right then. The Malitanians had them and were using them.

The armored strike had come as a complete surprise. Curt tried to figure out how they'd done it without G-2 or surveillance satellites finding it. Why hadn't Dale Brown's birdbot recce seen the tanks?

Either Modibo's forces had parked the tanks out in the suburban Dakar area nearby, or they'd managed to camouflage them as something else.

He would find out about that in the post-action debriefs. Right than, it was up to him to come up with a tactical plan to minimize his own losses against such a formidable array of weaponry while trying to stop them from attaining their mission goal, whatever that was. Curt thought he knew. All the pieces of the puzzle were now there.

Generalissimo Modibo *had* to be in that hidden underground bunker! The bunker entrance was reasonably close to the military ramp that had been demolished by the initial air assault. Modibo's limousine had been totalled along with some of his personal retinue. Curt guessed that the dictator had managed to make it into the bunker. He didn't know how many people were in there with the man, but it couldn't be many. They'd sat there quietly during the initial phases of the Dakar airport assault, working with above-ground scouts reporting in by fiber optical telephone. The information on the Bloodbath deployments and actions had then been passed along to someone in Dakar. The armored assault had undoubtedly been set up to rescue Modibo.

In the face of such offensive power, Curt knew he could do nothing but give way. A solid defense was impossible. A resilient one might work. He didn't know where the soft spots on the Type 640 were. No one in the intel community had gotten that much information on these vehicles.

The battle tank was almost a museum piece in the twenty-first century. Air- and ground-launched anti-tank guided missiles had spelled the effective end of heavy armor as a battlefield weapon. Even the Soviets had given up trying to make their heavy tanks impervious to armor-piercing ordnance. That said a great deal about anti-tank technology because the Soviets had been enamored of tanks for over a century.

Why had the East World resurrected the heavy tank, Curt wondered? Then it became clear why they had. With the emergence of the war robot on the battlefield and the disappearance of the heavy tank which required too much armor to stave off anti-tank missiles, powerful and expensive anti-tank weapons had also disappeared from military inventories. If you don't need them, you won't get funding for them.

That was going to change as a result of Dakar, Curt guessed.

Greys all, this is Grey Head! Listen up real good! Those of you involved in this Malitanian armored assault on the east gate, take cover and adopt a low profile, he told his people. Then he went on to explain what he had in mind. He knew if he told the Greys what to do, they would figure out how to do it. And they would surprise everyone in the process. They were professionals. He could count on them. However, he also knew he had to keep the big picture in mind. *These tanks are unstoppable from the front with what we've got. So let them through us and concentrate on the light-skinned quad-fifty air defense gear and APVs. I know this isn't our way of fighting, but we have no recourse. Why are the Malitanians making this irrational assault? I think Malefactor is in an underground bunker about four hundred meters inside the gate. The tanks are probably the shock force intended to*

270

break through to him. They may ring the bunker entrance which I'm marking on your displays. Modibo will probably climb into an APV. Then it's my guess that the force will retreat out the gate again. So keep a cool stool here. Don't be a hero. Grey Air may be able to cut them so they bleed if we can take out the quad fifties with Smart Farts and Saucy Cans. Questions?

Negatory from TACBATT Leader!

Okay, TACBATT Leader, make it so! Curt told her, stepping out of the line of direct command over the tactical battalion at that point.

Grey Head, Mustang Leader! Can we help?

Yes! Stay where you are and do what you're doing! Curt told Dyani.

You might need the manpower.

Negatory! You're covering our minus-x!

It doesn't need covering! The west side of the peninsula has been scrubbed clean from Pointe des Almadies down to Fann, Dyani reported.

Okay, Mustang Leader, circle around via the perimeter fence to the south. Don't try to cross the runway! It might get deadly out there in a few minutes, Curt said, giving in. She was right. He could use all the firepower he could get. Furthermore, Dyani's SCOUT platoon was fast and stealthy when it moved.

But she'd brought up the fact that Curt should check in with Battleaxe about all this. The Wolfhounds and Cottonbalers were moving away from the airport to the east, and the Malitanian armored assault had effectively gotten in behind them. Maybe they could turn their front and hit the Malitanians from the rear. It might be a possibility if the Wolfhounds and Cottonbalers weren't already engaging the enemy.

Battleaxe, Grey Head here. We've got serious trouble on the east side of the airport, Curt called in.

I've been watching, Grey Head, Gen. Belinda Hettrick snapped back. *What do you need?*

About a dozen old Em-Three Tee-Dee heavy warbots to tangle

271

with these tanks.

Get serious! The Fiftieth Division won't even have those when it comes ashore!

I was serious, but never mind. Can you ask the First Cav to send some of their heavier stuff back? Maybe they can cut off this Malitanian force before it gets to the autoroute up the east side of Dakar. The reason I ask is that we probably can't stop this Malitanian force.

Stop them on their way eastbound? You mean they're not trying to dislodge us from the airport?

I don't think so, and I'll tell you why. Curt went on to explain what was going on and his hypothesis that the armored force was intended to rescue Modibo.

I take it that you want to capture or kill Modibo? Hettrick asked.

Affirmative! If we can cut the brain off from the body, this fracas will be over in hours!

I know. That's standard campaign doctrine. Okay, go ahead and try it. Keep me informed. If I'm not on the horn here, let Wilkinson know. Or Atkinson. I'm going to have the Wolfers stop and hold in the area of Parc de Hann. And I'll swing the Cottonbalers south to provide reinforcements for the Wolfhounds. If you can hold the armored assault and keep them from crossing the airport, or if they're really here to rescue Modibo, then our best bet is to hit them very hard on the way out. They'll be tired. They'll have sustained some losses. And they'll have expended ammo. So you've got your work cut out for you, Grey Head.

In other words, Battleaxe, the Greys will be the ones that bust them down to size and cause them to shoot a lot of stuff at us, Curt observed.

You've got it straight, Grey Head! Stop them, turn them, and burn them. Preferably before they do it to you, Hettrick confirmed. Then she went on, *I hope to hell you can do it because we don't have anything left over here on the west side of the airport to serve as your reserves.*

Maybe I ought to have better sense than to ask Churchill's

272

question: *'Où est la masse de manoeuvre?'* *Where are the reserves?* Curt said glumly.

Right! I'd have to give you the same answer Churchill got: *'Aucune.'* *There are none.* After a short pause, Hettrick added, *Curt, you and the Greys are going to have to stop them yourselves!*

Twenty-eight

The heavy tank hadn't appeared on a battlefield in more than a quarter of a century. Faced with a nearly invincible enemy weapon, Curt found that his thinking processes were strangely focused.

He had a few minutes to think. Four Malitanian tanks rolled past his Sierra Charlies without trying to seek them or their warbots out as targets. It was obvious the armored force was on a dedicated mission. Killing Sierra Charlies and destroying warbots were apparently of secondary importance.

Curt decided that these damned tanks *had* to be vulnerable somewhere, somehow! Every weapon had its soft spot. Tanks had been driven from the battlefield because of anti-tank ordnance. Ever more effective armor piercing warheads had won the race against ever more effective armor. Now that anti-warbot warheads were puny in comparison to old anti-armor warheads, the Chinese had resurrected the tank.

Curt asked himself, *Where is its armor thinnest?*

Could the Greys get at a Type 640 tank where it was most vulnerable?

Other than the M100A Smart Fart rockets, what was the most dangerous anti-tank weapon they had?

If the explosive charge in a 75mm Saucy Cans round wasn't enough, how much explosive was required to damage one of those Type 640s?

The idea of explosives drew Curt's attention to the fact

that the 132nd Combat Engineers Battalion was attached now to TACBATT. The engineers had explosives with them. They'd been asked to knock down the sturdy perimeter fence. But the situation had changed and that was no longer required. Could their explosives do the job of knocking out the Type 640 tanks?

TACBATT Leader, where is the engine batt? he asked Kitsy by tacomm.

Right with me, Grey Head!

Is Engine Leader equipped with tacomm?

Affirmative!

Get him on the channel with me! And you stay plugged in, too!

Roger!

Grey Head, Engine Leader here, came the new voice of Maj. Richard Hermann. Curt didn't know the man. The 132nd Engineer Battalion had come along with the Greys at the last moment prior to departing the ZI. *Do you need something blown up over here. sir?*

That response was heartening. *A tank. Preferably several. Chinese Six-forties. Can you hack it?*

Yes, sir! I see the humpers! Big! Anyone know how much they weigh? How much armor do they carry and where? the engineer officer responded.

Hassan? Curt asked.

Engine Leader, this is Assassin Leader. The best guess on the Six-forty's weight is about fifty tonnes. according to the Armor Journal, Hassan fired back, calling upon his knowledge of modern armaments. *No one knows what the armor is. But I just saw seven-five mike-mike shells bounce off one. I'd say it has to carry about two hundred millimeters of Dinas composite layered armor on the front and the turret.*

Thanks, Assassin Leader, Hermann replied easily in a laid back fashion. *Sounds like a Six-forty may only have about fifteen to twenty millimeters on the belly, then. Otherwise, it would be too damned heavy. Where are the engine intakes? Top, sides, or rear?*

Don't know, Engine Leader.

Okay, we'll just have to go by guess. Means a bigger fireball, that's all.

Engine Leader, this is Grey Head. Mind telling what you have in mind?

Yes, sir. We brought along some alky and some Em-Nine thickener. Jellied alky does a nice job on a heavy wire security fence if you place it right. And just for the hell of it because we may be called on to blow a bridge or move some rocks, we've also got a lot of det cord and Comp H. And an OCV loaded with hundred liter drums. And some drum rollers. Hermann explained, using engineer terminology that Curt wasn't familiar with.

It had been almost twenty years since Curt had studied military engineering and ordnance expediency at West Point. Technology had forged ahead some since then. Combat engineers attached to divisions used a lot of manipulative warbots that were military mods of civilian robots. The Washington Greys had never worked with combat engineers. The sort of high mobility warfare developed by the Sierra Charlies nominally didn't require such support as heavy facilities destruction. Curt knew what explosives Hermann referred to, and he knew about alcohol and thickeners. But what Hermann was thinking of doing with all of this remained a great mystery to him at that moment.

Curt told Hermann this.

Hermann went on easily, *I think we can brew some mobile rolling mines loaded with HE and some full of jellied alky. We'll do a little log rolling exercise. Get them under the Six-forties where they're thin-skinned. Try to put out a big and persistent fireball that will get sucked into their engines. You want us to try for the lighter vehicles, too?*

Engine Leader, if you can whang those Six-forties real hard. I think we can get the APVs with Smart Farts.

Well, Grey Head, sometimes the Smart Farts won't cut it, either. I think we can whip up a Gorbachev Cocktail or two for them.

What the hell is that? Talk tactical, Engine Leader.

Sorry, sir. Some of your slang is kind of strange to us warbot jockeys, too. It's sort of a super Molotov Cocktail, Grey Head. Plastic MRE container full of jellied alky. Don't worry. We'll educate your Sierra Charlies on ways to do a real nasty job of blowing up things here shortly. Uh, Grey Head, you might want to warn your people. We may singe your eyebrows or burn your i-r sensors. But we'll let you know when we get ready to blow.

Curt suddenly got the feeling that they might be able to win this one, thanks to the help of the 132nd Engineers. Hermann and his batt seemed to be crazies. Curt had met a few explosives experts who were slightly nuts, and engineers often had the tendency to be even more so. Part of their job, in addition to building things, was to blow things up. To really be a good engineer, it probably helped to be into fire and smoke for kicks. Curt also knew that the combat engineers weren't pure warbot brainies. They used NE warbots when they had to in order to handle some heavy construction tasks and dangerous explosives work. However, they were in many ways like Sierra Charlies: They got their pink bodies out of the linkage vans and did a lot of the explosives work by hand.

Go to it, Engine Leader. And stay in tacomm contact now, please. We've never worked with you before, so it's important that each of us knows what the other is doing. Otherwise, this could turn into a big sheep screw.

Roger, Grey Head! Right now would be a real good time to pop smoke on them. Not much to start with, but enough to try to confuse them.

Negatory, Engine Leader! Hold the smoke! We'll want a lot of it once they turn around and start out again. That's when we'll need to confuse them.

And that's when we'll roll some barrels under them, too.

TACBATT Leader, try to take out those three quad fifty vehicles now. The Harriers need to begin working over the tanks and APVs, Curt told Kitsy.

Roger, Grey Head! We want to put our Smart Farts right up their rear ends and hit them with some Saucy Cans, too. Larry is

277

*about ready to fire. Says he's got good ranging direct on them!
Give us a few more seconds here!*

Coordinate it with the tacair!

*Roger! We're doing that! We'll both hit them about the same
time! Stand by!*

Curt had allowed the Type 640s and their tail of
lighter vehicles to get well into the airport. Now the
tanks and APVs had started circling around where he
and the Stilettos had been a few minutes before. As he
and Adonica watched from the shelter of some destroyed
vehicles near the undemolished hangar, a barrage of
M100 Smart Farts was launched by the Greys. The
smoke trails converged on the quad fifty air defense vehicles. Then Curt heard the close-in muzzle blasts of the
Saucy Cans guns firing at point-blank range.

Got two of the humpers! came Kitsy's excited call.

*The third one looks like its fire director computer went out. It's
spraying shells all over the sky,* was the report from Harrier
flight commander Paul Hands. *Let it shoot! It'll be out of
ammo in a few seconds! Then we can take it out with ease!*

Which the Harpies of Hands' Harriers did.

They got one of the APVs in the process.

The collection of Malitianian vehicles was partly hidden
in the smoke and dust of the Smart Fart attack. The
maelstrom was thick enough to make difficult the job of
aiming a Novia assault rifle with its laser sights. Curt got
his Novia to his shoulder and tried to draw a bead on
some of the human forms that began to scramble around
among the vehicles. But the laser sight kept telling him
that it couldn't get a range report.

*TACBATT Leader, the Novia sight won't cut the crap out
there! Tell everyone to go to ten shot bursts and put a lot of jackets into that mess! We can't do our usual orgasmic sharpshooting
job, but general fire into the mess may hit a few Malitianians!*
Curt advised her as he switched his Novia to the proper
burst command and started to stroke the trigger.

A ten-round burst from a Novia sounds like someone
tearing a box. The individual muzzle blasts merge into

one loud ripping sound. Three-round bursts were normally used for accuracy because the Novia didn't exhibit any muzzle climb; by the time the rifle reacted to ten rapid firings, the gun had started to climb or waver, and accuracy went to hell. But in this instance, it didn't matter much. The objective was to put fire into those tanks and vehicles for the purpose of making life very difficult out there.

I got some millimeter radar returns on people coming out of a hole in the ground and climbing into tanks and APVs! was the report from Capt. Larry Hall of GUNCO. *You hit two of them.*

Ginny, I want you to get in there as fast as you can after the tanks pull out! Those two may need a bio-tech! Kitsy told her former company bio-tech, Ginny Bowles.

Stop firing Novias into them! Dan Power called out. *Looks like they crawled behind armor now!*

Affirmative on that! Larry Hall confirmed. *Radar returns are gone!*

Stand by for their withdrawal!

Colonel, how did you know they were going to withdraw instead of barge on across the airport and wipe out Battleaxe? Pagan wanted to know.

Because I think they picked up Malefactor! He's probably in one of the tanks!

Which one? If we get it, we could bring this whole operation to a screeching halt! Matsu Mikawa said.

Any one of the four tanks is a prime target, Curt advised.

Suppose Malefactor is in an APV? Dan Power asked.

He isn't. My gut feeling tells me he went for the heaviest armor plate, Hassan guessed. *If he's like most dictators, he went for maximum protection for his skin and to hell with his followers!*

Grey Head, Engine Leader here! We're ready, Colonel.

Fire at will, Engine Leader, Curt told him.

Okay, first we'll pop a little smoke to hide the gate and confuse him a little bit.

Curt saw a battered Jeep—it wasn't exactly like the

Jeeps in the Greys—dash eastward along the road. It began to spew dense white smoke. The smoke was up-sun of the tanks. The combination made it very difficult to see through it. In effect, the tank drivers were suddenly blinded. They could see the asphalt road ahead of them, but the instant the smoke rolled over them, the road effectively disappeared.

Engine Leader here! Guard your eyes and i-r sensor suites!

The explosions that followed were deafening and spectacular.

They lit up the mid-morning surroundings. Some of them looked like fuel-air explosions. Others resembled the gasoline explosions used by Hollywood special effects people to enhance an ordinary explosion, which really isn't very spectacular at all.

The 132nd Combat Engineer Battalion had, in the space of a few minutes, loaded some 100-liter and 25-liter drums with jellied alcohol or Comp H explosive. They'd been laid on their sides so they would roll. Attached to them were small assemblies that looked like bicycle training wheels—except these were powered by batteries and small electric motors. Each also included a cheap and dirty sensor suite and guidance computer.

The drums rolled out on the road under power and positioned themselves under the Type 640 tanks which in turn rolled right over them.

At that point, det cord and other detonators were activated.

The barrels blew up.

Some blew up under the tanks and armored personnel vehicles. The quick-and-dirty mines didn't lift the 640 tanks. They simply blew holes in the soft underbellies.

The rolling drums full of jellied alky erupted in huge, persistent fireballs. Some of the flame was ingested by the engines in the tanks and APVs. They either stopped or blew up.

Jesus Christ! What the hell did you guys do down there? came the surprised call from Cal Worsham. *Goddammit, we were about to roll in on those goddamned tanks! Why the hell didn't you warn us you were going to touch off such fucking big explosions? You coulda killed us!*

Grey Head, Engine Leader. Sorry about that. But we had to take out some pretty big vehicles, Maj. Richard Hermann apologized on the tacomm. *My apologies to your air chief.*

Goddammit, you sure as hell overdid it! Worsham complained.

I'll buy you a drink after this is all over, Major.

Shit, I oughta buy you one! You fucking well did a job on those humpers! was Cal Worsham's respectful if vulgar accolade. Worsham may have been one rough son of a bitch, but he knew professional expertise when he saw it.

TACBATT Leader, this is Assassin Leader! I can see well enough through the crap to spot them bailing out of the tanks! Some of them are armed. Most of them just seem to be trying to save their asses! Some of them are on fire!

We got 'em! We got 'em! Move in on them! Move in on them! Shoot if they shoot. But take them if you can! If their clothing's on fire, help put it out! Kitsy's voice came over the tacomm almost like a full shout. Kitsy always liked spectacular displays. Curt remembered how she'd reacted to that fabulous fireworks display in Brunei many years ago. But this was combat, and Kitsy was really hyped-up now. She was almost too excited to be the sort of cool, calculating battalion commander she should have been. Curt figured he'd maybe better have a talk with her about it later. Much later.

Right then, they'd broken up a major heavy armored assault. If they reacted right and did everything properly, they might take a very important prisoner as a result.

Keep an eye out for Malefactor! He's the one they came in to rescue! Curt told his Sierra Charlies.

Almost simultaneously with Kitsy's order, the surviving Jeeps and Mary Anns of the Washington Greys began moving toward the now burning tanks and APVs. Behind them were the hunched, rapidly moving forms of the Greys, their Novias up and ready to return fire.

It was time Curt joined them. *Bucephalus, move now toward the burning tanks and vehicles. Keep your weapon at the ready. Shoot at any target shooting at you. I will be behind you! Move out!*

Turning to Adonica, he said almost needlessly because she was already up and moving, *Let's go!*

Yessir! Kos! Tullis! Move in! Dammit, I want us to be the ones who take Modibo!

Adonica, remember what I told you! Curt reminded her of his warning about shooting the dictator.

She didn't reply because she was on the run already.

The airport exit road was a mess where the engineer battalion had done the "log rolling job" on the tanks and APVs. All seven vehicles were burning. Behind them at the entrance to the bunker, the quad fifties were either silent or burning. All four Type 640 tanks were on fire, their composite armor melting in some places or blazing in others.

Some of the vehicle crews were rolling on the ground, trying to put out their flaming clothing.

Others were armed. A few shots were fired. The warbots of the Greys responded without hesitation, one round per person being all that was required.

Other former occupants of the tanks and vehicles tried to stumble to their feet, their hands in the air.

A tall, bearded Sikh in a turban that was a dirty and scorched white staggered to his feet as Curt dashed up. "I am all right! I am all right! I am a foreign military advisor! I have my papers! But please help Generalissimo Modibo here! He is badly burned! Help him! Help him, please!"

Twenty-nine

The sunset over the Atlantic Ocean as seen from the Club Méditerranée was spectacular.

"Much better than the sunrise this morning," Kitsy observed.

"I didn't see the sunrise," was Hassan's comment. "I was hunkered down in a Chippie."

"So was I. And scared to boot. That's why today's sunset is much better than the sunrise," Kitsy explained.

"I never thought that a hot shower and clean clothes would feel so good." This had been Lt. Matsu "Mickie" Mikawa's first hot combat mission. She'd led Mikawa's Marauders with unusually aggressive verve. The climax had been her apparently fearless participation in the defeat of the Malitanian tanks and the subsequent capture of Generalissimo Modibo. The campaign seasoned Greys were impressed. Which is why she and Lt. Dan Power, another fresh brown bar, were sitting on the patio of the Club Med with the others that evening. In brief, they'd become part of the extended "family" of the Washington Greys.

The Greys were kicking back and relaxing because Hettrick had withdrawn the regiment from the continuing combat action on the Cape Verde Peninsula. Of the three regiments in the 17th Iron Fist Division, the Greys had taken the heaviest warbot losses and most serious casualties.

Jerry Allen, Charley Koslowski, Lew Pagan, Robert Lee

Garrison, and Jay Taire has suffered wounds of various sorts. They were now in the sick bay that Maj. Ruth Gydesen had set up in the nearby Hilton Meridian Hotel & Casino.

The hotel also held Generalissimo Modibo. The dictator had second degree burns on his hands and some lung damage from inhaling flame and smoke. He'd gotten out of the Type 640 tank just before it blew. The 132nd Combat Engineering Battalion had sent a second rolling mine filled with jellied alcohol under that particular tank. The fireball had ignited turbine fuel leaking as a result of the Comp H rolling mine that had gotten under the tank first.

Colonel Pratihara had survived unhurt but shaken. However, the remaining two Malitanian Air Force pilots who'd gotten out of the bunker had been hit with Novia fire during the tank melee. All were being held as VIP prisoners of war in the hotel. In spite of the fact that no state of declared war existed, only a United Nations' Security Council resolution authorization, the Geneva accords were carefully followed in Operation Bloodbath.

Pratihara was complaining that he should be repatriated at once to India because he was a non-participating non-combatant, a foreign military advisor. But he was still being retained in the hotel so Bellamack's G-2 intelligence staffers could interrogate him.

Thus, the hotel was under heavy guard. That's what the Washington Greys had been assigned to provide. Their planned task of securing the Dakar airport had been successfully completed. And the 50th R.U.R. Robot Infantry Division hadn't shown up yet.

The old Club Med had been commandeered as quarters for the Greys. Actually, this delighted the Club management. As a result of the Malitanian invasion of Senegambia, tourist business had dropped to nothing. The Greys had not only helped save the city of Dakar and its inhabitants from further atrocities, but they had saved the Club Med from economic disaster. The manager now had a suitable contract for housing and feeding not only the Greys but also the 17th Iron Fist Division staff. Hettrick had set up her division headquarters across the road at the hotel.

So the early evening saw those Greys who were not on security duty getting some R&R in the midst of an ongoing armed conflict. They'd done their job and taken their losses. The other two Iron Fist regiments were now in action out on the peninsula.

Col. Curt Carson walked onto the terrace and joined the officers and NCOs watching the sunset. The Greys enjoyed relaxing with sunsets. They all knew there might come a time when a particular sunset might be their last one. And they were grateful that they were able to see this one.

"Colonel, you look whupped," Kitsy observed. She often observed her colonel more closely than other Greys. "Please sit down and take ten. Can we order you a drink? This place has lots and lots of Class Six supplies. Good stuff, too!"

Curt cleared the action of his Novia and leaned it against a palm trunk. It was obvious that he was weary as he slowly shucked his helmet and equipment harness, dropping them carefully to the ground. He withdrew his tacomm brick from the pack and clipped it to his shirt pocket. Then he sat down at the big circular table. "Thanks, I will. But no Class Six stuff for me, please. If I got a shot of ethanol in me right now, I'd probably have to be carried out of here feet first. And I've got work to do yet tonight. We're still not out of the slime."

"How's Jerry?"

"How's Kos?"

"How's Lew?"

"How's Bobby Lee?"

"How's Jay?"

The chorus of questions arose simultaneously from those gathered around the table.

Curt sighed and told them, "Jerry may lose his arm. He's got to be evacked to the States as soon as he can take the trip."

Regimental Sgt. Maj. Henry Kester said something

under his breath.

Curt caught part of it and asked, "Henry?"

Kester shook his head. "I just said that only the good die young, Colonel."

"Ruth doesn't think Jerry will die. But he's pretty badly torn up," Curt told him loudly enough that everyone else could hear it, too.

"What a goddamned waste!" Cal Worsham growled, banging his glass down hard on the table in frustration.

"It may not be a waste, Cal," Kitsy suggested. "Remember the general who lost a leg in Vietnam and went on to command a division in Operation Desert Storm?"

"Who was that, Kitsy?" Curt asked.

"In the condition I'm in tonight, I really don't remember."

"Look it up and report the information to me tomorrow night, Major. The simple answer is left to the student as an exercise," Curt instructed her. Kitsy was learning the hard way that her formal military education hadn't stopped when she graduated from West Point. Curt was pressing on her to continue her studies. He wasn't being chicken-shit and assigning make-work to a subordinate. Kitsy was smart and aggressive, and he knew she would do it.

It was also a necessary assignment. With Jerry Allen possibly out of the running and maybe even out of the army on a medical disability discharge, Kitsy could turn out to be Curt's obvious choice of the officer to recommend as his replacement at some point in the future. He didn't know when that might occur, but he had to have a replacement ready. At that moment, Curt was so weary that he almost wished it could be tomorrow.

But Col. Curt Carson wasn't ready to declare twenty-and-out yet. He was just exhausted right then, and exhaustion distorted his thoughts. He knew he would have to get some sleep that night. Otherwise, he could make a bad decision that would cost lives.

"How's Adonica holding up?" Hassan wanted to know.

"Dyani's with her. They're both over at the temporary hospital in the hotel," Curt reported. "I just came from

286

there. Jerry is in no shape to receive other visitors yet. Adonica is handling it very well. Dyani's helping a lot."

"How about the rest of our casualties?" Nick Gerard pushed for more information.

"Minor contusions and abrasions from taking small arms fire in their body armor. Jay Taire burned his hands trying to clear an automatic loader jam in one of his Saucy Cans."

"Those guns got hot," Edie remarked. "Heavy i-r signatures. Damned good thing the Malitanians either couldn't work their high-tech targeting gear or it was busted."

"All our guns got hot," Dan Power reminded them. "I didn't believe some of the war stories I heard when I came aboard. I do now. I honestly didn't think that combat could be that intense. Or that short."

"Mister Power, the more intense the fight, the shorter it is," Curt advised him. He liked the new man. Power had made his name shine during the day. Power had been where he was supposed to be when he was supposed to be there doing what he was supposed to be doing. And he'd showed surprising initiative. Curt was proud of the Greys but especially proud of the quality of its newcomers. "We like short fights. They create fewer casualties and losses. As for our other injured people, Doctor Ruth tells me everyone except Jerry and Jay should be on duty status within twenty-four hours."

"That's good! We're short-handed enough already. To say nothing about also being short-botted," Nick remarked.

"What's the status on our bot strength, Edie?"

"Lost some Jeeps. Couple of Mary Anns were totaled. Majors Hampton and Otis are on the ground with their units. They'll do an all-nighter to fix up the bots that can be fixed. Some parts can be cannibalized from the totaled bots. We may be short only three Jeeps and four Mary Anns by tomorrow morning," his chief technical sergeant ticked off the elements of her report in succinct terms.

"We need them now that Battleaxe withdrew us and slapped us with this guard detail," Curt said darkly. He didn't like guard duty. He didn't like to be on the defensive. But he knew the military and political battles of the past few years had pulled down the Grey's fighting strength and capabilities. The regiment had gone into Operation Bloodbath short of Sierra Charlies, short of warbots, and short on field experience for the newcomers. The Washington Greys had been on the edge of not being able to fight effectively at all. The fact that they'd done such a spectacular job at the Dakar airport made Curt feel very proud of all of them. He tended to forget that he'd led them and had come up with some of the tactical maneuvers which had allowed them to prevail.

"Being on guard detail is better than continuing to get shot at, Colonel," Henry Kester reminded his chief.

"Henry, you know damned good and well that we could still get shot at on guard duty!" Curt told the old soldier. "The Malitanian high command is still functional. They could attempt a rescue mission to get their Generalissimo back. They tried it earlier today, if you recall."

"Yessir. And we plowed their field when they did it. So we can and will do it again!" Henry said with confidence. He knew the outfit. In fact, he probably ran more of the activities of the Washington Greys than Col. Curt Carson, who was the notional regimental commander. Henry was a wise old soldier. He knew how to anticipate his boss and how to get things done without having to resort to the official, regulation, Army way.

"The Malitanians still have a very strong and powerful military force in being," Curt said. "Their chain of command still exists. Their command and control isn't suffering yet because we didn't have enough time to soften it up before we hit Dakar. And they've got good East World military advisors. The fight isn't over yet. In fact, we may be out of here before it is."

"Jesus, I thought for sure the bastards would cave in without their dictator," Cal Worsham said.

"The Malitanian Army knows Modibo is alive," Hassan told him. "As long as Modibo lives, his followers will nurse the idea that they can rescue him."

"Which is why we've got to stay on our damned toes and

288

not kick back here," Curt snapped, then changed the subject. He'd spent the past few hours working through those problems and scenarios with Hettrick. He needed a break. "Dammit, I'm hungry! And I'll be damned if I'll try to stuff another MRE into my complaining gut! Have they got anything to eat here? Is it any good?"

"Not much in the way of meat and veggies, Colonel," Kitsy said, picking up a huge menu and handing it to him. "The Malitanians came through here yesterday and took all of it they could carry. You were right; this is basically a food war. But there's lots and lots of outstanding seafood. The boats go out every day and come back with real fresh fish and shrimp."

Curt looked at the menu which was in French. He put it down with utter weariness in his bones. He was too tired to try to translate it. "You were right. I'm whupped. Order for me, please."

"You trust me that much?"

"Always."

"Dyani has spoiled you, but for the better."

"Oh? In what ways?"

"Colonel, your macho has changed." Kitsy was treading precariously on very personal ground, so she didn't say more. She signalled for the Senegalese waiter and ordered for her colonel.

"Where's Joan, Russ, and Pappy, Colonel?" Hassan asked when Kitsy was through.

"Where I was just before I came over here to get some chow," Curt told him. "With Iron Fist staff. Putting the final bricks in our wall around Modibo. And figuring out if we could respond to the requests from the Wolfhounds and Cottonbalers for any of our spare warbots we might not need for this guard detail. Don't worry; we're not going to lose our bots. What we've got left, at any rate. We fought off that assault on our gear. All battles don't take place out in the field. We need our warbots. They're excellent for guard duty tasks." Which they were. Warbots never sleep although their power packs eventually go flat after fifty hours or so and must be replaced or recharged. Their sensors can detect people and equipment in the dark whereas humans require night vision equipment. Warbots never slack off; they maintain a constant high state of alert. They're perfect guards. And they are outstanding force multiplier. The Greys might be desperately short of personnel, but one Sierra Charlie could operate up to a dozen warbots in guard mode.

"Any recent sit reps? What's going on out in the real world of war?" Kitsy queried.

"Bloodbath hasn't exactly been a walk-through, troops," Curt told them. "The Cottonbalers and the Wolfhounds are emplaced across the peninsula neck in the Pinkine area. The One-thirty-second Engineers have laid concertina razor wire and put up obstacles to concentrate any Malitanian assaults from the east. The Wolfers and Cottonballs are taking some probing assaults from Malitanians."

"How about the troops in the city? Urban fighting always has a very high pucker factor. Is Bloodbath making any progress without high casualties?" Hassan asked.

"The French Foreign Legion and the First Cav went in to clean out most of Dakar this afternoon. They discovered the Garamandes were pretty much in control already. The Malitanian command had to pull out units to assault the east gate today, and that left things lean for them in the city. The Garamandes have it pretty well secured by now. Yeah, there are a few isolated pockets of resistance left in the city. The Malitanian troops who were left in Dakar this afternoon saw what was happening. They decided to get the hell out before the gate across the peninsula neck slammed shut on them. But they were too eager to grab what loot they could and get out of town before they were cut off," Curt brought them up to date slowly as he began to consume the excellent fish almandine the waiter had brought in response to Kitsy's order.

"So they tarried. And got cut off. And were forced to surrender," Kitsy guessed.

"Or be slaughtered by the Garamandes," Hassan ventured.

"The Malitanians preferred to surrender to the First Cav. Americans are always perceived as being soldiers who fight with little hate," Curt reminded them.

"Yeah, I wouldn't want to surrender to the French Foreign Legion; those are tough bastards. On the other hand, the Garamandes are probably pretty damned pissed off about the way the Malitanians butchered the Senegambians," Nick Gerard observed.

"Sort of a reverse bloodbath," Henry Kester said quietly. "What goes around comes around."

Curt nodded and continued to eat. It was good food. The first good food he'd had since leaving Fort Huachuca. He discovered he needed food. He began to feel better with his belly full. Between bites, he went on, "Right now, the Foreign Legion is policing the city. As you pointed out, Nick, those guys are mean but disciplined. The First Cav is holding the port facilities. General Bellamack and the Operation Bloodbath staff were airlifted in a couple of hours ago and will be set up in Dakar tonight. Nyamia Lébou says the Garamandes will start working on the Malitanian units to the east of Dakar tonight. Talk about a reverse bloodbath, Henry, we haven't seen anything yet. And we can't do a damned thing to stop it because of our ROEs."

His voice was drowned by the roar of an aircraft passing overhead in the darkening sunset sky. "You can hear the airlift in operation. We've got the airport. As soon as the Fiftieth Robot Infantry Division cruises into Dakar harbor in the Navy boats, we'll probably load aboard one of the empty cargo haulers and let the Aerospace Farce fly us home."

"Good! I'm glad this war's practically over," Dan Power guessed.

"Mister Power, you'll learn that armed conflict isn't over until it's over, and sometimes it isn't over. Sometimes you have to either stay on the job or come back and do the job over again because someone screwed up," Curt advised the young officer, recalling in his mind the lessons of military and diplomatic history. "The Franco-Prussian War. World

War One. The German Reunification skirmish. Those three come to mind as examples."

"Yes, sir. History repeats itself," Power agreed.

"Only because we didn't learn the first time, Lieutenant."

"I'm really surprised that the Garamandes allowed us to hold Modibo as a POW," Mickie Mikawa said.

"So am I, Lieutenant."

And he wasn't the only one.

Thirty

Someone was shooting Chinese firecrackers.

Curt came awake enough to realize that what he heard wasn't firecrackers.

It was small arms fire.

That didn't seem right. Curt was still in a state of semi-exhaustion. He couldn't manage to make sense out of it as he slowly tried to come fully awake through the physical exhaustion that still gripped him.

An explosion rocked the room. The large arcadia glass doors leading out to the swimming pool area were blown in. Shards of glass were scattered throughout the room. This was followed by a shower of warm chlorinated swimming pool water.

That brought him fully awake.

A grenade in the swimming pool, he thought.

Before the electric power failed, Curt got a look at the bedside clock.

It was 0330.

Night assault! Best time of the day to initiate one! He'd done it himself in past campaigns.

Dyani was out of bed before him.

Curt grabbed for his clothes and began to dress. As he did so, he found his tacomm brick among the glass shards on the floor. "Grey Day, this is Grey Head! Report!" he put in a verbose call to the officer of the day.

Lt. Ted "Tiger" Kyger responded through the tacomm

brick's small speaker, "Grey Head, Grey Day! The hotel and Club Med are under assault! Paratroops!"

"Sound Red Alert!"

"Being done, Grey Head!"

"Where are they?"

"Don't know, sir! Everywhere, seems like!"

He cursed himself. He should have known better than to let down his guard. He'd taken a shower and washed his underwear before hitting the sack. His shorts were still wet in the humid maritime climate. He had trouble wriggling into them.

"Dammit, Dyani, put on the goddamned body armor! Don't go out there without it!" he yelled at her when he saw what she was doing.

"No time!"

"Take time! That's an order!"

"But I've got to get out there and start scouting this assault! Time is critical! You need tactical intelligence data!" she started to argue with him, then came awake enough to realize what she was doing. "Erase that last! Yessir! Will do!"

Dyani had spent most of the evening with Adonica. She'd seen Jerry in sick bay. Body armor had saved Jerry's life but maybe not his arm. Dyani had given Curt a full report on the Jerry and Adonica situation. It didn't look good from Jerry's point of view. And Adonica had required a lot of help from Dyani although she maintained she and Jerry had worked through this sort of situation in the past, just in case. When it happened, it was something else, however. After Battle Mountain, Adonica had helped Dyani "arrange her priorities." Now, Dyani had become the consoling big sister.

The assault outside appeared to involve mostly small arms fire and perhaps some grenades. The sounds were the popping of small arms fire punctuated by the occasional boom of a grenade explosion. Dyani realized she would be foolish not to take the few minutes required to get into the skin-tight body armor. She knew Curt was right. He wasn't just thinking of her well-being alone because of the order he relayed over the tacomm to Kyger:

"Grey Day, Grey Head! Inform all personnel, take time to get into body armor! Let the warbots and the present guard personnel take the incoming for right now. I want everyone in body armor! I don't want any more casualties! The warbots and guard detail can start providing us information on the extent of this assault and where its focus is."

"That's easy, Grey Head! The main paratroop force appears to be concentrated on the Hilton Meridian Hotel. What you've been hit with at Club Med is a diversionary attack intended to keep your heads down," the new artillery officer reported. Kyger's Saucy Cans wouldn't be useful in this sort of close-quarter fighting. So the lieutenant was doing his utmost as OOD to be the center of gravity until the Greys could get up and organized. That's what the OOD's job really was all about anyway. However, it wasn't intended as such in a combat situation, which this now was.

There was no need to open the terrace doors to get outside. Curt and Dyani walked through the empty frames. Going out the front door of the room would have put them in the hallway. That might be a dangerous place if an enemy paratrooper had gotten to either end of the long hallway.

With his combat helmet now on his head and its neuroelectronic pads in contact with his skin, Curt could "talk" via fast tacomm. *Grey Day, Grey Head and Mustang Leader are out of the motel in the swimming pool area. Do you know if the assault troops have concentrated on our vehicles in the parking lots?*

Negatory on that, Grey Head! The enemy troops appear to be concentrating on the Hilton with perhaps a squad over at Club Med. They haven't gone for your OCV. That's where I am! Kyger reported, then added, *Grey Chief, Grey Ops, Grey Major, and Grey Tech just came in!*

TACBATT Leader, Grey Head! You with us?

Just barely, Grey Head! TACBATT Leader and ASSAULTCO Bravo Leader are heading for the warbot vehicles. It was obvious that Kitsy and Hassan had been unwinding together. Kitsy was doing the right thing by heading for the ARTVs to get warbots powered up and rolling as backups.

Okay, Kitsy, detach about six Sierra Charlies and have them do a search and destroy around Club Med for the paratrooper squad reported to be there. Dumb bastards wasted a grenade throwing it in the pool!

Yessir, it woke me up too. But to be honest. I've always wanted to toss a grenade in a swimming pool to see what would happen! Now I know, so I don't have to do it, and you don't have to order me not to! Kitsy wasn't being flippant in the face of danger. It was classic Kitsy Clinton. Curt could see her running toward the ARTVs with Hassan. *I'll put Mickey on that job!*

Suggest you have her Marauders accompany the Hellcats. Larry isn't going to be able to use his Saucy Cans. This will be tight close quarter fighting! Curt suggested.

You're right! But Mickey can handle it. She's a female samurai!

Sorry! I shouldn't micromanage you. Do what's necessary. Let's see what's going on over at the Hilton. That's where I want to concentrate our counter-moves. This attack was laid on to get Modibo out of here, Curt reminded her.

Just like Colonel Otto Skorzeny's rescue of Mussolini! Grey Head, I've studied that! And I can beat it! Kitsy snapped back with confidence.

Yeah, but this is complicated by the fact that Battleaxe is headquartered and quartered in the Hilton! Curt told her. He was concerned that the enemy paratroops also knew this and might try to take Hettrick and her staff as hostages for the safe withdrawal of Modibo. *Our first job is to protect Battleaxe. Then we'll counter the Malefactor rescue!*

What do you mean, protect Battleaxe? I'm perfectly prepared to protect myself! This isn't Yemen. Gen. Belinda Hettrick's tacomm voice came on the channel. *We're ready for the bastards!*

We'll give you some support anyway, Battleaxe! Kitsy told the division commander.

Carson, control your eager officer with the tiger juice! Hettrick fired back. *We're okay. We're secure. They'll lose troopers trying to get us out of here! We've got the elevators turned off and the stairwell exits covered! Hell, we're not really staff stooges, you know. We've all had our share of combat! But Major Gydesen and her Bio-tech unit are unarmed and unprotected! If these paratroops are Malitanians, they could get in there and slaughter your bio-techs and wounded Greys just like they butchered the Senegambians!*

Jesus, I never thought about that! Bio-techs are always considered noncombatants under the Geneva conventions! Curt realized with a sinking feeling in his stomach. Hettrick could be right. The Bio-tech company and the wounded Greys could be in real danger here.

Don't count on it here, Grey Head! was the comment from Battleaxe.

TACBATT Leader, Stiletto Leader! Kitsy, Dyani and I were in the sick bay just a few hours ago. We know the area! I can get in there with some Sierra Charlies and seal off that place real quick! Adonica broke in. *You take the Jeeps and Mary Anns along with the rest of the Sierra Charlies to cover whatever escape route these bastards use out of the Hilton.*

If they came to rescue Malefactor, they'll have some sort of escape aircraft, Kitsy observed. *How did they get in here in the first place? Where's their aircraft?*

Parachutes! They dropped in! The chutes are all over the Hilton parking lot! Hassan reported.

Roger that! I saw them parachute in, Kyger agreed.

Okay, they'll need an aerodyne to get out. Where is there room to land a 'dyne the size of a Chippie around here? Kitsy asked.

Parking lot is full of our vehicles. Dan Power said.

Before everyone starts making plans based on the intellectual brilliance of these speculations, came Edie Sampson's slightly caustic remark, *Grey Tech would like to point out that our wimpy little regimental air defense radar on the OCV painted three small targets trying to hover out over the ocean behind Ile de N'Gor, bearing two-five-zero, range one-one-hundred meters. They're not trying real hard to be stealthy. They must think we're completely asleep over here!*

Thanks, Edie, we were asleep! But we're not now! Kitsy fired back.

Grey Tech, Grey Head, Curt put in, vainly trying to get tacomm protocol back on track. *I hope to God you didn't let them see you painting them!*

Grey Head, Grey Tech knows better than that! I got them on passive i-r first. Then I hit them with a single short pulse to confirm the i-r. And I'm reading some intermittent tacomm hop transmissions plus their ranging lidar.

Grey Head didn't underestimate Grey Tech! Can you make any sense out of the tacomm they're using?

Standard East World stuff that the Malitanians have been using, Grey Head.

Keep an eagle-type eyeball on them, Grey Tech. I may try to scramble the Harpies on them. I'll get the Harpies spooled up over at the airport anyway just in case we don't manage to kill them on the ground when they get here . . . wherever they decided to land around here, was Curt's quick assessment.

TACBATT Leader, Grey Major suggests they could put one of them down on the beach as a feint while the other two squat on the tennis court complex, was Henry Kester's observation. *Grey Head, we can cover potential landing spots around the tennis courts and overlooking the beach while Stiletto Leader and Mustang Leader do their work in the bio-tech portion of the Hilton.*

Yeah, I guess we can, Grey Major. We'll do that. Curt replied. Like any tactical action, the conflict was quickly taking on a flow of its own. Curt knew it was already beyond his control. The Greys were an organized team. They had the situation in hand right then. They knew what was required. And they were moving to take care of matters. Curt was no longer a company commander who could exercise direct control over his troops and warbots in a furball such as this. He was a regimental commander who could watch, advise, see things his subordinates might be missing because of their intimate contact with the fight, and move if necessary to close holes in the plan. But this time, he would take some Sierra Charlies and warbots, and he would cover the tennis courts and beach. No other unit commander in the regiment was available to run that show, so it was up to him. *Henry, let's collect as many bots and warm bodies as we can and set some sort of an action base. Round 'em up!*

Roger! Greys all, everyone not involved with Stiletto and Mustang Leaders rendezvous with Grey Head and Grey Major in the vicinity of the Hilton tennis court complex! Bring bots if you can!

Then the situation suddenly began to go to slime.

The emergency tacomm channel came alive. *Grey Day, Grey Day! This is Lieutenant Clark in the Bio-tech ward! I'm the on-duty nurse! Emergency! Emergency! Armed soldiers are entering the floor through windows from the roof of the terrace! They're shooting! I . . .*

The tacomm transmission was abruptly terminated.

Goddammit, Dyani they got around us! They outflanked us! Take your people up the south stairwell while I go up the north one with the Stilettos!

Stiletto Leader, Mustang Leader is already meeting heavy fire opposition in the south stairwell! I need a Bio-tech fast! One of the Malitanians dropped a grenade down the stairwell. Sergeant Sid Johnson's out!

You all right, Dyani?

To Curt's relief, Dyani replied to Adonica, *Affirmative! I saw it coming and went where it wasn't.*

Mustang Bio is here! I'm going in for Johnson! Bio-tech Sgt. Allan Williams didn't have to do that. Another grenade could come down that stairwell at any time. But he did go in.

Okay, I got the north stairwell without resistance! Adonica reported. *Stand back from that access door, Carol! I'm going to shoot through it just to make sure no one is on the other side waiting!*

Roger, Captain! I'm standing by to go through when you quit firing! Master Sgt. Carol Head was an experienced lead NCO. The big Moravian had been through many fire fights, including house-to-house urban combat. He knew exactly what to do and when to do it.

TACBATT Leader, this is Hellcat Leader! We've cornered the diversionary assault squad that blew us out of bed in Club Med! came the excited report from Larry Hall. His artillery gunners normally didn't become involved in close-hand fire fights, and Curt was worried that they would make lethal mistakes. But apparently they hadn't because Hall went on, *Six of them! We've got them trapped in the exercise room! Sort of dicey to go in there after them. It's one big humper of a room! Lots of places to hide behind equipment!*

Curt didn't want to lose any more people. If Hall had some Malitanians truly trapped, it would be better if the Hellcats held them where they were until the present furball was terminated. Then they could be reinforced by other Sierra Charlie groups. *Roger, Hellcat Leader! Hold them where they are! We'll get some help to you shortly!*

Grey Head, Mikawa's gone in with Elliott behind two Jeeps! Je-

sus, Mickie, that was stupid! You're . . .

His thought was cut off by Mikawa broadcasting in the clear to him, *Larry, the Jeeps will take them! They're going in ahead of us! They'll draw the fire. Then we can . . . Oh, my God, yes, the Jeeps did draw fire! And returned it! Only one Malitanian left alive. Guk! Not enough left of him to even try saving. Elliott, stand back while I give him the coup de grace! Okay, now let's get the hell out of here! Larry, these are the same uniforms we've seen the Malitanians wearing, but these guys aren't Malitanians! I don't know who they are!*

At almost the same time, Adonica's tacomm message came in to Curt, *We're on the sick bay floor of the Hilton! Trying to get through all the bio-tech equipment they've spread around the hallway to delay us. Pagan's okay. Madder than hell he didn't have his Novia at hand. Same for Koslowski . . . Garrison must have had a sleeping pill; he's logging sack time and otherwise unharmed. Jay Taire's okay. So is Jerry, but he's sedated, too.*

Adonica, they shot Julia Clark, the on-duty nurse! Dyani reported. *Any Bio-tech! To the sick bay Emergency! Right now!*

Hold it! One paratrooper wounded, down, bleeding in one of the rooms! Adonica went on in the flush of combat. *Okay, I've got him! He's disarmed! Tullis, get in here and help me!*

Captain, the Malitanian paratroopers are out the door with Modibo!

Let them go, Paul! We've got other Sierra Charlies waiting outside! Grey Head, Stiletto Leader here! These paratroopers are not—repeat are not—Malitanians! They look like Bengalis! Or Hindus. In fact, this wounded paratrooper I've got here is carrying Indian Army identification!

Thirty-one

A half-dozen private cars roared into the Hilton parking lot. As they came to a halt, people armed with rifles quickly debarked and went for cover.

Curt stopped his run toward the tennis court area and came immediately to the alert.

The yellow sodium lights of the parking area provided enough illumination that Curt could see they were in civilian clothing. Around their left upper arms were striped green and white cloth brassards.

The news that the parachute assault team was from the Indian Army plus the unheralded arrival of what he assumed to be partisans pissed him off.

He knew what the Indian Army parachute brigade was doing here. The East World nations had a lot invested in Malitania and its dictator, Generalissimo Modibo.

Colonel Pratihara didn't hide the fact that he was a commissioned officer in the Indian Army. But he wouldn't talk at all when he'd been captured with Modibo the previous day. Pratihara simply repeated his name, rank, and serial number. He demanded to be released at once as a noncombatant.

Curt also knew from intelligence reports that the Malitanian Army had no airborne units, paratroops, or special forces. Hence, it had no capability to carry out a rescue of their leader. Therefore, the Indian Army had come in to do the job. Judging by the rapidity of their response, Curt guessed that the Indian parachute unit had been holding in

reserve in Bamako. Maybe the East World supporters of
Modibo really didn't trust him all the way. Maybe there
were more East World military units being held in Malitania. That would make sense from the strategic point of
view, given the importance of Dakar.

The presence of military advisors had been tacitly accepted for a long time as no military provocation on the
part of the advisors' countries. But the presence of clandestine military forces was another matter. The whole Senegambian picture was now changed. It could be a precursor
to a larger conflict yet to come. Curt hoped this wasn't the
case. The Greys would probably be among the first units to
go out and get shot at if it happened. Like police forces and
fire departments, they concentrated on prevention and
were happiest when they really didn't have to do their jobs.

As for the arrival of the non-uniformed armed personnel, Curt guessed they were Garamandes partisans reacting to the sudden assault on Club Med and the Hilton.
Garamandes were all over this part of Senegambia. But
Nyamia Lébou was supposed to keep the Operation Bloodbath command informed of all Garamandes' movements.
Curt was upset that he hadn't been told about this one.
Maybe there hadn't been time. This paratroop rescue assault had been sudden.

However, Curt considered that he could always use the
help . . . providing the Garamandes would follow orders
and adhere to a tactical plan. He would have to anticipate
that they wouldn't. They were armed citizens fighting for
their country. It was hard to make them follow orders. In
fact, Curt had never made anyone follow an order since
he'd left West Point. Curt led by other means than threatened retribution.

Battleax, Grey Head! Curt reported to Hettrick. *Two data
points. One: The Malitanian parachute assault team isn't Malitanian. It's part of the Indian Army. We found Indian Army i-d on
one of the parachutists that we killed. Two: It looks like the goddamned Garamandes have arrived in the Hilton parking lot. About
thirty of them. Armed. Did we know they were coming?*

Hettrick came back very coolly for a divisional com-

302

mander who was under attack. She was obviously holding her own. *We shot one of the bastards who was dumb enough to walk in here without checking first. I confirm your finding. This guy was an NCO in the Indian Army. No insignia indicating nationality or rank on him. Direct violation of the Geneva conventions. I'm passing the word up the line to Bloodbath.*

This will raise some hackles in Fort Fumble for sure!

Not our worry. Answer to second question: Hell, no! Negative on communications from the Garamandes about getting over here to help out. Grey Head, you handle the Garamandes. You're out there in the heat of it already. We're sort of busy here at the moment, but we're not in any trouble.

Thanks a lot for nothing much, Battleaxe. Will do! Curt shot back. *Henry, get over to the tennis courts. Take command. Prepare for the arrival of those aerodynes.*

Hell, Colonel, I ain't no officer! Henry Kester pointed out.

You're my Number One non-com, and if I say you're in command, you're in command! Henry, dammit, you're experienced in this sort of thing. Think of it as a lethal barroom brawl!

Yessir! Whatever you say, sir! I just hope the officers won't get pissed and not follow me.

Henry, TACBATT Leader here! If Grey Head says to follow you, we follow you! Or do I have to tell you what you've told me several times? Soldier, shut up and soldier! Except you said it more nicely.

Quit talking and get to work, Curt admonished them. He recognized the chatter as a way his Greys let off steam before and during a fracas. But this was going to be a tight one, and he didn't want to lose a second of time in idle chatter. *I'll get this Garamandes group worked into the operation somehow. I hope.*

Roger, Colonel! Just make sure you keep in touch. Otherwise, someone is likely to take a shot at you because you didn't identify yourself, Henry warned.

Curt turned and walked toward the dispersing Garamandes group. In his parade ground voice, he called out, "Halt! United States Army! Identify yourselves! Where's your commander?"

Only a few members even hesitated, but one came over

303

to Curt.

In the light, Curt saw the black eye patch first.

"Madame Lébou?"

"Yes! Get out of our way, Colonel! Someone is trying to get Modibo out of here. We won't allow that to happen! He's got to be held to answer for his war crimes and atrocities!" Nyamia Lébou responded quickly. "That is why we wanted to guard him! But you wouldn't let us! We should have put up enough of a fuss to make you back down on that. Now we have to come in and break up this rescue operation!"

Curt held up his hand. "Back off, Nyamia! We've got the situation under control! If you and your partisans start running around without i-d beacons, my people will sure as hell shoot them!"

Nyamia held up the tacomm brick that had been given to her for communications coordination with Operation Bloodbath. It was chattering with conversations between the Washington Greys. "We have heard what is going on! You certainly do not have things under control! The Indian mercenaries are getting away with Modibo! We do not intend to allow that to happen!"

"Nor do we! So calm down and get into the flow of the fight here!" Curt snapped. "My regiment has already taken far too many casualties. So I'm not going to have you and your partisans running around here shooting at anything that moves! I'll give orders to shoot on sight any unidentified civilian. Do you want to try standing up against my Sierra Charlies and warbots!"

Nyamia started to bring her FAM AC carbine around to her hip, but looked at Curt and suddenly thought better of it. Curt was a big man. He was also wearing body armor that would stop any bullet from her carbine. And she wasn't wearing body armor.

"Good! I'm glad you thought about what you might have done in haste just now. I'd hate to cause a second wound to a valiant fighter." Curt didn't mind smoothing on a little soft soap right then. "Get your partisans, Nyamia! Follow me! We're going into a position where we can ambush the paratroops when they try to get Modibo aboard an aero-dyne."

"What aerodyne?"

"Three of them are hovering off Ile de N'Gor waiting," Curt explained. "Look, we've got excellent night fighting gear plus an overview of the operation you don't have. The Garamandes and the Greys can hit the Indian paratroops together. We know where they are and where they're going. So get your people, come along with me, and you won't get shot at. If you come, you'll have the chance to help us stop this rescue attempt!"

Nyamia Lébou apparently did not like taking orders, but she took them anyway right then. Going along with this American colonel was opportunistic. If she thought the American operation was failing, she could always retake command of the Garamandes and do what she felt neces-sary to stop the Indian paratroops and Modibo.

Her partisans had taken cover but were obviously watch-ing this exchange because she gave a hand signal. About twenty-four partisans appeared out of the tropical foliage.

Curt took off to follow Henry, calling on tacomm as he did so, *Grey Major, Grey Head here! I'm right behind you. I'm bringing about twenty-odd partisans with me. They don't have bea-cons, but I have one. So figure if non-identified signatures are fol-lowing my beacon, they're friends.*

Roger, Grey Head, Grey Major sees you! We can always use a few more guns and warm bodies to shoot them!

Grey Head, Grey Tech here! The aerodynes have come out of their holding hover beyond the island and have started inshore. ETA at the Hilton is about three minutes! Edie Sampson told him.

Roger! Keep me advised as to aerodyne positions! Grey Major, did you hear that?

Affirmative! Want us to hold fire until they start to squat?

You do that! But be prepared to turn the Mary Anns loose on them if we screw up somehow and let them get Modibo aboard! Where is the unit that has Malefactor?

Major Clinton and a few warbots are doing an orgasmic job of delaying them at the terrace exit doors from the lobby.

TACBATT Leader, this is Grey Head! Goddammit, don't try to make a big hero of yourself! Let those paratroopers get out of there and toward the aerodyne landing zone! Curt admonished Kitsy.

Grey Head, we're managing to slow them up here! That will give you more time to deploy forces around whatever point the aerodynes choose to squat! Kitsy tried to explain.

How many rounds have you taken in the body armor thus far?

Only one.

That's enough! Now withdraw and track the Indian paratroopers. Let the warbots hassle them if you want. But you stay the hell out of the line of fire, goddammit! I've lost too many Greys in this sheep screw already! Curt was angry for an irrational reason. Perhaps it was kindled by his usual concern for the ladies of the Greys in combat. Or perhaps it was partly the fact that he didn't want to lose yet another future regimental commander.

Is that an order, Grey Head!

That's an order, TACBATT Leader!

Grey Head, Mustang Leader! Harlan is tracking the paratroopers, too! I'm just exiting the hotel behind them. They don't know I'm behind them! They're heading for the beach! Dyani called in, giving her usual scouting report on the situation from her usual position behind the enemy.

Grey Head, Grey Ops here! came the tacomm voice of Russ Frazier. *I've got Mickie and her Marauders with me now along with Kyger's Tigers! We'll cover the tennis courts. We've got lots of Smart Farts, and we can sure as hell ding the shit out of an aerodyne with what we brought along!*

Dammit, Russ, you're a staffer now! Curt had to remind him.

Staff stooge I may now be, Colonel. But it will take a JCS Execute Order to keep me out of this sheep screw! Be aware of the fact that most of your staff deserted the OCV. Joan is with Henry. To answer your next question: Pappy, Nellie, and Edie are left in the OCV to run the show.

Curt didn't have time to argue. The situation was moving too fast. The finale of this assault was going to take every Grey who was available to fight. Furthermore, it was too late to stop those he didn't want exposed to enemy fire. Especially this night.

306

Two aerodynes heading for the beach! Signatures indicate Hindustani Aircraft Type H-One-thirty Agni tactical airlifters used in East World airborne units, Edie reported. *The other one isn't headed for any predictable landing spot. I thought originally it might he going toward the tennis complex, but I'm not sure now. And neither is Grady. We can't get a flight path prediction on it!*

Mustang Leader, are you still tracking Modibo? Curt asked.

Affirmative!

So is TACBATT Leader! Kitsy added.

Can you identify Modibo?

Affirmative! White bandages on both hands. They stand out, Dyani observed.

Jeez, you'd think these guys had planned this operation well enough to have brought along dark gloves for him! Hassan put in.

How could they know Modibo got his hands burned and we bandaged them? Kitsy asked.

How did they know where we'd stashed him in the first place? Hassan fired back.

Good question! We'll let the spooks figure that one out! Our job is to keep him around to enjoy our hospitality! was Curt's answer. He broke out on the beach and looked around.

Out over the ocean he could see the two holes in the star field. Those holes signified the presence of two aerodynes running without lights.

The beach itself was about a hundred meters wide and perfectly smooth.

But it was dotted with about a hundred beach umbrellas and other items of beach furniture.

A plan began to form in Curt's mind. After years of Sierra Charlie combat, he'd learned to survey a battle site quickly and come up with a tactical plan that would make use of cover and the strengths of the Greys.

Position the warbots in cover at the edge of the beach! Keep tacomm command contact with them! We'll need their heavy firepower. We'll want them to roll quickly toward the aerodynes. They'll serve as targets to draw fire and keep the paratroopers' attention directed at them. Set them to fire on whatever fires on them, single bursts, track convergence, don't fire again if convergence obtained, Curt snapped orders quickly over the tacomm. Neuroelectronic tacomm was much faster than verbal messaging. His "voice" was heard directly in the brains of all his Sierra Charlies. NE tacomm was often five times faster than voice communications. *While they're doing that, we'll hassle those paratroopers from cover. Use night vision laser sighting on your Novias! Three round bursts. Everyone who can, find cover under or around these umbrellas and such. Do it. And do it goddamned fast!* Curt ordered. *You've got maybe ninety seconds! Move!*

The beach was suddenly covered with human forms dashing in the darkness toward the cover of the beach furniture.

Warhawk Leader, this is Grey Head! How many Harpies you got available?

Six to spool up!

Get them in the air now and keep them low. Be prepared to whang some Hindustani One-thirties on the beach in front of the Hilton. Be advised we have Greys under cover on the beach, so be careful!

Roger, Grey Head, Hands' Harriers are breaking ground now!

Curt now had air cover for chase if the Greys failed on the ground. He didn't want to kill Modibo. But he wasn't about to let the Malitanians and the East Worlders get the Butcher of Bamako back in their hands to do this again in the future. Once was enough.

He found Henry Kester on the edge of the beach under cover in the palms. Henry had two tube rocket launchers strapped across his shoulders. *Where are the Garamandes?*

Behind us, I thought. It was your detail. I been kinda busy here, Colonel.

Garamandes, where are you? Nyamia, get on the tacomm! Curt called, trying to check on the partisans who were following him but who were nearly invisible in the dark.

We're right here alongside you, Carson. Nyamia was speaking into her tacomm, but it broadcast into Curt's neuroelectronic tacomm set.

Don't talk unless you have to, but talk to me when you must, Curt warned her. *When the aerodynes start to hover, there will be enough noise that you'll have to shout. But all hell will be loose by that time anyway!*

Share your tube rockets with us! Most of your soldiers are carrying two. They can't shoot two at once. Give one to each of us, and we can double the immediate firepower base, Nyamia suggested.

Curt didn't have an M100 with him. Henry unstrapped one of the two he was carrying and handed it to her. *Know how to work this?*

Yes. Pull the end release. Aim. Squeeze the trigger to the first notch. When the rocket says it has the target you've identified, pull the trigger all the way.

Keep that up and we'll recruit you, ma'am, Henry said. *Good troopers are hard to find. Especially ones as attractive as you are!*

Sergeant, flattery will get you everything, maybe. Keep talking!

It must be combat time, Curt told himself. Black humor was coming even from the partisan leader. Curt knew it was part of combat. People who hadn't been there would never know or understand it. In fact, some armchair generals were offended by it. Certainly, anti-war protesters were.

Let the enemy aerodynes come in and land, Curt instructed. *Anyone who's ever ridden a Chippie assault knows a 'dyne is most vulnerable when its landed.*

When it happened, it happened very fast.

The instant the first Indian aerodyne squatted on the wet, compacted sand, its loading ramps came down. Two dozen armed men with two unarmed people Curt recognized as Modibo and Pratihara broke cover at the edge of the beach and rushed the 'dyne.

Aim for the armed men, not Modibo with the white bandages on his hands! Commence firing! Curt snapped the order.

But the second aerodyne was suddenly overhead as well. It wasn't an unarmed Hindustani Aircraft H-130. It was the heavily armed H-130-A attack version mounting rotary cannon in several locations. It hovered and began to shoot back, apparently using infrared sensors to target the Greys and warbots. Bucephalus, Curt's Jeep, took one of those rounds. It didn't penetrate the Jeep's armor, but it knocked the warbot over and put it out of action.

Curt didn't need to tell his troops what to do. Four M100 Smart Farts lanced through the air with their tails of fire. Four homed on the H-130-A. All four hit it squarely. The

H-130-A was armored, but no aerodyne can take the warhead impacts of four Smart Farts at once. It staggered in the air. Then it began to blow thin yellow flames from its lift slots. Curt could see that the pilot was struggling to keep it in the air.

But the delay had given the Indian paratroopers enough time to get to the waiting airlift aerodyne. Some of them didn't make it. The Greys cut them down with accurate laser-directed Novia fire.

Get Modibo! Get him! He's going aboard! That might have been Hassan yelling.

Two of Modibo's escorts fell.

But the Malitanian dictator managed to disappear inside the aerodyne.

Its loading ramp swung shut even as it began to lift.

Curt could see that it was taking 25-millimeter fire from the Mary Anns. They were penetrating. The big tactical airlift aerodyne was a tough target to miss at a range of about a hundred meters.

As the aerodyne lifted, someone broke cover from beside Curt and dashed out onto the beach.

It was Nyamia. She was carrying the M-100 Henry had given her.

Without hesitation, Nyamia dashed under the lifting aerodyne. She ignored the rifle fire still coming from those Indian paratroopers who had been left on the beach.

She hoisted the launch tube to her right shoulder and with her remaining good eye, laid its sights in the center of its underbelly. When she fired, the M100 was still accelerating as it hit the aerodyne about thirty meters over her head.

The Smart Fart had found a vulnerable spot. Even the 'dyne's protective armor couldn't hold against a 100-millimeter rocket.

Turbine fuel began to gush out of the hole, but the explosion of the M100's warhead ignited it. The flames washed down. Then, without warning, the aerodyne began to settle. It crashed down on top of her and exploded in a fireball of orange and yellow flame.

Almost simultaneously, the attack aerodyne hit the beach on the edge of the incoming tide. Its landing jacks folded with the impact. Someone fired another M100 into it. Two Mary Anns targeted it with their 25-millimeter cannons. It was the second big explosion on the beach.

A third fireball erupted over by the Hilton. The third aerodyne had been destroyed by Frazier and his detail at the tennis courts.

Harriers all, this is Harrier Leader. Looks like we won't be needed! The ground pounders did it with their little rockets. Come right and return to Dakar Airport!

Curt stood up, but he didn't sling his Novia.

He didn't see how Nyamia Lébou could possible have survived. She'd been directly under the aerodyne when it crashed.

Oh, my God! It was almost a gasp, almost a sob from Kitsy. *What a hell of a way to go!*

Major Clinton, came the gentle voice of Henry Kester, *there ain't no nice way to go, even in bed. But she died for something she believed in. That sonofabitch won't ravage her country again. There may not be better ways to go.*

Thirty-two

"Mister President, the ambassador from Malitania is here!" the President's attractive secretary announced demurely from the door to the Oval Office.

The President looked up from where he was sitting in the conversation area before the fireplace. It was only September, but the weather in Washington was unseasonably nippy this year. So flames licked around a log in the fireplace. "Please have him escorted in," the President replied. He turned to his colleagues seated with him. "Ladies and gentlemen, I want you to know that this is perhaps one of the most difficult meetings I've ever had."

"We understand, Mister President," Sen. Dan Bancroft assured him. He knew damned well that the President would never have asked the Malitanian ambassador to come to the White House at all if it hadn't been for their insistence. Bancroft had damaging inside information about activities in the White House. Normally, the senator from Ohio wasn't a hawk. But the Senegambian matter had proved to be an opportunity. Bancroft was opportunistic. Ideology was for idealists and public consumption. The poll taken the day before clearly showed that the American public was in support of Operation Bloodbath. Bancroft knew he was on firm ground. The President had to be convinced, but the convincing part wasn't hard. However, those in the room were present ostensibly to back up the President. In reality, they were there to ensure that the Commander In Chief did what was necessary.

It was a diverse group representing many facets of American

government and life — Vice President Henrietta Hamlin, Secretary of State Andrea Pruitt, Secretary of Defense Nelson Fetterman, Senator Bancroft, and Congressman Jacob O. Carlisle.

Bancroft had insisted that Carlisle be present. The retired general had helped Bancroft by providing invaluable military and international background. This had made Bancroft a new power in the Senate. In reciprocation, Bancroft had used his influence to improve the freshman congressman's position on the south side of the Capitol.

Albert W. Murray of the NIA was also present, but only by "national technical means." The White House recorded all such meetings. So did the NIA in a highly discreet manner, and only one man ever saw the data. Murray liked his job. He was good at it. He wanted to keep it because he wasn't certain that any successor would operate with the nation's interests at heart. Murray believed he had, did, and would. He was never overt. As a result, Murray was respected, not feared.

The Hon. Kankan Moussa Mokhtar arrived, accompanied by two Marine guards in full dress uniform. They left once Mokhtar was in the Oval Office, but they remained outside the door.

The President didn't rise. Therefore, no one else did. Instead, the chief executive motioned to the empty chair. "Good morning, Mister Ambassador. Please be seated. I believe you know the others."

Mokhtar gave a Muslim bow. The failure of the President to rise and greet him was a protocol item that was lost on the former Berber tribesman. Mokhtar had struggled to learn enough to become his country's ambassador to the United States. But he definitely caught the chill in the room. The fireplace did little to dispel it. He'd also faced problems in his disapproval of the American lifestyle. Two women, albeit of high government position, were in the room for a discussion that had to be of the greatest international import. Mokhtar simply did not understand that the American culture was growing increasingly more gender-equal. It wasn't the Muslim way. "Good morning, Mister President. And good morning to the rest of you." Mokhtar didn't attempt to shake hands because

313

the President didn't offer to do so. It alerted the Malitanian ambassador that this meeting was far more serious than his chargé d'affaires had expected.

It was also cool on Mokhtar's part. American military forces were fighting against the Malitanian Army in Senegambia. But the ambassador had little current information. Nearly all of the telecommunications' services normally used between Bamako and Washington hadn't been working for over 24 hours. Mokhtar had gotten a little information from commercial television news services. But the American reaction had been so rapid that even the vaunted newshawks and newsharpies hadn't managed to get their remote reporting teams in place yet. Those who were in Senegambia had been caught out in the savannah reporting on atrocities when the Americans had made their rapid and surprise move against Dakar. Therefore, little news was coming from Dakar itself.

Except to the American government officials who were in that room.

So Mokhtar would perhaps find out what was going on in Senegambia. At least, he hoped so. He felt he could trust what he was told. Americans were far too open and candid when it came to international affairs. He believed them to be stupid for doing so. However, Mokhtar came from a culture where stealth and deception were the norm.

Once the ambassador was seated, the President went on in halting phrases. It was apparent even to Mokhtar that the American chief executive was having some sort of trouble delivering this edict, if that's what it was.

"Mister Ambassador, the United States of America regrets the sudden and untimely death of your president. Please convey our sincere condolences to the Malitanian people," the President said.

Mokhtar was shocked by this announcement. He'd received no such reports. And he'd heard nothing on commercial TV. He didn't know whether he felt relief or grief at this news. Mokhtar had been a minor government official in Bamako when Modibo swept out of the Sahara to take over what was then Mali. Loyalty and performance during the Mauritanian Anschluss had been rewarded by Modibo's appointment of

314

him to Washington. Mokhtar had been a Modibo supporter, partly to save his own hide and partly because he'd found himself a member of the winning team. He was relieved to think that perhaps Modibo's terrorism was at an end. But he grieved because he might find himself seeking asylum in the United States if the new government was hostile to Modiboites.

But Mokhtar reacted as many Muslims do: with carefully guarded skepticism and a refusal to believe what the infidel said. "Mister President, I have received no such information at the embassy."

"Of course you haven't. Our military activity has been designed to cut Malitanian information flow."

"If I may ask, when and under what conditions did my president's demise occur?"

"At about midnight, Washington time. He'd been detained by our military forces at Dakar Airport. He was injured while resisting detention. He was taken to the Hilton Meridian Hotel near Dakar where he was being treated by our medical teams. I'm told that he suffered burned hands while attempting to exit a Chinese Type Six-forty tank. Taken with him was a Colonel Pratihara, an officer in the Indian Army who claims to be a military advisor. Also captured and held as prisoners of war under the terms of the Geneva conventions were several members of the Malitanian Air Force."

The President had carefully memorized the information. It made him sick at heart to have initiated military operations in Senegambia. It bothered him greatly that these activities had resulted in the death of another head of state, although Modibo had provoked open aggression and permitted unmentionable atrocities in Senegambia. However, the President took solace in the fact that his actions had helped preserve a cultural heritage and protect the country's educational facilities.

"May I convey this information to my government?"

"Of course. This is no star chamber, Mister Ambassador. If you have trouble making contact, I've authorized Secretary Pruitt the use of American telecommunications' facilities to permit you to report to your government in Bamako. But I have other information that I must convey to you. And a specific message for whomever is in charge of your government in

315

Bamako at this time." The President didn't tell the ambassador that he would be flying to New York later today to report the results of the UN-backed military action to the General Assembly. But he had to let the ambassador have the information ahead of time.

Both Senator Bancroft and Congressman Carlisle had advised the President on the basis of their international expertise — more Carlisle's than Bancroft's — that no government probably existed in Bamako at this moment. When dictators such as Modibo fall as a result of a military embarrassment, the ruling party seldom prevails in establishing a replacement dictator. Opposition groups seize such opportunities to rise up and depose the ruling group.

Without giving Mokhtar an opportunity to comment because the President had been coached in maintaining absolute control of this meeting, the chief executive went on, "However, in spite of the fact that American and French troops were operating in Senegambia in support of resolutions of the United Nations Security Council, an attempt was made to release President Modibo by the use of force and violence. At eleven-thirty last night, Washington time, a battalion of parachute troops from the Indian Army made a vicious and forceful assault on the American medical facility at the Hilton Meridian Hotel where your President was under care. During the ensuing military engagement, the Indian Air Force aircraft attempting to evacuate President Modibo was shot down. No one survived. However, we're prepared to transport the remains of President Modibo to Bamako."

Mokhtar lost his cool at that point. "Mister President, my president's death is a direct result of your country's military invasion of Senegambia! You will be held responsible for President Modibo's murder!"

The President shook his head. "Mister Ambassador, the Indian Air Force aerodyne was shot down by Senegambian partisans. We have numerous eyewitness accounts of the incident. And, sir, may I ask why Indian paratroops and Indian Air Force aircraft were present in Senegambia? Were these foreign forces invited into Malitania and Senegambia by your government? Certainly, they were not there under the authorization of the United Nations!"

Mokhtar bristled. Again, the President had been briefed to expect this sort of behavior. "I do not have to answer that, Mister President! If Indian military units were indeed present as you claim, we of Malitania have the right to call upon our friends for help just as the Senegambians did! Certainly, your aggressive military invasion of Senegambia was of no greater perfidy than my government bringing in Indian military forces!"

"A difference does indeed exist, Mister Ambassador! But we won't argue that. We'll leave that up to the United Nations and to the World Court, especially when it comes to war crimes," the President said sadly, recalling the videotapes and other reports of atrocities that were just beginning to come out of Dakar. "Occasionally, we in the civilized world of the twenty-first century fall victims of our own belief that the rest of the world is also civilized. Frankly, the entire Senegambian affair has been very tragic in my view. It has only served to remind many of us that we have a very long way to go to bring the rest of the world up to the level of civilized behavior with which we try to conduct our affairs . . ."

"We Malitanians have the right to live! We have the right to eat! We were denied those rights more than a century ago when you and the European nations divided Africa to suit your interests. You left us with nothing, and it got worse!" Mokhtar objected strongly.

"You have the right to live only if you don't deny that right to your neighbor! You have a right to eat only if you don't take food from your neighbor!"

"If we do not have it, we must be strong enough to take it!"

The President shook his head. He suddenly realized that he could not bridge the cultural gap. Mokhtar was still an eighteenth century person. "And if you do, some of us will have to take action. You must understand that we will not abide naked aggression. I was mistaken in believing that this issue was settled once and for all in 1991. It was not."

The President sighed. This was far more difficult than he thought it would be. It was causing him to change some of his own beliefs. "Mister Ambassador, I have a message for you to

317

deliver to your government in Bamako. Basically, it says that we regret the death of your president. However, this occurred during a military operation conducted by troops of the Indian Army. Your president was killed by a Senegambian citizen. It was not our intention nor was it the intention of the United Nations to kill President Modibo. We sincerely regret that it happened. However, all that aside, the situation is such that American, French, and Senegambian military and paramilitary forces now hold Dakar and the Cape Verde Peninsula. Malitanian armed forces have been driven off the peninsula. We're holding as prisoners of war more than twenty-thousand members of the Malitanian Army. Your air force has either been destroyed or rendered ineffective. Senegambian interests are demanding a military offensive all the way to Bamako. In fact, we won't be able to prevent the Senegambians from doing this unless a cease-fire can be arranged at once. As for the American forces, I've ordered them into a state of unilateral cease-fire as of eight o'clock this morning. The French president has followed suit for the French forces. Our forces will cease all military operations unless they are fired upon. We therefore offer a cease-fire and demand Malitanian adherence to the various UN resolutions. If your government does not respond favorably to this within twenty-four hours, American and French forces will join with the Senegambian regular and irregular forces to eject your nation's military forces from Senegambia."

The President reached out, and Secretary of State Pruitt handed him a prepared diplomatic note. As the chief executive looked at it, he went on, "Mister Ambassador, these cease-fire terms are set forth in this official communication between my government and your government. You will note that it has been coordinated with the government of France and with the Secretary General of the United Nations. Please see to it that it's delivered to your government in Bamako at once. Secretary Pruitt will offer assistance in doing so because of the state of your telecommunications' systems. Thank you for coming, Mister Ambassador." He turned to Andrea Pruitt. "Madame Secretary, would you please be so kind as to show the ambassador out?"

When Mokhtar had left the Oval Office, the President sighed. "That was a very difficult thing for me to do," he admitted. "However, in a way, I'm glad I did it. We won, and the blood lust was beginning to take control of me. It isn't easy to be polite to a person who represents such a terrible man as Modibo was."

It was Congressman Jacob Carlisle who spoke up, "Mister President, I know how difficult it is to become involved in a war. But once the war is won, it's even more difficult to end it properly so it doesn't breed another one."

"Do you have an answer about how to prevent that?"

"No, sir, but we're working on it. We're working on it. The answer must be based on reality and experience, not theory and wishful thinking. We'll get there eventually."

"And the sooner the better."

Across the river in the Pentagon, American military telecommunications were working beautifully. Gen. Jeffrey Pickens reached Gen. Bill Bellamack with no problem. Bellamack's new headquarters in Dakar had been in operation for only a few hours. But the communications part of C^3I was up and running.

Pickens had to perform a task that involved eating crow, but he didn't have to tell Bellamack that. However, he suspected that Bellamack knew anyway. "Bill, congratulations! The cease-fire is in effect! You did an outstanding job with Operation Bloodbath! I just wanted to call and let you know!"

Bellamack's holographic image showed the Dakar harbor behind him. Riding on its surface were the huge, hulking black forms of two carrier submarines. Aerodynes were shuttling between the submarines and the city. The 50th "R.U.R." Robot Infantry Division was coming ashore. "Jeff, I appreciate your accolade. But I've got to hand the laurels to the divisions and regiments who actually did it. And to the French Foreign Legion. It surprised me, but Colonel Debas turned out to be the best French officer I've ever worked with. One thing for sure: I wouldn't want to get on the brown downwind side of his regiment!"

He didn't report right then that the French cooperation had helped make the operation successful when it had threatened to go down the tubes the day before. Bellamack knew he'd been given a force that was understrength for the operation. The sudden tank attack on Dakar Airport had caused the Malitanians to weaken their otherwise formidable defenses. The Foreign Legion took immediate advantage of that to capture the city of Dakar. Bellamack had said a silent prayer of thanks for having Belinda Hettrick on his otherwise vulnerable left flank to the north. Her Sierra Charlies had done what no warbot outfit could. He was proud of her and the SCs. But he was a Sierra Charlie himself. He felt strange about Operation Bloodbath. It was his first shot at combined arms command. It had taken a lot of hard work and a lot of give and take. He'd learned this when he'd commanded the Washington Greys.

"General Wool will be calling you later to congratulate you, but I wanted to be the first," Pickens told him. "You vindicated my faith in your capabilities, Bill. I'm putting you in for a DSM."

"I appreciate that, Jeff, but I want lots of medals for my troops. And especially for the Sierra Charlies. Promotions, too." He paused, then added, "Jeff, our casualties were extremely light. Typical of a high-tech war. But some of them were tragic. So I'm going to be calling on you and some of the other members of the staff for some special considerations for some of them. They may end up being disabled. But they're too good to lose. We've got to find slots for them."

"Always supporting your Sierra Charlies, eh? Okay, they deserve it! 'Do not bind the mouths of the kine who tread the grain.' I've never been one of those hard-asses who could find the regulation that said no. There are plenty of regs that can be interpreted so people can get what they deserve."

Bellamack knew the man was eating a healthy dose of crow, but the CINC of Operation Bloodbath had the horsesense not to rub it in. That wasn't the way career progress was made either in the military or in civilian life. So he changed the subject. "I'm ready to pull the Seventeenth Iron Fist Division out according to plan. They should be home in a few days."

"Bill, hold them where they are until we get word of the official cease-fire. You know what the Malitanians have sitting to the east of you."

"Yeah, but their glorious leader is gone."

"We can't take chances. Not until the cease-fire is firm. Hold them in position. Keep your recce up."

"Some of them have taken losses that reduce their combat efficiency below acceptable standards," Bellamack revealed. He didn't like the idea of Fort Fumble interfering in which had been a successful operational plan. Part of that plan was to bring home early those units that had done the hard initial fighting. "I've got to get the Iron Fist out of here. Especially the Washington Greys. They got hit hard. And I promised them they'd be the first to go home."

"You'll be able to keep that promise, Bill. They *will* be the first. But not until we're damned sure the Malitanian hordes won't break over you again. And not until we know that The Man won't tell us to forge on to Bamako."

"The Washington Greys aren't going to like it, Jeff."

"The Washington Greys will follow orders. The Washington Greys are professionals, Bill."

Epilogue

"So we're not going home?"

"We're not going home, Kitsy," Curt told her. "At least not right away. You know the drill: 'Haven't you heard? It's all been changed!' "

"Well, there are worse places to be stationed temporarily," she told him, looking out over the Atlantic Ocean from the terrace of the Hilton Meridian Hotel. "At least, they didn't shoot up this place too bad when they tried to take Modibo."

"And Hettrick got the word she could pull us all back here to be held as a mobile reserve," Curt went on.

"Party time!" Kitsy said brightly. "Some of the men in the Wolfhounds and Cottonbalers seem to be very interesting!"

"When you're not on duty, yes."

"Oh, my God, Curt, you're not going to keep us under Rule Ten, are you?"

Curt grinned. "Not only no, but hell no! However, we'll maintain some semblance of working hours. Like ten-hundred to fourteen-hundred or something."

"That's better!"

"But you'll be working your sweet little ass off from ten to two and maybe before and later every day," Curt reminded her. "You've got the TACBATT officially."

"I do?" Kitsy could still look like a surprised teen-ager.

"Yes, because I just said so."

Kitsy sighed. "I don't like the way I got it."

"Neither do I. But do not look a gift camel in the mouth."

"I know. Those goddamned beasts spit at me. Besides,

they've got fleas and they stink. Thank God there aren't many of them here! Just enough to remind me of the benefits of having a trike to move around in. How in the hell did they ever fight from camels?"

"You forget," Curt reminded her, "the time the Army tried to establish a camel-based cavalry outfit in the Arizona Territory."

"I want to forget it. It failed."

"Kitsy, not everything we do succeeds as well as this operation. The Army's made some classic blunders, misjudgments, and fuck-ups in the past. And we will in the future. I just want to make sure that you don't do it with the Tactical Battalion."

"Not if I can help it!"

"I know. I'm counting on you. I always have," Curt admitted. Then he became very businesslike. "How's Nick Gerard?"

"Okay now."

"Use him. He's a good battalion NCO."

"I know. I intend to lean on him heavily."

"We think we officers command the Washington Greys. We're wrong. The NCOs always have and always will. Nick still has steps up the career ladder ahead of him," Curt pointed out.

"I think I do, too."

"You'll have to earn every step, and you'll have to prove it every time," Curt advised. "Hettrick did."

"I know. She's my role model."

"You couldn't have picked a better one."

Kitsy held up her hand. "Except I'm going to do her one better. I think she picked a very lonely way up the ladder."

Curt recalled the past with a warm feeling, but he simply told Kitsy, "You're wrong. And you'll find that out." He looked at his watch. "So go take over your command officially. You've still got two hours left in the work day. Work!"

Kitsy got up but then looked down at her colonel relaxing in a beach chair on the terrace of the hotel. "Sir, since you're my regimental commander, and since I should look to you as an example, perhaps you can tell me something. If you're working now, can I get this sort of work?"

"I'm working, Major. I'm working. And even if I'm not, RHIP. If I could let you stick around, you'd see what kind of real work a regimental commander has to do this afternoon. But it's sort of a private chat, and I really don't want anyone else involved. You've had to do it from time to time as a company commander. You'll have an even tougher time doing it as a battalion commander."

Kitsy looked at him knowingly. "I hope it works out for Adonica."

"It will. Now scoot!"

He'd asked Capt. Adonica Sweet to come see him at 1400 hours. She was prompt.

Curt didn't expect that Capt. Dyani Motega would come with her. But he was not surprised at Dyani's presence.

Adonica looked fresh and clean and sparkling as usual. However, Curt could tell from her eyes that she was under a lot of stress. She was stiffly formal with him. "Captain Adonica Sweet reporting as ordered, sir!"

"Please sit down, Adonica. And you, too, Dyani," Curt motioned to two empty chairs. His chosen spot on the terrace was open but private. And he gave them both the clear signal that this was an informal meeting.

"Did Jerry get off okay?" he went on once the two ladies had taken seats. Maj. Jerry Allen was on his way to Walter Reed Army Hospital aboard a long-range airlifter.

"Yes, sir." Adonica seemed emptied.

"Do you want to be with him?" Curt asked unnecessarily, but he wanted the answer from her.

Adonica paused. "Yes, sir."

"I'll have Pappy Gratton cut travel orders and leave papers for you. How much leave do you have coming? I'll authorize emergency leave if you haven't got enough in the bucket."

"Sir, I have new responsibilities to the Greys and to my new assault company." Adonica was trying hard to keep it under control. Thus far, she was succeeding. Curt could see Dyani's stoic influence on the lovely young woman.

"You've also got responsibilities to your own life, Adonica," Curt reminded her gently.

"Sir, when I accepted my commission, my private life and needs became secondary."

Curt shook his head. "No, Adonica," he said simply. Then he

324

went on, "The instant our professional lives become more important than our personal lives is the instant we become zealots. When that happens, we lose sight of who we are and what we're doing. Each of us controls enough death and destruction that we're truly dangerous if we become zealous. Look at Modibo, the man responsible for all this mess."

"I'm sorry I didn't get the chance to kill him," Adonica said quietly, and Curt saw the relentless warrior personality in her come forth to mask the all-American beauty she possessed. "But I'm sorry Nyamia bought it in the process of doing it. I guess it was right that a Senegambian kill him. He certainly deserved it from her. He was the one who was responsible for killing all the Senegambians."

"Nyamia was a zealot. I don't want you to become one, too," Curt told her. "As your regimental commander, I'm responsible for your well-being, like it or not. If you won't accept leave to be with Jerry, I'll issue you a direct order."

"Curt, dammit, I don't want to let down all the people in the Greys who count on me!" Adonica suddenly blurted out.

"You won't be letting them down, Adonica. On the contrary, they'll worry themselves sick over you if you stick around here. If you reject your most loved one at this particularly critical time in both your lives, they'll feel that you'll reject them at some point," Curt tried to explain to her.

"Why did he have to get hurt?"

"I don't have that answer any more than you do."

"What do we do now? He's been badly wounded. Maybe deformed for life! I don't see how any medical miracle can bring him back to the Greys."

"I don't either. And it hurts me more than you'll know in a different way than you could know," Curt admitted. "For years, Jerry has been my Number Two officer in the Greys. I was grooming him as a potential successor. I knew that either he or Kitsy could cut it. Therefore, I set it up so we'd know beyond a doubt who'd prevail. Now that's gone. And I'm faced with the reality that I've lost Jerry and that I'll also lose you, a fine company commander."

"What do you mean? What else is there for me but Jerry and the Greys?"

"You and Jerry often assured me that you'd worked things out. Are you forgetting some of it now that it happened? Let me ask you: What would you do if he'd been killed instead of wounded?" Curt wanted to know.

"I'd still have the Washington Greys."

"But you're forgetting there are things in the world other than the Washington Greys," Curt told her. Thanks to Jerry and Adonica, he and Dyani had gone through a similar exercise. Dyani's eyes told him then that she knew what he was going to say to Adonica. "Let me tell you about a conversation I had today with both Hettrick and Bellamack. Jerry has a mind that's too good to waste. He's seen combat as both a warbot brainy and a Sierra Charlie. He hasn't forgotten one moment of it. And he can teach it to others because he's done so. Regardless what the biotechs can or cannot do for him at Walter Reed, his new assignment is pretty much set. He won't be coming back to the Greys." Curt said this with utter sadness.

"What . . . ?"

"The paperwork will start processing through DCSPERS tomorrow. Upon discharge from Walter Reed, Colonel Jerry Allen will be posted permanently as a professor of military history and tactics at the United States Military Academy. Major Adonica Sweet will receive orders to report to the United States Military Academy as an associate professor of military tactics and leadership," Curt announced. "I'm sorry that Jerry left before I could tell him, but we managed to put all the bricks in place only about an hour ago. The fix is in, Adonica. You're going to get orders. An order is an order. So go do it, and my love and support go with you. Don't forget: You won't be leaving the Washington Greys. Once a Grey, always a Grey."

Curt had never seen Adonica Sweet weep before. But now she cried. She didn't sob. She just cried.

In some ways, Curt wished he'd been born a Muslim. Grown Muslim men are permitted to cry. In fact, they're expected to.

There wasn't much more to the conversation. But Dyani didn't leave with Adonica.

"She no longer needs me, Kida," Dyani explained. "She didn't need me when she reported to you. But she asked me to

326

come along. And I did. But I can tell that you need me."

"I always have. For a long time, I didn't know it. Or I didn't know how much."

"I always have, too. The same." Dyani never had to say very much. She had other ways of expressing herself.

Curt sighed and leaned back in the chair. The afternoon was bright with sunsl.ine, and the ocean breeze was fresh and smelled of salt water. He finally looked at Dyani, which wasn't exactly an unpleasant way to spend time. "Well, Deer Arrow, either of us could buy it at any time, too. So what do you think? Is it time for us to move on to other things together?"

She slowly shook her head. "Not yet, Kida. Not yet."

"Well, we don't have to move on right now, anyway. Here we are. We have a lovely beach and lovely quarters. We're surrounded by lovely people who are our friends." Curt was beginning to unwind after several days of very intense living.

"We're warriors among warriors. And we don't have to fight today. Let's enjoy that while we can," Dyani Motega told him with the future in her eyes.

Appendix I

THE 3rd ROBOT INFANTRY REGIMENT
(SPECIAL COMBAT)
"THE WASHINGTON GREYS"
ROLE OF HONOR
WOUNDED IN THE LINE OF DUTY IN SENEGAMBIA

Maj. Jerry P. Allen
First Lt. Julian B. Clark, R.N.
Master Sgt. Robert Lee Garrison
Platoon Sgt. Charles P. Kowlowski
Capt. Lewis C. Pagan
First Lt. Jerome "Jay" Taire

Appendix II

OPERATION BLOODBATH

Lt. Gen. William O. Bellamack, commanding general,
U.S. Army Forces Command (FORSCOM)
Col. R. H. Rathbone, G-3
FORSCOMM, Operation Bloodbath
Rear Adm. Thomas A. Weaver, deputy commander
Naval operations, Operation Bloodbath
Maj. Gen. Roger Willcox, deputy commander
Air operations, Operation Bloodbath

50th "R.U.R." Division, Maj. Gen. Karl K. Chappick, commander.

1st Cavalry Division, Maj. Gen. Charles D. Palmer, commander.

17th "Iron Fist" Division, Maj. Gen. Belinda J. Hettrick, commanding officer.

Col. Joanne Wilkinson, COS, 17th "Iron Fist" Division.

Col. James B. Ricketts, G-1, 17th "Iron Fist" Division.

Lt. Col. Eleanor S. Aarts, G-2, 17th "Iron Fist" Division.

Lt. Col. Hensley Atkinson, G-3, 17th "Iron Fist" Division.

Lt. Col. Adrian D. Kleperas, G-4, 17th "Iron Fist" Division.

3rd Robot Infantry Regiment (Special Combat), the "Washington Greys":

Col. Curt C. Carson, commanding officer

Headquarters Company (HEADCO) ("Carson's Companions")

Lt. Col. Joan G. Ward, chief of staff

Maj. Patrick Gillis Gratton, regimental adjutant (S-1)

Maj. Russell B. Frazier (S-3)

Maj. Nelson A. Crile, regimental chaplain

Master Sgt. Maj. Henry G. Kester, regimental sergeant major

Sgt. Maj. Edwina A. Sampson, regimental technical sergeant

Tactical Battalion (TACBATT) ("Allen's Alleycats"):

Maj. Jerry P. Allen

Battalion Sgt. Maj. Nicholas P. Gerard

Reconnaissance Company (RECONCO) ("Motega's Mustangs")

Capt. Dyani Motega (S-2)

First Sgt. Tracy C. Dillon

Bio-tech Sgt. Allan J. Williams, P.N.

Scouting Platoon (SCOUT) ("Saunder's Scouts")

2nd Lt. Harlan P. Saunders

Platoon Sgt. Sidney Albert Johnson

Sgt. Zebulon P. Long

Birdbot Platoon (BIRD) ("Brown's Black Hawks")

Capt. Dale B. Brown

Platoon Sgt. Emma Crawford

Sgt. William J. Hull

Sgt. Jacob F. Kent

Sgt. Christine Burgess

Sgt. Jennifer M. Volker

Assault Company A (ASSAULTCO Alpha) ("Clinton's Cougars")

Maj. Kathleen B. Clinton

Master Sgt. First Class Carol J. Head

Bio-tech Sgt. Virginia Bowles, P.N.

First Platoon: ("Sweet's Stilettos")

Capt. Adonica Sweet

Platoon Sgt. Charles P. Koslowski
Sgt. Paul T. Tullis
Second Platoon: ("Power's Panthers")
2nd Lt. Dan G. Power
Platoon Sgt. Betty Jo Trumble
Sgt. Dennis W. Dent
Assault Company B (ASSAULTCO Bravo) ("Pagan's Pumas")
Capt. Lewis C. Pagan
Master Sgt. Robert Lee Garrison
Bio-tech Sgt. Marla M. Metford
First Platoon: ("Hassan's Assassins")
Capt. Hassan Ben Mahmud
Platoon Sgt. Isadore Beau Greenwald
Sgt. Maria Lunalilo
Second Platoon: ("Mikawa's Marauders")
2nd Lt. Matsu Mikawa
Platoon Sgt. James P. Elliott
Sgt. A. W. Guilford
Gunnery Company (GUNCO) ("Hall's Hellcats")
Capt. Lawrence W. Hall
1st Sgt. Forest L. Barnes
Bio-tech Sgt. Shelley C. Hale, P.N.
First Platoon: ("Taire's Terrors")
1st Lt. Jerome "Jay" Taire
Platoon Sgt. Andrea Carrington
Second Platoon: ("Kyger's Killers")
2nd Lt. Theodore "Tiger" Kyger
Platoon Sgt. Victor Jouillan
Air Battalion (AIRBATT) ("Worsham's Warhawks")
Maj. Calvin J. Worsham
Battalion Sgt. Maj. John Adam
Tactical Air Support Company (TACAIRCO) ("Hands' Harriers")
Capt. Paul Hands
1st Sgt. Clancy Thomas
1st Lt. Gabe Neatherly
1st Lt. Bruce Mark

1st Lt. Stacy Honey
1st Lt. Jay Kennedy
1st Lt. Richard Cooke
Flight Sgt. Zeke Braswell
Flight Sgt. Larry Myers
Flight Sgt. Adam Neiswader
Flight Sgt. Grant Brown
Flight Sgt. Sharon Spence

Airlift Company (AIRLIFTCO) ("Timm's Tigers")
Capt. Timothea Timm
First Sgt. Carl Bagwell
1st Lt. Ned Phillips
1st Lt. Mike Hart
1st Lt. Dorothy Peterson
1st Lt. Nancy Roberts
2nd Lt. Larry Rosenberg
2nd Lt. Jess S. Switzer
Flight Sgt. Kevin Hubbard
Flight Sgt. Jeffrey O'Connell
Flight Sgt. Barry Morris
Flight Sgt. Ann Shepherd
Flight Sgt. Robert Pritchard
Flight Sgt. Harley Earll
Flight Sgt. Sergio Tomasio
Flight Sgt. Joeseph Kalakava

Service Battalion (SERVBATT)
Lt. Col. Wade W. Hampton
Battalion Sgt. Maj. Joan J. Stark

Vehicle Technical Company (VETECO)
Maj. Frederick W. Benteen
Technical Sgt. First Class Raymond G. Wolf
Technical Sgt. Kenneth M. Hawkins
Technical Sgt. Charles B. Slocum

Warbot Technical Company (BOTECO)
Maj. Elwood S. Otis
Technical Sgt. Bailey Ann Miles
Technical Sgt. Gerald W. Mora
Technical Sgt. Loretta A. Carruthers

Air Maintenance Company (AIRMAINCO)
  Capt. Ron Knight
  First Sgt. Rebecca Campbell
  Technical Sgt. Joel Pruitt
  Technical Sgt. Richard N. Germain
  Technical Sgt. Douglas Bell
  Technical Sgt. Pam Gordon
  Technical Sgt. Clete McCoy
  Technical Sgt. Carol Jensen
Logistics Company (LOGCO)
  Maj. Harriet F. Dearborn (S-4)
  Chief Supply Sgt. Manuel P. Sanchez
  Supply Sgt. Marriette W. Ireland
  Supply Sgt. Jamie G. Casner
Bio-tech Company (BIOTECO)
  Maj. Ruth Gydesen, M.D.
  Capt. Denise G. Logan, M.D.
  Capt. Thomas E. Alvin, M.D.
  Capt. Larry C. McHenry, M.D.
  Capt. Helen Devlin, R.N.
  1st Lt. Clifford B. Braxton, R.N.
  1st Lt. Laurie S. Cornell, R.N.
  1st Lt. Julia B. Clark, R.N.
  1st Lt. William O. Molde, R.N.
  Bio-tech Sgt. Marcela V. Jolton, P.N.
  Bio-tech Sgt. Nellie A. Miles, P.N.
  Bio-tech Sgt. George O. Howard, P.N.
  Bio-tech Sgt. Wallace W. Izard, P.N.

27th Robot Infantry (Special Combat) Regiment, "The Wolfhounds,"
17th Iron Fist Division
Col. Frederick H. Salley, commanding officer.

Lt. Col. Martin C. Kelly, Operations Officer
27th Robot Infantry (Special Combat) Regiment, "The Wolfhounds,"
17th Iron Fist Division, AUS

7th Robot Infantry Regiment (Special Combat) "The Cottonhalers,"
17th Iron Fist Division
Col. Maxine Frances Cashier, commanding officer.

2e Regiment Etranger de Parachutistes, Legion Etranger
Aubagne, France,
Col. Robert Debas, commanding officer.

The "Garamandes" Senegambian irregular partisan
resistance forces,
Nyamia Lébou, leader.
Léon Keita, Garamandes tribunal member.
Georges Damas, Garamandes terrorism specialist.
Sundiata Linguére, Garamandes intelligence chief.
Mariama Fulani, commander, Garamandes irregulars.
Jasper Duckworth Greenway, videonaturalist.
Dr. Henri M. Mermoz, medical doctor, member of
Garamandes.

OTHERS

The President of the United States of America.
The Hon. Henrietta H. Hamlin, Vice President of the
United States of America.
The Hon. Dr. Andrea M. Pruitt, Secretary of State
The Hon. Nelson J. Fetterman. Secretary of Defense
Gen. Albert W. Murray, USAF (Ret.), Director, National
Intelligence Agency.
Gen. Daniel O. Gram, AUS (Ret.), National Security Advisor.
Sen. Dan G. Bancroft (D-OH), Chairman, Senate Armed
Services Committee.
Rep. Jacob O. Carlisle (R-AZ).
Gen. John E. Wool, Chairman, Joint Chiefs of Staff,
Washington D.C.
Gen. William H. Gill, JCS, COS, U.S. Army, Washington, D.C.

Adm. Lewis S. Joseph, JCS, CNO, U.S. Navy, Washington, D.C.

Gen. Frank R. Lahm, JCS, COS, U.S. Aerospace Force, Washington, D.C.

Lt. Gen. Oliver G. Hayward. JCS, Commandant, U.S. Marine Corps, Washington, D.C.

Gen. Jeffrey Winfield Pickens, Deputy Chief of Staff, Operations and Plans (DCSOP), United States Army, the Pentagon, Washington, D.C.

Generalissimo Modibo Ould Daddah Sidi Ahmed, President for Life, Savior of the Sahel, and Chief of the Military Forces of the United State of Malitania.

Col. Abdul Karim Kassem, military commander, Malitanian province of Dakar.

Col. Godavari Singh Pratihara, military advisor for the Malitanian province of Dakar.

The Hon. Kankan Moussa Mokhtar, Malitanian ambassador to the United States.

The Hon. Dr. Luther M. Jones, United States ambassador to Senegambia, Dakar embassy.

The Sultana Alzena Mahathis bint Muhamad, interior minister, Negara Darussalam Brunei.

Appendix III

PRINCIPLES OF NEUROELECTRONIC ROBOTICS

*Excerpt from
Department of the Army Technical Manual
TM-88-190, "Basic Theory and Applications
of Neuroelectronics")*

History:

In 1800, Count Alessandro Volta—the Italian electrical pioneer for whom the electronic unit, the volt, is named—discovered a phenomenon he called "electrophonic hearing." This was the sensation of sound created by the application of small electrical charges to the skin.

In the 1950s, a teen-aged amateur scientist, Gillis Patrick Flanagan, discovered that the sensation of hearing could be achieved by applying suitably amplified electrical signals to human skin anywhere on the body, creating the sensation of sound in the subject's brain. Flanagan's "Neurophone" was dismissed as a hoax by electronics scientists and neurophysiologists of the time.

At about the same time, Soviet researchers and a Rumanian scientist, Dr. Henri M. Coanda, working in France independently, discovered that the sensation of sight could be created in the human brain by application of both light and electrical signals to the human fingertips.

From this basic background, amateur researchers built a

theory that the Flanagan Neurophone and other electronic sensation producing devices were somehow creating signals in the nerves of the skin that the human nervous system recognized in the brain as being those "coded" for sound and sight respectively. It required years of study and the application of computer technology to be able to create the full range of sensations — sight, sound, taste, touch, and muscle kinesthetics — by application of passive, non-intrusive sensors pads to the human skin around the head and along the spinal column.

The neuroelectric activity of the human brain was first demonstrated in 1929 by Hans Berger of Jena, Germany, the inventor of the electroencephalograph or EEG. This used a passive skin sensor positioned on the head of a subject to pick up the electric fields induced by the neuroelectric activity in the brain.

In the 1960s, progress in solid-state electronics produced the Super-conducting Quantum Interference Device, the SQUID, capable of measuring even smaller neuroelectric brain activity than the ordinary EEG.

In 1968, David Cohen initiated the science of magnetoencephalography (MEG) when he used a SQUID to measure the magnetic fields generated by neural activity in the human brain.

By 1977, researchers were mapping the various centers of neural activity in the human brain, a job that was completed before the end of the twentieth century.

Basics of Neuroelectronics:

Progress in computer technology, artificial intelligence, and robotics early in the twenty-first century created the neuroelectronic robot when neuroelectronic stimulation and MEG were combined.

This allowed a robot operator to "get inside" a robot to see and hear and feel the same thing that the robot saw, heard, and felt by means of a "down link" from the robot's sensors through computers and thus by passive skin electrodes into the robot operator's brain.

The robot operator could also control the robot by merely "thinking" the action commands which were picked up by MEG sensors in the linkage harness that covered the head and spinal column of the operator. Sophisticated computers and artificial intelligence units translated these thought commands into commands for the robot. This made the robot an extension of the human operator's body.

In the commercial world, this two-way or "duplex" linkage between a human and a robot is carried out by means of hard-wire connections, radio transmissions, or laser links.

Military Applications of Neuroelectronics:

Military and naval applications of remotely-operated weapons go back to World War II and the German development of the Henschel Hs.238 glide bomb launched from a manned bombing plane and guided by radio control from a human operator in the bombing plane who watched the image transmitted by a television camera in the nose of the glide bomb. In the 1990s, thought commands based on MEG technology were first used in fighter aircraft.

The United States Army began introducing neurophonic robots into its infantry, armored, and cavalry units early in the twenty-first century when it was shown that the human soldier could direct war robots ("warbots") safely from the rear area of a battle. This removed the human soldier from the actual battlefield, a trend that had been developing for decades. This move was enthusiastically supported by Congress and the public.

War Robots:

"Robot" is derived from the Czech word *robota* meaning work, especially drudgery. It is applied to any device with humanlike actions directed either by a computer or by a human being through a computer and a two-way command-sensor circuit.

War robots, known as "warbots," are robots designed for military purposes. Most warbots are heavily armed and armored. In many ways, warbots are like miniaturized tanks capable of being operated remotely. Other warbots are remotely-piloted vehicles such as aircraft or scouting vehicles capable of going where it is very dangerous for humans to go. Many reconnaissance and surveillance warbots can be disguised as animals; bird-shaped warbots (birdbots) and rodent-shaped warbots (ratbots) are examples of these. Such disguised warbots can often be used without the enemy recognizing that they are different from the natural animals in a battle environment.

Warbots are operated using the principles of neuroelectronics. This branch of technology is a synthesis of bioelectronics and computer technologies. It permits a computer to detect and recognize command signals from the human nervous system and to stimulate the human nervous system with computer-generated electronic signals by means of non-intrusive skin-mounted sensors for the purpose of creating sensory signals in the human mind.

The connection between a warbot soldier and a warbot is by means of a linkage system. This is a remote connection or link between a human being and one or more neuroelectronically controlled warbots. This link channel may be by means of wires, radio, laser, or optics. The actual technology of linkage is highly classified. The robot/computer sends its data directly to the human soldier's nervous system through small nonintrusive electrodes positioned on the soldier's skin. This data is presented in such a way that the soldier's nervous system perceives the signals as sight, sound, feeling, or position of the robot's parts. The robot/computer also picks up thought commands from the soldier's nervous system, translates them into commands a robot can understand, and monitors the robot's accomplishment of the commanded action.

Linkage is assisted by artificial intelligence or AI modules. These are very fast computer elements with large memories which can simulate some functions of human thought and decision-making processes. AI brings together many apparently disconnected pieces of data, evaluates the priority of each, and makes simple decisions concerning what to do, how to do it, when to do it, and what to report to the human being in control. In intense situations such as combat, AI relieves a great deal of mental load from a soldier, permitting him to make better decisions.

Another important part of the linkage system is the intelligence amplifier or IA, a very fast computer with a very large memory. When linked to a human nervous system by non-intrusive neuroelectronic pickups and electrodes, an IA serves as a very fast extension of the human brain allowing the brain to function faster, recall more data, store more data, and thus "amplify" a human being's "intelligence."

The Robot Infantry (RI):

The Robot Infantry or RI is the primary warbot combat branch of the United States Army. It grew from the regular infantry when robots and linkage were introduced. The RI replaced the regular infantry in the early twenty-first century because warbots and linkage allowed the human being to be removed from the battlefield and from the hazard of being killed in combat. Other warbot combat arms include the Robot Armored and the Robot Cavalry.

Because a warbot soldier isn't actually exposed to the deadly hazards of actual combat, women were allowed to become qualified as warbot brainies and to be assigned to combat units. Women also showed themselves to be excellent and outstanding warbot operators with an operational mode that is far more devious and aggressive than most men warbot brainies. Male/female warbot teams were found to operate in combat with extremely high effectiveness. At the time the Robot Infantry was formed, female equality advocates were extremely vocal and effective in ensuring that women were afforded the opportunity to overcome what was termed "the final step toward equality: the right to fight alongside men for God and country."

However, being a warbot soldier or "warbot brainy"—a slang term implying that the soldier is basically the brains of the warbot—has personal dangers associated with it that are new to warfare. It is possible to be "killed in action" or KIA. This is a slang term used to describe the situation where a warbot soldier's neuroelectronic data and sensory inputs from one or more warbots is suddenly cut off. This leaves the human being in a state of mental limbo. It is a very debilitating and mentally disturbing situation because one reality—that of having the warbot as an extension of the mind and body—is suddenly replaced with another reality—that of the soldier in the real world depending upon his own sensory inputs and commanding his own body. This can lead, in the extreme, to catatonic withdrawal or, more normally, to confusion between realities, a new form of schizophrenia. Warbot brainies who have been KIA require highly specialized bio-electronic therapy. They may be out of action for three to six months. Some KIA warbot brainies have to be discharged or assigned to non-warbot administrative positions. The worst cases remain under intensive care for years.

Training and War Gaming:

Training of warbot soldiers begins in Basic Training. Neuroelectronics has allowed exceptionally good personnel evaluation techniques to be perfected. Those recruits volunteering for the RI and subsequently selected as a result of neuroelectronic screening show a high percentage of success in RI training. NE techniques permit a person to search out, identify, and disarm personal mental problems. An RI recruit and a warbot brainy are basically very stable individuals with a strong sense of purpose, a firm grasp on the real world, and an integrated personality capable of accepting full responsibility for personal actions.

341

In short, people in the RI have turned out to be extremely adult in their outlook and behavior. Except in cases of severe mental disturbance and disease, bioelectronic professionals and technicians are prohibited by the canons of practice—derived from the Hippocratic Oath and the canons of metalaw—from deep probing of another person's mind. An individual with mental problems is encouraged to and assisted in working out the problems personally, a procedure which results in much more positive solutions.

Thus, both officers and NCOs tend to be stable personalities. But the training and operational procedures do not eliminate a person's individual personality or personal differences.

Because of the realism created by linkage, it has become possible to simulate combat very effectively using computers which operate with pre-recorded or self-programming simulator programs. These simulators or "sims" use the sim computers as substitutes for real warbots and provide the databit stream on the down link. A warbot brainy can simulate multi-warbot operation and can be cross-linked with other warbot brainies of his platoon, company, or regiment in highly realistic war games.

Recent Developments:

RI doctrine and tactics were developed to counter massive offensive assaults by motorized infantry and armored units of the sort anticipated in Europe. Subsequent modifications allowed RI units to perform in an outstanding fashion in repetitive patrol and guard capacities where the United States government found it necessary to station military forces for the protection of national commercial and industrial interests such as petroleum extraction and pipeline transportation facilities and personnel stationed in foreign lands. Additional changes to warbot tactics were necessary to counter revolutionary mass infantry operations on the open savannahs and deserts of central Africa.

However, RI doctrines and tactics were found wanting

in situations involving terrorists, commando-type missions, and insurgent operations. Progress in robotics allowed the development of artificially intelligent voice- and radio-commanded warbots capable of limited self-action in combat. In a sense, these new warbots served as "smart tanks" or the ultimate modern embodiments of the not-very-bright cannon fodder infantry soldiers of the past. Human-like in their capabilities—they seem to have the human IQ equivalent of 70-80—they can operate alongside human soldiers on the battlefield.

The development of these new warbots led to the parallel development of the Special Combat or Sierra Charlie doctrines and tactics. The personnel of Special Combat regiments became known as "Sierra Charlies." They are trained to engage in personal field combat supported and accompanied by special high-tech artificially-intelligent warbots that are voice-commanded rather than run by linkage.

Thus, Sierra Charlies operate in the combat environment without neuroelectronic warbots and usually with less capability than RI warbot brainies to utilize the benefits of computers and artificial intelligence to relieve battle load. They appear to be evolving into the twenty-first century high-tech equivalents of the special forces of the past.

Sierra Charlie doctrines and tactics are still undergoing development in the United States Army.

Appendix IV

GLOSSARY OF ROBOT
INFANTRY TERMS AND SLANG

ACV: Airportable Command Vehicle M660.

Aerodyne: A saucer-shaped flying machine that obtains its lift from the exhaust of one or more turbine fanjet engines blowing outward over the curved upper surface of the craft from an annular segmented slot near the center of the upper surface. The aerodyne was invented by Dr. Henri M. Coanda after World War II but was not perfected until decades later because of the predominance of the rotary-winged helicopter.

ALO: Active Level of Operation readiness.

AOG: Aircraft on the ground.

AP: Anti-personnel.

APV: Armored Personnel Vehicle.

Artificial Intelligence or AI: Very fast computer modules with large memories which can simulate some functions of human thought and decision-making processes by bringing together many apparently disconnected pieces of data, making simple evaluations of the priority of each, and making simple decisions concerning what to do, how to do it, when to do it, and what to report to the human being in control.

ASAP: As soon as possible.

AT: Anti-tank.

Beanie: A West Point term for a plebe or first-year man.

Beanette: A female beanie.

Birdbot: The M20 Aeroreconnaissance Neuroelectronic Bird Warbot used for aerial recce. Comes in shapes and sizes to resemble indigenous birds.

Bio-tech: A biological technologist once known in the twentieth century Army as a "medic."

Black Maria: The M44A Assault Shotgun, the Sierra Charlie's 18.52-millimeter friend in close quarter combat.

Blue U: The United States Aerospace Force Academy.

Bohemian Brigade: War correspondents or a news media television crew.

Bot: Generalized generic slang term for "robot" which takes many forms, as warbot, reconbot, etc. See "Robot" below.

Bot flush: Since robots have no natural excrement, this term is a reference to what comes out of a highly mechanical warbot when its lubricants are changed during routine maintenance. Used by soldiers as a slang term referring to anything of a detestable nature.

Cee-pee or CP: Slang for "Command Post."

CG: Commanding general.

Check minus-x: Look behind you. In terms of coordinates, plus-x is ahead, minus-x is behind, plus-y is to the right, minus-y is left, plus-z is up, and minus-z is down.

CINC: Commander In Chief.

Chippie: The UCA-21C Chippewa tactical airlift aerodyne.

CIC: Combat Information Center. May be different from a command post.

CJSC: The Chairman of the Joint Chiefs of Staff.

Class 6 supplies: Alcoholic beverages of high ethanol content procured through non-regulation channels; officially, only five classes of supplies exist.

CNO: The Chief of Naval Operations.

CO: The commanding officer.

Column of ducks: A convoy proceeding through terrain where they are likely to draw fire.

CRAF: Civil Reserve Air Fleet.

Creamed: Greased, beaten, conquered, overwhelmed.

CTAF: Common Traffic Advisory Frequency.

CYA: Cover Your Ass. In polite company, "Cover Your Anatomy."

DCSOPS: The Army's Deputy Chief of Staff for Operations.

DCSPERS: The Army's Deputy Chief of Staff for Personnel.

D-M: Davis-Monthan Aerospace Force Base, Tucson, Arizona.

Downlink: A remote command or data channel from a warbot to a soldier.

ECM: Electronic Counter Measures.

FAM: The French arms maker, Fusil Automatique Mitrailleur.

FCC: The Federal Communications Commission.

FEBA: Forward Edge of the Battle Area.

FIDO: Acronym for "Fuck it; drive on!" Overcome your obstacle or problem and get on with the operation.

FIG: Foreign Internal Guardian mission, the sort of assignment Army units draw to protect American interests in selected locations around the world. Great for RI units but not within the intended mission profiles of Sierra Charlie regiments.

Fort Fumble: Any headquarters but especially the Pentagon when not otherwise specified.

Furball: A complex, confused fight, battle, or operation.

G-1, G-2, G-3, G-4: Elements of a general's staff; G-1 = Personnel; G-2 = Intelligence services; G-3 = Operations; G-4 = Logistics and supplies. In a regiment, these are known as S-1, S-2, S-3, and S-4 because they aren't part of a general officer's staff.

GA: "Go ahead!"

General Ducrot: Any incompetent, lazy, fucked-up, incompetent officer who doesn't know or won't admit those shortcomings. May have other commissioned officer rank to more closely describe the individual.

Go physical: To lapse into idiot mode, to operate in a combat or recon environment without neuroelectronic warbots; what the Special Combat units do all the time. See "Idiot mode" below.

Golden BB: A small caliber bullet that hits and thus creates large problems.

Greased: Beaten, conquered, overwhelmed, creamed.

Harpy: The AD-40C tactical air assault aerodyne which the Aerospace Force originally developed in the A version; the Navy flies the B version. The Office In Charge Of Stupid Names tried to get everyone to call it the "Thunder Devil," but the Harpy name stuck with the drivers and troops. The compound term "newsharpy" is also used to refer to a hyperthyroid, ego-blasted, over-achieving female news personality or reporter.

Headquarters happy: Any denizen of headquarters, regimental or higher.

Humper: Any device whose proper name a soldier can't recall at the moment.

ID or i-d: Identification.

Idiot mode: Operating in the combat environment without neuroelectronic warbots, especially operating without the benefit of computers and artificial intelligence to relieve battle load. What the warbot brainies think the Sierra Charlies do all the time. See "Go physical" above.

IG: The inspector general.

Intelligence: Generally considered to exist in four categories: animal, human, machine, and military.

Intelligence amplifier or IA: A very fast computer with a very large memory which, when linked to a human nervous system by non-intrusive neuroelectronic pickups and electrodes, serves as a very fast extension of the human brain allowing the brain to function faster, recall more data, store more data, and thus "amplify" a human being's "intelligence." (Does not imply that the Army knows what "human intelligence" really is.)

347

JCS: Joint Chief of Staff.

Jeep: Word coined from the initials "GP" standing for "General Purpose." Once applied to an Army quarter-ton vehicle but subsequently used to refer to the Mark 33A2 General Purpose Warbot.

J.I.C.: Just In Case.

KE: Kinetic energy as applied to KE kill weapons.

KIA: "Killed in action." A warbot brainy term used to describe the situation where a warbot soldier's neuroelectronic data and sensory inputs from one or more warbots is suddenly cut off, leaving the human being in a state of mental limbo. A very debilitating and mentally disturbing situation. (Different from being physically killed in action, a situation with which only Sierra Charlies find themselves threatened.)

LAMVA: The M473 Light Artillery Maneuvering Vehicle, Airportable, a robotic armored vehicle mounting a 75-millimeter Saucy Cans gun used for light artillery support of a Sierra Charlie regiment.

Linkage: The remote connection or link between a human being and one or more neuroelectronically controlled warbots. This link channel may be by means of wires, radio, laser, or optics. The actual technology of linkage is highly classified. The robot/computer sends its data directly to the human soldier's nervous system through small nonintrusive electrodes positioned on the soldier's skin. This data is coded in such a way that the soldier perceives the signals as sight, sound, feeling, or position of the robot's parts. The robot/computer also picks up commands from the soldier's nervous system that are merely "thought" by the soldier, translates them into commands a robot can understand, and monitors the robot's accomplishment of the commanded action.

Log bird: A logistics or supply aircraft.

Mary Ann: The M60A Airborne Mobile Assault Warbot which mounts a single M300 25-millimeter automatic cannon with variable fire rate. Accompanies Sierra Charlie

348

roops in the field and provides fire support.

Mad minute: The first intense, chaotic, wild, frenzied period of a fire fight when it seems every gun in the world is being shot at you.

Mike-mike: Soldier's shorthand for "millimeter."

MRE: Officially, Meal Ready to Eat; Soldiers claim it means "Meal Rarely Edible."

NCO: Non-commissioned officer.

NE: Neuroelectronic (see same below).

Neuroelectronics or NE: The synthesis of electronics and computer technologies that permit a computer to detect and recognize signals from the human nervous system by means of nonintrusive skin-mounted sensors as well as to timulate the human nervous system with computer-generated electronic signals through similar skin-mounted electrodes for the purpose of creating sensory signals in the human mind. See "Linkage" above.

NIA: National Intelligence Agency, supposedly the reorganized Central Intelligence Agency except that the NIA doesn't officially exist. Ask anyone.

Novia: The 7.62-millimeter M33A3 "Ranger" Assault Rifle designed in Mexico as the M3 Novia. The Sierra Charlies still call it the Novia or "sweetheart."

NSC: The National Security Council.

OCV: Operational Command Vehicle, the command version of the M660 ACV.

Orgasmic!: A slang term that grew out of the observation, "Outstanding!" It means the same thing. Usually but not always.

Oscar briefing: An orders briefing.

Papa briefing: A planning briefing.

POSSOH: "Person of Opposite Sex Sharing Off-duty Hours."

POW: Prisoner of war.

PTV: Personal Transport Vehicle or "Trike," a three-wheeled unarmored vehicle similar to an old sidecar motorcycle capable of carrying two Sierra Charlies or one

Sierra Charlie and a Jeep.

Pucker factor: The detrimental effect on the human body that results from being in an extremely hazardous situation such as being shot at.

RI: The Robot Infantry combat branch of the United States Army.

Robot: From the Czech word *robota* meaning work, especially drudgery. A device with humanlike actions directed either by a computer or by a human being through a computer and a two-way command-sensor circuit. See "Linkage" and "Neuroelectronics" above.

Robot Infantry or RI: A combat branch of the United States Army which grew from the regular infantry with the introduction of robots and linkage to warfare. Replaced the regular infantry in the early twenty-first century.

RPV: Remotely Piloted Vehicle, an early form of birdbot.

RTV: Robot Transport Vehicle, now the M662 Airportable Robot Transport Vehicle (ARTV) but still called an RTV by Sierra Charlies.

Rule Ten: Slang reference to Army Regulation 601-10 which prohibits physical contact between male and female personnel when on duty except for that required in the conduct of official business.

Rules of Engagement or ROE: Official restrictions on the freedom of action of a commander or soldier in his confrontation with an opponent that act to increase the probability that said commander or soldier will lose the combat all other things being equal.

SADARM: Search and destroy armor, a type of warhead.

Saucy Cans: An American Army corruption of the French designation for the 75-millimeter "soixante-quintze" weapon mounted on the LAMVA.

SC: Sierra Charlie. (see below).

Scroom!: Abbreviation for "Screw 'em!"

SECDEF: The Secretary of Defense.

Sheep screw: A disorganized, embarrassing, graceless

350

chaotic fuck-up.

Sierra Charlie: Phonetic alphabet derivative of the initials "SC" meaning "Special Combat." Soldiers trained to engage in personal field combat supported and accompanied by artificially intelligent warbots that are voice-commanded rather than run by linkage. The ultimate weapon of World War IV.

Sierra Hotel: What warbot brainies say when they can't say, "Shit hot!"

Simulator or sim: A device that can simulate the sensations perceived by a human being and the results of the human's responses. A simple toy computer or video game simulating the flight of an aircraft or the driving of a race car is an example of a primitive simulator.

Sit-guess: Slang for "estimate of the situation," an educated guess about your predicament.

Sit-rep: Short for "situation report" to notify your superior officer about the sheep screw you're in at the moment.

Smart Fart: The M100A (FG/IM-190) Anti-tank/Anti-aircraft tube-launched rocket capable of being launched off the shoulder of a Sierra Charlie. So-called because of its self-guided "smart" warhead and the sound it makes when fired.

Snake pit: Slang for the highly computerized briefing center located in most caserns and other Army posts.

Snivel: To complain about the injustice being done you.

Spasm mode: Slang for killed in action (KIA).

Spook: Slang term for either a spy or a military intelligence specialist. Also used as a verb relating to reconnaissance.

Staff stooge: Derogatory term referring to a staff officer. Also "staff weenie."

TAB-V: Theater Air Base Vulnerability shelter.

TACAMO!: "Take Charge And Move Out!"

Tacomm: A portable frequency-hopping communications transceiver system once used by rear-echelon warbot brainy troops and now generally used in very advanced

351

and rugged versions by the Sierra Charlies.

Tango Sierra: Tough shit.

Tech-weenie: The derogatory term applied by combat soldiers to the scientists, engineers, and technicians who complicate life by insisting that the soldier have gadgetry that is the newest, fastest, most powerful, most accurate, and usually the most unreliable products of their fertile techie imaginations.

Third Herd, the: The 3rd Robot Infantry Regiment (Special Combat), the Washington Greys (but you'd better be a Grey to use that term).

Tiger error: What happens when an eager soldier tries too hard.

TO&E: Table of Organization and Equipment.

TRACON: Terminal Radar Control facility at an airport.

Umpteen hundred: Some time in the distant, undetermined future.

Up link: The remote command link or channel from the warbot brainy to the warbot.

VLF: Very Low Frequency radio wavelength.

Warbot: Abbreviation for "war robot," a mechanical device that is operated by or commanded by a soldier to fight in the field.

Warbot brainy: The human soldier who operates warbots through linkage, implying that the soldier is basically the brains of the warbot. Sierra Charlies remind everyone that they are definitely not warbot brainies whom they consider to be grown-up children operating destructive video games.

ZI: Zone of the Interior, the continental United States.